RIGHT MOVE

A.M. ARTHUR

carina
press

carina
press®

Recycling programs
for this product may
not exist in your area.

ISBN-13: 978-1-335-40182-3

Right Move

Copyright © 2020 by A.M. Arthur

This edition published by arrangement with Harlequin Books S.A.

For questions and comments about the quality of this book,
please contact us at CustomerService@Harlequin.com.

Carina Press
22 Adelaide St. West, 40th Floor
Toronto, Ontario M5H 4E3, Canada
www.CarinaPress.com

Printed in U.S.A.

RIGHT MOVE

Prologue

Levi Peletier had long ago learned to trust his instincts, and instinct was what prompted him to pull over to the side of a country road in Wyoming to inspect an abandoned cardboard box. He wasn't usually much for checking out other people's trash, but he trundled onto the shoulder, mindful of the brand-new tiny house he had hitched to his pickup. Levi didn't want to risk hurting his first major adult investment.

There was nothing special about the box, no markings beyond the moving company logo stamped on the sides, but something still drew him to it. He shifted into park and got out. The two-lane road stretched out for miles in all directions, and he'd chosen this route because of its remoteness. After getting sober six months ago, Levi preferred solitude with nature over the bustle of city life. Or even small-town life. Give him open skies or thick forests any day.

The mewling sounds from the box clued Levi in before he could peer inside. Three kittens were curled up in a bundle of fur and tails and spindly legs, and two of the three were crying. They were young, he couldn't guess how young, and someone had left them here. Three tiny, precious lives. Abandoned.

"Hey, you guys." He squatted beside the box and reached inside. The striped ginger kitten immediately tried suckling his fingertip. He didn't know a lot about cats, having grown up spending most of his life in a traveling rodeo, but he did know this suggested they hadn't been properly weaned. And they were hungry. Poor little things. "Well, I hadn't planned on having roommates this soon, but I guess you're all coming with me."

He picked up the box, grateful he'd listened to his instincts and stopped to check.

Since the only thing Levi had in his tiny house that the kittens could eat was bottled water, he found the smallest bowl he had and gave them some. The little babies mobbed the bowl, and it infuriated him to think how long they'd been without food. He tried not to think about it. His phone's GPS said the nearest town was about ten miles ahead, so once he had them settled in the box with a towel to keep warm, he headed out again.

Naturally, the town didn't have a veterinarian's office, but a nice lady at the post office gave him directions to another town with options. She also thanked him for rescuing the kittens. "Any decent person would," he said as he tipped his hat. Maybe Levi didn't ride anymore but he still loved his cowboy hats.

He'd lost all his old hats last year when he ended up homeless, and the hat on his head had been a gift from his father after Levi completed rehab.

He took a photo of the post office's exterior before rolling out of town. He'd definitely be writing about this newest adventure on his blog, and he liked including photos. The blog idea had come up during his stint in rehab, as a method of remembering his past in a positive way, instead of letting the agony of his little brother's accidental death a year and a half ago darken and distort his entire life. At first, Levi had written in a notebook. Once he realized what an incredibly unique life he'd lived, he decided to share it with the wider world.

And he was also documenting his decision to take his home on the road on the blog. He enjoyed blindly traveling the states and landing wherever he landed for the night, even if it was just on the side of the road.

The next town was large enough to have several grocery stores and vet options. The first vet he visited squeezed them in, since the kittens were so young and vulnerable, and Levi instantly liked the young man who examined them. He explained how he'd found the trio.

"I don't understand people who abandon innocent creatures like that," Dr. Clark said as he looked over the black-and-white baby.

"Agreed." Levi watched the careful way the vet handled the kittens as he weighed them, looked at their teeth and into their ears. The calico meowed the entire time it was handled.

"They're all girls, and I'd guess them to be around six weeks old. Should be old enough to figure out drinking formula from a bowl so you don't have to bottle-feed them. Assuming you're going to keep them."

Levi stroked the top of the ginger's head. "They ended up in my life for a reason. If the universe decided I need three cats, I'll keep them."

Dr. Clark smiled and held eye contact a hair longer than most men would hold with other men. Unless they were interested. "Can I assume you'll be bringing them back for future shots and checkups? Because they'll need names."

He hadn't decided for sure on settling in this area but sticking around might have its merits. "I have no idea what to call them. I'm used to naming horses, not cats."

"Well, for now we can designate them by their breed and your last name. Mister?"

"Levi Peletier." He spelled his last name for the vet, who typed it into a computer. "Um, I guess Ginger, Tuxedo and Calico for now." Actually, he liked the name Ginger for his little ginger kitty. Maybe he'd keep that.

"You're new in town, I take it?"

"Very new. I've got my house hitched to my pickup."

"How's that?"

Levi explained a bit about his blog. "As I told the kittens, I hadn't intended on getting a roommate, much less three, but here we are."

"If you need a place to park, Lakeview Campground is only a few miles outside of town." Dr. Clark grinned. "I've been fishing out on that lake. It's a beautiful area. Peaceful. Not too crowded, even at the height of summer vacation season."

"Then maybe I'll check it out. Stick around for a little while."

"Then welcome to town, Mr. Peletier."

"Thank you, and Levi is fine." He couldn't decide if the vet was flirting with him or not. Levi was bisexual, and Dr. Clark was all kinds of cute and kind.

They shook hands and Levi liked that Dr. Clark didn't let go right away. He wasn't ready for a relationship, not after only being six months sober, but maybe living out here wouldn't be as lonely as he expected.

If nothing else, he could make a new friend while he was in the area.

"I'll get you some cans of kitten formula," Dr. Clark said. "You should be able to transition them from the formula to wet food fairly soon. The biggest question is litter box training."

Ginger chose that moment to prove the doc right by squatting and pooping on the exam table. Levi laughed. "I guess we'll figure that one out," he replied.

"Have you ever owned a cat before, Levi?"

"Not a day in my life but I'm a fast learner. They came to me for a reason, and I'll honor that reason. And I also believe in karma, so whoever abandoned them better watch their ass."

"Agreed. There's a special place in hell for people who abuse animals." Dr. Clark seemed to be stalling, looking for things to talk about. "You mentioned earlier you're used to naming horses. I take it you ride?"

Levi quirked an eyebrow. "I do. Did. I grew up working with horses but I left that life behind. Needed a change."

"A change you're finding here?"

"We'll see. The best part of my house is I can take it with me when I get itchy feet. I spent most of my life traveling, so settling down in any one spot for a long time will be a challenge." But Levi needed the stability while he figured out his future. He missed his father and he missed his best friend, Robin, but distance was best for everyone for now. This was where the kittens had led him, and this was where he'd settle for a while.

"Sounds as if you've got some interesting stories to tell." Dr. Clark wrote something on a business card and handed it over. "If you ever want to tell some stories over a beer, give me a call. I'll get your kitten formula and meet you at the front desk."

Levi tucked the card into his pocket and took his time gathering the little floofballs back into the box. The tuxedo kitty started purring immediately when he scratched behind her ears, the sound impossibly loud for such a small beast. But maybe now they'd all start feeling safe. Because they were.

"I have no idea how this is going to work in my little house. Every spot is precise. I don't know where I'll stash a litter box, but we'll figure it out, right ladies?"

Ginger looked up and meowed at him, as if agreeing with his words. Despite getting his shit figured out in rehab and back on a good path, Levi still floundered most days. Still wondered if he was making the right choices, doing the right things. He was used to being given a schedule, to knowing which town he'd be performing in next, to a nomadic existence that made real, long-term relationships impossible.

Now he had a new town, three kittens, and a potential new friend. After completely losing himself to alcohol and drugs for a year of his life, this truly felt like the beginning of his second chance.

Chapter One

After living an incredibly solitary life for the last seven years, having friends was a huge mind fuck for George Thompson. He and his twin brother Orry had lived in their apartment for close to six months, and neither had done much to endear themselves to their neighbors except to stay quiet and not bother anyone. Now, half a year later, they had four good friends in their two sets of downstairs neighbors, and George was still getting used to being around people again.

Being around people before was essentially what sent the twins into hiding in the first place.

George was just finishing up his latest video-captioning assignment when his phone startled him with a text. Orry used to be the only person who ever texted him, but Orry was currently napping in his bedroom in between jobs. He worked his ass off doing multiple jobs to help pay rent and car insurance, but neither of them wanted to move out of their San Francisco neighborhood. They needed to stay close to their grandparents.

He grabbed his phone off the corner of his desk.

Slater: Pizza in the living room.

The text made him smile. The apartment was one of four inside a renovated old house—two upstairs and two downstairs. Their sextet of friends had started referring to the home's big lobby as the living room because it had furniture, magazines and books that all residents were free to use. The other upstairs residents, a quiet father-daughter duo, weren't very sociable and that was fine. Once upon a time, George hadn't been sociable either.

George responded he'd be down, then went to check on Orry. He'd been napping for a few hours and would probably like to eat. Orry never turned down free food. His brother was sprawled on his bed, face pressed into a pillow, his phone playing a white noise app. Even though George used headphones when closed-captioning, so Orry couldn't overhear the videos, Orry said it made him feel less like he knew George was in his own bedroom watching porn.

Closed-captioning for porn was definitely a thing, and George had seriously lucked into a job that didn't require him to leave the house.

"Dude, you want pizza?" George asked.

Orry jerked upright in bed, as if summoned from the deep by the mere mention of the p-word. He yawned and rubbed at his face. "M'kay. Where?"

"Living room. Slater offered."

"Cool. Gimme a minute." Bro code for *I gotta whiz.*

George waited in the living room for Orry's rumpled emergence from the tiny hallway beyond their open living space. His attention went to the floor near a section of wall where a photo had broken a few months ago. Broken because of George's stupidity. He thought they'd cleaned up the glass but Orry had cut himself a few days later, because George had missed something.

Small things like that loved to take up space in his head, and George was tired of it.

Having friends meant new things to take up space in his head, instead of letting the past crowd everything out.

Orry appeared a few minutes later, and together they went downstairs to the "living room." Slater and Derrick were there with two pizza boxes and a six-pack. At almost the same moment George and Orry appeared, the door to the other downstairs apartment opened, spilling out Dez and Morgan.

Morgan used to scare George because of his general size and muscles, but he was the epitome of the gentle giant. His partner, Dez, on the other hand, was roughly half his size, nonbinary, and preferred she/her pronouns. Today, Dez wore leggings, a button-down shirt and a tie, and her hair had grown out a bit. Slater and Derrick were a now-committed couple whose relationship had started as fake and ended up as something way more permanent—a truth Slater had finally revealed to George and Orry around Halloween. George had genuinely believed they'd been a couple the whole time because chemistry oozed off them.

"Hey," Morgan said once their sextet had collected themselves around the food. "What are we eating today?"

"I decided to be nice to Dez," Derrick replied, "and one of the pies has vegan cheese and vegan pepperoni. You're welcome."

Dez pumped her fist in the air. She was a part-time vegan, from what George understood, eating her tofu while also catering to Morgan's taste for meat. Seemed odd to George, but whatever made the pair's relationship work. Dez had volunteered to cook for the twins a few times, but they always found a polite excuse.

Curious, George tried the vegan pie instead of the other, which looked like supreme. Pizza wasn't the healthiest thing anyway, and while George wasn't as militant about his diet as he once was, he'd never be the guy who pigged out on junk food and soda.

"Who has plans for Thanksgiving?" Derrick asked once everyone had pizza, his deep voice booming in the large lobby. Like Morgan, Derrick used to intimidate George because he was tall and broad, but the guy was one of the kindest, most easygoing people George had ever met. And he was clearly in love with Slater, which sometimes made George a little jealous.

Not that he had a crush on Slater, or anything, but in the last two years since he began to caption gay porn almost exclusively, he'd...noticed men more. A former cowboy who'd left the country behind for his boyfriend and a new start, Slater was handsome in a way that appealed to George. Just like the trick rider he'd met this past summer on the Fourth of July had appealed to him.

Levi.

"We're going north to see my folks," Morgan replied to Derrick's question, and for a split second, George forgot what time of year it was.

Thanksgiving.

"That's cool," Derrick replied, then looked between George and Orry. "You guys?"

"Same as every year, I guess," Orry replied. "Frozen turkey dinners and work."

"That sounds boring. Think you guys can take a day off work? My in-laws are throwing a big Thanksgiving dinner out in Garrett. Did the same thing last year, and I think it's becoming a new tradition. I mentioned inviting some of my friends and Wes said, 'The more the merrier.'"

"That's very Wes," Slater drawled.

George vaguely remembered Wes from one of his visits in the city with his boyfriend. Another cowboy. Slater's old coworkers from his ranch job still regularly came by to see him, but George avoided the lobby when they were around. Too many unfamiliar people. And now he was being invited to a house full of them?

"What do you think?" Orry asked him, holding George's gaze. Orry wouldn't go if George said no, but George needed to stop being selfish. It had been seven years, damn it. His encounter with Adrian this past summer only proved that George needed to stop hiding. He had to find a fucking backbone and take his life back.

"Okay, let's go," George replied, his voice more confident than he expected.

Orry's eyebrows rose. "Are you sure?"

Nope. "Yeah, I'm sure. Besides, you never turn down free food."

Orry threw a wadded-up napkin at his head.

"Great," Derrick said with a grin. "I'll text Wes later and let him know we're bringing guests. And don't worry about bringing anything. They had a freaking feast last year and plenty of leftovers. Actually—" he looked at Slater "—I don't remember seeing you there."

"I wasn't," Slater replied. "The ranch is closed to guests that week, and since I wasn't part of the skeleton crew tending the horses, I went up to see my family."

"Ah, makes sense."

George knew from casual conversation that Slater

had a daughter in college, and he made frequent trips to Sacramento to visit her. "Is your daughter coming down for the big feast?"

"Yup." Slater beamed like the proud dad he was. "She's excited to see the ranch where I worked and meet some of the people I talk about, especially Wes. When she found out I knew someone who made movies and television, she practically begged to come."

Nerves made his belly squirm, but the odds of anyone at this week's upcoming Thanksgiving meal recognizing him from his ice skating days were slim to none. He'd grown up, changed his hair and in the world of competitive sports, seven years was a lifetime. "Will the trick riders be there?" George asked without thinking.

Derrick shrugged. "Probably. Why?"

"Just curious. I enjoyed watching their show back in July. What they do is very athletic and takes a lot of training." Kind of like figure skating but he hadn't told Dez or Morgan about that part of his life yet.

"I have a lot of respect for Robin and Levi," Slater said. "It's hard enough for some folks simply to mount a horse, never mind the tricks those two do. You thinking of a career change?"

"No." Not really. George liked his job but he didn't want to do it forever. He wasn't sure trick riding was in his future, but he still had a lot of his old flexibility and muscle control. It might be a fun thing to try.

If he got up the courage to ask. Which he probably wouldn't.

Dez started talking about her newest upcycling creation, and the meal resumed like usual, attention finally off George. He didn't mind the vegan pizza, even though he picked off most of the pepperoni. Too spicy.

Orry tried a piece, though, and liked it. But he'd always been a more adventurous eater. Orry hadn't had to stay slender and light to perfect his triple axel. Didn't have to carry the weight of their parents' hopes, dreams and financial investment on his shoulders...

"Dude?" Morgan snapped his fingers in front of George's face, and George reared back. "You okay? You zoned."

"Yeah, sorry." He offered what he hoped was a passable smile. "Lost in thought."

"No kidding."

George avoided looking at Orry. Orry waited until they were both back upstairs, alone, before bringing it up. "What upset you?" he asked.

"Nothing upset me." George adored his twin and how attentive he was, but sometimes Orry could be a little overbearing when it came to watching George's mood. "I started thinking about food and it swept me into the past. I'm okay."

Orry studied him a beat. "Are you sure you want to go to this big Thanksgiving meal?"

"Yes. It'll be good for me. And it's been a long time since either of us had a big, home-cooked dinner."

"True. Okay, well, you can still change your mind before Thursday."

"I know." He had no intention of changing his mind—or telling Orry even if he did—because he knew how much Orry needed this. Orry worked so hard he barely had a social life, and Orry had the kind of personality that thrived around other human beings. George was the extreme introvert who'd spent a third of his life avoiding people at all costs.

But he was also...bored with this life. He used to

live for the glamor and spectacle of the rink, and now he lived for…well, to live and that was it.

There had to be more to life than just existing.

Right?

With Bentley Ghost Town shut down for the next two months, Levi had more time on his hands than he knew what to do with. He hadn't been so content living in one place since his first homestead up in the Lakeview Campground in Wyoming, and he wanted to stick around, but boredom gave him itchy feet.

Moving to Northern California to be closer to Robin Butler, a man who was still his brother no matter what legal documents said, had been a calculated risk. Robin used to work at Clean Slate Ranch, and when the owner of the ghost town wanted to do a grand reopening this past January, Levi had agreed to help. He and Robin had been trick riders once upon a time for Lucky's Rodeo, and Levi still remembered everything he'd picked up after a lifetime of practice. When the reopening show was a resounding success, Levi and Robin became a permanent part of the ghost town experience.

Being on the beautiful property outside the tiny town of Garrett, California, settled Levi in a way he hadn't felt in a long time. He'd planted his tiny home on a piece of land lent to him by the owner, and his three cats loved the freedom they had to explore. Those crazy animals had been his most consistent allies from the moment he found that box on the side of the road. No matter how far into the wilds they traveled, they always came home to him at night.

Unlike lying, cheating boyfriends.

Nah, not going there. It was Thanksgiving, and Levi

wanted to be in a positive mood when he walked down to his hosts' home for a midafternoon dinner. Despite being told he didn't need to bring anything, Levi had used his small oven to cook up a batch of his father's infamous cornpone. Thicker and wetter than cornbread, the treat was a family favorite.

Xander had adored it.

A bit of melancholy settled over Levi as he combed his hair in the small-ish bathroom, as it still sometimes did when he remembered his late little brother. Hard to believe he'd have been gone four years this Christmas Day. Xander and Robin had loved each other hard and for a long time, but Levi was glad Robin had moved on. He was house hunting still with his boyfriend, Shawn, and they were a lovely, committed couple.

The sort of relationship Levi craved more and more, but he lived in a semiremote area now, which made meeting people kind of tough. Dating apps hadn't netted him much success in the past. And visitors to Bentley were usually not locals so flirting there was a waste of time. Maybe some people simply didn't get that one big love of their life, while other people like Robin got two.

Didn't mean Levi would stop trying. Hell, today's Thanksgiving dinner would be full of people he didn't know, including ranch staff and Garrett locals. Maybe he'd luck into someone—if for nothing else, a good roll in the hay.

Dinner officially began at two but guests were allowed to start arriving any time after noon. Since Levi lived a brief five-minute walk from his destination, he left at right around arrival time with his platter of cut cornpone. He loved the bit of land he was currently parked on, secluded from all roads without feeling too desolate or remote. Levi had gotten used to camp-grounds and similar areas to park his home, so the isola-tion was new. Ginger darted out of the brush and trailed him for a few dozen yards before retreating, as was her habit. Even when he went running in the morning, she followed him for a bit before turning back.

Such a mama cat.

Not that she'd ever be an actual mama, because he'd gotten all three of his kitties spayed as soon as they were old enough.

The collection of vehicles parked around the Garrett-Bentley house came into view before the ac-tual structure. Levi hadn't been around last year for the celebration but he had to wonder how that many people fit inside the smallish, two-story cabin. Robin had mentioned that a lot of the ranch staff who attended carpooled but that was still a heck of a lot of vehicles.

He was more familiar with the employees of Bentley Ghost Town than of the neighboring Clean Slate Ranch, but he was very good with faces, and Levi exchanged greetings with several people as soon as he entered the house. It had a log cabin exterior, but the inside was an eclectic mix of styles. The first floor had a huge open living space, with the social area near the door and a long dining table in the rear near a bank of wide win-dows. The view was gorgeous. To the left were stairs to the master loft, and below that was the kitchen and spare rooms.

Levi liked the design of the place a lot, and it was already swarming with people.

Wes Bentley, one half of the duo who owned the place, popped right over with a bright smile. "Hey, wel-come! You didn't have to bring anything."

"I know but this is a family favorite." He handed over the platter. "Cornpone. Like cornbread, only way better."

"Excellent. Drinks are in coolers over there. Please help yourself. And there are appetizers on the table already." Wes bounced away with the platter, his energy already infectious when the guy had probably been cooking for hours by now.

Levi had liked Wes from the moment he met the high-strung actor, much like he'd liked Wes's bear of a boyfriend Mack Garrett, who was also Levi's boss up at Bentley. The names could confuse folks a bit—after all, how many couples lived between towns named after them—but they were good people. He spotted Mack in the kitchen with an older lady he guessed to be Wes's mother, as she'd been named one of the primary participants in cooking today's menu.

While Levi could hold a conversation with just about anyone, he poured himself a plastic cup of root beer and lingered by the coat closet, watching rather than participating. The slowly growing crowd was a mix of straight and queer couples, as well as single folks like himself. He spotted the owner of Clean Slate Ranch, along with the man's foreman and the lady who ran the guesthouse. More ranch hands. One of the servers from the ghost town's saloon.

When Robin and Shawn arrived, Levi exchanged brief hugs with both men. He genuinely liked Shawn, who was quiet and polite and made Robin shine like the sun when Robin smiled at him. The kind of in love Levi missed, but he also wasn't sure he wanted to risk another heartbreak just yet. It had been over a year since

Grant, and his libido was definitely on board with something casual—if he could find someone.

"What are your plans for the next two months?" Shawn asked Levi. "I'm donating my time down at the ranch in the guesthouse, so I've got something to keep me busy."

Shawn was the pastry/sous chef at the ghost town saloon, and he lived in a cabin with Robin down at the ranch while they house hunted. Last year, the ranch cook Patrice had broken her collarbone right before Thanksgiving, and Shawn was hired to cook for guests in her place. It was how Robin and Shawn began their flirtation and eventual romance, and this year Shawn had the same two-month break as everyone else from the ghost town.

"I'm honestly not sure," Levi replied. "Maybe I'll spend some time exploring local attractions for my blog. Haven't had much time to do that yet." Even though he'd been in Garrett for ten months, he was usually too exhausted after work to do anything except stream television shows. And on his weekend—the ghost town was closed Tuesdays and Wednesdays—he was often practicing or wandering the land.

"How about you, man?" Levi asked Robin. "Gonna sit on your ass and whittle another chess set for Shawn?"

"Ha ha." Robin flipped him off. "No, I've got some woodworking commissions to keep me busy. With Christmas coming up, I got a few extra orders through the general store."

Wood whittling had been a hobby for Robin for a long time, until he started selling pieces in the ghost town's general store this past spring. Now he had a good little side business to help supplement his income, es-

pecially during two months without pay. Levi would
be fine. He had an income from his blog and no rent to
pay on the land. Only monthly payments on his house
and truck, and insurance every six months.

He just needed to stay busy so the road didn't call
him too loudly.

Not that he couldn't travel for a while and come back
to roost in two months...

"Hey, there's the crafty cowboy!" someone shouted.

Levi glanced at the front door. Former ranch hand
Slater and his boyfriend, Derrick, had arrived, and they
had a pair of unexpected companions: the Thompson
twins. Levi knew immediately which was Orry and
which was George, because George had haunted eyes.
He'd met them this summer on July 4th when the pair
visited the ghost town. George had been enchanted by
the horses and seemed intrigued by Levi and Robin's
trick riding routines. But there was something about his
big, blue eyes that had captivated Levi five months ago,
and he was a little ashamed that he'd actually searched
George's name online.

He had been shocked to realize the young man he'd
met had once been rising-star figure skater Georgie
Thompson. Levi respected the hell out of athletes like
figure skaters and gymnasts because he knew all about
technique and precision. One wrong move on a racing
horse, and Levi could fall and break his neck.

Just like Xander had.

Levi straightened, intending to go reintroduce himself. Maybe start up a conversation with George.

Except George took in the crowded room, went exceptionally pale, and then bolted back outside.

Chapter Two

I can't do this, I can't do this, I can't do this. Fuck!

George hadn't woken up this morning with butterflies in his stomach. No, he'd woken up with a gut full of angry, buzzing hornets that stung his insides and insisted he cancel Thanksgiving dinner in Garrett. But Orry had been excited all week, and George wouldn't be selfish. So he'd taken his meds, along with antacids, and tried to relax.

Hah.

He'd barely kept his legs from bouncing the entire hour-long car trip outside the city, and even though the Garrett area was now slightly familiar after having been here once before, the big sign advertising the ghost town did nothing to calm him. He swore it somehow made his anxiety worse, and he was a jumpy mess when Derrick parked his car near a sea of other vehicles. Way more than George had anticipated.

It had taken a quiet pep talk from Orry before he could even get out of the car. Derrick and Slater waited patiently, though, aware of how hard this was for George. "Come on, it'll be okay," Orry whispered, one hand on his right elbow.

Walk, you idiot. Walk.

He somehow managed to walk onto the spacious front porch, noting the furniture and people chilling outside. The log cabin exterior of the place. The chill in the air and smell of nature all around him. He followed his brother inside, trying to focus on the back of his head and not see the crowd right away. To absorb the warmth and wonderful scents of turkey, spices and other things.

Then the very loud, "Hey, there's the crafty cowboy!" seemed to put all eyes on Slater and their quartet. All eyes on George. He saw a sea of disappointed fans and all the old shame came rushing back. Crushed down on him. The house was too small, the fans too close.

So he ran like a coward.

Ran all the way back to Derrick's car and pressed his forehead against the cool metal of the door. Regulated his breathing the way he'd been taught during panic attacks. Felt the car beneath his touch. Smelled grass and the faint odor of wood char.

"You're okay." Orry stroked his back with a firm, familiar touch. "Jesus, I didn't think you were this bad."

"I'm so sorry I embarrassed you."

"You didn't embarrass me, bro. I feel like an ass for not realizing how anxious you were about this."

"Didn't want you to see. You wanted to be here. You deserve this."

"Yeah, well, *you* don't deserve *this*." By "this" Orry meant more than just today's panic attack.

But George was tired of letting his anxiety cripple him. His friendships with his downstairs neighbors had reinforced that fatigue and made him truly face his loneliness. "I'm going back inside, I just need a few minutes. I wasn't prepared for all those people. It's been a while."

"I know. But if the people in that house are anything like Slater, they won't judge you for having a
panic attack."

"Thanks." George released his grip on the car long
enough to hug his brother, then leaned his back against
it. Stared up at the sunshine and blue sky. "This is nice."

"Real sky and sun on your face is always better than
through a window." Orry hesitated, as if about to comment again, then smiled and went back to the cabin.

George closed his eyes and allowed the sun to warm
his face for a little while as he worked up the courage to
go back in. His attacks embarrassed the hell out of him
when he had them in front of other people. But unless
Orry told everyone that's what had happened to him,
folks could simply assume he left something in the car.

Except for the handful of folks on the porch who
could probably see him standing here like a fool. Oh
well, it couldn't be helped. As his adrenaline waned and
his fingertips stopped twitching, he caught the sound
of rough scuffling nearby. George opened his eyes to
an unexpected sight: Levi the trick rider.

He blinked hard, sure he was imagining him because
of the sun glaring against his eyelids, but no. Levi stood
a few feet away with a bottle of water in one hand and a
small, almost shy smile on his face. "Hey," Levi said. He
held out the bottle. "Thought maybe you could use this."

"I...thank you." George was crazy thirsty now, and
Levi surprised the hell out of him by cracking the top
before handing it over. George gulped the cold water,
thankful for the man's unexpected kindness. "I mean
it, thank you."

"Happy to." He tucked both hands in the pockets of
his low-slung jeans. In a long-sleeve blue cotton T-shirt

and sneakers, Levi seemed different from the cowboy George remembered. More peaceful. And the man was good looking in a way that made George feel very plain.

"It's a nice day." Stupid small talk was stupid but George still wasn't good at handling conversations with near-strangers.

Levi's smile broadened. "It is. We've had a string of really nice weather up here this week. Glad it held up because I think Wes invited the whole county to this shindig. Some folks might have to eat outside."

"Probably me."

"Not used to big crowds of people, huh?"

"No." Words were coming more easily now, and it had everything to do with his conversation partner. Something about Levi simply...put him at ease. "No, I haven't been around a group like this in years. But Orry really wanted to come today, and I knew he wouldn't if I stayed at home."

"That's a brave thing to do, George. Step outside your comfort zones for your brother."

"He's taken care of me for a long time. It's my turn to do something for him." Determination straightened George's spine. "I can do this."

"Sure you can. Take it in baby steps. Instead of looking at all the faces, focus on the ones nearest you. The ones you're talkin' to. Then look at some new ones if you want but don't push yourself."

George studied Levi's serene expression. "Are you, like, a life coach or something in your spare time?"

Levi laughed and it rippled over George's skin in a pleasant, unexpected way. "No, but I spent a lot of time studying philosophy and various religions when I got out of rehab. I learned a lot of coping mechanisms."

The blunt way Levi admitted to having been in rehab startled George into momentary silence. Who said that to a total stranger? Levi, obviously, and he didn't seem embarrassed at all. His expression hadn't changed. And as curious as he was about why Levi was in rehab— *drugs or alcohol addiction, duh*—he didn't want to ruin this pleasant conversation by being nosy. He liked talking to Levi and wanted to keep doing it for as long as possible.

"Well, you give really good advice," George said.

"Thank you. I appreciate and accept your compliment. Whenever you're ready to go back inside, let me know."

"Might as well give it a whirl. I need to at least meet and thank the hosts for having me. I just don't know who they are."

"That's okay, I can introduce you, if you like."

"Really?" George wasn't sure why that surprised him as much as it did. "Don't you have someone to get back to?" He didn't see a ring on his left hand but surely someone as kind and handsome as Levi had a girlfriend inside.

"No, no one inside." Levi's lips twitched. "But I do have three beautiful ladies waiting for me at home."

George's mouth fell open. The guy had three girlfriends? "You have what?"

"Cats. Ginger, Baby and Sporty."

"Oh." Okay, that made a lot more sense. "I like cats."

"Me too. And they're completely housebroken. My home has a little cat door so they can do their business outside and enjoy wandering."

"Wow." George knew cats could be trained to use the toilet, but to housebreak them like a dog? "How did you do that?"

Levi's smile flickered. "I didn't. An ex did."

Pursuing that felt wrong, so he didn't. "Our building has a cat who uses the toilet. Lucky. He's old and he came with the place when our landlord bought it. He wanders in and out of everyone's apartments. We all keep the lids up so he doesn't poop in our shoes."

Levi laughed again, and yes, it rippled over George a second time. "Sounds like a cat I'd like to meet."

"Lucky's great. Although he's gotten really attached to Slater since he moved in with Derrick. Probably because Slater likes to sit out in the main foyer when he's home and working on a project."

"Robin described the setup once. Sounds really cozy."

"It is." George sipped his water. "It's funny, because until Slater moved in, Orry and I avoided talking to any of our neighbors. We just wanted to get through our days quietly and unnoticed. Now we all have pizza lunches and board game marathons together."

"Slater's accident led to some very positive results."

"Yeah." Time for more positive results. "Okay, let's go inside."

Levi couldn't explain the impulse that had led to him taking water outside to George. Maybe it was Orry's unhappy expression when he came back from checking on his brother. Maybe it was his own innate curiosity about the former figure skater. Or his haunted eyes. Whatever the reason, Levi had done it and was glad.

He'd enjoyed their conversation, and he got the distinct impression that George didn't open up to people easily. George was guarded but his walls seemed to crumble with Levi. And he got extra respect points from Levi for not pressing on the rehab comment. Most people would have wanted to know details, like rubber-neckers at a traffic accident, but George hadn't asked.

George's bravery in coming today when he was clearly uncomfortable spoke to something deep inside Levi. It made him want to befriend the guy in a way he hadn't felt since Robin Butler ambled into the office trailer of Lucky's Rodeo, looking for a job.

"Okay, let's go inside," George said. Slumped against the car before, he now stood with his back straight and his haunted eyes determined.

Levi allowed George to go first, following slightly to his left. They were close in height, Levi a bit taller, but George was on the skinny side of slender, so Levi instinctively moved to watch his back. No real reason for it because they were entering a house full of friends. Still, Levi listened to his instincts.

Except for the new, unexpected urge to take George's hand. That was a quick way to end this newfound quasi friendship they were forming. The younger man gave off zero vibes on his gaydar, so he'd protect from a distance. Maybe even be the guy's friend.

George's hand trembled once as he reached for the screen door but he clasped the handle and pulled. Stepped back inside the full house teaming with both people and pleasant food smells. Orry stood close to the door with Robin and Shawn, and George went directly to his twin's side. He seemed to be following Levi's advice, keeping his attention on the three people in front of him, rather than the house at large, as Robin made introductions. George impressed Levi by shaking their hands.

Orry met Levi's gaze and offered a friendly smile. A nod. Levi nodded back.

Shawn chatted a bit about working at the saloon before asking, "What do you do, George?"

Levi was curious about that, as well, with as bad as his anxiety seemed, but he hadn't wanted to pry too much. He preferred when people offered up personal information.

"I do closed-captioning for online videos," George replied. "It's really flexible hours and lets me work from home."

"That sounds pretty cool. Any particular type of videos?"

George's shoulders stiffened slightly. "All kinds. I like the work."

"At least you have a single, steady paying job," Orry said in a joking tone. "I work, like, four at once."

"Hey, our generation didn't create this economy," Shawn replied. "We're just trying to survive in it. Trust me, I know. I was homeless for two years while still working full time."

Levi blinked, surprised by the blunt admission. But Shawn possessed a strong inner spirit and had a survivor's aura to him. He could believe Shawn would make it through such an ordeal and still be able to smile at the world.

"Dude, it sucks you were homeless," Orry said.

"It did suck, but it's what eventually brought me here." Shawn leaned his shoulder into Robin's and smiled at his boyfriend.

A pang of loneliness struck Levi in the chest. He was beyond happy for Robin's good fortune and newfound love; Robin more than deserved it after losing Xander the way he had. But Levi had needs too. Needs not being met stuck out here in the middle of nowhere, instead of on the road traveling to the next exciting location. Needs frequently met by rodeo fans or casual gawkers. His only serious adult relationship had ended in disaster.

Their group chatted amiably for a while, until Levi said, "George, you wanted to meet today's hosts, right? Should I introduce you?"

George flashed him a wide-eyed stare an instant before the expression gentled. Went more carefully neutral. "Sure, okay. Let's do that."

"One face at a time."

Levi led the way, keenly aware of George sticking close to his back as Levi threaded their way through the packed living room to the kitchen. He introduced George to Mack, Wes and Wes's mother. Levi introduced George to Miles Arlington, who was also helping in the kitchen, but George remembered Miles from his visit to the ghost town. Slater had apparently gotten his friends kitchen access.

So far so good.

George's fingertips were starting to twitch. Not a good sign. Levi steered him back toward Orry, who was chatting with Slater and some other ranch hands. Orry was definitely the more sociable of the pair, and he was heavily engaged in the conversation. George stood there mutely, and Levi stuck close, unsure why he felt the need to when his twin was right there.

Eventually, Wes stood on one of the two long benches on either side of the dining table to thank everyone for coming, thank the other cooks, and announce that it was time to eat. A line began to form for food but George stayed put. Levi stayed too, and Orry did the same. Folks with full plates began to settle at both the dining table, and at spots all around the living space. A card table with folding chairs. The sofa with TV tray tables. Others migrated outside.

Once the majority of people had their food, Orry headed for the line and George followed. George always seemed to follow and that sort of bothered Levi. The guy had strength for sure, and he needed to find that strength again. Learn how to lead himself forward.

Levi got in line behind George and filled a plate with all kinds of delicious-looking food. While he tried to limit his meat intake, he indulged in both ham and turkey, along with gravy and different sides. George's plate was more simplistic with white meat turkey sans gravy, mashed potatoes, some fresh veggies from a snack tray sans dip, and—to Levi's quiet delight—a piece of cornpone. Levi refrained from taking one of the few remaining pieces, because he'd had it before and wanted others to enjoy the amazing taste.

Orry accepted one of two remaining seats at a card table, then looked expectantly at George. George headed for the door. Curious, Levi followed him. With the patio furniture full, George went down the steps and found a patch of grass he liked before plunking down. Levi did the same, not surprised George preferred the open air to the stifling house. All the faces and cacophonous voices.

They ate in silence for a few minutes, and Levi enjoyed the simplicity of it. Existing without expectation. With a cute boy he kind of liked but didn't want to scare away, because the cute boy was likely straight.

"So why did you name one of your cats Sporty?" George asked, apropos of nothing.

Levi tilted his head. "She's one of the Spice Girls. All three cats are named after former members."

"Oh. I mean, I know who the Spice Girls are, kind of, but I didn't know their names."

"Not a fan of nineties girl group pop?"

"Not really, I'm not sure. Growing up, we listened to mostly classical music, and that's all I ever skated to, and now I just listen to whatever streams on my app." George's eyes went wide as he realized what he'd let slip.

He probably didn't talk about his former career anymore, and Levi didn't want to make a big deal out of it. "In the interest of full disclosure, I know you used to figure skate competitively."

George's pale skin stained bright red. "Oh. How?"

This time it was Levi's turn to be slightly embarrassed. "After we met back in July, I got incredibly curious about you. You seemed familiar somehow, and I searched your name online."

"You cyberstalked me?" This time, George looked ready to bolt.

Fix this, you fool.

"No," Levi said firmly. "Once I realized you were Georgie Thompson, I stopped looking. Believe it or not, I genuinely admire figure skaters for their artistry and flexibility. I recognized your name, and I remember the…" Drama wasn't the right word. "I remember how your departure from the sport was depicted in the news."

George snorted. "Departure is one word for it, I guess. I quit right before a skate that could have helped get me on the Olympic team. Shit, I never talk about this stuff." He gazed at Levi with a kind of wonder on his face. "Why is it so easy to talk to you?"

"Because I'm a neutral party, a relative stranger, and

I like listening to you talk." That had come out a tad flirtier than Levi intended, but George didn't seem to notice. "I'm sure you had your reasons for quittin'."

"I did. My sanity and my health." He didn't elaborate on those things, and the topic was far too serious for a holiday, so Levi didn't push.

"Then let me ask you a tough question." George tensed, so Levi didn't draw it out; he liked the kid too much to make him uncomfortable. "What's your favorite scary movie?"

George burst out laughing. A lovely sound he should make more often. "I like your brand of tough questions. I'm not sure if I have one. I don't watch a lot of scary movies, but I did get the cultural reference for once."

"Okay, then favorite movie genre."

"Romantic comedies, I guess. I like knowing it'll have a happy ending. I'm not much for watching the violent stuff."

"Understandable. I watch pretty much anything, depending on my mood. Okay, I know you live in San Francisco, but are you from the Bay Area?"

George poked at his slice of turkey. "I guess I am. We were born in Fremont and grew up there, but when I showed a real talent for ice skating at five years old, my parents moved us to Los Angeles because my mom decided I'd find the best coaches there." His gaze flickered with something unpleasant Levi wanted to ask about but didn't. "After I quit, Orry and I moved back here to live with our grandparents, until we were older and could live on our own."

"Do you still see your grandparents?"

"Orry does. They live together in an assisted living center. I try to visit but mostly I call them on their tablet.

At least that way we can at least chat face-to-face. Sort of. It's just…hard seeing people who were so strong for me weak now. Grandpa had a stroke two years ago, and he has a hard time taking care of himself, and sometimes I feel so fucking selfish for not doing more."

George's sad expression hardened slightly, as if his grief was joined by annoyance or anger. Anger at exactly what, Levi could only guess. Himself and his crippling anxiety? His social isolation? But anger was a better emotion sometimes than grief. Anger was more likely to motivate someone to change their situation, while grief often left them resigned to it.

"What more do you see yourself doing in the future?" Levi asked.

"I don't know. Take a walk around the block without wanting to throw up." He waved his hand at the cabin. "Come to a Thanksgiving dinner without running out of the room. Honestly, today was a huge step for me. Maybe too huge. But it's hard not to try and take these huge steps when I've been sitting still for so long." George's eyes flickered briefly lower on Levi's face before rising again. "A lot of different steps."

Had he looked at Levi's mouth? "George, how old are you?"

"Twenty-three. Why?" A new sort of stubbornness crept into George's expression. "How old are you?"

"Thirty-four."

His eyes briefly widened. "You don't look that old."

Levi snickered. "Thank you, I think."

"I'm sorry, I didn't mean to imply thirty-four is old, you just look younger." He blushed again, which was kind of adorable. "Shit, I'm fucking this up, aren't I?"

"You aren't fucking up anything. We're new friends

getting to know each other." Levi took a chance and gently squeezed his wrist, a brief contact that he shouldn't have indulged in, because his skin buzzed with awareness.

Even George seemed surprised, staring at his wrist for a long moment before meeting Levi's gaze again. A new sort of wonder spread across his face, as if he'd discovered something new and amazing through one simple touch. He glanced at Levi's mouth again. George was so sweet, so innocent, so…kissable.

And probably a damned virgin. Don't be that guy.

"Are you almost done eating?" Levi asked, desperate to redirect their conversation into something less problematic. He was no saint and not above fucking a near-stranger, but George was special. And not for Levi.

"Um, I guess." George had a few scraps of his food left but no longer seemed interested in it. And his guard was back up, damn it.

"Do you want pie? They always have a ton of dessert options."

"No, thanks. Um, do you mind taking my plate? I'm going to take a walk." George sort of shoved his paper plate and fork at Levi, then scrambled to his feet and began walking toward the tree line behind the house.

Damn it, I fucked up.

Part of Levi wanted to chase after him, but George wasn't his to chase. They were newish friends who barely knew each other. Levi wanted to get to know him better, but if their single touch was any indication, that could be a bad idea. Or it could be an amazing one.

Only time—and the universe—would tell.

Chapter Three

George strode across the lawn to the back of the property, his face flaming, hands in his pockets, positive he was the biggest idiot on the planet. After years of self-isolation, after years of pretending he had no physical desire or need to touch, because that meant human interaction, he'd managed a real connection to another person. And somehow, he'd fucked it up.

Never in his life had the casual touch of someone else warmed his skin so quickly. It had both scared and excited him, because he liked talking to Levi. Levi was kind, inviting, and he didn't push. Didn't ask invasive questions, even though he had to be thinking them. And he was damned attractive.

George had never given much thought to his sexuality, because he'd never had time to date as a teenager. Always busy with practice, tutoring and more practice. Sure, he'd roughhoused a bit in the locker room with other skaters, and enjoyed the physical contact, but that was typical teenage boy stuff. Wasn't it? He sure as hell hadn't liked it when Adrian touched him.

Levi's touch, though? It made George feel something he didn't understand. Talking to Levi today, hanging around him for over an hour, had been a breath of fresh air in his otherwise stuffy existence, and he wanted that air back. But he'd humiliated himself by trying to flirt, and Levi was definitely not interested.

George wandered near the edge of the forest that made up the back of the cabin's property. In the far distance, he could see the very peak of the mountain that he remembered from the ghost town. The land up here was absolutely gorgeous, even with the weather easing into winter. Peaceful in its quiet. Completely different from living in the city with its constant noise and people everywhere.

The brush rustled nearby and George froze. He'd wandered a long way from the cabin, and there were wild animals out there in the mountains. Slater had said so. The rustling got closer, and then a small black-and-white creature streaked out from the underbrush. George yelped, terrified it was a skunk about to spray him.

Instead, the cat stopped by his ankles and bumped her head on his leg. George smiled and squatted to pet her. "You must be one of Levi's kitties."

She let him scratch her head a few times before swatting him away with one paw. "Hey, sassy britches, you came over to me for pets. Are you Baby, Sporty or, well, I guess you probably aren't Ginger."

She meowed at him, then turned and started walking toward the underbrush. George stood, amused when she stopped and looked back at him, as if expecting him to follow. If these cats were smart enough to use a cat door and always come home to Levi at night, maybe he was supposed to follow. Curious, he did. She darted behind a tree, and a few steps into the woods, George heard it.

Yowling. Distant, but he followed the sound and the

cat deeper into the woods until he found the source. A striped ginger cat lay on her side, meowing in distress, and at first George couldn't figure out why. He knelt, heart aching for the poor creature's obvious pain. Then he noticed the odd angle of one hip, protruding too far from the joint. She must have fallen out of a tree and hurt herself.

"It's okay, baby, we'll get you help." He yanked out his cell and called Orry.

"Dude, why are you calling? Where—what's that noise?"

"Where's Levi? I need to talk to him."

"Why? Are you okay?"

"I found one of his cats in the woods and she's hurt. I don't know what to do."

"Shit, okay. One sec." The hum of voices filled a line for too damned long, and the ginger's distress was starting to freak George out.

"George?" Levi asked. "Where are you?"

"In the woods."

"North or south?"

"I have no idea."

Levi's voice was coming in shorter pants, as if he was running and talking at the same time. Knowing he was coming helped George keep a lid on his panic. "When you walked, did you go left or right along the tree line?"

"Right."

"Okay, good. Which cat and what's wrong with her?"

"The ginger, and I think maybe she dislocated her hip but I don't know. She isn't bleeding, she's just in pain."

"I know, I can hear her. She's Ginger. I'll be there soon, okay?"

"Okay."

Levi hung up, and George waited, making what he hoped were soothing sounds, but the poor cat's meowing had begun fucking with his anxiety. His hands were shaking, and he really needed Levi to get there. To fix this, because George didn't know how.

He finally heard Levi shouting his name; George shouted right back, and it helped Levi zero in on them. His face was flushed but he seemed outwardly calm, and George was surprised to see Orry following right behind.

"Are you okay?" Orry asked George, while Levi fell to his knees and stroked Ginger's head.

"I've been better but I'm not hurt." George watched Levi gently run his fingers along the cat's flank, down to her protruding hip. She hissed. "Your black-and-white one led me to Ginger."

Levi looked up, his eyes a bit too shiny. "That's Baby. I think you're right about Ginger's hip."

"What do we do? Vets aren't open on Thanksgiving."

"There's an emergency vet about thirty minutes from here. Orry, can you do a favor for me?"

"Sure," Orry replied.

"My house is only a few dozen yards farther north. My pickup's there, and the keys are in the ignition. Can you bring it down here? I don't want to jostle Ginger more than I have to."

"Of course, I'll be right back." Orry took off at a run.

"I'm so sorry, little girl," Levi said to his wailing pet. "I wish I could make it stop hurtin'." The heartbreak and tenderness in his voice made George's own heart ache a bit for the older man's pain.

George risked reaching out and squeezing Levi's

shoulder. "I'm sorry she's hurt." *I'm sorry you're hurting, too.*

"Thank you. Me too."

The leaves rustled nearby. Baby came back out of the underbrush, trailed by a calico with gorgeous mottled fur in all shades of brown, tan, black and gold. Sporty. The pair stopped nearby and watched, seeming confused by their sister's problem.

"They were six weeks old when I rescued them," Levi said. "Littermates, I believe. They've got this hive mind that's a little scary when they conspire to steal whatever I'm cooking for dinner."

"It's sweet how close they are."

A truck engine rumbled toward them. "Okay, you aren't going to like this, little girl." Levi took his jacket off and spread it on the ground. As gently as he could, he lifted Ginger up and put her on the coat. The cat yowled and hissed but didn't actively try to bite him. Levi wrapped her up, then slowly stood. George helped him with a hand on his elbow for balance. He kept his hand there. It was just practical. They didn't need Levi tripping as they picked their way out of the woods.

The truck was idling, Orry standing by the fender. George opened the passenger door for Levi, who seemed torn about putting Ginger on the seat. No one to hold and support her. "I'll go with you," George said without thinking. "I can hold Ginger so she isn't alone."

Surprise flashed across Levi's face for an instant before something softer replaced it. "Are you sure?"

No. "Yes."

"Okay. Thank you, George."

"Of course." He climbed into the passenger seat,

buckled up, and held still while Levi carefully arranged the coat-bundled cat on his lap.

Orry appeared before Levi could shut the door. "Call me, bro. Keep me updated on everything." His expression clearly said he didn't trust Levi alone with his brother on a long car trip to an unknown destination. But George trusted Levi.

"I will."

Orry flashed Levi, who was getting in on the driver's side, an odd look, then gently closed the door. George closed his eyes and focused on his breathing. On the scents of leather and a light, spicy cologne in the truck cab. On the constant whine of the cat on his lap. The vibrations of the truck as Levi drove. The radio wasn't on, leaving the truck mostly silent when Ginger wasn't voicing her displeasure.

"You doing okay over there?" Levi asked after a few minutes.

"I think so." He opened his eyes. "This is...really outside my comfort zone."

"Are you sure—"

"I'm sure I want to be here." George met and held Levi's gaze briefly. "I need to do this. Baby found me and brought me to Ginger to help her. Let me help."

Levi grinned so sweetly George couldn't help another glance at his lips. Lips he'd first noticed while they ate, watching them open and close around bites of food. Unbidden images had begun stirring in the far recesses of his mind. Images and urges that Levi had promptly quelled with his obvious disinterest. Not that George was entirely sure what he, himself, wanted.

To feel things. To stop being cut off from the world and the people in it.

"I'm grateful for your help and acknowledge your intentions," Levi said.

That was a strange way to phrase things, but once in a while, odd words seemed to come out of Levi. But he'd mentioned studying religions and spirituality; maybe that was his Zen way of saying "You can help."

Ginger's cries lowered a bit the longer they drove. Maybe it was the comfort of being on a warm lap, in the warm truck cab, versus laying on the cold ground alone. George stroked her forehead with his fingertips, wishing he could do more for her and for her daddy. They soon left Garrett behind and were on the interstate heading west toward San Jose.

"How do you know where this clinic is?" George asked.

"Had a scare with Baby a few months ago. She came home one night with a swollen bite on her hip, and the regular vet over in Daggett was closed, so I had to find this one. Couldn't risk it had it been a venomous snake."

George shuddered. Snakes freaked him out. And Baby was obviously fine if she was out there saving her sister today. "Are there a lot of venomous snakes around here?"

"Not really, and they're mostly varieties of rattlers, which makes them easier to stay away from. The Garretts do a good job of keeping the lands closest to the ghost town and ranch clear of dangerous animals. Most of them seem to stick to the wilder parts of the land, like the mountain lions."

"Have you ever seen one? A mountain lion?"

Levi grinned as he eased into an exit lane. "I have. I run every morning, have for a while now. It wakes me up and gets me goin' for the day."

George hid a grimace. He'd been a runner too, once upon a time, and not because it woke him up. It burned calories and kept him slender.

"I moved here back in January, and it was March 13th when it happened. I was runnin' on a new trail, trying to change up my routine, and I got into a pretty isolated area by accident. And that's when I saw her." He negotiated another turn, wonder visible in his face and audible in his voice. "She was sunning herself on a boulder, and I froze solid when I spotted her there. I had no idea what to do, but runnin' felt idiotic. I stood there for a long time. She just...watched me. She was breathtaking."

He couldn't imagine happening upon a mountain lion while out for a run. He'd have freaked the fuck out and probably gotten himself eaten. But George had usually run at the gym tracks or on a treadmill, not out in the California wilderness.

"I very quietly thanked her for meeting me that day," Levi continued, "and for allowing me to experience her beauty. Her long tail flicked once and it felt like a dismissal, so I began backing away. One step at a time. When she yawned at me, I felt safe enough to turn and walk to a safe enough distance to start runnin' again. It was an amazing moment."

"It sounds amazing, but if that had been me I'd have probably peed my pants."

Levi chuckled. "I think a lot of people would. I wasn't calm because I'm super brave in the face of danger. I've just...reached a kind of peace with the world and my own existence in it."

"I'm jealous of that." George stared out the window at the passing suburb, unable to remember being at peace with his life. Maybe when he was out there skating, doing his routine and living in the jumps, spins, and the timing with the music. But once the music stopped, that peace had stopped.

Levi pulled into a space at the emergency clinic before they could continue the discussion, and George was glad. Levi got out and collected Ginger. George rang the buzzer and a few seconds later they were let inside—apparently, that was a thing, even during the daytime. A friendly nurse took Ginger straight back to their exam area, while Levi filled out a clipboard of information. George hung back, surprised they were the only people there.

George forced himself to read a magazine so he didn't pace the waiting room. He'd never been inside a vet's office before, but it felt like any regular doctor's office, except all the posters were about animals instead of people. It had that same medicinal smell. The same hard waiting room chairs. Just like the hospital he'd been in for a while after he quit skating.

Fuck, I can't do this.

"I'm so sorry, Levi," George said. "Can I please wait in your truck?"

Levi handed him the keys without a word, his expression impossible to read.

George fled.

The simple fact that George had volunteered to come all the way out here for one of Levi's cats meant a great deal, and it had endeared the younger man to him in ways Levi couldn't voice. Not only had George found and rescued one of his cats, he'd braved his own anxiety to hold her and comfort her while Levi drove them all to a strange town.

George had held out longer than Levi expected, given what he knew about how sheltered George's life had been up until recently. It didn't hurt his feelings at all when George asked to wait in the truck. He still missed George's presence and that was an odd new feeling.

So he stopped thinking about George. When he finally spoke to a vet, an X-ray confirmed a hip dislocation. Since it was recent, they could manually reset it under general anesthesia. She'd have to wear a bandage for a while and—the hardest part of all—be confined so she didn't dislocate it again before it properly healed.

His cats were used to wandering the wider world. Seeing Ginger in a cage for days, maybe up to two weeks, sucked in the worst way. She also had to be carefully monitored, which sent his thoughts of traveling for his two-month hiatus from work right out the window. On the plus side, he had the time to keep an eye on her. But the idea of kicking around his house with nothing to do for days on end…not appealing at all.

While he waited, he fielded a few concerned texts from Robin—Orry had apparently told several people why Levi had abruptly fled the Thanksgiving gathering—making sure Levi was okay. Levi wasn't entirely sure, because today had rattled him. His kitties were part of him in ways he couldn't explain, and hearing Ginger wailing so loudly had torn out a bit of his heart. But she'd be okay because George had found her.

Stop thinking about George.

Easier said than done. George was under his skin and digging in deeper with each new moment they shared today. He was kind and brave and scared and sensitive, and he wasn't the kind of person Levi was usually attracted to. He enjoyed loud personalities, people who challenged him in new, unexpected ways.

George is very unexpected.

He was and in brand-new ways. He was soft and contemplative, instead of brash and loud. George tried hard not to be noticed, even when he was the most beautiful person in the room. He was also so freaking young and inexperienced, and Levi was terrified of getting too close. Of exposing him to the darkness in Levi's past. To all the things he'd done to feed his addictions.

George came back into the waiting room—which had grown by four people who'd brought in various pets—around four with an unhappy frown on his pretty face. "Derrick and Slater are ready to head home," he said. "I texted them the address here. They're going to stop by and pick me up."

"Oh. Okay." Levi wasn't sure what else to say. As much as he wanted the comfort of having George nearby, the guy had a life in San Francisco to return to.

"I hate to leave you alone, but they're my ride home."

"I know. It's okay. I should be able to take Ginger home soon." Home to a tiny house he shared with three cats and no one else.

George frowned, then sat in the chair beside him. "Look, give me your number. Please? I need to know how Ginger is doing." The bubble of hurt those words produced burst when George added, "And you, too."

Levi happily exchanged information with George, grateful his new friend wanted to stay in contact. "Excepting my cat getting hurt, hanging out with you today was fun, George. I'm glad we got to know each other."

"Me too. I have a hard time making new friends, and I think you're, like, a really cool person."

"Same. Not as much the making new friends part, but the cool person part. I truly hope you keep testing your comfort zones and trying new things."

"I'll do my best."

"That's all any of us really can do." Levi resisted the new, strong urge to kiss George goodbye. That was a bad idea for a whole host of reasons, the least of which was George's likely inexperience when it came to dating and sex. The inexperience, Levi was guessing at, but it was a pretty good guess based on what little he knew about George's life. He was also uncertain if George's apparent interest was because of Levi specifically, or because Levi was the first person in a long time to show him a lot of direct attention.

"Ginger is going to be okay?" George asked.

"Yeah, they're fixing her up. She's gotta stay in a carrier for a few days or more so that's not going to be fun. I've gotta watch her, make sure she doesn't mess with the bandages. I'm not looking forward to spending my winter break cooped up inside with one cat and my laptop."

Levi abhorred the idea of losing his hour-long morning runs. Runs that woke him up and made him feel like part of the wider world. He hated the idea of being stuck inside his tiny home all day long, instead of outside and moving around, reminding himself of why he was sober—so he could live his life in honor of his baby brother. Sure, he could take Ginger's carrier wherever he went to watch her, but too much jostling would hinder her recovery. Maybe even negatively affect it. But she was his cat, and he didn't have any other options than to stay home and care for her.

"It's too bad she isn't my cat," George said. "I spend my entire day in my bedroom working. I could watch her easy."

Levi studied George's face, the idea striking him hard. George preferred staying indoors, versus going out, and he worked from home. Watching Ginger would be easy enough without hindering his routines. And visiting Ginger every day would be the perfect excuse to spend more time with George. Get to know his new friend better. And it would give Ginger a better environment for her to recover, while also keeping Levi on his own path forward. "Is taking Ginger temporarily something you'd seriously do?"

George blinked at him several times. "I mean... I've never owned a cat before but Lucky is fun to play with."

"Cats are very independent creatures, which I'm sure you know from Lucky. The hardest part is going to be her whining to be let out and keeping the litter box clean, since she'll be in an enclosed space. But no pressure to do it, I know that was probably an off-the-cuff comment, not you volunteering."

"You'd really trust me to take care of Ginger? We barely know each other."

"True, but you strike me as a sincere person. And selfishly, the idea of being inside all the time..." Levi searched for a way to explain that didn't dump his past all over George, or make himself sound like an ass. "I love my cats, but being outdoors gives me a sense of peace I don't get from anything else right now. Keeps me centered. As strange and impulsive as it sounds, I think this is a great option for her recovery." *And my continued sobriety.*

Determination crept over George's face. "I'll do it. I can do this. It's not as if I really go anywhere. Sure."

"Yeah?" Something like pride warmed Levi's chest and, despite knowing how much he'd miss and worry about her, this still felt right. "I really appreciate this. I'll be over every day to visit her, if that's okay."

"Of course, she's your cat." His eyes flickered briefly with panic. "Um, so how do we do this?"

"Well, I'd offer to drive you guys home, but I'll need to swing by Walmart for a carrier, food, and a litter tray. Plus, I bet you've come pretty close to your limit of pushing boundaries today. Why don't you go home with Orry and the others as planned. I'll be by later with Ginger and the supplies."

"Okay. Okay, that sounds like a good plan." George's shoulders relaxed a bit. "Thank you. I do need to get back to familiar surroundings again. I'll text you the address." He did, then made a call. "Hey, brother, we're going to have an extra roommate for a couple of days to two weeks."

Orry squawked.

Chapter Four

George had gone into today's Thanksgiving meal expecting to be exhausted when it was over and needing a nap as soon he got into the car. Instead, he was a ball of nervous energy on the ride back to the house, telling the tale of his cat rescue afternoon to Derrick and Slater while Orry shot him annoyed looks over the new roommate announcement. George was rarely an impulsive person, and while he hadn't expected Levi to take his offer seriously, he was glad he'd volunteered.

It meant seeing Levi again soon. And often.

He liked his new friend. He liked Levi's overall positive attitude toward life. His love for his cats. His... well, pretty much everything. He just really liked Levi.

"You might want to do your best to keep Lucky out of your apartment," Derrick said. "He's always been king of the house, and he might not like having another cat around."

"Good idea," George replied. "But Ginger has to stay in her carrier anyway, so even if he sneaks inside, she'll have protection." He'd be careful, though. Levi was entrusting George with his little girl's care and George couldn't fuck it up.

"Ginger is an outdoor cat, though, right? She's not going to like being locked up."

"I know. Hopefully, she doesn't yowl loud enough for it to go through the walls to the other apartments. And I apologize ahead of time if it does." George didn't want to alienate his new friends with noise but doing this for Levi felt important in a way he couldn't explain. Not only important to Levi but also for George.

I'll prove I can take care of another living creature, instead of always being taken care of.

"Don't worry about it," Slater said. "You're doing a really nice thing for Levi by taking in his cat."

Derrick reached out to squeeze Slater's shoulder. "Kind of like when I took in you and your busted ankle this summer?"

"Exactly."

George snorted. "Yeah, well, I'm not allowed to fall in love with Ginger. She has a daddy." Derrick started laughing but George wasn't sure why that was funny. Slater punched Derrick in the shoulder. "What did I miss?"

"Nothing, Derrick is being childish," Slater replied. "So you and Levi hit it off, huh? I don't really know him but he's got a long history with Robin. Robin was married to Levi's brother Xander."

"Oh wow. *Was* married? Did they divorce or something?"

"No, Xander died in an accident about…it'll be four years this Christmas. From the gossip I've heard, Levi and Robin lost touch for a while but got back in contact last year when Mack brought up the idea of a big rodeo show to reopen the ghost town."

"And now they do the trick riding demos together.

Huh." Funny how life randomly brought people together.

"Robin was saying that he and Shawn might have
decided on a house. They've been looking for a while."

"Good for them," Derrick replied. "You think Reyes
and Miles will ever move out of cabin row?"

"Doubtful, not while Reyes is head cowboy at the
ranch."

"What's cabin row?" Orry asked. Neither of the
twins had ever been to Clean Slate Ranch, only Bentley Ghost Town, despite both attractions being on the
same property.

"It's the row of two-person cabins behind the main
house where the horsemen live. Early last year, when
Miles was hired to be head chef at the ghost town saloon, he moved into a cabin with Reyes, and eventually
they fell in love. And with both of them still working on
Garrett land, it makes sense to keep living there. They
seem happy enough."

"But Robin and Shawn want to move out of their
cabin and buy a house?" George asked.

"Yes, because Arthur needs the cabin space, and neither of them work for him now. They work for Mack.
Plus, Shawn is teaching Robin how to cook."

Arthur Garrett was the owner of Clean Slate Ranch,
and he owned the land that the ghost town—and his
grandson Mack—resided on. George knew that much
from studying the websites for both places. He'd heard
enough stories by now of people he'd only briefly met
that some of them felt like old friends. And maybe he
could get to know more people through Levi.

At home, Orry and George each thanked Derrick for
driving before going up the private staircase to their

apartment. Lucky was nowhere to be seen, which wasn't unusual when the lobby was quiet. Orry unlocked their door, and as soon as it was shut, said, "You should have asked me first."

"It's just a cat." George hung his jacket on the hooks by the door. "And it's for less than two weeks, just until she doesn't need to be closely monitored anymore."

"But why did you have to do it?"

"I didn't. But I work from home and I have the time to basically look at her every five minutes and make sure she isn't ripping the bandage off. I don't get the sense Levi would handle that as well as I can. Being stuck inside all the time."

Orry crossed his arms. "How do you know? You just met him."

"We talked a lot." George crossed into the kitchen to get a soda from the fridge. "He used to live a nomadic life and genuinely seems to love the outdoors. He's also got this Zen vibe going that's very…peaceful."

"So you guys are best friends now?"

George stared at his brother, a little confused by the cold attitude. "No, but we are friends. Come on, Orry, he's the first new friend I've made in years that doesn't already live in this house."

"And who's single."

"What?" What the hell did Levi being single have to do with anything? "So?"

"So I'm worried about you getting attached to an older, single guy after knowing him for a few hours. You have been in a bubble for years, and I don't want you to get taken advantage of."

George scowled, equally grateful that his brother was always watching his back and also annoyed by the same. "Come on, Levi isn't that guy. We're friends and I'm helping him take care of his cat. He loves those cats to bits, I could tell the minute he saw how hurt Ginger was."

"Yeah, I saw it too. His face when you told him on the phone." Orry uncrossed his arms. "He seems okay."

"He is okay, and you worry too much. Now if you're done haranguing me, I have to go clean my room. I'm having a guest."

"Your room is spotless like the rest of the apartment."

"I need to know the exact right spot for Ginger's cage. I might have to rearrange something." Plus, they were going to have a visitor inside the apartment for the first time in ages, and George wanted everything to look good.

His bedroom didn't have much in it besides a basic single bed, a flimsy side table, and his desk. Hamper. The closet was tiny, but he didn't own a lot of clothes because he worked from home. Why not wear the same T-shirt three days in a row as long as it didn't smell? Saved on laundry, too. His desk was near the room's only window and there was a bare spot on the floor by the wall to his right. Should be a good spot for Ginger. She'd at least have a small view of the outdoors during her confinement.

The bed was made, because George always made his bed after taking a morning shower. He'd read once that if you accomplished one task first thing, you'd had a successful day already. His grandmother had crocheted the afghan on his bed, and he smoothed a hand over it. She was dealing with a lot, and he really needed to visit. It had been too long. She still crocheted things she occasionally sent back to the apartment with Orry, like winter hats and scarves. Others she sold at craft fairs held by their assisted living center.

With nothing else to do in his room, George grabbed his tablet and opened the last book he'd been reading. Perched on the bed, he let time pass. Maybe an hour went by before the buzzer rang out in the living room. He stood, unsure where Orry was, and left his room. Since Orry wasn't in sight, George hit the button.

"Hello?"

"It's Levi and Ginger."

His pulse jumped. "Okay. Come inside and we're the staircase on the right."

"Cool."

George pushed the button that unlocked the front door for visitors. Every tenant had two keys: one shared to get into the house and a second key unique to each apartment. He opened the apartment door to the pleasant sight of Levi ascending the stairs with a cardboard carrier in his hand and a shopping bag in the other. It only occurred to George then that Levi probably had more stuff in his truck, and that he should have volunteered to help.

Ginger was no longer meowing her head off, which George appreciated. Once he reached the landing, Levi met his gaze and smiled. "Hey again."

"Hi," George replied. "Uh, please, come inside. Do you have more stuff to get?"

"I do." Levi put the bag on the floor near the door, then handed the carrier over to George. "But I can manage in one more trip, if you want to get to know a slightly stoned Ginger a bit better."

He laughed. "Okay."

Levi disappeared again, and George left the door

partly open for him. He peeked in through the wide holes in the cardboard carrier, likely from the emergency vet. Ginger's hind leg was wrapped up in a white bandage, and the poor kitty did look stoned. A tiny slip of her tongue stuck out between her lips, and that was strangely adorable. "Hello, new roomie."

She blinked.

"These are your new digs for a while. Welcome."

Orry wandered in from his bedroom. "Levi gone already?"

George resisted the urge to roll his eyes. "No, he had to go get more stuff. Want to meet Ginger?"

"I guess." He bent over and looked inside. "Hi, kitty. Don't cry too loud, okay? I have a hard time sleeping as it is."

That tidbit surprised George a little. Sure, Orry worked several different jobs that varied hours, but he wasn't sleeping? Even more reason for George to get his shit together. Maybe he could go out and find his own second, part-time job so Orry didn't feel like he had to do all the work keeping the rent paid and food in the fridge.

"Why do you have trouble sleeping?" George asked. "For how long?"

"A few months, and I don't know why. Probably just stress, and I don't want to take those over the counter drugs. I'm fine."

George wanted to believe him but Orry always downplayed things when he was sick or stressed out, because he didn't want to worry George. They were going to address this again, like adults, but not while they had a guest. Levi returned a few minutes later with

another bag and a box containing some sort of metal
crate meant for small dogs.

"Since I couldn't bear to leave her in an enclosed
carrier for days on end," Levi said, "I bought this for
her. She'll be able to see a lot more."

"That's really cool of you," George replied. And it
really was. "I have spot in my room picked out where
she can see out the window."

Levi beamed. "Show me the way."

They left Ginger with Orry for now, and George's
stomach wobbled weirdly as another person not his
brother entered his bedroom for the first time since he
moved in. He pointed out the spot, and Levi immediately set to work building the crate. George watched
him, once again impressed by his calm presence now
that the crisis had passed. Even if Orry hadn't been
home, George was perfectly safe with Levi.

Levi wasn't going to get angry, yell at him, and then
shove him like Adrian had.

"Hey, you okay?" Levi asked.

"Huh?" George looked up to find Levi watching him
with open concern. "Yeah, sorry. I got lost in thought."

"Not good thoughts, I take it. Are you having second
thoughts about keeping Ginger for a while?"

"No, this was totally unrelated. I've never had a pet
before. I'm kind of looking forward to the experience."

Something odd flickered in Levi's eyes. "I look forward to the experience, too. Visiting Ginger every day
is a good excuse to explore San Francisco more. Might
as well since I'm out here."

"I'd offer a guided tour but I…haven't been out much
since I came back to the city. I'm sure a lot has changed
since I was younger."

"Probably." Levi went back to work on the crate. "I bought a small litter pan that will fit inside the crate and still give Ginger room to move around a bit. I know scooping poop every day isn't all that fun but the litter is flushable."

"Um, okay." They made flushable cat litter? Curious, George went to inspect the bag of other items Levi had brought. Orry was sitting on the floor poking his fingers through the holes in Ginger's carrier, making weird little noises at her. George grinned. Looked like she had a new fan.

Cat food, food and water bowls, litter, a small litter tray, a plastic scoop, some treats, and pill pocket things for medicine. All the basic things they'd need to get through the next few days to a week. Ginger couldn't exactly play with toys if she was expected to stay as motionless as possible so her hip could heal. George put some food in the bowl, then stored the bag and treats on top of the fridge. Added litter to the pan. He hedged on where to keep the rest of the litter, but in the end chose the bathroom. If he was flushing the pee clumps and poop, might as well refill at the dumpsite. He didn't want to leave a dirty scoop on the floor, so George found a plastic container with no lid that he could see, and he put the scoop in that near the toilet.

When he returned to the bedroom, Levi had just finished assembling the crate. The spaces between each slim metal bar were wide enough to get three fingers through. Miss Ginger wouldn't lack for petting.

"Is she a snuggler?" George asked.

"Ginger?" Levi shook his head and began stuffing extra bits of garbage into the box. "Nah. Baby is the snuggler. Ginger likes to be scratched right between her shoulder blades but isn't much of a lap cat. Mostly, she's going to hate being confined."

"I can kind of relate. I used to live for self-isolation and being alone, but lately I've been… I don't know. Craving social interaction in a way I haven't in a long time. I can definitely relate to poor Ginger's predicament, but at least she's alive. She can heal and go back to her life."

Levi stood and held his gaze for a long moment that made George's belly wobble again. "Is that what you're trying to do? Get back to life?"

"Yes. And if having a real life means taking care of a friend's cat, then that's what I'll do."

"I admire you, George. Not everyone would be brave enough to step this far outside their comfort zone. Especially to help a near-stranger."

"I don't think of you as a stranger anymore, Levi. Maybe it's only been a day but you are my friend. I hope."

Levi grinned. "We're friends." He opened his mouth to say something else, but a loud yowl preceded Orry walking into the small room with Ginger in her carrier.

"She's tired of me, I guess," Orry said. He handed the carrier to George. "Here. She's your guest." Then he strode out of the room.

George chuckled. "For all my issues, Orry can be a drama queen, too. Do you think Miss Ginger is tired of her box?"

"Most definitely," Levi replied. "Come on, baby girl, let's give you more light, at least."

George gave Levi the carrier, and he gently eased Ginger from the cardboard prison to the more open crate. Ginger blinked dumbly at them, then sniffed at her new litter box. It only took up about a third of the crate, giving her room to move around. But not enough room to hurt her newly set hip. Levi sat cross-legged by the crate and petted her through the bars, whispering things George couldn't hear. His reluctance to leave his cat was almost painful to see, and George flailed for the right thing to say.

"Does she, uh, have any medication to take?" George asked.

"Yes, it's in one of the bags. I bought a bag of those pill pocket treat things because she hates taking pills. That way you don't get all scratched up trying to pry her mouth open, and she won't traumatize her hip from struggling."

"Smart plan. Um, it's getting late. Do you want to stay for dinner?"

"That's very kind of you, but I should probably go soon. I've disrupted your day enough already."

It isn't a disruption anymore.

George genuinely liked being around Levi. "Well, I'll let you sit with Ginger alone, then."

"You don't have to leave." Levi looked up with that familiar, warm smile, and he seemed to mean it.

"It's okay, I need to ask Orry something." He didn't really but it was a good excuse to leave the room, and it wasn't until he'd tracked Orry to his own bedroom that George realized what he'd done: he'd left someone alone in his room near all his personal things. His stomach rolled with acid but Levi was safe. He wouldn't go snooping.

Orry lay stretched out on his stomach across his bed, playing a game on his phone, and he didn't acknowledge George's arrival.

"Are you sure you aren't mad at me?" George asked.

"Why would I be mad at you?"

"For bringing a cat into the apartment without asking you first? I don't know, you just seem weird."

"It's been a long day." Orry paused the game and sat up. "I'm just tired, I promise. Actually, I need to take a power nap because I have a bartending shift tonight."

George frowned. "I didn't know that. You said you took the whole day off."

"My boss just texted that they have an opening while you were playing with your cat."

"Oh. Okay."

He left his brother alone and wandered into the kitchen, not really hungry but unsure what to do with himself while Levi was in his bedroom. Pacing a bit helped, and he hated the sad expression on Levi's face when he came out. He collected his reusable bags and then stood by the door, uncertain. They talked briefly about how much food to give Ginger and when she got her pain pills.

"I'll take good care of her, I promise," George said. "And I'll text you pictures and updates."

"Thank you." Levi tried to smile but it didn't reach his eyes. The man was truly attached to those cats and it showed. "I mean it, George, thank you for doing this. I'll come by tomorrow around noon, is that okay? I can bring lunch with me."

"Okay."

"Cool. Pizza?"

His stomach pitted. "Um, I'll eat it when it's all there is but it's not a favorite food."

"What is a favorite?"

"I'm actually very basic with food. You can just pick

up some subs or something, and I'll be cool with that. Honestly, I usually just have a sandwich for lunch."

"Okay." Levi opened up a note app on his phone. "Give me your order. I'll look online for a recommended place nearby."

"Whole wheat roll, turkey, lettuce, tomato, sweet peppers, salt and oregano, and mustard."

"Sounds interesting. Turkey's your favorite?"

"Turkey or chicken, but not every sandwich shop has chicken as an option."

"If they do, would you rather chicken?"

The care Levi was taking with a sandwich order made George's heart trill in that bizarre way again. As if Levi really cared about making lunch perfect for George.

It's because you're caring for one of his furbabies. He's grateful.

"Yes, okay," George replied. "And we've got chips and pretzels here, so don't worry about those. Drinks, too."

"Got it." Levi flashed him a brilliant smile. "I'll see you tomorrow, then. Give Ginger extra pets for me before bed."

"I will. Bye, Levi."

"Later."

George stood on the landing and watched Levi descend the stairs, sad to see him go even though they'd spent hours together. Something in George's life had shifted profoundly today, and he had no idea what would happen next.

But for the first time in years, he was excited to find out.

Chapter Five

Levi's nervous anticipation was his constant companion on the drive into San Francisco to both visit Ginger and bring lunch for him and George. The anticipation made sense because he missed his kitty. Baby and Sporty had seemed to sense the absence of their sister last night, because they both snuggled close in bed until dawn. After feeding them, he went on his usual run, then spent some time drafting a blog post about yesterday's adventures.

He only ever used first names, sometimes nicknames, when writing about real people, and he mostly stuck to his feelings over yesterday's fright with Ginger and the kind new friend who'd taken her in. Since his followers loved seeing kitty pictures, he uploaded the one of Ginger that George had sent last night at bedtime, along with the adorable caption "Good night, Dad." He'd sent back a heart emoji.

Once he'd edited and uploaded the post, he called and chatted briefly with Robin about the house he and Shawn had made an offer on. Levi was thrilled for his best friend, and also amazed that someone who had thrived in the mobile lifestyle of a traveling rodeo was actually settling down. But Robin was a man in love, and Levi wished the couple all the best.

He'd found a highly reviewed deli in George's neighborhood, and he left early enough to order their food in person rather than using an app to order ahead. Then he knew it would be freshly made, instead of sitting on the counter waiting for him. They did have sliced chicken, which delighted Levi, and he ordered a loaded veggie sub for himself. The staff was quick and kind. Levi put cash in the tip jar and thanked them for serving him today.

The nervous part of his anticipation hadn't amped up until he left the store with their food. He couldn't remember the last time he'd been nervous to visit a friend's house with lunch. But something about his friendship with George was different. Bigger in a way he couldn't explain. The guy volunteered to take care of Levi's cat, for goodness' sake, with no prompting and no real reward. It had been incredibly selfless of George.

George. A humble name for an exceptionally complex human being. And he was impressed with George for stepping out of his comfort zones and testing his own limitations, rather than continuing to hide behind old habits and familiar things. George was charming and sweet, adorable in his own way, and Levi genuinely liked him.

Maybe more than he should, given their age difference. Eleven years was kind of a lot and George had been sheltered for so long. Not that he had any reason to think George was interested in him…beyond those glances at Levi's lips.

Not going there.

Levi rang the buzzer for the Thompson apartment.

"Levi?" George asked, his voice a bit dull today, and that worried Levi.

"Yeah, it's me."

"Cool."

The door unlocked, and Levi went inside the spacious lobby. He loved the layout of the house, with its shared living room and separate apartments. He was a touch surprised to find Slater and his neighbor Dez sharing the love seat, each working on a craft project of some sort. Slater had taken up needlepoint during his convalescence from a broken ankle this past summer, and most of his patterns were of the adult variety. He was sewing fabric stretched out on a big wooden hoop, while Dez stitched what looked like a shirt by hand.

"Hey, dude," Slater said. "You here to see your cat?"

Levi chuckled. "I see the gossip has gotten around. Yes, George is watching my cat because she needs a lot of supervision. It's a huge favor. That's why I'm bringing him lunch as a thank you." He hefted the cloth bag he'd put his takeout order into. He preferred using the bags he already owned instead of plastic ones whenever possible.

"George is really cute," Dez said. Her devilish smile suggested all kinds of things Levi wasn't ready to explore with George.

Slater poked her in the ribs. "He's also been through a lot and has just begun coming out of his shell. Don't play matchmaker. The kid's probably straight, and even if he isn't, he's still learning how to walk, let alone run."

"Fine, fine."

Levi left the pair to their craftwork and ascended the stairs to the Thompson apartment. Knocked sharply twice. The sounds of Ginger's meowing greeted him at the same time George opened the door on a terse, "Hey."

"Hi, everything okay?"

"Sure, Ginger's just been a bit unsettled this morning." He let Levi inside and took the bag from him. "Go see her. Please."

The words sounded like a direct order, so Levi did as told. Ginger meowed pitifully in her crate, and she swished her long tail when she spotted him. Levi sat beside her and stuck his fingers through the slim bars. She immediately rubbed both cheeks against his knuckles and started to purr. "I missed you, too, baby girl."

Tears smarted behind his eyes, and Levi rubbed at them with his free hand. Ginger was safe and purring, so why was he so emotional? Probably because he hadn't spent a night with only two of his three girls since he found her and her siblings. They hadn't even needed to stay overnight at the vet when he had them all spayed. The most difficult week of his life had been last December when Levi had come out to the ranch to see Robin again. Separated from his girls that entire time.

He petted her for a while, until his stomach grumbled for food. "I'll be back in a few, okay?"

He started to stand, only to spot George in the doorway with two plates. "I thought maybe you'd want to picnic with Ginger and me," George said, his cheeks stained pink.

"I'd love that."

George handed Levi a plate with his sub and a handful of potato chips, then put his own plate on top of Ginger's crate. "I'll be right back with drinks. I have ginger ale, water and almond milk."

"Water is fine, thank you."

"Of course."

Levi waited for George to return with drinks and napkins, and to settle before he tried the veggie sub. The flavors were amazing, with lots of crisp vegetables and a drizzle of Italian dressing, and he'd eaten three big bites before he realized George was staring at him. Watching him eat.

"You are definitely enjoying that," George said.

"It's delicious. Oh, and they had chicken."

He grinned. "I saw the marking on the wrapper, thank you."

"You are very welcome. Especially considering I imagine Ginger was being a bit whiny this morning?"

"She wasn't too bad until about an hour ago. I think the pain pills help, and I gave her one with her breakfast, but I also think she just misses being outside."

"I'm sure she does." Levi popped a chip into his mouth and chewed, noting George had chosen a few sourdough pretzels for himself. "I'm sorry if her fussing brought down your mood."

"She didn't. I wear headphones when I work and can kind of tune her out, and Orry isn't home." His lips bunched into a frown before he ate a pretzel.

Levi's own mood drooped. "Is Orry upset about Ginger?"

"He said he isn't." George put his sandwich down and huffed. "He lied to me last night, and he doesn't lie to me. At least, not that I've ever noticed before."

"What did he lie about?"

"Having a bartending shift. I checked the website of the place he works for and they were closed last night. It was Thanksgiving but that didn't really occur to me until this morning."

Levi couldn't hope to understand the complex relationship of the Thompson twins, but he didn't like seeing George upset. "Did you ask him about it?"

"Not yet. He's working one of his other jobs. The

food delivery one, I think. I just…he can tell me any-thing. We've always been honest, ever since we were sixteen. He knows all my secrets, and he's never judged me for them. I can't fathom what he thinks I won't un-derstand."

"Maybe he was embarrassed to tell you he was going out on Thanksgiving to shop Black Friday deals for a cheap flat-screen?"

George snorted. "Unlikely. Did you notice we don't have a TV? We do everything on our phones and live as cheaply as possible, because rent is crazy expensive, even in this neighborhood. The only reason I have a laptop is because I can type faster on that keyboard for my closed-captions job."

"That makes sense." Levi hadn't actually noticed that the living room didn't have a television until George mentioned it. "And I'm the same about not owning a TV. There wasn't a great place to install one in my house, and I have a tablet to stream stuff. And I usually prefer to read in the evenings, versus watching movies. Most of my TV watching happens on my days off."

"Same. But I also watch videos all day long for my day job, so getting my eyes off the screen for a while helps. I have ebooks, but Orry also brings me physical books from the library when I ask him to."

"Well, maybe one day soon you'll want to go get your own books."

George nodded slowly. "That's part of the plan. Do more for myself so Orry doesn't have to keep doing ev-erything for me."

"And you're taking steps to get there. As your friend, I look forward to helping you take more of those steps."

"Yeah?" George's smile sent an odd warmth through

Levi's belly. "Thank you. And thanks for lunch, the sub is really good."

"Happy to." Before Levi could think through the intelligence of it, he blurted out, "We could make this a daily thing. You and me having lunch with Ginger. And it doesn't always have to be subs, if you want something different."

"Nah, subs are great. Like I said, I usually have a basic sandwich for lunch anyway." George stared down at the portion of his six-incher remaining. "Honestly, I'm not sure I can eat the whole thing."

"They have a four-inch option if six inches is too much meat." Levi realized what he'd said and tried to hide his embarrassment behind sipping his water. George, thankfully, seemed oblivious to the innuendo.

"Maybe the four-inch tomorrow, then. I'll finish the rest of this with my dinner." He put the remaining quarter of the sub back down and ate his last pretzel.

Levi finished his food in between petting Ginger. She seemed content with her human companions, and the bandage on her hip looked as clean and new as yesterday. "Has she been messing with the bandages?"

"Not really, no." George petted the other side of her neck. "She really is a doll baby when she isn't yowling at the top of her lungs."

"She cried quite a bit as a kitten, but I also kept them fairly confined to the house until I thought they were old enough to run around outside. And, of course, they were confined whenever we were driving to a new spot."

"How often do you move around?"

Do, not did. Interesting.

Levi pondered how much to share about Grant. "Well, when I first found the kittens, I settled at a campground in Wyoming, and I stayed there for a while. Then I needed a fresh start, so we traveled around before settling in Colorado. That's where I was when Robin called me about the rodeo attraction."

"And then you came here. About a year ago?"

"Almost a year, yes." Levi saw the unasked questions in George's wide eyes. "I love my job here, and I love working with Robin again. I like to think I'm here for a while longer. At least one more season at the ghost town."

Something like relief flashed in his eyes. "Okay, cool. I mean, you bought a tiny house so you can travel, but it's also nice to have roots."

"I'm honestly not sure what it's like to have roots. Growing up, we had a home base where we'd winter the rodeo in New Mexico, but it wasn't like having a real house with Sunday dinners and all kinds of memories. My family moved around as a unit. I guess it's sort of in my blood. But I do like to think I'll settle down one day. Maybe find someone to settle with."

George scratched beneath Ginger's chin, his lips pursed together. "Maybe that's it."

"What's it?"

"Maybe Orry is seeing someone and he lied last night so I wouldn't know."

"Why would your brother lie to you about dating someone?"

"I don't know. I know he's had casual things over the years, but he's never really dated because he's busy working and worrying about me. Maybe he's met someone and doesn't want me to know yet, so I don't feel guilty and push my limits before I'm ready."

Levi turned that over for a moment and it made sense. "How would you feel about him dating someone?"

"I'd be over the moon." George's entire face lit up. "Orry really deserves a great girl in his life. Or guy, I'm not totally sure who he's into. We've never talked about it."

"His sexuality?"

"Yeah. Or mine. But I was always busy with skating and didn't have time to really notice people, and then I isolated myself, and it stopped mattering."

Levi blinked several times, surprised at how many personal things George was telling him today. And also kind of honored. "You don't know your sexuality?"

George shrugged. "It never really mattered before now."

"Why does it matter more now?"

Those pretty eyes briefly dropped to Levi's lips again, and his heart kicked. "Because now I'm getting out into the world. Meeting people. Stuff that didn't seem important before is suddenly important."

"That makes sense." Levi risked a brief squeeze to George's knee. "You're still young, George, you have time to figure yourself out."

"When did you know?"

Levi put his plate on the carpet and scratched his chin, his other hand still stroking Ginger, pulling out long, rusty purrs. "Well, I consider myself bisexual. I've dated women but my only serious relationship was with a man. I guess I figured it out during puberty, when I was noticing both the hot cowboys in their tight jeans, and the hot cowgirls in their denim skirts. My first kiss was a girl, but my first under-the-clothes encounter was with a boy." Off George's wide-eyed surprise, he added,

"But I was also a very social person from a young age, and my brother Xander had a knack for goading me into things. You've lived a very different life."

George watched him with an indecipherable expression, when the guy was usually easy to read. As if stuck between surprise over everything Levi had confessed and...something else. Understanding, maybe?

"Have you ever been attracted to another person, George?" Levi asked.

"I'm not sure. I mean, back when I skated I noticed other boys in the locker room. I admired the girl skaters for their abilities but not the same way I admired some of the boys. Especially Andy Jaworski. He wasn't as good as me in the long program but damn, he could do an amazing triple axel-double salchow combination."

Levi turned that over, needing to proceed with caution, because George was giving him a lot of sensitive personal information, and he didn't want to take advantage of that—of George having someone else to open up to besides his brother. "Did you ever want to kiss Andy?"

His cheeks and neck flushed red, and George looked at his lap, shaggy blond hair falling over his forehead. That was all the answer Levi needed. "Hey," Levi said, giving that same knee a second brief squeeze. "You don't have to be embarrassed about it, especially not around me. You haven't had a chance to really explore who you are as an individual person, and I know revealing truths can be scary, but I am a safe place for you. I promise."

After several long moments, George finally looked up, eyes so shiny Levi half expected the guy to burst into tears.

* * *

George hadn't expected the surge of emotion that flooded him when Levi asked if he'd ever wanted to kiss Andy. Yes, George had wanted to kiss Andy more than once. Tall, lean, athletic, and cute, Andy had drawn George to him, even though they were competitors. He'd covertly observed Andy in the locker rooms more than once, curious about the other teen's body. But he'd never acted on those impulses.

He'd been too scared of losing focus, losing his spot in competitions, losing his dream if he admitted he might be gay, even though it wasn't exactly unheard of in figure skating. Hell, Johnny Weir was one of his personal heroes. He'd also been scared of what his parents might think. So, he'd locked those feelings up tight and buried them deep, not acknowledging them again until he started doing closed-captions for gay porn. The bodies, the mouths, the abs, the dicks…they'd briefly awoken long-suppressed feelings and thoughts. But acting on those thoughts had still been impossible, this time because of his anxiety, so he had once again ignored them. Pressed them back down and pretended they didn't exist. Until now.

And sitting this close to Levi, a kind man with a gentle soul, who spoke to George's heart, was a very bad idea.

Especially when his knee still felt warm from those two brief touches.

He held Levi's gaze, his own eyes filling with tears he refused to shed. Levi watched him with so much patience and understanding, George wanted to fling himself into the older man's arms for a hug. But he didn't. "I wanted to kiss Andy," he admitted. He kind of wanted to kiss Levi but that was a very bad idea.

Levi's smile brightened. "Okay. Thank you for sharing your truth with me."

"Orry doesn't know."

"Your brother doesn't know you're gay?"

George shook his head. "I mean, I've only started to really admit it to myself recently, and until now no one has ever directly applied the label to me. But yes." He swallowed hard against a rush of acid in his throat. "I'm gay."

"Thank you again for sharing your truth. I'm honored to be the first to know, and I promise I won't out you to anyone. This is your truth to tell."

"Thank you." Not that George thought Levi would run out and blab it to the whole house, but the words relaxed some of his anxiety over this entire conversation. "Wow, I did not expect to come out over lunch."

Levi laughed. "Life comes at you fast."

"Very true."

The serious conversation seemed to be over, so George changed the subject. "Tell me a story about the rodeo. Please?"

Levi did, painting an amusing scene of his brother Xander, as their clown/opening act, being randomly pooped on by a pigeon hiding in the rafters of the arena they were performing in, and incorporating the accident into his routine. They were both laughing by the end, and Ginger was asleep from their constant petting. Nearly two hours had passed from the time Levi arrived to when he stood to leave.

They carried their drinks and plates into the kitchen as a pair, and the odd domesticity of it made George

yearn in a new, intense way. Yearn for a real life with
a partner who didn't judge him, who loved him, and
who'd protect his heart. Things he'd told himself for
years that he didn't need, because alone was safer.

But was it really?

George walked Levi to the door, and they stood there
a moment. Levi stuck out his hand, and George shook
it. More warmth against his palm that woke him up inside. "I'll see you tomorrow," George said.

"Same bat-time, same bat-lunch."

"Same what?"

Levi chuckled. "I keep forgetting how young you
are. You have an old soul."

"That's a compliment, right?"

"Yes, it is. It means you feel things deeply and have
great empathy for others. Even though you hide from
it, you are very attuned to the world at large. I'm glad
you're starting to live in it again."

"Me too. Thank you for helping me do that."

"My pleasure." Levi tipped an imaginary hat at him
then left.

Like yesterday, George watched him descend the
stairs until he was out of sight. Since Ginger was still
asleep in her crate when he returned to their room,
George put his headphones on and settled in to work
for a while. But instead of pressing play on his current assignment, George stared at the still image.
One big, bearish guy was in the process of fingering
a younger twink. Because of this job, George probably knew more about gay sex mechanics and positions than Levi—unless Levi was a porn connoisseur,
of course—and he wasn't sure how he felt about that.
Would Levi think him writing closed-captions for porn

was weird? Maybe. But Levi was the least judgmental person George had ever met.

Not really saying much, since he didn't know very many people, but still.

His entire workday was focused around sex, but George had never had sex. Hell, he'd never even been kissed. He wanted to be kissed, though. He wanted a lot of things, he just wasn't sure how to reach for them.

Tomorrow, he'd ask Levi for ideas on getting out there, meeting people, possibly even dating. Yeah, Levi would have good advice.

If George actually drummed up the courage to ask.

Chapter Six

George did not, in fact, drum up the courage to ask Levi for help for the next four days. Ginger was less yowly, which he assumed meant she was in less pain and her hip was mending. Levi continued to bring them lunch, same subs every day from the same place. They talked about all kinds of things but not George's sexuality or anything too serious. He enjoyed these casual conversations, more than he enjoyed chilling downstairs with Dez, Morgan, Slater, and Derrick.

Levi understood George in a way no one ever had. Not even Orry. And he adored their friendship and the casual touches they shared.

He also hadn't confronted Orry about his Thanksgiving night lie, because he was afraid Orry had some terrible secret that could hurt them both. Or worse, that Orry might lie to him again. It also made him wonder how truthful Orry had been in the past about his various part-time jobs and where he was really spending his time. Ignorance was better than a devastating truth, so George kept quiet.

On Wednesday, the sixth day of George watching over Ginger, Levi arrived early in the morning because Ginger had a vet appointment to assess her hip. George was sad to see Ginger leave, but Levi promised they were coming back with lunch no matter what the vet said about her confinement. He tried to work on a video while they were gone but his mind kept wandering. Would Ginger go home today? Would their amazing lunches end?

Would he ever see Levi again after today?

Levi texted that they'd both be back by twelve thirty, and George resisted asking how the appointment went. He managed to get a little bit of work done, but he didn't find the male-on-male action as captivating as before. Probably because he was too busy worrying about his own personal life—now that he actually had a personal life. And a friend he really wanted to keep in contact with.

The buzzer went off at twelve twenty and George nearly flew to the door to hit the unlock button on the downstairs door. He unlocked and opened his apartment door, heart pounding, stupidly eager to see both man and cat again. Levi appeared with the carrier in one hand and his cloth bag in the other. Ginger meowed a few times but it sounded more like annoyed meows than pained ones. George had gotten pretty attuned to her this past week.

"Miss Ginger," Levi said as he walked inside, "is free of her bandage, thank goodness, and she doesn't need constant supervision anymore. She does, however, still need to spend a few more days confined to the crate, which we can do at home."

George's heart dropped and he worked hard to keep his disappointment off his face. "Oh. Cool. I bet she misses her siblings."

"I know they miss her." He put the carrier on the

floor near the kitchen table. "They practically sleep on my head every night now. Ready for lunch?"

"Yeah sure." Hoping to keep things light and not reveal how disappointed George really was, he joked, "Are we picnicking on the kitchen floor today instead of in my bedroom?"

Levi flashed him a blinding smile, his joy at taking his fur baby home clear. "She seems okay for now. Maybe we could eat at the table for a change?"

"Okay."

Since they were using the table and could just eat off the waxed paper wrappers, George forewent plates and fetched them their preferred drinks and the bag of pretzels. Levi took their subs out of his bag, and then he produced two plastic-wrapped brownies. "To celebrate, if you like chocolate," Levi said. "If not, maybe Orry wants it?"

"I like chocolate." George didn't indulge often but part of him agreed to eat whatever Levi put in front of him simply to please the man. They sat opposite each other and unrolled their lunches. "So Ginger is on the mend?"

"Yep, she's still fairly young for a cat, you took great care of her, and vet says she healed quickly and well. Thank you so much for that, George, you have no idea how much it means to me that I can take her home." Levi's eyes shined with emotion. "They've always been a trio, so it's been hard only having a pair."

"I can't imagine." George meant that. He'd get a tiny slice of the feeling once Ginger was gone but he'd only had her a week. Levi had had the three of them for two years. George would just have to pay more attention to

Lucky when she came around. "I'm glad Ginger can go home. Your family will be together again."

Levi looked up from his sub and a charge of emotion seemed to shoot across the table from him to George. "I bet she'll miss you. But you and I are going to keep in touch. You are free to come visit at any time, and while the ghost town is shut down, maybe I'll make some trips into the city. We can hang. Here or maybe other places. I've been here almost a year and I've never been to Golden Gate Park."

George placed a hand over his heart and feigned shock. "I'm a severe introvert, and even I've done that."

"See? You can show me stuff. And maybe one day I can give you a private tour of the ghost town."

The ghost town thing sounded strangely like a come-on, so George tempered his surprise with laughter. "I guess we'll see. But I do want to stay friends, Levi. Not just for Ginger, but we have really good conversations. I can let my guard down with you." *I want to kiss you every single time I see you now.*

George kept that one to himself.

"I feel the same," Levi said. "You're important to me, George. Our friendship is important to me."

They held eye contact a beat longer, something new and unspoken there, before they both started eating. George didn't enjoy his sub as much as the previous ones, because this one was the last. The end of a new tradition. While they ate, he got the name of the deli from Levi and plugged it into his phone, grateful to see the place delivered. He wanted to hold on to something of theirs.

He nearly asked if Levi would want to occasionally have lunch together via video chat but that seemed excessively needy. After a meal full of casual, occasionally awkward conversation, they washed their brownies down with water and ginger ale, and then it was time. Levi carried the crate down to his pickup, while George spent a few minutes petting Ginger. Silently saying goodbye to the sweet kitty he'd come to love.

When Levi returned, George got the extra food, litter and pill pockets for him. "Want me to carry the stuff so you don't jostle Ginger too much?" George asked.

"Sure." Levi winked. "You need some sunshine on that pale skin."

George laughed. He didn't care about the sun; he wanted to prolong this as much as possible. He grabbed his keys and they trooped downstairs together. The living room was empty for a change. His heart skipped once and his stomach sloshed with acid when George walked outside to the small front porch. He silently followed Levi nearly half the block down to his pickup.

Levi opened the passenger-side door. George deposited the cloth bag on the middle of the bench front seat, a little sad he might never see those bags again. Then Levi surprised him by hefting the carrier up into both arms, putting Ginger closer to eye level for George. George poked his fingers through the grate. Ginger licked them, then started purring.

"Bye, pretty lady. You were a great roommate, but I'm glad you're going home to your sisters."

Glad for you and your daddy, but sad for me.

George straightened, so Levi put the carrier in the truck and shut the door. Ginger immediately began yowling, and the sound made George want to cry.

"Again, I cannot thank you enough for what you did

for us," Levi said. "It was very selfless. I will repay your kindness."

"You don't have to."

"I want to. I'm just not sure how yet. The universe will show me the way."

George smiled. "You are such an odd person sometimes, Levi, but I think that's why I like you. Us odd ducks need to flock together."

"Agreed." Levi's eyes flickered briefly downward, as if he wanted to kiss George, and George would let him. By God, yes, he would let Levi be his first kiss. "May I give you a hug goodbye?"

The request warmed George all over. Some people would have just impulsively hugged him, no matter what George thought, but not Levi. Levi was too thoughtful for that, and it meant everything to George. "Yes." He hadn't been hugged by anyone except Orry in a long damned time. Too long.

Levi took a single step into his personal space, arms open. When he didn't advance, George closed the distance between them and draped his arms loosely around Levi's waist. The man's taller frame and work-earned muscles felt great against George's body. He smelled good, too, a faint fragrance of something reminiscent of pine. Levi rested his chin on George's shoulder, and they held each other in a loose embrace. Sweet and wonderful and George never wanted to let go.

"You're my hero," Levi whispered, then pulled back.

George's body mourned the loss of Levi against him, and he wasn't sure what to do with that. He'd never craved another person's hug as fiercely as he craved Levi's. All his muddled brain could think to do was say, "Drive safe."

"I will." Levi hesitated a beat longer, then walked around the truck. Got into the driver's seat and shut the door.

George shoved his hands into the pockets of his jeans, thoughts and emotions tumbling all over themselves. As Levi and Ginger drove away, they took a tiny piece of his heart back to Garrett with them.

Levi spent the hour-long drive home confused and annoyed by his conflicting emotions. He had enjoyed this entire week of daily visits with George, bringing him lunch and picnicking with Ginger. He was thrilled to finally bring Ginger home to Baby and Sporty. So why did he also feel as if he was betraying George somehow? It made no sense.

And that hug. *That hug.*

He hadn't expected George to agree to more than a handshake goodbye, but the instant that slender body pressed into his? Levi had wanted to hold on and never let go. To take George with him back to his tiny house, their three cats, and a wonderful, happy life together. But life wasn't that sort of fairy tale and they both knew it. They each had their lives to return to and they would remain in contact. Remain friends.

A friend Levi kind of wanted to kiss until they were both breathless.

Ginger yowled in the passenger seat, and he tried to keep his fingers inside the carrier for her to rub against. She hated being confined more than the other two, even for brief trips to the vet, so he imagined this past week had been horrible for her. But she was healing and that's what counted. In a few more days, she'd be free to wander again with her siblings. Small price to pay when the injuries from falling from a tree could have been catastrophic.

Hopefully, she'd be more cautious where she climbed in the future.

"You'll be okay, baby girl. We'll be home soon."

Her chirp sounded strangely annoyed but he didn't blame her. Levi couldn't imagine being caged for an entire week. The closest he'd ever come to being imprisoned had been detox and rehab, and even those situations had come with their own set of freedoms. He, like his kitties, was meant to wander, not remain trapped in one place.

More and more, he considered uprooting his tiny home and hitting the road again. Taking the ghost town closure as a chance to travel and wander for a while, maybe find some new, exciting blog material. But every time he considered uprooting his life, even temporarily, his thoughts wandered back to George. To not seeing him again for weeks on end, when this entire past week of visits meant the world to Levi.

He drove up the familiar, pitted dirt road and the familiar split. Going straight led to Clean Slate Ranch. The left road ended at the ghost town, and Levi turned that way. Went down the long driveway to Mack and Wes's place, and then onto a grass track that his tires had begun wearing into the earth. He'd already promised Mack he'd reseed any areas where his truck or home caused real damage.

Baby was sleeping in the sun near the house when Levi parked, and she barely twitched when he opened and shut his truck door. Then Ginger began yowling, and Baby surged to her feet. Sporty came racing out from beneath the house, and they were both winding around his ankles, chirping for their littermate. Levi gently lifted the carrier out and, since it was sunny and not too chilly, he put the carrier down in a sunspot. The siblings sniffed and chirped, and Ginger reached out with one paw to swat at Sporty.

Levi closed his eyes and sent positive energy out to the universe, thanking her for bringing his girl home safely.

His phone dinged with a text.

Robin: You back yet?

Levi sent back an affirmative, and less than fifteen minutes later, he and Robin were sitting out on deck chairs together, each holding a cold bottle of cream soda from a local soda maker Robin knew he loved. The cats had all settled together around the carrier, and Levi had never seen a sweeter sight.

Except maybe George's smile.

"Now that the family's back together," Robin said, "you give any more thought to traveling during our break?"

"Some. I might wait until January, though, so I'm here for Christmas." Levi needed to be there with Robin on the four-year anniversary of Xander's death. "Plus, Ginger has just spent the last week cooped up. I don't want to coop her up in the house right away."

"Good point." Robin pulled from his bottle, and Levi noticed the way his lips kept twitching.

"What?" Levi knew Robin's tells. "You're hiding something."

"Just wanted to celebrate the good news with you in

person." He broke out into a full-on smile. "The seller finally accepted our offer on the house."

"That's fantastic." He hauled Robin up into a hug, mindful of their sodas. "I'm thrilled for you and Shawn. I mean it."

"Shawn is over the moon. From living in his car to a homeowner in a year's time."

"Things are working out for you both exactly as they're supposed to."

Robin gently clinked the lip of his cream soda to Levi's. "For us both. I'm not sure if I've really said it this bluntly before, but having this past year with both Shawn and you in my life has been…a blessing. I never thought I'd be this happy again."

"That's all I want. And Xander would want it, too."

"I know." Robin's eyes went briefly sad. "I'll always miss him. But this is my life now and exactly where I want to be."

"Same, brother." Only now, a tiny piece of his heart was tugging back in the direction of San Francisco. How had George gotten under his skin in a week? Then again, he'd heard of folks who hooked up one night as perfect strangers and were living together days later. Stranger things had happened—just not to Levi.

Then again, he hadn't been the guy who wanted to settle down. He'd fucked his way through his twenties, probably breaking hearts along the rodeo circuit, but he hadn't cared. Not back then. Not until he lost his baby brother and nearly lost his own life. But George was so young and inexperienced, and Levi didn't know if George was even into Levi, or if Levi was simply a convenient person to explore his sexuality with. Sometimes

Levi wondered if George even knew what he wanted, deep down.

They settled in their chairs again, and Levi tried to enjoy his soda and the company of his best friend. Robin nattered on about Shawn's plan for the house for a while before he caught on that Levi wasn't completely paying attention. "How do you feel about a zebra print couch in the living room?" Robin asked.

"Sounds good."

"Okay, man, what is it? You're miles away right now."

Levi tapped a fingernail against his glass bottle. "Truth?"

"Always."

He didn't have to ask Robin to keep this a secret and not tell Shawn, or anyone else. Truth always was their shorthand. "I think I've got feelings for George Thompson."

Robin's eyebrows crept up. "The shy twin who just babysat your cat for a week?"

"Yes."

"Are you sure those feelings aren't just a lot of gratitude for him rescuing Ginger and taking care of her for you?"

"I don't know. I think that's part of it, yes, but there something about him that I find appealing. Maybe it's his vulnerability, maybe it's his kindness. Both? I like how I feel when I'm around him, and I've really loved our lunch dates. I definitely want to see him again."

"Lunch dates, huh?" Robin wiggled his eyebrows. "Does George know they were dates?"

"You know what I mean."

"I know, sorry. Then hang out with him more. Get a better read on the guy. Is he gay? Bi?"

"Not my place to say." George had confided in him and Levi wouldn't crap on that trust by outing him. "There have been moments where I thought he was looking at my lips, and he let me hug him today. I'm probably the first new person he's hugged in years. He's been so sheltered, Robin."

"You worried you've got too much experience, or something?"

"Maybe. I did some really questionable things at the tail end of my...spiral. Stuff I barely talked about in rehab. I can't imagine openin' up to someone like George about all that ugly."

Robin thumped his knee. "Hey, I bet you and me have some similar ugly in our pasts. And for all intents and purposes, Shawn was pretty damned sheltered when we first got together. He listened when I talked. He accepted the stuff I'd done once, and he knew who I was in the present. If there's something real between you and George? He'll do the same thing."

"Maybe." Levi didn't usually doubt himself like this but something about George made him want to be as gentle and kind as possible.

"You can tell me to fuck off, but man, did you catch something?"

Levi shook his head. "I was lucky. Had a bad scare in the hospital while waiting for test results, but no. It's not about that, I just...can't explain it."

"Then maybe you should pursue it. See if there's something between you."

"How? Bring him another sandwich with no real excuse other than I want to see him again?"

Robin stared at him for several long moments before a smile spread across his face. "So don't take him a sandwich. Take him something else that will help him test his comfort zones."

"Dude, I am not going over there for a booty call. He'd slam the door in my face."

"So not what I meant."

Curious what his friend had in mind, Levi leaned in closer. "Okay, good. Then what?"

Chapter Seven

George tried to work after Levi and Ginger left, but all he could do was stare at the indented carpet where the crate had once been. He already missed his coworker and it had been less than an hour. Part of him wanted to leave the apartment door open just to see if Lucky would wander inside, but he couldn't do that and work in his bedroom. And the terms of the lease prevented him from adopting a cat of his own.

One week. How had his life changed so dramatically in one week? He wanted a cat and couldn't stop thinking about Levi and that hug. His smiles and odd mannerisms. His unique way of looking at the world.

When Orry texted that he was on his way home with Chinese takeout for dinner, George realized he'd been staring into space for most of the afternoon. Since he'd accomplished nothing productive, he gave up. Shut down his program and went into the living room to read on his phone. Orry looked exhausted when he finally got home. He dumped his keys and the food on the coffee table and thumped down on the futon next to George.

"Cat gone?"

George grunted and reached for the bag of food, stomach already rumbling from the familiar scents. "Yeah, a few hours ago. Levi was thrilled to take her home."

"Excellent. Now I can sleep again."

"Her yowling wasn't that bad."

"You wear noise canceling headphones all the time. Hand me the pot stickers."

George found the labeled carton and passed it over, along with a plastic cutlery set. He could manage with chopsticks but Orry had never bothered to try. George had wanted to learn when he was younger so he could catch flies with them like Mr. Miyagi in those old karate movies, and while he'd never caught a fly, he could eat fried rice with them. He found a carton of Black Pepper Chicken and went to town on it.

"Where did you work today?" George asked between bites.

"Ride share job. Might have to get the car checked soon. The engine is making a weird rattle sometimes and I don't want it to affect my customer rating."

"Okay. You off the rest of the night?"

"Nah, got a bartending shift that starts at eight."

"Oh." Intellectually, George understood his brother worked all the time to help pay rent here, keep the car maintained, and cover any additional expenses their grandparents might have, but he also missed his brother. This was the first meal they'd shared in days.

And he still hadn't asked Orry about that mysterious shift on Thanksgiving night.

"You know you can talk to me about anything, right?" George asked.

Orry paused with a pot sticker right in front of his mouth. "Duh." Then he shoved the whole thing in.

"I just… I guess I feel like we don't really talk much anymore."

"If I had anything interesting to share, I'd share. I mean, I could probably come up with some funny customer stories but I'm exhausted. After I eat, I'm going to power nap."

"Okay." Disappointment swamped George, and he pushed it aside in favor of stealing a pot sticker out of Orry's carton.

Orry pretended to stab at his hand with his fork. "Thief!"

"We always have joint custody of the pot stickers. You don't get to hog them all."

"You're annoying when you're right."

They had a joint account for household expenses like rent, utility bills and food, and George insisted takeout fell under the food category. They both ate it, after all, so why should one or the other pay for it out of their personal money? The only time it didn't count was if Orry was working and grabbed a solo meal. So far, the system had worked well for them for years.

After they ate their fill, George volunteered to store the scant leftovers and sent Orry to take a nap. George tidied up, then stood in Orry's bedroom doorway and watched his brother sleep. He didn't completely buy that nothing was up, but it was also possible George was overthinking everything—as he often did—and that Orry was simply overworked and stressed out. Orry was so used to being the one who took care of George, and for too many years, George had relied on that. It was far beyond time that George step beyond his comfort zones and do more for his brother.

He went back to his room, put on his headphones, and got to work.

* * *

The next day, George was deeply focused on transcribing a three-way fisting scene when he thought he heard the faintest of noises. Maybe the front doorbell, but he wasn't expecting anyone, so he paid closer attention to the words coming out of the mouth of the guy who was punching his fist in and out of the bottom's ass. Mostly words of pleasure and praise, but the bottom's response was harder to decipher. George had a list of noise words to use from this particular studio, but none seemed quite appropriate for the sounds the poor bottom made.

Orry was home—napping, George was pretty sure— and a bit later Orry filled his doorway. George paused the video and took off his headphones. "What?"

"Door's for you," Orry said. "Your boyfriend's back."

George blinked dumbly at him for several seconds.

"It's Levi," Orry finally said. "He says he has something for you."

George nearly overturned his desk chair in his haste to stand, shocked to his core that Levi was back after only a day. Was something wrong with Ginger? Had he done something wrong? Forgotten the bag of treats?

"Dude, relax," Orry said, hands up. "He's calm and I'm here. Go talk to him. Your porn can wait."

Annoyance burbled up inside George at the porn dig. It wasn't as if he sat there and masturbated all day to the videos he transcribed. It was his freaking job. Whatever. George turned his computer screen off—just in case—then gently pushed past his brother and walked into the living room, his insides jumping all over the place the instant he set eyes on Levi.

Levi stood a few feet beyond the front door, his familiar smile in place, and an envelope of some sort in his hand. George tried to downplay how happy he was to see Levi again and probably failed miserably. "Hi," George said.

"Hey." Levi's smile brightened. "I know it's kind of soon, but I think I figured out a way to thank you and your brother for being so kind to Ginger this past week."

Of course, it's about the cat.

"Um, okay." George beckoned Levi toward the futon, where Levi perched on one end; George did the same. "I volunteered. You don't owe us anything."

"Yes, I do. When people do me favors I like to pay it forward somehow. Do something kind. Usually for someone else but I really wanted to do something for you."

Levi seemed intent on doing this something, so George nodded. "Okay."

"Here." Levi handed him the envelope. No name on the front but it had Clean Slate Ranch's logo on the upper left corner.

Intrigued, George lifted the unsealed flap and pulled out two rectangles of paper. It took him a moment to understand what he was looking at. Two paid-for vouchers for a week's vacation at the ranch. His insides shook and his pulse raced. George pushed the vouchers at Levi. "No, I can't. It's too expensive." And in his experience, expensive gifts led to bad things.

"I got the family discount, and the regular rates aren't as high as you think. It's also winter and the business gets slow, so they drop the prices anyway. There will also be fewer other guests to interact with."

George met Levi's gaze, impressed by how well Levi had read him again. He did want to experience the ranch and its amenities, and he'd never ridden a horse in his life. Or been camping or any of the other things he'd read about on their website. "I, um, I'm still not sure." He glanced over his shoulder, unsurprised to see Orry hovering in the hall. "What do you think? He's giving us a ranch vacation."

"I can't," Orry said flatly, the tone annoying George when Levi was being this generous. "I have to work. We can't afford both of us not working for a whole week."

"I apologize if I overstepped," Levi replied. "I didn't even think about you being able to take time off work."

"That's life, huh? If George wants to go, I can't stop him. He's a grown man. Thanks for the offer, dude, but I can't go."

"Heard and understood. I'll repay your patience and kindness another way."

"Whatever." Orry rolled his eyes and disappeared down the hallway.

"I'm sorry he was rude to you," George said, a little embarrassed by his brother's behavior when Levi was only being nice.

"I've dealt with ruder tourists, it's fine," Levi replied. "Is there someone you want to give the second voucher to? Maybe one of your downstairs neighbors? I bet Slater would get a kick out of being a guest at the ranch, instead of one of the horsemen."

George smiled but he wasn't sure about a vacation with Slater and a bunch of strangers. Besides, Slater probably wouldn't want to do it. Dez might. Then the solution hit him solidly in the heart, and he knew exactly who would make him comfortable all week at the ranch. "You come with me."

Levi blinked several times in a row. "I'm sorry?"

"With the ghost town shut down, it's not like you'll

miss work. You take the other voucher. Then I know I'll
always have a friend around, even if I do something like
have a panic attack. I know there will be people on staff
I'll recognize but they aren't people I consider friends."

They aren't you, Levi.

"I mean…" Levi's gaze went distant. "I could probably ask Wes or Mack to check on the cats every day and
make sure they have food. Or maybe get permission to
borrow an ATV. That way I can check myself once or
twice. We've hardly been apart since I rescued them."

"Oh." George's heart dropped to his feet. "If being
away is too hard, you can say no. I get it. They're, like,
your kids."

"No, I can manage it. I just rarely have to. Which
probably says a lot about my lack of a social or dating life."

"Join the club." George winked, and Levi chuckled.
"So what do you think? Come on vacation with me?"

"Sure. Is next week too soon?"

George swallowed back an embarrassing squeak of
surprise. "Next week?"

"It's the last week they're open to guests until January. Closing for Christmas and New Year's, and I know
they have openings. But if that's too soon, we can wait.
Only the weather next week is supposed to be unseason-
ably warm. Midsixties most days, low fifties at night.
We might even be able to do a camping trip."

"Um." George had never been impulsive. He liked
to plan, to know, to schedule his life. But if he worked
longer hours for the rest of the week and got ahead on
his work, he could take a solid week off. Unplug for a
while and enjoy the ranch. Spend time with Levi.

Except Orry…because of his fluid work schedule,

they hadn't spent more than one day apart in the last seven years. How was George going to manage an entire week without his twin?

"This is a big step for you, isn't it?" Levi asked. "Leaving your safe space and your brother for a week."

"How do you do that?"

"Do what?"

"Get into my head and pull out exactly what I'm thinking. Orry has been my rock since we were sixteen. Not having him around…" It would be painful and weird and borderline crazy-making but George was an adult. If he ever wanted to have a real, adult life, he had to start putting space between himself and Orry. "It'll be weird but good. Healthy, I think. And it helps knowing you'll be around. My friend."

Levi's tender smile sent strange, warm feelings through George's chest. "I am definitely your friend, George. So next week? All I need to do is call Reyes and we're on the guest list."

"Okay, yes." George jumped off the plank and into the cold, dark water with both feet, confident he'd surface before he drowned. "Yes, next week. Um, I can't exactly take Orry's car, though."

"If you can work a deal with him to meet halfway, I'll pick you up. We have to be in the visitor parking area by ten a.m. Sunday morning for transport to the ranch. Pack comfortable, warm clothes. Boots if you have them."

"I have sneakers."

"They'll be fine. I didn't see any rain in the forecast but you know that can change on a dime."

"True." George couldn't believe he was doing this. An impromptu vacation at a dude ranch with his new friend with only a few days' notice. "I'll work it out with Orry. And then I'll text you with a meet spot."

"Great. I was not expecting to go on this vacation with you, George, but now I'm looking forward to the experience."

"Me too. I think it's the first real vacation I've had since… I don't know, maybe since I was eight? Our parents took us to Disneyland. But after that, skating took up all my free time, and we didn't really do much as a family. It was always practice, school and tutors."

"I'm sorry." Levi squeezed George's knee in a warm, comforting touch that lit George up from the inside out. "Having grown up with my family always around, I can't imagine how lonely you might have been."

George took a chance and covered Levi's hand with his own, and the touch cemented his impromptu decision to go on the trip. "You lost your little brother. I cannot fathom that kind of pain. I don't think I'd survive losing Orry."

Levi turned his hand and clasped their palms together. "I sincerely hope you never have to find out."

The moment seemed to stretch out for ages—their joined hands, the long and meaningful look they shared. The new intimacy that had begun to grow. George didn't know what to say or do, only that he liked it a lot. But he didn't know what to do with it. If he should push or pull back. He latched on to the first thing that buzzed through his whirling brain.

"How's Ginger today?" George asked.

"Grumpy. I think she resents being close to her siblings but not being able to play with them. She's got another checkup Saturday morning, though, and I really hope her doc says the leg is strong enough for me to let her out. I haven't had to clean a litter box regularly since they were kittens." Levi's cheerful wink made George laugh.

"So you're telling me they hold it for eight hours on your road trips?"

"Nah, I let them out at rest stops for bathroom breaks. I've even got a clicker they're trained to respond to and return to the house."

George stared at Levi, more impressed with the man with each conversation they had. "How did you learn to do that?"

"The internet. And I, uh, spent a lot of time with a veterinarian after I first found the kittens. He had some good ideas."

Levi rarely hesitated or self-censored himself when he was around George, and the hesitation over the vet didn't pass his notice. It heightened his curiosity about that period in Levi's life. He was also polite enough not to pry.

"I will admit, though," Levi added, "I do keep a small emergency litter box stored away in case of terrible weather. They don't mind a little rain but refuse to go out during torrential downpours or too much snow."

"Makes sense. Most cats hate water, right?"

"In my experience they do, but I've seen videos on social media that suggest some love it. I saw one once of a cat swimming in a full bathtub."

"You're kidding."

"Nope." Levi whipped out his phone and a minute later, George was watching the evidence. He was leaning in close to Levi so they could both see the screen, and he caught that familiar pinelike scent on Levi's skin. Something sweet on his breath. So enticing…

Once the video ended, George scooted away. "I guess at this point, you can find a video of anything online."

Levi's eyes twitched with something unpleasant. "Yeah, you can."

The levity of the moment seemed to vanish, replaced by an awkward silence George wasn't used to feeling with Levi. But something in George's comment had struck a bad chord, and George needed to fix the musical score before Levi changed his mind about this vacation.

"What else should I pack for next week?" George asked.

Levi's face brightened. "There's a more complete list of suggestions on the website, but warm clothes for sure. If you want to do an overnight campout and own long johns, I'd suggest packing those. I guess growing up in ice rinks, you don't get cold too easily?"

"Not very easily, no. Orry doesn't like the cold much, though. I think it reminds him of—" George snapped his mouth shut, aware he'd been about to blurt out one of Orry's most private secrets. That he'd run away from home when he was sixteen, in defiance of all the attention their parents showered on George, and he'd prostituted himself to survive. Orry had chosen to share the secret with their downstairs friends but it wasn't George's place to tell Levi. "Um, a bad time in his life."

"I can understand that. We all have different triggers for our traumas."

Don't I know it.

"But Orry's good now?" Levi asked gently.

"Yeah, I think so. It was a lifetime ago. But thank you for caring."

"You're my friend, George. I care about the people

you love. I'd like to be Orry's friend, too, but he seems hesitant about me, and I can't figure out why."

"He's just overprotective. Has been ever since I quit skating. But he knows I'm trying to be the person I used to be, to be part of the world. He's trying to temper his instincts to question the motives of every person who comes near me."

Levi studied his face for a moment with those beautiful, expressive eyes. "Someone betrayed your trust. Someone besides your parents?"

George's gut shriveled. "Yes, and I don't want to talk about it."

"Heard and backing off."

"Thank you. I trust you, Levi, but there are some things I don't talk about, not even with Orry."

"I get it. I hear you. I went through a horrific period of time in my life, and I did things I have only ever told my therapist. There are probably a few things I didn't tell her because I blocked them out. But you will always have a safe place with me, George. I promise."

"I know, thank you. And same. I'm not much of a talker but I'm a pretty good listener."

"Yes, you are." Levi looked like he wanted to say something else, but instead deflated George's good mood with, "I should probably go."

"Oh, um, okay." George didn't want their pleasant conversation to end, but he couldn't be greedy with Levi's time. The guy had an hour's drive home and a whole other life beyond his friendship with George. "I'll text you a spot to meet on Sunday morning."

"Sounds good."

They both rose and George walked him to the door. He hoped Levi would ask for another hug, but all Levi did was extend a hand. Slightly disappointed, George shook with the firmest grip he had, resigning himself to the fact that yesterday's hug had been gratitude over Ginger. Nothing more. "Thank you again for the vacation voucher," George said. "I'm nervous but excited. I've never done anything like it before."

"Then I am honored to be there for your first time." Levi held eye contact a beat longer than George expected before releasing his hand.

George immediately missed his touch, and he didn't allow his mind to spin out on why. He was simply starved for human contact; that was all. That was all it could be.

Right?

Chapter Eight

Over the course of his lifetime, Levi could count on one hand the number of times he'd been seriously nervous to do something. First time riding a horse solo when he was four? No big deal. She was a gentle mare named Starling, and he'd loved every second of being on the majestic beauty. First time standing up on the saddle of a galloping horse? Cake walk because he was confident in his physical abilities.

The two most recent times were last December, when Levi showed up at Clean Slate Ranch to surprise Robin with a visit—someone he'd truly missed and hadn't seen in nearly three years. The other time was when he let himself fall in love with Grant, and that had gone spectacularly wrong.

And then there was today, driving to the pickup spot George had texted him. They'd chosen a truck stop because it was easy to get in and out of, and it was very public. Not that this was a hostage negotiation or anything, just a passenger exchange. But Levi imagined Orry had some personal anxiety about his brother going off on his own for a solid week.

Levi texted that he'd arrived and tried not to fidget while he waited. George sent back that they were about five minutes out and he'd be there soon. That made him smile and his heart beat a little harder. He sipped from the thermos of water he always kept on hand and hummed to whatever was on the radio. After not seeing him for the last two days, George was almost here.

He'd never thought to ask what Orry's car looked like, but an older-model gray sedan pulled into the spot next to Levi's truck. Levi got out to help, but Orry was the one who hefted George's suitcase into the bed of his pickup. Then Orry pulled George to the other side of the car and whispered to him. Levi held back, giving them a moment.

The twins embraced in a long hug that hinted at the strength of their bond. George pulled back first and said—from what Levi could see of his lips—"Go, I'm safe."

Orry turned and gave Levi a stern look. "Take care of my brother. His safety is in your hands, dude."

"I'll take good care of him and return him to you in pristine condition."

A woman holding a plastic bag of groceries from the plaza's convenience store walked past and shot them all a funny look. George blushed, then moved to stand by the passenger side door of the truck. He watched Orry back out and drive away, waving once. Whether or not Orry could see the gesture, Levi didn't know. He resisted the urge to go around the truck and open George's door for him; this was not a date, just an outing with a friend.

They both climbed into the truck. It was about three years old now, and while it didn't have all the newest bells and whistles, Levi made do with it. It had driven him a lot of miles and across a lot of states since he bought it slightly used. "I'm a little surprised your brother didn't hand me a written list of personal care instructions," Levi said.

George burst out laughing in that lovely, lyrical way he had on the rare occasions he laughed around Levi. "I kind of am, too. But I'm under strict orders to text him at each meal, and to send pictures."

"Proof you're not damaged?"

"I guess. I do think he's a little jealous he can't go. Maybe we can save up and come back together in the summer."

"If you want to do that, don't wait too long to make your reservation. The slots fill up fast these days." Levi backed out of his spot and got them on the road.

"That's good business for the ranch, though, right?" George seemed to look everywhere at once while Levi navigated his way back onto the interstate. "Slater has told me stories about how Mack built the ghost town to keep the town of Garrett from dying off and the ranch being threatened."

"Yeah, it's definitely good for business, and Robin's told me a lot of the same stories. They deserve to be proud of everything they've accomplished, especially Mack."

"I agree."

Levi glanced at George's profile, unable to get a good read on the kid's mood. Was he anxious? Excited? A little bit of both? "I take it your boss was okay with you takin' off a whole week?"

George's head swiveled in his direction, lips twisted in confusion. "I freelance, I don't have a b—oh. Ha ha."

"I thought it was funny."

"I worked longer hours Friday and yesterday so I

won't lose much income. I'll just do more videos when I go back to make up for it. Hey, how's Ginger?"

Nice deflection away from your job.

"She's been sprung from jail." One of the most joyful moments of his new life had been watching Ginger walk out of the crate and join her siblings outside in the grass. They didn't wrestle like they often did, seeming to sense Ginger needed to take it easy for a while. Around lunch, he'd found them sleeping by the house in a pile of fur and limbs, soaking in the sunshine.

"Awesome. I am thrilled she's doing better. I guess you arranged for people to feed her?"

"Yes, Wes agreed to feed them and check their water bowl. But I might have to sneak up and visit them some afternoon. I've only been away from them for a whole week one other time, and it was torture. But they were also in another state, not a shortcut through the trees."

"I get it. If I could sneak away for an hour to visit Orry, I would. I won't lie, Levi, parts of this week are going to be tough for me, so I'm glad you'll be around."

Those words settled in Levi's heart and he held them tight. "I'm here for whatever you need."

They didn't talk much more on the drive, but the silences weren't awkward. "I'm starting to remember the way here," George said when Levi turned off the interstate that eventually led to Garrett. "Which I guess I should, since it's my fourth time in, like, a year and a half."

"I'm glad you decided to come up to the July 4th celebration the first time. Glad we got a chance to meet." If Levi hadn't already briefly met and interacted with George both times at the ghost town, he might not have been confident enough to approach him at Thanksgiving. To be his friend.

"Me too." George gazed out at the road ahead of them, his profile distant. "I'm grateful Slater and Derrick came home when they did that night, or me and Orry might never have gotten to know them."

Levi searched for a "that night" reference but found nothing familiar. "What night?"

George blushed and looked at his lap. "Why do things keep slipping out around you?"

"Because you trust me. But you don't have to explain anything to me. Not unless you want to, and I won't share your secrets. I promise."

"I know." He stared at his twisted fingers as he spoke. "When I quit skating, my coach was furious. Like, beyond furious, because he'd spent so many years training me. Grooming me. He was so desperate to get one of his athletes into the Olympics, and he was sure I'd be the one. When I refused to compete anymore, he trashed me to any reporter who'd interview him. After Orry and I moved in with our grandparents, Adrian, my coach, came to their house to try and reason with me. When I refused and Grandpa ordered him out, Adrian got physical. Gramma had to call the police to remove him."

"Damn," Levi said, aching inside for what had clearly been a traumatic moment for a teenager.

"Yeah. I didn't hear from him again for years, so I assumed he'd moved on. But this past summer, he showed up at the apartment. He was so polite and contrite over the speaker, said he wanted to formally apologize in person, that I took a chance and let him in. Orry wasn't home or he would have talked me out of it. As soon as

I let him in, he put the chain on the door and started yelling at me. I tried to stand up for myself, but he was just there. In my face."

They were maybe a mile from town but Levi didn't care. He pulled over to the shoulder, because George was getting upset, and this story deserved Levi's full attention. He shifted into park, took off his seatbelt and slid closer to George on the bench seat. Took on a chance on squeezing George's knee.

George covered that hand with one of his and met Levi's eyes. Grief and anger stormed together in their depths. "I finally told him that everything that happened, all the reasons I quit were his fault and to fuck back out of my life. He hit me in the face hard enough that I knocked the futon over backward and a picture fell off the wall."

"Fuck." Fury blazed deep inside Levi where he tried to hide his quick temper. Running and meditation helped but he couldn't do either of those things in this moment. All he could do was twist their hands until they were palm to palm and listen.

"Derrick and Slater had just gotten home from a date and they heard the thump. Came upstairs and knocked. Adrian tried to send them away, but Derrick threatened to call the police. Adrian said some mean things about us and left. I haven't had contact since."

"Thank the universe for Slater and Derrick. You could have been hurt a lot worse."

George trembled once. "Believe me, I know. Orry came home a few minutes later, and they were so kind to us both. Supportive. After that, Orry and I started hanging out with them in the living room more."

"We're all put in the places we're meant to be."

"I don't think I always believe that but it's a nice sentiment. However—" George's eyes brightened a bit "—I do believe it in our case. You're the first person I've told about that night with Adrian, beyond the people who witnessed it firsthand."

"I'm honored that you continue to trust me with your secrets, George. Sincerely."

George released his hand and rubbed at his own eyes. "I didn't mean to share all that in your truck. Fuck, we won't be late, will we?"

Levi glanced at the dash. "Nah, we aren't too far, and Reyes knows we're coming so even if we were a few minutes late, he'd hold the wagon."

"Okay. I'm okay."

"All right." Levi slid back across the seat, buckled up, and got them back on the road.

They didn't speak again as they drove through Garrett. Main Street was decorated with Christmas lights and pine garlands, and some of the businesses had decorations in the windows. George seemed completely charmed by it all, and too soon they were through town. The two big boulders announcing the entrance to the ranch lands appeared. A few dozen yards down the bumpy dirt road was a four-sided chain-link-fence enclosure that served as the parking lot for that week's guests. Three other cars were waiting, folks still in their vehicles thanks to the morning chill likely still hanging in the air.

"I read about this on the website," George said, leaning forward, eyes fixed on the trail. "They pick us up in a wagon."

"Yup. It's something Arthur always insists on, unless the weather is super bad."

Maybe a minute passed before two horses came into view on the horizon, cresting a small hill, followed by two men riding on a buckboard. Even from the distance, Levi recognized the familiar forms of head cowboy Reyes Caldero and ranch foreman Judson Marvel. Both men wore long-sleeve ranch polos, jeans, boots and cowboy hats.

When other folks started getting out of the cars, Levi shut off the engine and climbed out. They each got their bags from the pickup bed and joined the eleven other folks waiting by the parking lot gate. Levi studied the people he'd be spending time around for the next week. A pair of men and a little girl stood together, the men's elbows brushing, both obviously excited to be there, and the looks they shared suggested not just best friends on vacation. The girl was practically bouncing on her tiptoes.

A family of four were squabbling over something. The parents looked tired, and their two teenage daughters… well, he wasn't sure. Probably missed their cell phones. The other group was four older adults, late thirties or early forties. Two men, two women. Couples or simply friends. They were too far away to properly clock their fingers for wedding rings.

Excitement charged the air when Judson brought the buckboard to a stop by the gate. "Ho, there," Judson said in a familiar, booming voice. "Welcome to Clean Slate Ranch!" A scattering of applause. "Name's Judson Marvel. I'm ranch foreman. This here quiet fellow beside me is Reyes Caldero, our head cowboy. You wanna work with the horses, chances are you'll have to face his ugly mug."

The speech felt slightly canned but that was only

because Levi knew the men. Arthur Garrett, the ranch owner, was no longer actively involved in the ranch itself, but he still insisted on a little bit of theatricality for the guests.

Reyes tipped his hat at the crowd and climbed down from the wagon. "You can leave your luggage here," he said in his lightly accented voice. "We'll lock the gate and send a truck down to retrieve it all and have it brought up to the guesthouse. Don't worry, we've never had anyone's things stolen."

Everyone made a small pile with their luggage. Levi noticed a flash of fear on George's face but it was gone fast. He lightly squeezed George's elbow and winked when George met his eyes. George nodded, then let out a long breath.

Reyes helped everyone climb onto the buckboard. It had benches along both sides, and Levi waited until last so he could make sure George was on the end with Levi on his left side, instead of sandwiched next to a stranger. Reyes gave him a knowing smile but didn't comment. He returned to the front of the wagon, and once he was situated, Judson turned them around.

Levi relaxed into the gentle rolling of the wagon and the easy pace of the horses. The land stretched out all around them in hills, grass and trees, and in the far distance, huge crags of mountains teeming with wildlife. While Levi was familiar with the property, he'd never experienced it as an actual ranch guest before. Not like this, and he wanted to enjoy the experience.

Even the hard parts he expected to face with George and his anxiety.

George looked everywhere, even snapped a few pictures with his phone. Levi sucked in the familiar country air. The other guests chatted amongst their own groups but folks mostly looked. Experienced. Admired the beauty all around them.

Eventually a big, three-story building appeared on the horizon, followed by a smaller, two-story one. A barn and corral. Another barnlike building beyond it where staff hid their cars.

Judson circled the wagon past the main house, which had a sign that read Office over it, and stopped in front of the guesthouse. Patrice, the den mother who took care of guests and cooked all the meals, waited patiently on the wide front porch. She was a genuinely kind woman who also struck Levi as an old soul.

Reyes helped everyone down, while Judson went onto the porch to stand beside Patrice. When everyone was down, Judson said, "We are very excited to see all your smiling faces today, on our last full week before the holidays, and we thank you for joining us. We're an open-minded, family-friendly place here at Clean Slate Ranch. Everyone is welcome here as long as they remember that."

Levi glanced at the other pair of men in time to see their wide smiles.

"While we do our best to give all our guests the most authentic experience possible, this isn't the eighteen seventies. Among the injury release forms you have to sign, there's also a conduct form. Discrimination of any kind will not be tolerated, and we reserve the right to keep your deposit and send you home at any time. Clear?"

Lots of nods and murmurs of clear went up around the crowd, and Levi basked in the broad grin on George's face.

"Now that we've reviewed the serious stuff," Judson

continued, "let's talk about your stay this week. This land has been in the Garrett family for generations, and I'll repeat some wisdom that's been handed down for generations: respect the land, and the land will respect you. There are wild animals out there on this land, mostly harmless but we've seen evidence of mountain lions out in the wilder areas. Stay on the marked trails and don't go wandering, and you'll be fine."

Reyes now stood at the base of the steps leading up to the porch.

"You've all met our head cowboy, Reyes Caldero," Judson said. "He's in charge of the horses, and he'll help guide you through the process of learning to properly saddle, mount, and ride your assigned horse. Most of the animals are rescues, but they work extensively with them down at our horse rescue facility, so they're safe to work with.

"This pretty lady to my right is Miss Patrice, and she's in charge of the guesthouse. She'll be cooking your breakfasts and most dinners, and we'll offer cold sandwiches and salads for lunch."

Patrice stepped forward and commented on about various things, from food allergies to guests cleaning up after themselves and leaving the common areas tidy. A pickup carrying their luggage arrived right as her welcome speech wound down. Judson invited everyone inside to get their welcome packets and room assignments.

George started tapping his fingers against his thigh. Levi leaned in and whispered, "Don't worry, we've got our own room. No strangers."

The tapping stopped.

A younger horseman named Hugo and an older veteran of the ranch named Ernie were already inside the bunkhouse, and Reyes went to stand beside them. Because of Robin's motor mouth, Levi knew they were on standby to carry luggage for the female guests. The first group called to sign things was the older quartet. The Sanchezes and the Porters. Two couples, probably friends on vacation together. Reyes and Ernie carried the two ladies' suitcases up the stairs on the far left. Straight ahead, beneath the stairs, was the entrance to the dining room.

He and George were called next, so he didn't learn the names of the other guests yet. They signed the appropriate spots and got their packets. "It's nice to see you taking some time off, Levi," Patrice whispered. "You enjoy your week here. Both of you."

"Thank you, ma'am," Levi replied.

Hugo guided them to the second floor. It had four rooms with four bunk beds and a private bathroom each. Every door had an animal symbol on it, and Hugo gave them the room with the coyote. The rooms weren't huge but they also weren't cramped for personal space, and theirs had a huge window with a gorgeous view of the land. George gravitated to the bunk beds on the left and put his bag on the bottom mattress.

"You probably know the spiel," Hugo said with a friendly grin, "but make sure to look over your welcome packets. Meet the other guests but don't wander beyond the main yard yet. A cold lunch will be ready downstairs at noon."

"Thank you," Levi replied, mindful George hadn't spoken a word since they'd gotten on the buckboard.

"Enjoy your vacation, man. You, too, George."

George startled, apparently not expecting Hugo to

know who he was. "Um, thanks. You too?" Awkward but he was clearly outside of his comfort zone and struggling.

"Yeah, thanks. Uh, I'll see you guys in the corral later." Hugo left with an imaginary tip of a hat.

Levi put his bag down on the other bunk then closed the door. Put both hands on George's shoulders. "Breathe for me, okay? I know this is new, this isn't what you're used to, but you are perfectly safe. I'm right here."

George sucked in a ragged breath, held it, and released. His color got a little less pasty and more lifelike as he took a few more long, cleansing breaths. "I'm not used to this."

"I know. And the good news is, all the activities are voluntary. If you need to stay in the room until lunch, do it. The only thing is if you want to ride this week, we do have to be at the corral for today's first lesson."

"Right. I think, uh, maybe I should stay in here for a little while. Get my bearings."

"If that's what you need, then do it. The ranch Wi-Fi password is in the welcome packet. Make sure you get it and text me if you need anything. Unless…you'd rather I stay?"

George hesitated before shaking his head. "No, you go explore. If we both stay in here behind a closed door, people will talk." His wry smile was somehow both worried and teasing.

A fresh wave of tender feelings warmed Levi's chest. "Wouldn't want rumors on the first day."

"No. They'll figure out I'm a basket case soon enough."

"You are not a basket case. You're George Thompson and you are a fighter. We've got this."

They held eye contact for a long, lovely moment in time, and Levi really, really wanted to kiss George. But he wouldn't. He was along on this vacation as chaperone, nothing more. George needed a friend, and Levi would give him friendship and support.

George took a small step back and broke eye contact. "Thank you, Levi."

"I'll see you in the little while." Levi didn't want to leave him alone this early in their trip, but he had to trust George to know what he needed.

With a sad sigh, he went downstairs to meet the other guests.

Chapter Nine

George hated that he needed a break less than an hour into their vacation, but being alone inside the room, door shut against the world, helped immensely. He sat on the floor beneath the window and concentrated. He breathed in and out. Noticed the brown and gray shades of the wood floor and walls. The simple ivory blankets on the four bunked beds. The scents of detergent and something vaguely floral. The creaky sounds of the old guesthouse as people moved around inside it.

Those things grounded him.

He pulled out his phone and did a voice-to-text because his fingers were shaking too hard to type. "I'm here. Settling in. The place is beautiful. I miss you already." Send. He played a word puzzle on his phone for a while. This particular game relaxed him because it forced him to focus on making multiple words out of a jumble of letters. It took all his concentration to complete each level, and he could block out everything else.

Orry replied about fifteen minutes later: Miss you too, bro. You okay?

Had a minor panic attack but I'm okay now. Handling it.

He could only imagine the face Orry was making.
The conversation seemed over for now. George set an
alarm for eleven fifty so he didn't miss lunch, then continued playing his game. Managed quite a few difficult
levels before the alarm went off. His ass was numb
from sitting on the hardwood floor for over an hour.
He stretched carefully as he stood and popped a verte-
brae in his neck, too.

Then came the new challenge: opening that door and
going downstairs alone. He stared at the door handle.
And stared. And stared. Somewhere outside, a loud bell
clanged, probably the call for lunch. But George still
couldn't open the door. Too many strangers out there.
Even after the opening speeches, even knowing he was
in a perfectly safe environment, he couldn't—

Someone knocked. "George, you still in there?"

Levi. "Yes."

The door opened and Levi popped half his body inside. "It's lunchtime."

"I know. I, uh, I tried."

"It's okay, that's why I came up."

"Thank you." Instead of feeling like a child for not
being able to do something as simple as open the door,
he was grateful to Levi for thinking ahead. For coming
to get him so George wasn't alone.

Levi winked in a familiar gesture of both amusement
and affection. "Come on, I'm starving."

They left together and descended the big staircase.
The dining room was full of the other guests, plus Patrice. A big sideboard against the far wall held a commercial drink machine, as well as plates, paper napkins,
utensils, and a bowl of snack-size bags of chips. The
long dining table was loaded with a platter of assorted

deli meats and cheeses, cold salads, and all kinds of pickles and condiments.

The family with the teen girls had already settled in the big communal living space to eat, which calmed George's racing heart a fraction. They weren't all expected to cram around the table to eat and reach around each other for food. Good. The two men with the little girl got their food and stopped in passing.

"Guys, this is my friend George," Levi said to them. "George, this is Samuel and Rey Briggs-King, and their daughter Faith. We got to chatting a while ago, and I've already sold them on a ghost town visit if they're ever back in California."

"You can sell the ghost town to anyone, I bet," George quipped. "It's nice to meet you guys."

"Please, come join us for lunch," Rey said. He was shorter than Samuel with dark hair that contrasted Samuel's blond. The affection between them was clear simply from the way they stood together, and Faith definitely favored Rey.

Levi deferred the request to George. "Sure, okay," George replied.

The little family moved off. George got a plate and surveyed the options. Pretty similar to his typical lunch fare, even though at home he preferred low sodium brands. They'd been added to the guest list just in time to fill out the form about food allergies, and while George didn't have any that he was aware of, he was generally a picky eater. Everything here was fine, though, and the online menu for dinnertime sounded great. Mostly simple food.

He made a turkey sandwich on whole wheat, with a smear of mustard, sliced tomatoes, and some dill sandwich-sliced pickles from a jar. Took a small scoop of potato salad and what looked like some sort of broccoli salad in a white dressing. Levi made a much thicker sandwich with all kinds of fixings, and he helped himself to a little of each salad option. Food done, they got their drinks.

They found the Briggs-King family in a cluster of chairs around a wide, round coffee table. Faith was sitting on the floor, using the coffee table for her food. Samuel and Rey were sharing a love seat. George chose a chair across from the couple, and Levi sat on his left. George was curious about the pair but he wasn't used to initiating getting-to-know-you questions with perfect strangers.

"So Samuel and Rey are here for their honeymoon," Levi said after a few minutes of eating in silence.

"Really?" George stared at the pair. "You brought your daughter on your honeymoon?"

"It's a second, longer honeymoon vacation," Rey replied with a chuckle. "Samuel and I did the whole marriage thing backward. As soon as it was legal we went down to the justice of the peace to get hitched, and then our friends threw us a bachelor party. But Samuel and I are both workaholics, and I have a small business back in Pennsylvania. We haven't been able to have a real vacation in years, but the stars aligned this month with vacation time and Faith being out of school."

"Why here?"

"I love horses," Faith piped up. "I got to ride a pony once at the state fair, but not a real horse yet, and we've been learning about the Old West in school. And Papa and I like to watch old western movies together on weekends."

Samuel pointed at himself, indicating he was Papa.

"You guys are from Pennsylvania?" George asked, surprised by the distance they'd traveled. "How'd you hear about Clean Slate way out there?"

"A client, actually," Rey replied. "I'm a private caterer, and one of our regulars mentioned vacationing here this past spring. Once I looked at the website and saw how tolerant and gay-friendly the place was, I was sold. Selling Samuel was a bit harder, but he's also a city boy."

"Former city boy," Samuel said. "I love our small town and can't imagine moving." The pair exchanged lovey smiles, and George's insides burned with jealousy. Would George ever have that kind of genuine affection for a life partner? "And before you ask, I'm a police officer. Have been for a long time."

"Oh, wow." George had mad respect for police officers and first responders, putting their lives on the line to save others. "Sounds intense."

"TV makes it way sexier and more dramatic than it really is. Most days, it's just walking around and helping everyday folk fix everyday problems. Especially in Stratton."

"So what do you do, George?" Rey asked.

George carefully chewed and swallowed his bite of broccoli salad. "I create closed-captions for video content for various websites. It's freelance work so I make my own hours."

"That's cool. I've never met anyone with that job, but I guess someone has to do it, right?"

"Yeah." He took a big bite of his sandwich in case Rey decided to pry into which websites. The conversation had him squirrely but not anxious. The two men were kind and polite, and Faith was adorable and sweet. This was…sort of fun.

As if sensing George's discomfort—how did he always do that?—Levi asked, "So how did you two meet?"

George vaguely listened to a story about a diner, a broken mirror, and a head injury while he finished his lunch, while also observing the room. Everyone seemed to be in their own clusters. The family of four. The quartet of friends. The gays.

Except Levi wasn't technically gay if he identified as bisexual. Either way, this thing George had with Levi was just friendship. It couldn't be more.

Faith finished eating first and got up to explore the wide bookshelf full of various board games. Not exactly authentic to the Old West but people needed ways to entertain themselves in the evenings, because George didn't see a television anywhere. Levi and Samuel volunteered to take everyone's plates and utensils to the bus bin in the dining room, and George found himself sort of alone with Rey. He was older than George, probably a bit closer to Levi's age.

"Your daughter looks like you," George blurted out.

Rey grinned. "Biologically, she's mine, but Sam is her father in every other way that counts. And we have a great group of friends. My family is everything to me."

"That's good. Sometimes family is too complicated."

"Like yours?"

"Understatement. But I have my brother and he's my best friend."

"You have a brother? Older or younger?"

"Older by about four minutes. We're identical twins."

Off Rey's surprised look, George found a photo of them on his phone.

"Holy crap, I can't tell which one is you," Rey said.

George wasn't sure if Rey was telling the truth or if he really couldn't see the differences in how much thinner George's face was. How less haunted Orry's eyes were. Then it didn't matter, because Levi and Samuel returned, and Rey showed Samuel the photo.

"I've never met identical twins before," Samuel said. "Why didn't your brother want to come this week?"

"He couldn't get off work. This was very last minute for me and Levi. Thanks for a favor I did for him."

"Must have been some favor in exchange for a week's vacation."

George deferred that to Levi, who told the Thanksgiving story and about Ginger's recovery at George and Orry's apartment. And he showed off pictures of all three cats. Faith cooed over them for a while, so Levi brought up a video of them tussling in the grass for her to watch.

"Wait, George and Orry," Rey said. "Why do I know those names?"

"*North and South*, babe," Samuel replied. "The one with Patrick Swayze?"

"Oh, right. I guess your parents were fans."

"My mother was obsessed with it before we were born," George replied. The food he'd eaten sat heavily in his stomach with the mention of his parents.

Rey seemed to understand right away. "What are you guys most excited to do this week? To be honest, I'm most looking forward to having someone else cook for me, three meals a day, for a whole week."

Levi laughed. "Patrice is a great cook. I've had her

food on more than one occasion. And tonight's welcome barbecue is a real treat. Best barbecue in Northern California, even if Arthur Garrett says so himself. He can't eat it anymore for health reasons, but he's still down here every Sunday cooking for his guests."

"He's the owner, right?"

"Yeah, he's a great man. There's a reason people come here to work and don't want to leave."

"Hey, if you find a place that makes you happy, why leave?" Rey leaned more heavily against Samuel's shoulder. "And we got completely off track. What do you guys want to do this week?"

"Well, I'd say I'm looking forward to riding horses," Levi said in a perfectly deadpan manner, "but that's sort of my day job, and that job is way more exciting than trail rides. However, I am a fan of camping. The weather is supposed to be nice enough that we should have at least one overnight camping trip available."

"Faith likes to camp in the backyard in the summer but we've never been out in the wilderness before." Trepidation flashed briefly across his face. A father's fear for his child's safety. A look George didn't remember ever seeing on his own father's face, not even when George was hospitalized.

Levi leaned forward. "Don't worry, the guides keep a shotgun on the chuck wagon in case of emergencies. My best friend used to be a horseman here, and he told me they've never had a camper injured on an overnight. Well, except for Wes Bentley, but that's also part of the ghost town legend at this point."

"The legend?" Samuel asked.

Levi launched into another amusing story George also knew, about a camper whose horse spooked and dragged terrified Wes across Garrett land to the remains of an old ghost town. He liked listening to Levi talk. He had a soothing cadence to his voice that kept George grounded and calm, despite being in a strange place, surrounded by strangers.

The guesthouse door swung open and heavy boots thumped inside. A tall, older hand George didn't know stood there, eyeballing everyone. "Just a reminder, folks," he said, "that for anyone hoping to ride our horses this week, there is a required lesson in the main corral that starts at two o'clock. I hope to see everyone there in about thirty minutes." The cowboy tipped his hat and left.

"Damn, have we been talking that long?" Rey asked. "I'm sort of nervous-excited about this. I've never been near a horse, much less on top of one."

"It can be intimidating at first," Levi replied. "But these are all gentle mares with good temperaments. And the horsemen are trained. You'll all be fine, I promise." He met George's eyes and the sentiment reflected silently back.

George nodded slightly, trusting his friend.

"What do you say, Faith?" Rey asked. "Ready to go see the horses?"

"Yes!" She gave Levi his phone back and rushed toward the door. Rey sprinted to catch up with her, laughing the entire time. Samuel followed them at a much more leisurely pace.

George remained seated until the guesthouse emptied, everyone apparently on board with learning to ride. Or at least watching their loved ones learn. George was curious, and he probably could have gotten a private lesson from Levi at some point, but this was part of the vacation package. Might as well take full advantage of the amenities.

The other guests were scattered around the perimeter of the large main corral. No one was inside the corral yet, but just inside the entrance to the big barn, George spotted a person moving around, putting gear on a horse. He and Levi stopped near the Briggs-King family. Faith was already bouncing on her toes, and he guessed her to be around nine or ten. Making happy childhood memories with her parents.

George had to think hard to find many of his own.

Don't go there. Enjoy the moment.

Reyes entered the corral leading a big horse saddled up and ready to go. "Good afternoon everyone," he said. "As Ernie announced earlier and as is explained in the welcome packets, anyone interested in riding one of our mares this week must take today's basic lessons. We'll go over mounting, riding and leading the horse. It also gives myself and my fellow horsemen a chance to observe everyone's basic skills, so we know which horse to pair you with this week."

One of the teenagers raised her hand. Reyes nodded. "Why do we have to ride the same horse all week?"

"For your safety as well as the horse's. Horses are more sensitive than a lot of folks give them credit for, and we need to match their temperament with yours. I tried riding a horse once that didn't like me, and I ended up sitting on an ice pack for the rest of the day."

"Got it."

George wasn't entirely sure how true that story was, given Reyes's experience, but it definitely made his point. Then again, George had once been a novice skater and had fallen on his ass on the ice dozens of times. No one was born knowing how to do every physical skill.

"Mounting a horse is fairly easy once you get the hang of it." Reyes pointed to wooden set of three steps. "But for you younger riders and folks who are a little nervous, we do have steps. However, we do not have steps out on the trails if you get off your horse, so it's best to give it a try at least once."

A soft murmur went through the guests. Two more cowboys, Hugo and the older guy from the guesthouse, came out of the barn leading horses of their own.

"Now, this beauty to my right is Attitude, or Tude for short," Reyes continued. "Hugo over there has Valentine and Ernie's with Hot Coffee."

"Tude is Mack's horse," Levi whispered. "And Hot Coffee is Reyes's."

Huh. Seemed odd to use personal horses for ranch demonstrations, but maybe that was part of keeping them in the barn? George had no idea how the ranch worked behind the scenes, and he was glad Levi knew a few of the details. It kind of gave them an advantage over the other guests.

"We've also got another experienced horseman in the group this week," Reyes said. "Mr. Levi Peletier over there works up at the ghost town during the on season, doing trick riding and demos. Maybe we can persuade him to do a little demo for us later in the week."

"Yes!" Faith piped up. "Let's see that."

Levi chuckled, then braced one foot on the bottom of the corral fencing and raised himself up off the ground. "I can be persuaded with a six-pack of Grand's Cream Soda," he joked before stepping back down.

"You work cheap," Reyes replied.

"Eh, I'm on vacation."

The easy banter relaxed George even more as they watched Reyes demonstrate the right way to brace their left foot in the stirrup, grab the pommel, and push off with the right leg. He made it look so damned easy, but the guy also had years of practice under his belt. Reyes talked about adjusting the stirrups to the correct height for each rider, followed by an admonishment not to ride too long the first time.

"Sitting astride a saddle stretches your thigh muscles a lot, and the longer you stay in the saddle, the more uncomfortable you'll be once you dismount."

Levi's lips twitched, as if finding a joke in the phrasing but George didn't get it.

Hugo mounted Valentine and showed them how to make the horse start walking by nudging her flank with his heels, leading with the bit, and gently pulling the horse to a stop. Seemed like basic things George had seen time and again in movies and on TV, but he'd never done any of it himself.

Hell, this was the closest he'd ever been to a live horse in his life.

Reyes did a demo of dismounting, and by that time, George noticed a new, familiar face had joined them at the corral: Miles Arlington. Reyes's husband and head chef at the ghost town's saloon. He was out of work, same as Levi, and from what gossip George remembered the pair lived in a cabin here at the ranch. Probably watched the tourists for something to do.

"Now," Reyes said, "we're going to separate you all into three groups and give you each more hands-on time with the horses."

Hugo ended up with the older quartet, while Ernie

took the family unit. George let out a breath, grateful to be working with Reyes and Levi his first time mounting a horse. Everyone was let inside the corral and their groups broke apart. Miles remained outside the corral but followed them to where Reyes led them.

"Have you ever ridden a horse before, Miss?" Reyes asked Faith.

"Only a little pony, but Dad says I'm big enough to ride a big horse on my own if I want," Faith replied in a soft, earnest voice. "Am I big enough?"

"I'd say so but how about I walk beside you the whole time." To Rey, he said, "We do have safety helmets if you prefer she wears one."

Rey cast a look at Samuel, who shrugged with his eyebrows. He'd only known the men for a few hours, but Rey definitely seemed like the nervous parent in the pair. "I'd prefer a helmet, yeah. Sorry, sprout, but at least this first time."

She frowned but didn't question him.

Reyes shouted at someone to bring a junior helmet and the steps. "You're old enough to ride, but definitely not tall enough yet to mount without help."

"Okay, sir. I've never ridden a horse before but I really want to."

"And you will in just a few minutes, Miss."

"Faith."

"Miss Faith."

The entire exchange was both touching and adorable. George leaned against the corral with Levi nearby, watching while Reyes helped Faith adjust the strap on her helmet. He led her to the steps and gently showed her how to put her foot in the stirrup and swing her other leg over. She let out a giggle of delight when she was finally on Tude; the horse barely twitched.

"Look, Dad and Papa!" She grinned so widely she showed off a single missing tooth. "I'm on a horse!"

Both dads had their phones out, snapping pictures, and it was one of the most affectionate, familial scenes George had observed in a long damned time. Reyes adjusted her stirrups, and then carefully led her around the corral. He let her try to rein Tude in herself, sticking close the entire time. Samuel filmed the whole thing while keeping a tight grip on Rey's hand.

Faith rode for a while, having the time of her life up on Tude, until Reyes asked who wanted to go next. She said her dad had to go. It took Rey a few times—and a bit of a boost from Reyes—to get up, but he managed. Samuel went next, and since Levi didn't need to practice—the lucky son of a bitch—all eyes were now on George.

Reyes impressed the hell out of him by allowing Levi to coach George through it. "The saddle gives a little," Levi said. "Don't let it scare you. You just pull yourself right on up. You're an athlete. I know you've got the muscles."

His confidence in George boosted his own self-confidence a bit more. He put his hands everywhere Levi indicated, got his left foot situated in the stirrup. Took a strong hold of the pommel...and shocked the crap out of himself by actually dragging his ass up and into the saddle. "Wow," George said, keenly aware of exactly how high off the ground he was now. "Dude."

"Great job. I am so proud of you." He clapped George's thigh once, then went about helping to adjust his stirrups. He had shorter legs than Samuel. "Get yourself situated and then nudge her in the flank with your heels."

George adjusted himself so his junk wasn't pressed painfully into the hard leather saddle and his feet were more secure in the stirrups. Then he risked starting the big beast by pressing his heels against her where he'd seen everyone else do it. Tude lurched forward, and George swallowed a yelp, reins tight in bloodless fists. After that first lurch, she plodded forward, and George figured out how to roll with her steps to avoid feeling seasick.

This was a completely new experience for him, and it was…kind of fun.

"Turn her to the left, George," Levi said.

He carefully pulled the left rein, and Tude angled her big body in that direction. They circled back to their group, and Levi talked him through a trot—really bouncy—and a canter—really, really bouncy. But despite the physical discomfort, George was enjoying himself. Experiencing something brand new with his friend. He kind of wished Orry was here to share it with him, but George liked having something private, all his own.

Something that was his and Levi's only.

Once George carefully dismounted—something he was pretty good at, thanks to his training—he stood a bit straighter and beamed at Levi. "I loved that. I understand better why you love working with horses so much."

"They're amazing animals." Levi's eyes gleamed. "You looked very natural up there."

"It was a little terrifying being that high up, but I got over it."

I knew you were there in case I fell.

George kept that thought to himself.

"When do we get to ride again?" Faith asked.

"Tomorrow," Reyes replied. "Tonight, my coworkers and I will figure out which horses are best for which riders, and then we'll introduce you before the first trail ride. How does that sound?"

"I can't wait!"

"Everyone," Reyes said to the corral at large. "Our welcome barbecue will begin at six. You're free to explore the main areas and trails, but we will have a guided walking tour of the land that begins in twenty minutes. You'll meet your guide over there." He pointed to a large sign that indicated the various trails.

As everyone else filtered out of the corral, Levi hung back with Reyes and Miles, and George stuck close. Levi started doing something on his phone.

"What do you think of this week's group?" Miles asked after he'd climbed through the wood fencing and into the corral to kiss his husband.

"They seem a calm bunch," Reyes replied. "No one who appears to be the troublemaking sort."

"Unlike my first time here."

"Exactly."

George saw an interesting story there but he didn't want to pry into their shared past. He wasn't really friends with either Reyes or Miles, and it wasn't his place to insert himself into their private lives. His phone pinged with a text. Expecting it to be Orry checking in, he was delighted to find a message from Levi with three pictures of George riding Tude. George almost didn't recognize himself or that wide, bright smile.

Reyes said, "You did well on Tude, George. You

have a natural grace that seems to put the horse at ease. You'll make a good rider."

His face went hot. "Um, thanks."

"You're welcome. I have to get Tude untacked and brushed down. Miles? Join me?"

"With pleasure," Miles replied. The couple headed toward the barn with the horse.

"How are you feeling?" Levi asked once they were alone. "You up for the trail tour, or do you need some time alone?"

"I'm not sure." George leaned against the corral, hands sliding into his jeans pockets. "Everything here feels so different from the city. Open. Freer. Less stifling. I loved riding Tude, and I can't wait to ride again tomorrow. I just…"

"It's okay." Levi relaxed beside him, their shoulders nearly touching. "You take all the small steps you need. I am right here, George. I promise. I didn't bring you here this week to overwhelm you. Just to help you have a little fun."

"I am having fun." George couldn't help a quick glance at Levi's mouth. A small part of him wanted to flee to their room and hide for a little while. But what if Levi came with him? Alone together in a small bedroom? Bad idea, and not because he didn't trust Levi. George didn't trust some of his own stray thoughts about his friend. "I think maybe the guided hike could be fun. You know the land but I don't."

Levi smiled that charming, disarming smile of his. "Then let's do it."

Chapter Ten

Levi swore he was watching George blossom right in front of his eyes. Before lunch, the shy blond had been nervous and twitchy, his gaze constantly wandering around the guesthouse, and later the corral. But something had shifted after his ride on Tude. A new confidence Levi didn't recognize. The face of a man who once skated in front of audience of thousands and knew he would be the best. Do his very best.

During the trail tour, George paid attention to what Burt had to say about the land and the paths they were free to use. They got a glimpse of the horse rescue in the distance, the bright red roof of the training pavilion difficult to miss on such a clear, sunshiny day.

"Do they do tours of the rescue?" George asked Levi quietly, rather than directing the question to Burt.

"Hey, Burt, do you do tours of the horse rescue?" Levi said, because he honestly wasn't sure. He'd never thought to ask before.

"We can arrange guided tours, yes, for folks who are interested," Burt replied with a grin. "Only small groups at a time, though. We don't want to overwhelm the horses or their trainers. They do important, delicate work there, rehabilitating those magnificent animals."

"Thank you," George whispered.

"Not a problem." Levi squeezed his wrist briefly. "You want to visit the rescue."

"Yes." His blue eyes shined with determination. "Is it weird that I feel a kind of kinship with the rescued horses? Like, what happened to them wasn't their fault, and they just want to get better and live again."

"Kind of like you?"

"Yeah. Like me." His gaze flittered to Levi's lips again, and Levi's heart fluttered with tender feelings for the younger man. Feelings he was pretty sure George reciprocated. If they hadn't been on a public trail with other people, Levi might have lost his mind a little and kissed George.

Kissed him like he'd wanted to for two weeks now. Find out how those pretty pink lips felt against his. But the tour group was getting farther down the trail, and they needed to catch up, not start making out against a tree. It was also their first day at the ranch, and the last thing Levi wanted to do was making the rest of the week awkward if he was reading George's signals wrong.

He wasn't but kept telling himself that anyway.

"I'll make sure and ask Reyes about a tour of the rescue, then," Levi said. "We better catch up."

"Huh?" George blinked like he'd been a hundred miles away. "Oh, right."

As they walked, elbows casually brushing once in a while, George snapped a few photos of the land that he texted to Orry. "Did you send one of you riding?" Levi asked.

"Yup. I can almost feel the first flash of terror, followed by pride and maybe even a bit of jealousy that I'm here and he isn't." George's smile dimmed. "It really does suck that he can't get a solid, well-paying job that actually offers benefits, but that's what we were dealt, I guess."

"I can't imagine the struggle. Some years, money was tight for the rodeo, but my dad had a good head for investments so we never went hungry. Never really went without."

"Can you tell me more about that? Having a loving, happy family around you?"

"Sure can." Levi had a lot of stories to choose from, most of them centered around Xander, and it didn't hurt to talk about his brother like it used to. He spun one of those stories for George while the hike continued, slowly circling the group back toward the main buildings. George listened with a serene expression, completely unlike the nervous man Levi had picked up this morning. Levi had heard Robin, Reyes and the other horsemen say that the land had a magical air to it that whispered to everyone who cared to listen.

George was definitely listening.

When they arrived back, some of the horses were wandering the corral, and several folks headed in that direction. George's cell rang, and his entire face lit up. "Hey, did you get my pictures?"

Levi gave him privacy for his call to Orry and turned toward the barn, unsure of his exact destination. Colt Woods intercepted him halfway there. Colt was a handyman on the ranch, married to a history professor who worked in San Francisco, and one of Mack and Reyes's best friends. Levi and he were friendly but didn't have very many private conversations.

"Hey, man, fun to see you as a guest this week," Colt said in a familiar, sunny tone.

"I figured since I'm on vacation, I might as well try taking a vacation."

"With one of Slater's twin neighbors?"

One of Slater's hot twin neighbors who is sweet and way too appealing, yes.

"I owed George for a favor," Levi said instead. "Please, tell me someone told you about my cat on Thanksgiving?"

"Yeah, I heard about it from Mack, Reyes and Robin. And I think from Derrick, too, but I've lost track at this point. Y'all are definitely the hot topic for ranch gossip."

Levi swallowed a groan. "Why? We're friends. The kid needs more friends."

"Because we're an insulated bunch, and we're also gossipier than a group of grandmas in a sewing circle. Hugo said he thinks George was a figure skater once, that he kind of recognized him."

"Okay."

Colt quirked an eyebrow. "So was he?"

"If he was, it's George's business."

"Well then that's a yes. You know why he quit?"

Colt was obviously not letting this go, so Levi gave him a little bit. "Not the specifics, only that the training and performing got unbearable. He didn't want to do it anymore. Doesn't want to be a celebrity or his life to be a spectacle." He put just enough force into his final sentence that Colt visibly backed off.

"Right, sorry. Point taken, man."

"Thank you."

"George is still hella cute, though."

Levi snorted. "Do people our age really still say hella?"

"I don't know about you, but I do. Anyway, I just

wanted to say hi, and if you and George are ever in the city at the same time as me and Avery, maybe we can do a double date."

"George and I are not dating."

"Says you." Colt winked before strolling into the barn.

Levi stared for a long time, turned around by the conversation. It didn't matter if Levi wanted to date George, kiss George, or do all sorts of things with George. George was coming out of his shell—and the closet—for the first time in years, maybe even his whole life, and Levi couldn't be selfish. Couldn't keep George's attention all to himself. George deserved the freedom to explore the wider world and all the people in it.

No matter how strongly Levi wanted to keep George all to himself.

"Dude, are you okay?" Orry asked.

George rolled his eyes as he strode toward a big tree opposite the guesthouse. "I'm perfectly fine, why?" He hadn't expected Orry to open the call like that but he also wasn't surprised.

"I don't know. I mean, you were on a horse. How was it?"

"Scary, but really cool. Getting up into a saddle is not as easy as it looks on TV, but I had a lot of fun once I was up there. I can't wait to ride again tomorrow." George ran his hand over the tree's rough bark. "It really is beautiful out here, bro. And peaceful."

"I believe you. You sound different."

"In a good way?"

"Yeah. Stronger. Maybe we should have put you on a horse years ago."

George laughed. "Maybe. I really think this week is going to be good for me. Levi and I have already met a couple with a little girl, and they are crazy nice. I'm talking to people, having conversations. It's weird but also kind of amazing. I'm even looking forward to an overnight camping trip."

"Camping? Ugh." Orry made a weird noise. "Then again, I know what it's like to sleep on the streets, so camping really isn't ever going to be my thing."

"Sorry." George didn't know all the details of the few months Orry had spent homeless when they were both sixteen. They simply hadn't talked about it because Orry didn't want to. But he'd seen enough and read enough to imagine what his twin had gone through as a homeless teenager.

"I'm not trying to guilt you," Orry said. "I want you to have fun this week, I swear. I guess I'm a little jealous that I couldn't get the time off to be there with you."

"Levi's been a great chaperone. I think he's even having some fun of his own. Reyes asked him to do some trick riding demos for the guests."

"Working on his vacation?" Orry blew a raspberry.

"How are you doing? It's gotta be weird being in the apartment by yourself."

"I've been working all day so I won't know until later. I'm actually about to pick up my next fare, so I gotta go. Be safe."

"You too."

George hung up but remained by the tree, observing the grounds from a distance. Judson and an elderly man in overalls and a bright pink long-sleeve shirt were working around a big brick barbecue pit, and the scents of burning wood and slowly roasting meat had begun to fill the air. Several of the hands were bringing picnic tables out of the barn and arranging them near the pit. Other guests were petting the horses in the corral and feeding them treats through the fencing.

Peaceful was too small a word for how this tiny slip of the world felt to George. He couldn't remember ever feeling this good or hopeful.

As the daylight waned and time inched closer to dinner, Reyes brought out one of those portable kerosene heat lamp things and set in in the middle of the picnic tables. The rising moon was close to full, and lights from a few oil lantern stakes kept it from being too dark. Patrice and Miles brought dish after dish out of the guesthouse kitchen and put them on a long table. George watched this practiced dance from his spot under the tree, grateful to Levi for giving him these precious moments alone before the socializing began again.

More of the ranch hands began emerging from a row of cabins behind the main house and milling with the guests. George was the only guest not currently over there. Levi was chatting with Robin and Shawn near the grill. He liked seeing how animated Levi got around Robin, and it made sense given their long history together as friends. It also made him a little jealous because George didn't have that.

Okay, so Orry was his best friend but that didn't count. Orry was related to him. His twin. George didn't remember what it was like to have a best friend who wasn't related to him. For a few years, he'd somewhat thought of Adrian as a BFF. They'd spent hours a day together training, usually seven days a week. They talked about all kinds of things. Looking back, George saw how Adrian had overshared with him, telling him private things that a fourteen-year-old didn't need to know about their coach and mentor.

It had all been meticulously orchestrated from the beginning.

Until Adrian pushed him too far and George had snapped.

Hugo sprinted up to the guesthouse front porch and rang the same bell that had announced lunch. George stood straighter and strode across the yard to the gathering. Mack and Wes had also joined Judson and the elderly man by the grill, and all eyes seemed to turn to them. George joined Levi by one of the picnic tables and returned his friendly smile.

"Good evening, friends new and old!" the elderly man said. "My name is Arthur Garrett, and I'm the owner of this beautiful piece of land you're visiting this week, and I want to say welcome. That big, strapping lad over there is my grandson Mack, and I'm glad to have him with us. He's usually too busy with his own attraction to bother visiting with this old man."

"Hush up, there, Arthur," Mack replied. "You'll start seeing so much of me you'll be begging me to reopen the ghost town."

George chuckled at the easy, familial banter between the pair, even as his heart lurched with grief. He missed his grandparents immensely. Maybe he'd go visit them next week if Orry was able to drive him.

"Anyhow," Arthur continued, "this here barbecue is a long-held tradition here at the ranch. Gives us all a chance to get to know who we'll be spending time with this week. It might seem a little silly, and it's not a requirement, but I hope some of you fine folks will tell us who you are, where you're from, maybe a bit about yourself and why you're visiting us."

George had absolutely no desire to do that, and Levi had already been introduced to everyone earlier at the corral, so George sat at the nearest picnic table and kept his gaze down. Rey introduced his family with a big smile. The Porter and Sanchez couples were all best friends, and they were here celebrating Mr. Sanchez's recent promotion. The Harrison family, it turned out, had a tradition of taking unusual vacations right before Christmas as their presents to each other.

That one was actually kind of cool. Gifting experiences instead of material objects.

He glanced up at Levi's profile. Levi had done the same thing for George by giving him a vacation instead of, say, a gift card or other material things as an expression of his thanks. Levi chose that moment to look down, and their eyes met in a new way that lit George up deep inside where he'd hidden his attraction to men for too damned long. George tumbled into the blue depths of Levi's eyes and gentle smile and the entire character of the man.

"Thanks for speaking up," Arthur said, breaking that beautiful spell. "It's a right pleasure to get to know y'all a bit better. I can hear your stomachs growling from the mouthwatering scent of this here meat. So I think it's time we all line up and eat!"

The words felt canned and practiced in some ways, but also authentic. Maybe it was the country-bumpkin persona Arthur exuded with his overalls and intonations. The man knew how to play an audience.

Other guests started getting in line, along with the hands, but George held back. Levi stood beside him, hands in his jeans pockets and perfectly at ease. No one gave George a cross look for not introducing himself. Once the line thinned, George stood and Levi followed him to the line. The table had an array of cold salads, baked beans, fresh fruit, and yeasty dinner rolls. George took a small selection of each salad, no beans, and a pile of fresh fruit.

The grill was a harder decision. His own diet consisted of mostly chicken and fish, and while they had some barbecue chicken breasts that looked delicious, George chose this rare opportunity to indulge in the ribs. He asked for two, and Arthur gave him three. Levi got ribs and a sausage.

They ended up eating with Robin, Shawn, Reyes and Miles, and George was thankful for the familiar faces. He wouldn't have minded eating with the Briggs-King family again, but they had a whole week to spend with the pair, and Levi seemed happy to share the meal with his best friend. Shawn showed off pictures of their house to anyone who'd look at them, and that familiar pang of jealousy shot through George at how happy and in love Shawn and Robin were.

I want that. I really do.

First, he had to trust enough to let another person in.

The food was, as promised, amazing, and George was thankful for the extra rib. The sauce was tangy with just a hint of spice. Even though anyone could go back for seconds or thirds, he limited himself so he didn't end up with a stomachache later. The fresh fruit tasted boring after all that delicious meat.

"What do you think of the ranch so far?" Miles asked George.

"It's amazing." George forked a piece of sliced strawberry but didn't eat it. "I feel at peace here. Like it's this entire planet separate from the rest of the world."

"I know the feeling. I remember thinking the same thing the first time I came here on vacation. Like nothing in my past mattered. I could just exist for a while and be me."

"Yeah, except I'm still figuring out who me is." He glanced across the picnic table at Miles, whose compassionate smile spoke a thousand words in his silence. No one else at the table seemed to be listening to them, thank God, so he risked adding, "Nature seems like a great place for people to find themselves."

"It is. I can't imagine what my life would be like right now if I hadn't come on vacation with Wes that week. All I know is that it would a lot more dreary. Less filled with life, color and love."

I want those things.

"Do you think you'd ever leave the city?" Miles asked when George didn't speak.

"I don't know. My brother and grandparents are there. I can take my job wherever I go but I can't imagine leaving my brother. We've been so close for so long, especially after our parents…it wasn't pretty."

"I kind of envy you your brother. I'm an only child and I haven't spoken to my parents in years. I was always a prop for them, a way to boost their social status and careers."

Long ago speeches about George's skating abilities, the need to practice over all else, and the drive to be the best filtered through his memory like a bad smell. "I can empathize with those kinds of parents, believe me. Nothing I did was ever good enough. No title, no medal. It was always about the Olympics."

George's gut churned as he realized what he'd said. Miles didn't press, though, simply looked thoughtful.

"It's funny how so many of us have a similar story," Miles eventually said. "Disappointed parents, I mean. But we all found family here at the ranch. And I have a feeling you've been adopted into it, George, whether you want to be or not."

"Guess I'll have to get used to it, then." George loved the idea of having friends and family here. More people who gave a damn about him and Orry than just their grandparents and neighbors.

Arthur chose that moment to stand on a chair and say, "While y'all continue to eat, and please do continue because we've got plenty, I want to tell y'all a story."

Everyone at the table except for Levi and George began to chuckle. They obviously knew what Arthur was about to say and it was likely another semirehearsed speech to intrigue the guests. He spoke about thieves being chased by Pinkertons and how they possibly left a treasure trove of gold out in the wild lands surrounding Garrett, but the family never found it because of the ghost protecting its location.

Arthur spoke with such earnestness that George believed the old man believed his own ghost story, and it was incredibly charming. Arthur ended the story with an admonishment to explore the land but to stay on the marked trails for their own safety. No issue there. The closest things to wild animals George had seen in his life were pigeons and squirrels. He did not want to risk running across a skunk. Or worse.

Once Arthur's speech ended, Ernie brought out a guitar and began playing the old-time song "Oh Susannah!" A few folks clapped along. Others went for more food. George was full and a little peopled out at this point but he wasn't sure how to excuse himself when the atmosphere was so bright and joyful.

Levi's elbow pressed into his ribs. "You want to take a walk? Enjoy the quiet night?"

"Please," George replied.

"Come on."

They left their plates on the table—George didn't see a bus bin and assumed someone would come around later to clean up—and followed Levi toward the rear of the house. Toward the row of cabins where the hands lived. They didn't stop there, though, just kept walking past the last cabin, away from the light of the torches and into nature and her dimmer skies.

"When I first came here to visit," Levi said, "I stayed in Robin's cabin, because he was pretty much living in Shawn's. I got up every morning to run around the land. I know where we'll be safe."

A tiny fist of worry loosened around George's heart. "Cool. I just…today has been so fun, but…"

"It's okay. You're not used to bein' around this many people for so long, I get it. How about we come up with a safe word for this week?"

"A safe word?"

Levi squeezed his elbow and George stopped walking. Shadows from the moon's silver light made the planes of Levi's even sharper. Almost more handsome. "If you feel overwhelmed during a social situation, it's something you can say that will tell me that, so I can get you out of it. I'm getting to know you pretty well but I don't ever want to assume."

That made sense. "Okay. What should it be?"

"Something innocuous. How about 'Did you hear that?'"

"That sounds good. I was pretty close to a 'Did you hear that?' moment at the end of dinner there."

"I assumed as much, which is why I asked to take a walk." Levi's hand hovered near George's cheek, as if he wanted to touch. Or brush hair away. George wasn't sure but he did welcome the touch. He *wanted* the touch.

So he leaned into it. Warm fingers brushed his skin, featherlight, but George felt it in his bones. He was on a moonlit walk with a handsome man, and George yearned for more. He glanced at Levi's lips, then parted his own. Levi's palm cupped George's left cheek and he took a step closer. George swore he felt Levi's body heat all over, despite them only touching in one spot.

The moment stretched out for an eternity, neither of them moving. Holding eye contact. Levi seemed at war with himself, and George saw the moment he made a decision. Those beautiful blue eyes softened. Levi leaned in closer. "I don't want to screw this up," he whispered.

"You can't," George rasped, unsure when he'd gotten short of breath. "Please. I want it to be you."

Levi let out a soft moan. "Your first kiss?"

"Yes."

Warm breath gusted across George lips and he waited for the gentle pressure of—an abrupt blast of music from Levi's pocket startled them both apart. George's heart kicked up and he nearly fell over from the shock of the noise.

"Damn it, Robin." Levi pulled his phone out and glared at it.

With the spell broken and the moment over, George said. "Answer it. It's fine."

Levi hesitated then answered. "Hey, what?"

In the quiet of the night, George could clearly hear Robin say, "Hey, man, are you going to chill at the guesthouse and play checkers like an old man, or do you wanna come to our cabin and watch a movie? George, too, if he wants."

"You go," George said before Levi could. "I'm going to head back to the room and read."

"Are you sure?" Levi asked, probably more to be polite than anything.

"Definitely."

"Copy all that," Robin said. "I'm helping with some of the cleanup. See you around eight."

"Okay. Eight." He hung up and let out a deep sigh.

"It's okay," George said, even though it wasn't. He wasn't okay and needed to be alone. "Just walk me back, please? I have no idea where I am."

Levi watched him for a few moments but George couldn't bring himself to meet the older man's eyes. He waited, hands in his pockets so Levi couldn't see them shaking, until Levi silently turned and started walking.

Chapter Eleven

Levi paced around cabin row while he waited for Robin and Shawn, unsettled by what had happened on the trail with George, and unsure what to do about it. He'd wanted to kiss George like crazy and he still did. His palm was still warm from touching George's face. When George had looked at him with those wide, begging eyes, Levi hadn't been able to say no.

He wasn't sure if Robin's call had been fortuitous or the worst timing ever, because Levi had never been anyone's first kiss before. It had been a perfectly romantic moment with the moon out and the stars twinkling overhead. They were the only two people who existed in the whole world. Levi had never felt so alive, so seen, as in that moment.

It had also scared the crap out of him.

George seemed delicate on the outside but he had a core of steel. Levi simply wasn't sure he was the person George really wanted. Levi was the guy who was available.

Trust him to know his own mind.

Xander's voice sometimes peeked out as his conscience, and it did again tonight. Back when Xander and Robin first got together and were hot and heavy, Levi had cautioned his little brother about getting involved with a coworker. Getting involved with someone he'd known for a day. Xander had told Levi to trust Xander knew his own mind. That Robin was who he wanted. And they'd been happy for eight amazing years.

"He's so young, Xan." Levi stared up at the stars and imagined one of them was his brother, smiling down at him. "I'm scared of screwing this up."

"Talking to yourself now?" Robin asked. "Maybe you need to go meditate more."

Levi pivoted. Robin and Shawn were walking in his direction, hand in hand, goopy smiles on their faces. "I probably do. Um, you mind if I bend your ear about something before we go in?"

"You guys talk," Shawn said. "This just means I get to go inside and pick the movie."

"Nothing with a sad ending," Robin replied, adding a pinch to Shawn's ass. "This feels like a serious conversation."

"I'll look for a comedy."

As soon as Shawn was inside the cabin, Levi walked to the porch and sat on the built-in bench that each cabin had. Robin plunked down beside him with a curious head tilt. "Okay, what's wrong?"

"I almost kissed George tonight."

"Almost? What stopped you?"

"Your phone call."

"Oh shit, sorry." Robin made an exaggerated grimace. "Didn't mean to cockblock you, man."

"It definitely would not have gone that far, trust me. I just…we were walking and it was peaceful, and the moon was up, and the way he looked at me… I've never felt so seen in my entire life, Robin. Not by anyone."

"Not even Grant?"

"Definitely not by Grant. There were so many things about him I never saw, because I wanted to give everyone the benefit of the doubt back then. He definitely taught me to be cautious again." Levi had admitted to his relationship with Grant a few months ago when he and Robin were out on a horse ride together. The fabulous mistake he'd made in falling for Grant and the horrible way Grant had betrayed him.

"Hey, sorry to bring that asshole up," Robin said.

"It's okay, he's a relevant part of my past. George is completely unlike him in every way, and I have no reason to think he would do what Grant did. George is young and vulnerable, and all I want to do is protect him. But he's so innocent."

"How innocent?"

"Tonight would have been his first kiss, innocent."

"Damn. Maybe my phone call was a good thing, then. Instead of in the heat of the moonlit moment, you can talk and make sure it's really what George wants."

"He asked me to kiss him. But again, I can't decide if it's because he wants *me* or if I'm just convenient. Which is why we need to talk."

"Exactly. I mean, a vacation fling worked out real well for Wes and Mack a few years ago, but you and George are completely different people. In different places in your lives. But I know you, Levi. I know you'll do the right thing by George."

"I hope you're right." The last thing Levi wanted to do was ruin his friendship with George. Or worse, break his already fragile heart.

George had probably reread the same three paragraphs in his book at least two dozen times, and he still had no idea what he'd read. He put his phone down and walked to the big window. Moonlight cast a beautiful silver sheen on the vast land in his view in a way that was almost haunting. Gorgeous. He longed for a way to properly photograph its magic so he could share it with Orry.

"I need your advice, big brother," he whispered to the sky. "But I'm scared to tell you, and I don't know why." Orry wouldn't care that George was gay, so why was he able to tell Levi and not his own twin?

He'd wanted Levi to kiss him tonight. Wanted the man to be his first kiss. The entire moment had been pulled out of a romantic movie and made real. George had felt truly seen by another person for the first time in his adult life, and he didn't want to lose that. But maybe preserving their friendship and forgetting the kissing stuff was a better idea.

Someone knocked, startling George into spinning around and tripping over his own ankles. He grabbed the windowsill to steady himself so he didn't fall on his ass. "Who is it?"

"It's Levi."

He'd come back instead of staying to watch a movie with his friends? "I didn't lock it."

The knob turned and Levi slipped into the room, a sheepish smile on his face.

"You don't have to knock," George said. "It's your room, too."

"I know, I just didn't want to barge in and scare you."

A little late for that but the sentiment was sweet. "How come you didn't stay to watch a movie?"

"I'd much rather talk to you about our walk earlier."

His stomach dipped, and George used the excuse of sitting on his bed to curl his now-trembling fingers into a ball on his lap. Levi sat on his own bunk, his expression so open and kind that some of George's fear of this conversation dimmed to a less disruptive level. When Levi didn't speak, George drummed up his own courage to start. "I meant what I said about wanting you to be my first kiss."

"I believe you. I wanted to kiss you, George. Still want to kiss you. But that also scares me a little and for a few different reasons."

Levi was scared? The man road horses sideways for a living, and he was scared of a kiss. That seemed impossible but this wasn't George's truth. It was Levi's. "What scares you?"

"How young and inexperienced you are. That I'm way more experienced than I'm comfortable telling you until we know each other a lot better."

"I may be sexually inexperienced, Levi, but I'm not oblivious to how sex works or how infinitely unique it is depending on the participants. In the last seven years, I've probably watched more porn than you have in your entire life." Shit. He hadn't meant to say that and his face went hot.

Levi quirked a single eyebrow. "That sounds like a challenge, Thompson."

"It's the truth." Might as well explain himself so Levi didn't think he was some sort of horny homebody who whacked off for hours a day. "It's my job. Not porn, but that's what I write captions for. Porn sites."

The other eyebrow joined the first briefly before settling. "I have to admit, I would have never guessed that you captioned porn, but deaf people should able to enjoy it too, right?"

"Right." George eyeballed Levi, surprised by his

calm reaction—and he really shouldn't have been. Levi didn't seem like the type of person who was quick to anger or judgment. "I've seen some pretty hardcore stuff, and maybe I've never done any of that stuff, but I know it exists. And since you're probably wondering and are too polite to ask, no, I don't sit around all day with a boner. It doesn't affect me much at all, even the gay stuff. I can compartmentalize sex from work."

"Okay. Thank you, George. I hear and accept your truth."

"Um, thanks. I've also got life experience. Maybe I've spent the better part of a decade locked away from other people, but I went through stuff when I was a teenager. Stuff that sticks with you."

"I know you did. I don't want to play a comparison game about our pasts. We both have darkness. Things that I hope, even if this thing between us never goes beyond a kiss, we can share with each other one day as really good friends."

George's heart gave a funny lurch at the idea of things not moving further than a kiss. He trusted Levi, was attracted to him, and wanted to explore those feelings. Badly. He stood. "Does that mean we're going to kiss?"

Levi bit his lower lip in a way that was both sexy and shy. "You still want to tonight? We sort of lost our perfect romantic moment in the woods."

"No, we didn't. This is better because it isn't in the moment. We talked and now we're positive we're both on the same page." He drummed up the rest of his courage and finally said what he needed. "I want to kiss you. Please, Levi Peletier, be my first kiss."

"How can I say no to that?" He stood and walked

a few steps to stand in front of the window. Held his hand out.

George took it and held tight, already a bit out of breath from the simple touch. Levi stepped closer until only the smallest breath of air remained between their bodies, and an odd flush heated George's skin from head to toe. With his free hand, Levi stroked the backs of his knuckles down George's cheek and that internal flush intensified. George licked his lips, needing this kiss now more than he needed air to breathe.

"Please," he whispered.

"Your trust means everything to me." Levi brushed his lips across George's forehead briefly before pressing a warm mouth against George's. Instead of tensing, George relaxed even more, melting against Levi's taller, broader form, his own free hand grasping at Levi's shirt. Levi's lips whispered across his, a delightful pressure that George carefully deepened. He parted his lips a bit, accepting Levi's gentle nips and sips. It seemed to go on for an eternity like that before it changed.

Levi's tongue lightly licked at George's mouth, taking little tastes, and George moaned. He really, truly moaned, and his dick began taking notice of how much he loved this. When Levi's tongue retreated, George advanced, exploring the soft lips of the man holding him so carefully. Trying this new, wonderful thing. Arousal rippled down his spine in wave after wave, and he grew bolder. Licked deeper into Levi's mouth. Got a stronger taste of the man and loved it. Hot and sweet. Pure male.

Perfection.

The world faded away, leaving George in a blissful state he never wanted to leave. He lived inside the sensual kiss and all the feelings surging through his body.

From his head to his toes—and especially his groin—
he was alive for the first time since he'd left the ice rink
behind. Alive and aware and so fucking good.

Levi pulled him in tighter, and the brush of another
man's erection against his thigh made George jump.
Levi immediately ended the kiss but didn't release
George, only put a bit of space between them. "You
okay?" Levi panted, breathless himself. Eyes wide with
arousal and concern.

George sucked in a ragged breath and silently reminded himself why Levi's erection was entirely appropriate, given their current situation. This was nothing
like with Adrian. "Startled me is all. That was…wow."

Levi, bless him, actually blushed. "Yeah?"

"Very much yeah. I never imagined kissing could
be so sensual."

"It can be a lot of things with the right person." Levi's
fingers lightly stroked his neck. "No regrets?"

"Absolutely not." He'd never felt more alive in his
life, and if kissing was this awesome, he would probably
have a bliss stroke when they finally had sex.

Not when I had sex. They. Us. Please, God, yes.

"Can we kiss some more?" George asked.

Levi's lips twitched. "I'm not sure if kissing you
more this close to all these beds is a good idea. I promise I'll behave, but man, you're putting thoughts in my
head."

"I trust you to keep them to just thoughts." And he
did trust him. Zero worry of Levi losing his mind and
doing something George didn't want or invite. That
level of trust after knowing the man for only a handful
of weeks was dizzying but also…nice. "I like feeling

close to someone who isn't related me. And it's a completely new kind of trust."

"Oh George." Levi traced a single fingertip from George's temple to his collarbone. "I like being close to someone who makes me feel as innocent as he is. Unmarked by all the turmoil in my past."

"I'm glad I can give that to you." George leaned up on his toes to kiss Levi again. "Lock the door."

Levi did, reacting to the order as if George had zapped him with a Taser. Then they were sitting together on Levi's bed, hip to hip, mouths fused in a long, unending kiss that left George floating on the best kind of joy. Hands didn't stray lower than their chests or arms. Levi seemed to love running his fingers through George's hair, and it felt a lot like being petted, and George loved it. They kissed until George was pretty sure they'd have to take turns in the shower to relieve themselves of the arousal, and he didn't care.

It was all worth it. His first kiss had turned into dozens, and George had never been happier in his life.

Levi woke the next morning with a boner so intense he gasped once he realized he was on his stomach, boxers twisted in such a way that said boner was not in a comfortable position. After making out with George for ages last night, he'd barely been able to calm his dick down enough to take a whiz before falling asleep alone.

Sort of alone. George was in the room, but on his own bunk, while Levi desperately wanted the younger man in his arms. He shifted around to gaze at the lump of George beneath his blanket. George faced the wall, back to him, and seemed to be asleep. As much as Levi wanted to palm his dick and get off to the memories of last night, he wasn't about to do that with George less than six feet away.

The rooms were not very big.

Instead, he untangled from his own bedding and went into the small bathroom. It was serviceable, like a cheap roadside motel. He brushed his teeth before climbing into the shower. Since his dick showed no signs of calming down, Levi used a bit of his own soap to handle the problem. He refused to let himself fantasize about George, though. Instead, he pulled on one of his favorite unexplored kinks: someone younger and smaller than him going to town on his ass. Unfortunately, the nameless, faceless younger top very quickly morphed into George, and Levi turned the cold water on full blast.

In no universe was he perving on his roommate.

The cold water helped, and Levi finished his shower. Since George was still asleep when Levi was dried and dressed in his regular jogging clothes, he left their room and wandered downstairs. Food smells filtered out from the kitchen; Levi took a chance on poking his head inside. Patrice, Miles and Shawn were working in tandem to create the Monday morning breakfast, and Shawn noticed him first.

"Hey, dude, you have an okay night?" Shawn asked.

Levi appreciated his discretion. "A really good night, thanks. It's odd being here as a guest, but it's also kind of fun being on vacation for the first time in forever. And speaking of vacation, aren't you and Miles supposed to be on your own?"

Patrice's warbling laughter filled the room. "These boys can't seem to stay out of my kitchen. Once a cook, always a cook. But I will never say no to the company. I love all my boys, even the ones who leave the nest."

"I was never technically in the nest," Miles said. "Just an observer who enjoys making sausage gravy for Patrice's famous buttermilk biscuits."

"The young lad has improved upon my own recipe for his diners up at the ghost town saloon."

"Hush, Patrice, no one will ever beat your gravy."

Levi chuckled at the banter. He'd tried both Patrice and Miles's version of sausage gravy and each had their own merits in terms of flavor. It also wasn't something Levi indulged in often, though.

"Plus, for me," Shawn said, "once Robin and I finally close on the house and can move in, I won't have any more chances to cook breakfast here. I'm okay with getting up early but not that early."

"We'll definitely miss you in the kitchen," Patrice replied. "He did a remarkable job taking over for me last year when I broke my collarbone."

"It was my pleasure."

The pair shared a fond, secretive smile that Levi didn't completely understand. He excused himself through the backdoor and began a light jog toward cabin row. Some lights were on in various windows as the hands slowly came awake for the new day. Levi ran familiar paths through the lands he'd come to memorize over the last year of his life, thankful to live in such a beautiful place. And to work with people who treasured this gorgeous piece of nature, rather than taking it for granted.

His mind constantly wandered back to last night's kisses with George, and he really wanted to kiss him again. Kiss him all the time. Do other things with him.

Show him so much pleasure that they'd both burst from it. One step at a time, though. One very slow step at a time. Levi never wanted to push or accidentally do something George was not genuinely ready for.

Besides, Levi wasn't sure how thin the guesthouse walls were, and he didn't want to embarrass George in front of the other guests with loud sex noises. His tiny house was a much better, much more remote option for that.

Noooope, not going there.

The morning was cool enough that he hadn't broken much of a sweat by the time he circled back to the guesthouse. He went in through the front and waved at the Briggs-King family, who were lounging in the living area waiting for the breakfast bell. George was in the bathroom when Levi entered their room, shower running, so he changed into regular clothes. George exited the bathroom dried and dressed a few minutes later, hair still damp and a little unruly.

"Hey, you were up early," he said.

"Old habits," Levi replied. "I got a good run in, though. Favorite way to start the day."

George smiled but something about it seemed forced. "So apparently guests are woken up by some sort of terrifying rooster call. It definitely got me out of bed."

"I must have been too far out to hear it, but Robin's told me about that. It makes sure everyone is up in time for the breakfast bell." He checked his phone. "Which should be any moment."

Sure enough, the bell clanged a few seconds later.

"Come on," Levi said. "Let's go see what Patrice, Shawn and Miles cooked up for us."

"All three of them?"

"Apparently, during their vacation time Shawn and Miles can't help themselves. Cooks like to keep busy in kitchens."

"I guess if something is a calling." George smiled but still seemed subdued on their walk downstairs.

The dining room's buffet was set up with all kinds of breakfast foods, and Levi made an eclectic plate. George took one biscuit and a lot of fresh fruit, and Levi started making a connection between his early run and George's mood. George had once been an athlete in a very competitive sport that required dexterity and leanness. Had George battled an eating disorder during his figure skating days? His modest food choices in the few weeks that Levi had known him suggested maybe. But since asking was hugely inappropriate, Levi ignored his worries and ate his breakfast.

Most of the guests sat around the big dining table. George had chosen an end seat to prevent him from sitting next to a stranger, and everyone chatted amiably about the day's activities. The weather tonight was supposed to be warm enough that they were offering the overnight camping trip. During warm weather, guests could go out Monday, Wednesday or Friday night (or all three if they really loved it), but during the colder months Reyes called the trips based on the overnight temperatures. The sleeping bags were warm but no one wanted to risk a guest getting sick.

Faith was excited for the camping trip, her dads not as much, but they agreed to sign up after breakfast.

George didn't speak during the meal, and once they were done and had cleaned up their dishes, Levi gently nudged him outside to the front porch. "What do you think about camping tonight?"

"I'm curious because it's something I've never done before," George said. "Do you want to go?"

"Sure. I've slept in way more uncomfortable places than a sleeping bag on the ground."

"Sounds like an interesting story."

"I've got a lot of those." George seemed more settled now than earlier but something still wasn't quite right. "Does it bother you that I run every morning?"

"No, your running is different than mine was. You run for your health, sure, but you also run to feel close to nature. To appreciate her beauty and gifts. I used to run because my coach demanded it. Twice a day for miles. He said the better my endurance the better I'd skate, and it was true, but…he was a little extreme in some of his coaching techniques."

Levi took a calculated risk with his next question. "Do you miss running?"

"Sometimes. I miss the exhilaration and the freedom of moving through the world really fast. It's how I used to feel when I'd land a hard jump combo. Or when I'd medal in a competition. The pride of accomplishing something. All I seem to accomplish anymore are my work assignments."

"You accomplished quite a few things these last few weeks, George. You befriended me. You saved my cat. You left your apartment and are here with me. Hanging out with perfect strangers. I am so proud of you for all of that."

George's expression cleared, and he smiled. "Thanks. You being proud of me means a lot." His gaze flickered to Levi's mouth. "A whole lot."

As much as Levi wanted to drag George into his arms and kiss him breathless, other guests were filtering outside on the porch. Making out was best left to the privacy of their room or the walking trails. "So camping?"

"Why not? Let's do it."

"Excellent. I'll run over to the office and sign us up. From what I remember Robin saying, we'll have to work with the horses for a while again this morning."

George grinned. "Good. I'm excited to ride again."

The old Levi would have had a heck of a lot of fun with the innuendo in that statement; this Levi behaved. "You'll get your chance, soon. I'll be back in a few minutes." He strode off the porch, eager for today's activities and every single minute he got to spend with George—in and out of the saddle.

Chapter Twelve

George settled in one of the porch chairs to wait for Levi's return, stomach pleasantly full from his fruit breakfast. He'd wanted to put some of that delicious smelling sausage gravy on his biscuit, but his overreaction to Levi's early-morning run had pressed his guilt button too damned hard, and he'd refrained from the extra fat and calories. Now he regretted the choice but there was no fixing it.

He'd just add extra mayo to his sandwich at lunch or something.

The diet/exercise urges had diminished over the years but certain things never completely went away. Not when he'd spent so many of his formative years battling eating disorders, thanks to Adrian and his parents. The only person in his past who'd never demanded perfection from him was Orry. They'd been competitive, yes, but in their own unique ways.

He took a picture of his view of the main ranch and texted it to Orry. These last twenty-fourish hours were the longest he'd been away from his twin in the last seven years, and while he missed Orry like crazy, he was also…okay. No imminent sense of panic or doom.

A longing, sure, but also a lot of excitement for the rest of his day here with Levi.

Levi.

George had woken with morning wood for the first time in ages, and he'd been insanely grateful that Levi wasn't in their room. It allowed him to escape into the bathroom with some dignity and rub one out in the shower. All he'd needed to do was remember making out with Levi for hours the night before—some of the best memories of his entire life, next to his first junior gold medal.

And while they didn't have lube or a condom be-tween them—at least, he assumed not but he hadn't searched Levi's luggage—George hoped they did more than kiss while sharing a room for the rest of the week. There were so many things they could with just hands, mouths and spit, and George wanted to try them. And the only person he trusted enough to give his body to was Levi.

Someone plunked down in the chair beside his. The mother of the two teenage girls. Mrs. Harrison? "I thought you looked familiar but older," she said in a faux whisper. "I was a huge figure skating follower when my girls were younger. You're Georgie Thomp-son, right? You quit right before Worlds?"

George's chest constricted. What were the fucking odds that someone would recognize him in the middle of bumfuck nowhere on a dude ranch? "My name is George," was all he managed to say.

"George, Georgie. You're the twin. You were really good, kid; why did you quit like that? I mean, the real reason, not all the random crap in the newspapers, like you and your brother running off to join a cult."

That was in the fucking paper?

George's stomach curled in on itself and his vision briefly blurred. Fingers began trembling. He tried to latch on to something tangible before the panic attack took over and embarrassed the hell out of him, but not even the faintest scent of dirt and horse kept him there.

Orry. I need Orry.

Then a somewhat familiar voice was there, talking to him or the woman, George wasn't sure. He didn't protest the firm hands that pulled him up and forward. Indoors and out of the fresh December air. Somewhere that smelled like food and warmth and safety, and then slender arms were pulling him into a hug.

"You're okay, it's okay. You're safe, George, you're okay. Listen to my voice. You're safe."

The constant reassurances helped George latch on to specific things: the smell of cooked bacon; the warmth of the person holding him; the murmur of other voices; the sound of what might have been a dishwasher. He was in a kitchen. The man holding him was roughly his size, maybe a bit taller, but just as slim.

When George thought he could look up without bursting into tears, he met Miles's eyes. Miles watched him with equal parts compassion and understanding, and without asking, George saw an ally in his panic attack. "Thanks for the save," George rasped, hating how much his voice wobbled.

"Happy to." Miles drew back a bit but didn't let go of George's forearms. "I don't know what Mrs. Harrison said to you but I saw how you reacted. I've been in a similar place. Where something unexpected triggers you."

"I don't want to talk about it."

"And I'm not asking. Only offering an ear to bend if you need one. Everyone who lives here has a story, George. Even our guests have stories. I just hope I helped today."

"You did." George twisted his arm so he could clasp one of Miles's hands. "Thank you. I was not handling that well."

"Do you need Patrice or Reyes to speak to Mrs. Harrison about whatever it is she said that upset you? They will. We want all our guests to feel welcome and safe here."

"She wasn't being mean." As much as George hated talking about his abrupt departure from competitive figure skating, he also believed the woman had simply been curious. She had no way to know what sort of hornet's nest of bad memories she'd stirred up with semi-innocent questions. "If she's an empathetic enough person, she won't bring it up again."

Miles snorted. "You give people a lot more credit than I do."

George gazed around him, not at all surprised to see he was in the big, semi-industrial kitchen of the guesthouse. Long prep counters, a huge oven with a bunch of burners on top, and a walk-in fridge.

"I'm just really out of my comfort zone here," George said. "I'm not used to being recognized anymore."

Miles didn't ask or question the statement. "Speaking as someone who has also had to work to challenge their own comfort zones, it can suck but it's usually worth it. The newfound sense of freedom. And Clean Slate is…a really good place to find yourself. Not physically, exactly, but emotionally and spiritually. I first came here for a week's vacation with my best friend, and it changed me in more ways than I can ever express. Moving here was the best choice I ever made."

George pulled on what bits of personal history he recalled. "You moved here for Reyes?"

"No, I moved here to start over and leave my past behind. Reyes was the most amazing bonus feature ever, and loving him changed my life." Miles chuckled, his green eyes crinkling at the corners. "Not that I'm advocating you move here to find true love, but keep your heart and mind open to possibilities. The world can be scary but it can also be a very beautiful place."

"Thank you." George carefully extricated himself from Miles's gentle hold. "I don't know what I want right now other than more than I used to have."

"It's a good first step. And if you ever need to talk, you can call me anytime."

"I don't have your number."

They swapped phone numbers, and by the end of things, George's confidence was back up and swinging for the fences. Miles was easy to talk to, and he spoke like a man who understood fear. George didn't want to imagine what the guy had gone through, so he didn't ask or ponder as he tucked his phone back into his jeans pocket.

"George!"

Levi's voice broke through the quiet of the downstairs, and George was not prepared for the way Levi thundered into the kitchen and yanked George into a fierce hug. "I'm okay," George said, several times in a row.

"You weren't outside," Levi said to his hair. "Samuel said he saw one of the staff take you into the house, that you looked weird, and I guess I panicked."

George pressed his cheek against Levi's shoulder. "No, I panicked. One of the guests brought up my skating past, and I had an attack, but Miles saw it and he got me out. Calmed me down. I'm okay, I promise."

Levi growled softly, and the protective sound went right to George's dick. "Who do I have to speak to?" Levi asked.

"No one, it's okay. At least now I know someone here knows who I am. Or who I was, I guess. I can prepare for it." George pulled back to stare into Levi's angry blue eyes. "I haven't faced this in years because I hid from it. If I want to be in the world again, I need to be able to face people who remember who I used to be. If that first step is on a rural ranch with a dozen other people, then so be it. I can do this."

Levi brushed his lips over George's. "Yes, you can."

George glanced around the kitchen but they were alone. He pressed his mouth to Levi's for a long time, basking in the heat of the man holding him. In their physical and emotional connection. "Your faith in me is everything."

"You are very easy to believe in."

The instant and confident way Levi said that he believed in him curled around George like a warm blanket and left him a bit gooey inside. "Saying stuff like that will get you dragged back up to our room, and we have horses to ride soon."

Levi's eyes sparkled with mischief. "I guess we'll have to save your ideas for later tonight when we're sharing a tent."

His insides wobbled. "A tent. Right."

"It's a two-person tent and we'll have separate sleeping bags. In the summer the campers usually sleep

under the stars but it's too chilly for that. But I can ask
Reyes to make sure you have your own tent if you'd
rather."

"No, it's okay." George shook his head, trying to
clear out the mental cobwebs. "I guess I didn't think
the camping trip through, and us sharing a tent is totally fine." He didn't mind the idea of snuggling up
close to Levi with two sleeping bags between them.
Sharing body heat with someone else for the first time
since the womb.

"Okay." Levi kissed his forehead once before letting him go. "You feel up to facing the other guests?"

"Yeah, I think so. Mrs. Harrison probably thinks
I'm a basket case. Maybe she'll stay away from me
from now on."

"You're irresistible."

"You're biased." One more forehead kiss from Levi
left George feeling all kinds of gooey inside.

"Come on, let's go mingle a bit before we have another horse riding lesson I really don't need."

George laughed, truly and joyfully, at the comment.
"Well, the rest of us aren't talented trick riders like you,
so you can suffer a while for us mere mortals."

"I suffer for one mere mortal alone." Levi winked.
"And that is little Miss Faith."

George tried to pinch him as he chased Levi out of
the kitchen.

One of the processes of the morning horse riding was
the hands pairing each rider up with a specific horse.
If yesterday had been about assessing talent and skill,
today was all matchmaking, and Levi leaned against the
corral while this happened. He was confident he'd end

up riding Zodiac. She was the horse he performed with at the ghost town, and she'd probably love the quiet exercise of an overnight trip after working hard all season.

Reyes was leading this trip, and Levi was not surprised to see Miles nearby, saddling up his horse Tango while Reyes assisted the campers. George was paired with Figuro, a horse Levi wasn't familiar with but he trusted Reyes's judgment. And George seemed perfectly comfortable in the saddle, as if the younger man had been waiting his entire life to discover horse riding. It definitely seemed to bring out a joyful innocence Levi had never seen in him before.

Once the campers—every single guest had signed up—were on their mounts, Reyes led the group around the corral several times. "The horses are trained to follow each other and stick to our trails," he said. "But if your mount wanders away from the group, gently lead them back on-path with the bit. To go right, use the right rein. Left, use the left rein. They're unlikely to fight you."

"Unlikely?" Samuel asked. He and Rey were each mounted on their own horses directly behind Faith, and Levi couldn't blame the young parents for being wary.

"The horses are highly trained, but they're still animals, and as such can be unpredictable under certain circumstances. I've got a story about exactly that to tell tonight when we reach our campsite."

Levi hid a smirk; he knew that story by heart at this point but it would be new to the other guests. Except maybe George, if Slater or Derrick had already told him about Wes and Blizzard discovering the ghost town a few years ago.

After a bit more instruction, the group tied their

horses to the corral fence and broke for lunch. "We're leaving in one hour," Reyes said in a booming voice. "Anyone who isn't here gets left behind. Also, if you have a hat, wear it. It might be winter but the sun is still out and you can burn. If you don't have a hat, you can purchase one in the canteen in the main house. And you won't need your phones unless you want to take pictures. After we're a half mile out, the Wi-Fi will drop. Wear clothes you'll be comfortable in for the next twenty-four hours." He gazed around the corral. "All right, see you soon."

"I packed a 49ers cap in my suitcase," George said as they walked toward the guesthouse for lunch. "Will that work?"

"Should be fine." Levi had packed his favorite cowboy hat, and he was curious what George looked wearing one. "It's mostly to keep the sun off your face while we're riding. Plus, actual cowboy hats are a fun fashion statement."

George chuckled. "I'll take your word for it. I have zero fashion sense. Then again, I work from home, so who cares what I wear?"

"What about your skating outfits?"

"My coach always chose those. Besides, those outfits were about performance not style. Something flashy to match the music and moves. I never kept a single one."

Levi partially regretted bringing up George's old career, but George didn't seem glum or upset. Only matter of fact about those years of his life. Very different from the man Levi had first met.

They each made sandwiches and a few salad selections, then went out to the porch to eat. They were soon joined by the Briggs-King family, and little Faith barely stopped talking about the camping trip long enough to eat her lunch. Levi loved seeing the girl vibrating with excitement, even though her dads seemed a touch reserved. But they loved and were indulging their daughter, and that was a beautiful thing.

After a quick trip to their room for hats and a bathroom break—Levi might have spent a few quick minutes kissing George by the window—they headed down to the corral to meet up with their group and guides. Hugo was the other horseman on the overnight, and he was riding lead while Reyes rode on the chuck wagon, led by his own horse Hot Coffee. The wagon had their food supplies, sleeping bags, tents, and a shotgun for safety.

Before they entered the corral, George's phone rang. He immediately walked in the opposite direction, his face expressing guilt that Levi didn't like. Levi watched from a distance, giving George privacy, and fairly certain the caller was Orry. Probably unhappy about the camping trip and George being unreachable until tomorrow around lunchtime. Too bad. This was George's life, and he was allowed to live it.

George looked defeated when he returned to the corral, and Levi resisted the urge to hug him. "Everything okay?" Levi asked.

"Orry being his usual, overprotective self. He's scared I'll get eaten by a mountain lion or fall off a cliff like Slater did."

"Slater's fall last spring was a freak accident. There's also a shotgun on the chuck wagon, but no guest has ever been threatened by a mountain lion."

"You were."

Levi squeezed George's wrist. "I wasn't threatened. I experienced the beauty of the land and then I backed away unscathed. There's a lot to be said for what Arthur, Judson and Reyes always say: respect the land and it respects you. We'll all be okay out there, George. Besides, you've got me to protect you."

Affection gleamed in George's eyes, and it took all of Levi's self-restraint not to drag him into the privacy of the barn. "I'll hold you to that. All of this is brand new for me." Something in his tone suggested he meant more than just the camping trip.

"I'll do my best to make it memorable," Levi whispered. "All of it."

"I know you will."

Someone nearby cleared their throat. Miles stood a few feet away, smiling. "We're heading out soon," he said softly. "You guys good?"

"We're perfect," George replied. "I'm excited for the trip."

"It's fun. I've been out with the guests before, and Reyes and I love to camp, just the two of us. It's that special thing we share." His knowing gaze seemed to hint that Levi and George could find a special thing to share, too—only he and George weren't married like Miles and Reyes. They weren't even technically a couple. Friends with brand-new benefits, maybe.

Whatever they were, Levi was here for it. He only hoped George was, too.

The first leg of the trip left George sore and exhausted by the time their entire party stopped by a long, babbling creek of water that bisected the land. They'd been riding for about two and a half hours, and his butt hurt more than he'd ever imagined. Figuro was a great horse and easy to manage, but damn, the constant rolling and up-and-down movements weren't easy to get used to. He had no idea how Levi managed to ride at a full gallop, never mind do all those tricks.

Everyone dismounted at the creek and the horses were allowed to drink. George took some time by himself to stretch in familiar routines from his skating days. Warming muscles and getting blood flowing again. He probably should have stretched before the ride began but too late now. Once his body felt less wound up, he took a few pictures of the scenery to send to Orry tomorrow because, as promised, the Wi-Fi signal was gone.

His conversation with Orry had been terse and uncomfortable, and not because of anything George had done. All he wanted was to go on an overnight horse ride/hike. What was wrong with that? His worrywart brother had made a much bigger deal out of it than it was, and it had taken all of George's patience to calm his twin down. To assure him he'd be perfectly safe in a large group of people, headed by very experienced members of the Clean Slate staff. He also promised to stay far away from the edge of the bluff in the morning—the bluff their neighbor Slater had fallen over saving a kid's life.

He had *not* mentioned that one of the staff overseeing the trip was his own age. Hugo was young but seemed perfectly capable.

Once his muscles were properly loosened, he glanced at his fellow campers. Levi, Miles and Reyes were chatting together, while Hugo made conversation with the two married couples. The Harrisons were keeping to themselves, which suited George just fine. He had no desire to relive his experience with Mrs. Harrison and embarrass himself again.

Rey approached with a cell phone in his hand. "Hey,

Faith really wants a picture of the three of us by the creek. Do you mind?"

"Not at all." George accepted the phone and took several shots of the adorable family in different poses by the rushing water. "These are great. You having fun, Faith?"

"The best time ever," she replied. "Are you?"

"Lots of fun." Even if his butt was sore. He handed Rey his phone back. "Your family is precious. I envy you."

Rey offered him a kind smile. "If kids and a partner are what you want one day, you can have that. For a long time, I didn't dare reach for my dreams. I existed one day at a time. One hour at a time. Until I met Samuel. He taught me how to dream again. You meet someone like that, you hold on tight, okay?"

George glanced briefly across the creek at Levi. "That's good advice, thank you."

"Anytime. I learned the hard way that family doesn't always have to be blood. Just the people you choose to love who also love you back."

The beautiful sentiment made his eyes sting as he thought about his brother and friends back in the city. "I've started learning that recently. Thanks."

Rey winked and returned to his husband and daughter.

George wandered down the creek and stopped at a shallow spot to dip his fingers into the icy water. Something shiny caught his attention, and he fished it out of the gravel and mud. Flat and round, like some sort of old coin, but time and the water had smoothed the markings down, making it difficult to know how old it was. It was about the size of a penny, though. He smiled at the unique find he'd randomly plucked out of the creek.

A shadow appeared nearby, so George didn't jump when Levi asked, "Going fishing?"

"Yup." He stood and held out the coin. "Found this."

"Huh." Levi squinted and held it up to the light. "I wonder how old it is."

"I don't know but as a trip souvenir, it's pretty unique."

"Very true." He handed it back, and their fingertips brushed.

George wanted to hold his hands again like last night, but they were surrounded by people, and he wasn't ready to out himself to the group. He hadn't even come out to his twin yet. But everything about Levi made George want to do things he'd never imagined doing— like pushing him against the nearest tree so they could make out, audience be damned.

He could behave himself until they were in a tent. Maybe.

Chapter Thirteen

They reached the campsite at dusk, just as they were losing sunlight. Levi had never been on one of the overnights before, and he marveled at the beauty of the area. They were on flat land near the base of a rocky crag that crept up into a much larger mountain that cast long shadows from the setting sun. Stones had been laid out in a large circle in a sandy area free of grass, which was their fire pit. Another creek—or maybe the same one as before—babbled nearby, giving the horses a place to hydrate before they were tied off at a long rail made out of thick, rough-hewn logs.

He couldn't wait for the sun to fully set and the stars to come out.

Once the horses were untacked, brushed, and tied up with bags of oats for their dinner, Reyes divided the group in two for campsite chores. Everyone pitched in. Levi joined the group of campers assigned to gather firewood for the big fire pit to provide light, heat, and cook their supper. George was part of the group unloading the chuck wagon, and he seemed perfectly at ease with Hugo, Faith, Rey and the Harrison teens.

Reyes oversaw the firewood collection with the wagon's shotgun in his hand, muzzle pointed at the ground. "Only dry wood, please," he said. "Don't break anything off a tree, because it won't burn and it hurts the tree. We need all sizes, so carry what you can manage best."

Mrs. Porter didn't seem thrilled with picking up sticks and mostly poked around. Levi rolled his eyes and collected the larger pieces that would keep the fire going throughout the night. When Reyes deemed they'd collected enough, the group headed back to the main site where the wood was sorted into piles based on size. Mr. Harrison asked about "personal business" and Hugo pointed out a rocky area with a few thick scrub trees as the watering hole.

Good to know.

"This is one of our traditions with new campers," Reyes said. "Who here knows how to build a campfire properly?"

Levi resisted raising his hand, curious about the other guests. Miles looked like he was trying to hide a smirk.

Faith's hand shot right into the air and she bounced on her toes. "I've been watching videos online to learn. I know."

"All right, Miss," Reyes replied. "How about you build it and I'll light it for you?"

"Okay."

Reyes handed her a wad of newspaper, and Faith quickly began to build it, using the paper and some dry grass as the tinder, smaller sticks for the kindling, constructing a textbook perfect pyramid of sticks that got bigger with each layer she added. The largest of the logs were left for later, once the fire really got blazing.

"Very good job," Reyes said. "Thank you."

"You're welcome." Faith scooted back, and Reyes

used a barbecue lighter to catch the tinder. It began to burn and grow, until soon a crackling fire warmed the chilly winter air and heated Levi's face and bare hands.

Hugo got a big, cast-iron pot situated over the fire and heated up bean and beef chili. After traveling all over the country, and especially the south, for most of his life, Levi had tried and appreciated a lot of different chili over the years. Texas-style meat only. Blow-your-head-off spicy and sweet, mild, smoky versions. Beans and meat. Even a few vegetarian chilies. But he definitely ranked Patrice's at the top of the list. Reyes toasted up crusty bread over the fire, and it was the perfect accompaniment to the meal.

All Levi needed to make it outstanding was a beer. But—out camping or not—he also didn't drink anymore for very good reasons.

After everything was cleaned in the creek and stored away in the wagon, Hugo brought out a few decks of cards and a box of matches for betting. Levi was pretty good at poker but he didn't like to gamble anymore, not even for matchsticks, so he wandered a bit, looking up at the beauty of the star-filled sky. Admiring the gorgeous sight he was blessed to sleep beneath tonight.

"Thank you for this moment," he whispered. "Thank you for your beauty."

He swore one of the stars winked.

"Do you know any constellations?" George asked, his soft voice a pleasant sound on the night air. He stopped an arm's reach from Levi, hands stuffed in his jacket pockets.

"A few. Columba is one of my favorites. It means dove, and it's named for the mythical dove that Noah sent from the ark during the great flood to search for land. The dove brought back an olive branch and hope. It's hard to see from here but—" Levi pointed "—it should be right about there."

George's gaze followed his direction. "I never used to notice the stars. But I grew up in the city and with all the light pollution, stars were things you saw in movies, not real life. This sky is incredible. I really wish Orry was here to see it, because no picture I take on my phone will ever capture the true glory of it."

"You're right. Pictures can capture moments in time but they can't often capture the emotion of the experience. Only the human heart can do that."

"You know, you could probably make extra money writing poetry and inspirational quotes."

"I kind of already do."

George tilted his head, his blond hair seeming to glow under the starlight. "How's that?"

Levi hadn't kept his blog a secret on purpose; he simply wasn't used to talking about it with other people besides Robin. It was too personal. "I have a travel blog that I started about two years ago. Mostly it was for fun. A way to document my travels in the tiny home, and then to show off my cats. I upload pictures I take and write brief essays on different things. Spirituality, how precious nature is, my perspective on the places I visit. It doesn't make me a lot of money but I do get some ad revenue."

"Oh wow, that's really cool." George's hand jerked, as if reaching for his phone, only to remember there was no Wi-Fi. "When we get back will you show it to me?"

"Of course. It's not a secret, it's just personal, so I never bring it up."

"I think it's kind of amazing." His smile dimmed. "Do you post about me?"

"Only in a vague way when I wrote about Ginger getting hurt and a very kind new friend was taking care of her. I didn't mention you by name, only referred to you as G. I wanted to protect your privacy, since I hadn't told you I was writing about you."

"Okay, thanks. I mean, I didn't figure you would, but..." He shrugged.

"I'm not offended that you asked. But I do agree with you about no picture accurately capturing this sky." Levi tried, though, taking a long panoramic shot of the beauty above them. "Do you mind if I write about our vacation? Vaguely, of course."

"I don't mind. How could I say no? You write about where you travel to, and this is a new part of the land for you."

"Thank you, George." He shoved his hands into his own jacket pockets so he didn't haul George into his arms and kiss him soundly under those magical stars. What was it about moonlight and nature that made George so hard to resist? They'd shared a similarly intense moment last night on their walk. Arousal buzzed across his skin, and Levi bit his tongue hard to stave it off.

The last thing he needed was to return to camp with a boner.

George was staring at his mouth, and that was a problem. Levi took three steps backward and gazed up at the sky. Pointed out a few more constellations he recognized to pass the time before the night air got uncomfortably cold. They headed back to the campfire. Two-person tents had been pitched, and the Porter-

Sanchez quartet was nowhere in sight; two tents were zipped up. Miles pointed out the last unclaimed tent.

"I think I'm going to read on my phone for a while," George said. "Get a little solitude."

"Of course." Levi sat on a log next to Hugo and watched George disappear into their tent. Good grief, but they seemed a lot smaller in person. At least they'd have two sleeping bags between them. Still, Levi didn't want to be the guy who woke up humping his friend because he couldn't control his dick.

So he'd stay up as late as possible and hopefully be too exhausted to do more than pass out.

"You and George seem really friendly," Hugo said quietly, their conversation mostly masked by the cracking of the fire.

"We're getting there." When Levi first came to the ranch last winter, Hugo had flirted with him pretty heavily, and Levi had been flattered. And interested. But their single date in Levi's home proved they didn't have any real chemistry. They'd remained friends, though, no awkwardness over the brief encounter. "George is a special guy. It's nice to see him opening up. Pushing against his comfort zones in positive ways."

"Well, you be good to him, then."

Levi blinked. "I—what? Of course I'm good to him. He's a terrific friend."

Hugo snickered and leaned in closer. "Dude, anyone with eyeballs can see how you two look at each other. There's no sense in pretending."

Oh great.

"Please, don't gossip about it," Levi whispered. "George is an intensely private person and gossip will make him hugely uncomfortable."

Hugo mimicked locking his lips with a key. "And if you don't want others to gossip, maybe stop making moon eyes at him when he isn't looking."

"Duly noted, and I thank you for your discretion."

"No problem. I mean, you never spread my stuff around, so I won't spread your stuff around." During their single date, Hugo had told Levi a bit about his past, including the tidbit that he had—by some epic twist of fate—grown up in Texas one town over from fellow ranch horseman Colt Woods and gone to school with his younger brothers. Colt had disappeared while Hugo was just a kid, so he'd never recognized Hugo, and Hugo wanted to leave it that way.

He'd left a lot of hurt behind in his old hometown. Levi could definitely empathize with needing to get away from your past. Levi just wished he'd gotten away from his own in a less painful, self-destructive manner.

Reyes added a log to the fire. "Hugo, I'll take the first watch if you want to get some sleep."

"Cool. Night, Levi."

"Night," Levi said with a grin.

Reyes replaced Hugo on the log, and they sat in silence for a while. Not even the brightness of the fire could dim the beauty of the stars. "They make you feel very, very small, don't they?" Levi asked. "The stars."

"Yes, they do. When Miles and I go camping, just the two of us, we'll lay on a blanket and watch them for hours."

"I do that at home sometimes, just to hear them whisper." Robin always said the land whispered to him in the darkest hours of dawn. He used to sit on his porch for hours whittling before he'd gotten a handle on his insomnia. Levi had always believed nature spoke to you if you knew how to listen.

"Can't say that I've heard the stars whisper," Reyes said, "but this land does sometimes feel magical. It gave me my husband, and I can't imagine how lonely my life would be without Miles in it. He's everything to me."

That Reyes was being this open with him surprised Levi a little. They were friendly but not what Levi would consider friends. "Thank you for sharin' your truth with me, Reyes. Sincerely. I can only hope to have that sort of love in my life one day."

"If you do find it, hold on tight with both hands. And be as honest with them as you can. I kept something bad in my past from Miles, and I almost lost him. I thank God every day that he forgave me."

Levi glanced at the tent, uncertain how George would react to certain parts of the year he'd spent drunk, high and eventually homeless. "I'm glad he did. I don't think I've ever seen two more in-synch people than you and Miles. Except maybe Robin and Shawn, but I also spend a lot of time with them at the ghost town."

"True."

They stared at the fire for a while longer. The other campers had all retired and the night was silent, save the crackling of wood as it worked to keep them warm. The tree had sacrificed its branches to the earth, and tomorrow those ashes would be buried back in the very ground that birthed it. The circle of life.

Eventually, Levi's eyes drooped and he could no longer ignore the siren's call of sleep. Tents and sleeping bags weren't the most comfortable things on earth but it beat the bench seat of a rusty, abandoned pickup truck in the freezing rain with only a ripped tarp to cover himself. The tent itself was sort of warm, probably from George's body heat, and George's soft, steady snore was a very comforting sound.

As quietly as he could, Levi shucked his boots and slid into his sleeping bag. Zipped it up about halfway and used his jacket to bulk up the small, attached pillow. Tired though he was after a long day of riding in the winter sunshine, Levi lay awake for a long time, listening to George breathe.

George woke to the sound of voices outside his tent, and it took him a few seconds to remember why he was so stiff and sleeping in a tent at all. The camping trip. He blinked his tentmate's face into focus. Levi slept facing him, a wave of dark hair fanning over his forehead. Peaceful. He'd never woken up in bed with another guy before, and while this wasn't technically a bed, they were maybe a foot apart.

Close enough.

Yesterday had been both a joyous and stressful day for George. Joyous for all the new experiences of trail riding, looking at the stars with Levi, and simply being around a crowd of people again for the first time in years. And stressful for all the same reasons. He'd tried hard not to use his safe word with Levi, and being able to separate themselves from the group during the card playing had helped immensely. It had also left George aroused and with a desperate need to kiss Levi again.

They'd both refrained, and George had managed to fall asleep. But just observing Levi's sleeping face sent blood where he didn't need it. He did have to pee, though, so he quietly untangled from his almost-too-hot sleeping bag, put his sneakers and jacket on, and braved the chilly morning.

Hugo was stoking the fire with small branches, waking the embers up into a full roar again. With the Harrison family the only others moving around yet, George took advantage of the watering hole to relieve himself. The sun was still low on the horizon, rising slowly over the rolling landscape, and George took a few pictures of the gorgeous shades of pinks, reds and oranges that swiftly brightened to brilliant blue.

Over a filling breakfast of biscuits and gravy and coffee, Reyes informed them they'd be leaving the wagon behind and riding up to a summit, before the long trail ride home. After hearing the stories of Slater's heroic rescue, George was eager to see this summit in person. Levi seemed a bit standoffish during the meal, sitting with a lot of room between them and barely speaking.

Odd but George was in too good a mood to read anything into it.

Reyes unhooked his horse from the wagon and actually rode her bareback. Their group rode for a few miles before stopping near the edge of a cliff that overlooked a vast green valley. The view was beyond breathtaking, and George kind of wanted to cry for how lovely the land was. Down in the valley full of plants and another creek was a small herd of deer all grazing together. He took as many photos as he possibly could while keeping a safe distance from the edge. Even Levi seemed in awe, if his wide-eyed, slack-jawed expression was anything to judge by.

"I remember my first time here," Miles said to George, coming up on his left. "I couldn't believe it either. That I'd ever see something so pretty in person."

"It's exquisite." George didn't know what else to say.

"More than two and a half ago years ago," Reyes said in a clear tone, "one of our guests named Wes Bentley let his horse wander from the group. Said horse was spooked by a skunk and sped off at gallop. Took Wes miles north of here before stopping in the remains of what had once been an old gold rush town. Arthur Garrett's grandson Mack decided to invest in rebuilding the town and turning it into a living attraction. While it's currently closed for the season, if you ever find yourselves back in these parts from February to November, it's well worth a day of your time."

"I can't imagine that," George said to Miles. "My horse galloping away. I'd have probably peed myself."

Miles snickered. "Wes was terrified. He's my best friend, and it was kind of incredible to live through. The ghost town, rebuilding it, being asked to be the head chef at the saloon. Opening day. But all the work has been worth it. It's amazing to think of all the good that came out of one little skunk."

"True story. I can't stop thinking about Slater going over that cliff back in May and being in one solid piece again."

"Yeah, I remember when that happened. Reyes was up here with him, and I don't think I've ever heard him so panicked. But somehow Slater came out of it with only a busted ankle and a concussion, and him being with Derrick brought you and your brother into the family. We're a very eclectic bunch but we're loyal."

George loved the sentiment but wasn't as sure he and Orry were really part of the huge, extended Garrett family yet. Maybe soon, if things went the way he hoped they did with Levi. "It's nice being part of something again."

"If you ever need anything, please reach out."

"I appreciate it." George wandered over to stand by Levi, curious at his continued quiet when he'd been all smiles and conversation the day before. "You okay?"

"Yeah, just thinking a lot. Had a good talk with Reyes last night. It was about as personal as we've been with each other."

"Anything you want to share?"

Levi shrugged but one corner of his mouth turned up in a half smile. "I guess I'm jealous of the strong relationship he has with Miles. The last time I trusted a man with my heart, I got burned. No, more like scorched. But I do want what Reyes and Miles have. One day. With the right person."

George didn't let himself hope he could be that right person. Not when everything between him and Levi was still so young and fresh. Untested. "I think I'm jealous of them, too. Happier *for* them, though. I keep trying to get Orry to date but he always says he's too busy working."

"Speaking of Orry working, did you ever ask him why he lied about bartending Thanksgiving night?"

"No." He'd mostly convinced himself not to think about it, that it wasn't a big deal. But it still tickled at the back of his mind.

"Do you think he's lied about work before?"

"I hope not. I mean, unless he's out there drug dealing, I won't care. Money is money."

The dig Adrian had made about Orry's past this summer nudged its way under George's skin like the tiniest shard of glass and stuck there. No way was Orry out there hooking for money. The only reason Orry had done it when he was sixteen was because he'd run away from home and lived on the streets. He'd been desperate and once confessed to George that he'd been ashamed of it. But it had allowed Orry to survive and come home to George when he'd needed him most. George's income was steady, so even if Orry had lost one of his gigs, they weren't cash strapped or anywhere close to broke.

"You just went away on me for a while," Levi said. "You don't think he's doing something illegal, do you?"

"No." He trusted his brother not to do anything that might separate them for the long term. "Maybe I'll finally bring it up when we go home. Let's not talk about sad stuff. It's too fucking pretty up here. And also…" George glanced over his shoulder for someone nearby. "Hey, Rey, can you take our picture?"

Rey grinned as he approached. George handed him his phone and positioned himself and Levi with the valley behind them. He kind of wanted to put his arm around Levi's waist. Levi slid a friendly arm across his shoulders and leaned in slightly. Good enough. Rey took several from different angles before handing it back.

"You two look good together," he whispered, then wandered off toward his family.

George's face got hot but he still scrolled through the images. They did look good together. A great contrast of Levi's tall and dark to his own slender and blond. He zoomed in on a close up and damn, but their blue eyes shined. Levi's were a deeper, more cerulean blue, while George's were a paler shade.

"I think I agree with Rey," Levi said.

"Me too." Even though Levi had introduced George as a close friend, Rey was clearly an observant guy. Or he was just projecting. George was unused to being around near-strangers on a regular basis, so his people-reading skills were pretty lacking. Thankfully, Levi never seemed to hold that against him.

George took a few more pictures before they were all asked to mount up. He was getting better at that but still needed a boost from Levi to get himself situated properly. Then he stealthily took some video of Levi expertly swinging himself up into the saddle. Maybe ten seconds' worth but damn, it showed off his ass nicely in those jeans.

The group was mostly quiet on the return trip to the campsite, where Reyes and Hugo hitched the horse back up to the chuck wagon, before setting off to the southeast and the ranch. At least, George was pretty sure of the direction but without a compass, he was just guessing. He trusted the horsemen to get them home safely.

Home. No, Clean Slate isn't home, it's just a vacation.

But hot damn, George felt at peace up here with the big, open skies and millions of stars at night. The quiet beauty of roving wilderness and the animals that lived peacefully near their respectful human neighbors. As long as he had Wi-Fi for work, George could be happy living in a place like this. But Orry wouldn't.

And George couldn't imagine moving this far away from his beloved twin.

As soon as he had Wi-Fi again, George texted a bunch of pictures to Orry, assuring him that he was safe, undamaged and almost back from the camping trip. Orry replied fast, complimenting the pictures and thanking him for the update. George wanted to call and hear his brother's voice, but he'd wait until he had more privacy.

His stomach was growling for lunch by the time they got back, but everyone had to untack and brush down their horse first. A few of the other hands helped with the saddles and blankets—many hands made light work—and George nearly cheered when they were released to the guesthouse for lunch. A simple turkey sandwich with mustard and pickles had never tasted more like heaven. A platter of sliced vegetables and dip replaced the fruit bowl this meal, and George tried not to go overboard on his portions. He'd always loved raw veggie trays.

He and Levi ate on the porch, sharing the steps instead of the furniture, because the sun was shining right on them, and it felt amazing against his face. George couldn't remember the last time he'd been exposed to this much constant fresh air, and he wanted to bask in every moment.

"There aren't any specific activities this afternoon," Levi said after he'd polished off half of a loaded sandwich. "I was thinking of asking Reyes if I can borrow an ATV. Go home for a little while and visit my cats. Make sure Ginger is doing okay."

"Oh, cool." George dipped a carrot stick in dip but didn't eat it, disappointment tightening his belly. "I bet they miss you."

"I miss them and don't normally worry this much, but after Ginger's accident…"

"You're an overprotective cat papa. I get it."

Some of his unhappiness must have bled through in George's voice, because Levi nudged one shoulder against his. "You want to come with me?"

A few hours of privacy in Levi's tiny home? Hell to the yes, he wanted to go. That disappointment dissolved, quickly replaced by anticipation. "Definitely." He couldn't bring himself to meet Levi's gaze, though, worried he didn't have a very good poker face on right now.

"Excellent."

When they were both done, Levi took their plates and cups into the guesthouse with the promise of hunting down Reyes, or someone else who could give them permission to use an ATV. Riding horses might have been fun, but George's ass needed a bit of rest after today's long return trip.

"Permission granted," Levi said upon return. "Reyes said the keys are in the ignitions, so we can take whichever."

"Cool. I've never actually ridden on one before."

"Want me to teach you how to drive it?"

His gut wobbled with nerves. "Um, maybe on the return trip? I'd rather watch you do it first."

"Sure. No problem. I'm happy to share new experiences with you, George."

"I hope you mean that."

Levi quirked a single eyebrow. "I do. Some things you may need to ease into more slowly, but I think I'm up for the challenge."

George glanced around but no one was close enough to hear the blatant flirting. "Then let's go check on your cats."

Chapter Fourteen

Levi was both excited and nervous to spend a few hours alone with George, far away from other people for the first time since Sunday night's epic make-out session. He craved the taste of George in his mouth again, the sensation of his slimmer body pressed close to Levi's. The chance to eventually do so much more.

Riding the ATV down the worn path to Mack's place was a special kind of torture, with George pressed up close to Levi's back and butt, arms cinched around his waist. Neither of them had showered since the previous morning, and George smelled faintly of sweat and horse, and Levi loved those scents. Craved them on George's skin. He drove slowly over the rutted path that was easier to travel on horse, he imagined, but they managed.

The cabin came into view, and Levi steered past Mack's place to the small patch of land Levi currently called home. No one came out right away, and he imagined it was because his girls didn't hear the familiar roar of his truck engine. Just the unusual sound of the ATV. But as soon as he shut it off and clucked his tongue, Baby zoomed out from beneath the house and jumped into his lap.

"Well, hello, Baby girl." Levi scratched her ears and

chin, absorbing the familiar sound of her purr as it rumbled from her throat. "I missed you."

George climbed off, and Levi immediately missed his body heat. Ginger and Sporty both came out of the brush, and Sporty jumped onto the ATV, too, trying to push Baby off his lap. Ginger headbutted George's shin. George gently picked her up, and Levi's heart fluttered at how sweet the pair looked together. Ginger had the loudest purr of the trio, and she filled the quiet air with her contentment and joy.

"I think the girls are happy to see us," George said.

"Definitely. I owe them some treats for being away this long." Levi freed his lap of wrestling cats and got off the ATV. He'd nearly tripped more than once walking to his home, because they wouldn't stop weaving around his ankles. He didn't bother locking the door right now because they were in the middle of nowhere with no tourists coming and going—plus Wes was walking over to feed the girls—so he went right inside.

George hesitated.

"Please, come in," Levi said. "Welcome to my very humble abode."

"I've never been inside a tiny house before." George stepped inside, then put Ginger down. The trio of cats stared up at them expectantly.

"Feel free to explore. Everyone always wants to see the composting toilet."

George chuckled. "I've heard of them but never seen one."

"You have to get used to them. Oh, and if you don't mind, will you remove your shoes? I'm not a clean freak or anything. It's just something I've done since I got the place."

"Of course. This is your house, your rules." George put his sneakers on the small mat next to Levi's boots, then began to poke around the simple living and kitchen space. The bathroom was beneath the lofted "bedroom," which was little more than a queen-size mattress and built-in dresser for his clothes. Levi grabbed a bag of their favorite treats from a cabinet and offered a few to each of his girls. Then he sat on the floor and petted them for a while, enjoying their soft fur and excited purrs. Three beautiful little lives he'd had the great fortune to rescue from a box on the side of the road.

One of the reasons he'd chosen this particular home model was because the design turned the steps up to his loft into tiered shelves/cabinets that he used for storage. Plus, the litter box when they were traveling or experiencing bad weather. George ascended those steps carefully, one hand on the wall for balance because there was no rail. It had taken Levi a few weeks to get used to it, but the cats loved chasing each other up and down them.

George gazed around a moment, then sat on the top step to look out over the compact living space. "This is pretty cool. A house you can take anywhere you want."

"That was the point. I missed the nomadic life I'd had with the rodeo. I wanted the freedom to just go where I could drive to, but I didn't want to have to rely on motels."

"Did you stay in a lot of motels with the rodeo?"

"Not very many. We had a bunch of RVs. I used to share one with Robin, my brother Xander and a guy named Petey. It was cramped but we loved what we did and we made it work. Although sometimes the sound of Xander and Robin fucking through a wall as thin as a bedsheet got to be a little much. But I think some of that was just me envying how in love they were."

"I know I said it before but I'm so sorry about Xander. I can't imagine how devastated I'd be if something ever happened to Orry."

"Thanks." Levi's throat didn't tighten the way it normally did when he talked about his late brother. "It's hard to believe it'll be four years this Christmas Day."

"I guess that's a hard holiday for you, huh?"

"Yes and no." He stroked Baby's soft head. "I have hundreds of amazing Christmas memories from the first three decades of my life. And last year was a huge turning point for my grief, because I spent it here with Robin. The brother I'd missed. I fell in love with this land. The peace and the beauty."

"How long do you think you'll stay?"

Levi didn't miss the subtle tremble in George's question. He looked up and held George's gaze. "I don't know. I love trick riding and I love working at the ghost town with Robin. Shawn's great. Everyone who works here, be it the ghost town or the ranch, is great."

"But?"

"No but." He didn't like that they were having this conversation so far apart but if this made George feel comfortable, Levi wouldn't complain. "Sometimes I get itchy feet. A rolling stone gathers no moss and all. I'd actually hoped to spend some of the ghost town's down time traveling a bit. Seeing more of Northern California."

"Shit, I wrecked those plans."

"Hardly." Levi pulled Sporty off his lap and went up three steps. Sat. "Ginger getting hurt put those plans off, and I do not regret being here with you right now.

Not even a tiny bit. You have been a breath of fresh air in my life George, not a burden. Never a burden."

Ginger darted up the steps and climbed onto George's lap.

"I think someone else has gotten attached, too," Levi added.

George swallowed hard, his expression softening. "I've gotten a bit attached myself."

They weren't talking about the cat anymore, and George was too close to a comfortable mattress. Levi needed to be the mature one and keep his ass where he was, but George licked his lips and Levi had to taste them again. To remember what it felt like to kiss George. He avoided stepping on Sporty during his ascent of the steps. George eased Ginger off his lap and scooted a bit to the side so Levi could sit next to him.

Levi cupped his cheek in one palm, arousal heating his blood. An abundance of naked emotions shined in George's eyes. "I didn't ask you here to seduce you, George."

George rested a hand on Levi's thigh. "Maybe I came here because I want you to seduce me."

"George."

"Not all the way. Not this soon, but I trust you, Levi. I'm attracted to you, and I've never felt this way about a guy before. I just…want to feel good with you. Make me feel good?"

How was a guy supposed to say no to such a sweetly asked question? "If I do anything you don't like, tell me and I'll stop."

"I promise."

Levi swooped in before George finished speaking, and the sweet taste of George was back on his lips.

His tongue. George fisted the front of Levi's shirt and hauled him closer—as if Levi was going anywhere. Levi made sweet love to George's mouth while careful to keep his hands from slipping below George's shoulders. He loved the thickness of George's hair and the soft noises he made in his throat as they kissed. Needy noises that went straight to Levi's dick, but he wasn't going to push anything on George.

George's free hand dropped to Levi's hip and squeezed, reminding Levi which part of his body was not getting any friction right now. "Anything...you...want...George," Levi said between kisses.

That wandering hand circled forward and squeezed Levi's erection. Levi nearly bit George's tongue from the bold move and amazing sensation of a hand on his dick. Ginger ruined the moment by jumping into Levi's lap. She bumped against George's hand, and they both laughed as they drew back.

"Someone's protective," George teased.

"Of you or of me? Silly girl. We're a little busy right now."

Ginger purred.

"I never expected my first time to be cockblocked by a cat," George said with an impish smile.

"Around these parts, you've got to learn to expect the unexpected." Levi glanced at George's impressively tented crotch. "Do you want to lie down on the bed with me? It's a lot easier to cuddle than sitting on these steps."

"Okay."

Levi rose first, unable to fully stand in the short space, then offered George his hand. George took it and held tight for the few brief steps it took to reach the mattress. They stretched out together, facing each other, and Levi pulled a pillow down for them to share. He nuzzled his nose against George's, adoring the innocent smile on George's face. The eagerness, too. The face of someone who truly wanted to have a new experience, and he wanted it with Levi.

I don't deserve such a precious gift.

Maybe he didn't deserve it but he would absolutely take care with it.

"I kind of feel like a teenager again," Levi said. "Sneaking off into another boy's bedroom."

George rested his hand on Levi's hip. "I wish I knew what that feels like but this is also pretty damned amazing. Being here with you. You make me feel so many things, Levi."

"I'm going to have fun making you feel a whole lot more."

"Bring it on."

Levi brought it by easing George on to his back and sliding half his taller, broader body on top of him. Inserting his leg between George's so his erection rode Levi's thigh. Levi's rode George's, too, and George let out a soft gasp. Thrust up once in a way that made Levi want to skip foreplay and simply slide his dick home. But he wouldn't. Couldn't. He wanted to show George all the possible ways for them to pleasure each other before crossing that border—if George wanted to go there with him.

"You are so beautiful," Levi whispered. "Not just physically but your soul. Your heart. Your trust is a gift, and I thank you for it."

"I love the weird way you talk sometimes."

"It took me a long time and a lot of bad choices before I learned the true value of trust and kindness. I want to shower you with both."

George's eyes went adorably half lidded. "Shower away."

"I will. One step at a time."

Levi did his favorite thing and made love to George's mouth with long, leisurely strokes of his tongue. Mimicking how he'd adore making love to George's body one day. If they went that far. Levi wouldn't dare presume at such an early stage. When he first presented the vacation vouchers to George, he had never imagined being at this point so quickly. But Clean Slate Ranch was a magical place, and George was blossoming under her big blue sky and vast, rolling lands.

Once George began humping up against him, Levi thrust down, enjoying the friction on his erection. It had been ages since he'd gotten off with another person, and George was amazingly addictive. Innocent and raw and needy. George squeezed his hips, fingers spread low without quite reaching Levi's butt. Levi rutted harder, urging him to touch more. Lower.

"Oh fuck." George nipped at his jaw. "If you keep doing that, I'm going to come in my jeans."

"That wet spot might be hard to explain." Levi met his gaze. "Do you want to take them off?"

"Yes." Not a moment's hesitation.

"Can I take off mine, too?"

"Yes."

Levi moaned. "You're absolutely sure?"

"Fuck yes. Please." George proved his point by shoving Levi sideways and yanking at his own belt buckle.

Levi did the same, leaving his shirt and boxer briefs on for now, while stripping out of his jeans and socks. The loft was getting warm but he didn't want to presume—George surprised him by yanking his long-sleeve T-shirt off, revealing a long, pale torso of lean muscle and a small scattering of blond hair. Levi licked his lips; George's boldness was a huge turn on.

"You can take your shirt off, if you want to," George said.

Sporty chose that moment to jump into bed and pounce on George's foot. He yelped from what Levi knew were needle-sharp claws in his skin. "Shoo, you," Levi said, swiping at Sporty's tail. She swatted at him once, then bolted away. "You okay?"

George snorted. "She didn't draw blood. Mostly surprised me. Guess they're possessive of their dad."

"Yeah, well, the last guy I let come around frequently ended up being a righteous mistake."

"I'm sorry."

"It's okay, it was a long time ago." Levi did not want to bring Grant into bed with them, so he took his shirt off. Observed the way George's eyes went wider, how his lips parted as he took in Levi's mostly naked body.

"Working with horses is good for you," George blurted.

Levi chuckled. "If I can't control my body, my face will end up in the dirt. But you haven't skated in years and you are in amazing shape."

"I still have issues with food." His face reddened. "Um."

The instant, embarrassed reaction from George told Levi to pull back and settle him. "You don't have to tell me anything you don't want to. But I will be here to listen when you're ready."

"Thanks. I just…" He faltered.

Levi clutched one of his hands. "You don't have to explain. I understand having darkness in your past, remember? I also think everything about your heart, mind and soul is beautiful. You are beautiful, George Thompson, inside and out. I am humbled that you chose me to be part of this new journey you're takin'."

Those must have been exactly the right words because George pounced. He tipped Levi on to his back and climbed on top of him, their underwear-covered erections pressed together as George began to thrust. A light, slow rhythm, testing this new thing out, before becoming more aggressive. He remained annoyingly out of kissing range, hands braced on Levi's pecs without teasing his nipples. Exploring these new sensations that left Levi a moaning, panting mess. Just enough to feel without being close enough to get off.

George was losing himself in this new, amazing thing he was sharing with Levi. To the sight, scent and feel of another man beneath him, giving George all the control. Letting him explore and go at his own pace. To the unique sensation of another hot dick rubbing against his own.

So. Good.

"You feel amazing," Levi said. "Wow."

George splayed his fingers wider on Levi's chest, the tips of both middle fingers nearly touching his nipples. "I've seen this, I just…never imagined…fuck." He was slowly losing the ability to speak.

"The real thing is better than a video, for sure. Can I hold your hips?"

"Yes." He adored the man for asking. Being so goddamn respectful of the fact that George had never done any of this before. "Please, Levi…you can touch wher-ever. Anywhere you want."

Lust burned in Levi's blue eyes. His hands slid up George's thighs and squeezed his hips, a firm hold with-out directing him. After a series of thrusts, Levi's hands moved a bit farther, stopping with his fingers over the very top of George's ass. The touch spurred George on, and he rolled his hips harder. Grew brave enough to rub Levi's nipples. Levi moaned again, his own hips snap-ping up against George's. Seeking his own pleasure.

Levi was always so controlled and well mannered, and George loved watching him fall apart. Loved know-ing he'd done that for Levi. And as much as George was loving watching Levi's face, he needed the comfort of Levi's kisses. He plunged back into Levi's mouth, seeking that familiar heat and taste. The slide of Levi's naked torso against George's had his balls drawing up tight, release imminent.

"Getting close," Levi panted.

George lifted his hips and shoved his briefs down as far as he could, releasing his dick. Purposely revealing himself to an adult man not his doctor for the first time in his life. "Get yours down."

Levi let out a sharp, almost-growl and pushed his underwear down as far as he could reach with George kneeling over him. As much as George wanted to ad-mire Levi's dick, he wanted to come a hell of a lot more. Precome and sweat helped slick their way, and George hadn't thrust more than a half dozen times before he shattered into a thousand pieces.

Pleasure unlike anything he'd ever experienced raced up his spine, and he couldn't censor the sounds he made. Levi writhed below him, and the extra wetness on their bellies told him Levi had come, too, but George was too boneless to do anything except remain plastered to Levi's body. His pulse raced and he tried to get his breathing back under control. He needed to find words. Any words.

"Fuck," Levi said. "Wow."

Two very good words. Then surprise jolted through him, and George raised his head high enough to see Levi's very blissed-out face. "I don't think I've ever heard you cuss before."

"I trained myself out of the habit. But back when I was in the rodeo, I could put Samuel Jackson to shame."

He laughed, and the movement reminded him of the mess they'd made of each other. "We're all sticky."

"I would hope so, considering that was one of the best moments of my life. And I have to admit, it was a heck of a turn-on when you ordered me to get my underwear off. I love seeing that take-charge side of you."

"I kind of surprised myself with it, but I didn't want to come in my briefs. I wanted us to share it more intimately."

Levi leaned up to kiss him. "I'm glad. No regrets?"

"None. And it's something I'd like to do again. Naked the whole time."

"Oh, we are definitely doing that."

"Good."

"We should probably go shower." He squeezed George's hips. "Believe it or not, the bathroom is big enough to share if you want."

For as in control as he'd felt during the sex he'd just had, George faltered over such a simple thing as a shared shower. Levi wasn't going to maul him if they were squished together in a shower for ten minutes. It

might even be fun. Everything he did with Levi—even
the slightly scary stuff like riding a horse for the first
time—was fun. "Okay."

"Yeah?" Levi kissed the tip of his nose. "Thank you
for your trust."

"You've more than earned it." He rolled off Levi,
careful to keep his sticky skin off the coverlet, and
untangled his legs from his briefs. Levi did the same.
They both gathered up their discarded clothes and carried them downstairs. The cats were lazing about in a
patch of sunshine, all three staring at them like they
knew exactly what their daddy had just been up to.

George had thought the bathroom was pretty spacious when he'd first inspected it—he still didn't understand how the composting toilet worked but he'd search
on his phone later—but with Levi's broad body in the
room, it suddenly felt cramped. The tub had a clear sliding door instead of a curtain, which Levi pushed back
to access the spigot.

"I'll warn you," Levi said with a wink, "sometimes
the cats come in and just stare at me while I'm show-
ering."

"They're just admiring you." George admired everything about Levi's body, from his taut ass to his hairy
upper thighs. He'd yet to completely ogle the man's dick
yet, though. It seemed impolite now that the sex was
over. And Levi wasn't blatantly staring at him, either.

"Good answer."

Levi set the water and while it warmed, he draped
his arms around George's waist and pulled him close,
their bodies aligning nicely, despite the height difference. George felt safe and cared for when Levi held

him. Levi didn't kiss him, simply stared until the room began filling with steam.

"What?" George finally asked.

"Nothing. Just admiring you. I have feelings for you, George, and I guess I'm a little worried that once you start peeling back my layers, you won't like what you see."

"Doubtful." George had occasionally thought the same in reverse. If or when George admitted to how badly he'd screwed up his life, thanks to Adrian and his manipulations. Maybe George had been an impressionable teenager but Levi might not see it that way. Except Levi was the least judgmental person he'd ever met. Levi was a safe place. "Now let's shower before we waste all your water."

Levi brushed his nose against George's once before releasing him. "Good point."

They didn't linger in the shower long, because the water was cooling fast, but it was a fun tangle of elbows and legs. The cats didn't bother them so they dried and dressed in peace, and even though George loved admiring Levi's naked body, he was grateful for the modesty of his clothes. To hide what old fears and habits still saw as an imperfect shape. Never skinny enough, fast enough, able to jump high enough.

The mood stuck with him on the brief walk into the kitchen.

"Are you thirsty?" Levi asked. "I've got cream soda, water or oat milk."

No calories. "Water is fine, thanks." George used the excuse of petting the cats to keep his back to Levi. Ginger purred before he even stroked her soft head. Usually, when the voice of doubt got too loud, George would put his earbuds in and play loud rock music until it quieted. But he didn't have his earbuds on him, and how would he explain it to Levi?

Levi handed him a cup of water with a few ice cubes in it, and George's hand trembled when he accepted it. Instead of commenting, Levi sat across the cat pile from him with a bottle of soda and started petting Sporty. They were who he'd come up here to check on, after all. Sex had just been a side bonus.

"George, are you sure you don't regret something we did?" Levi asked after a few minutes of silence. "You seem off."

"It wasn't anything we did. I don't regret having sex with you, I swear. I just…" He desperately wanted to be home in the apartment with his brother, who didn't ever ask because he knew and accepted George's quirks. "Can I get away with saying that it's not you or us, it's me? It's cliché but accurate."

"Of course. As long as I can get away with saying you can trust me with anything that's bothering you. I'm a good listener and I don't gossip."

"I do trust you. It's just not something I like to talk about. Ever. Maybe one day in the future, but not yet."

"Heard and understood. Thank you for your truth, George."

"You're welcome. Thank you for not pushing."

"Never. I respect your feelings, and I will do my best never to pressure you into anything."

Somehow, that still sounded like Levi doubted himself and that maybe he'd pressured George into sex too soon. And that simply wouldn't do. George did not regret a single thing about their day together, other than his own little internal episode about his appearance.

He put his water on the nearest flat surface, scooted right into Levi's personal space, and pressed their foreheads together.

"How's your recovery time, old man?" George teased.

"Old man, huh?"

In an unexpected display of strength and dexterity, Levi had George up and over his shoulder in a fireman's carry, and he took them both over to the built-in sofa for round two.

Chapter Fifteen

Their second time rubbing off together lasted longer than the first because Levi was a sadistic bastard who loved to pull George right to the edge, and then refuse to let him come. George adored and hated him for it. They didn't touch intimately beyond frotting, except for the one time Levi needed to arrange their dicks into a more comfortable position, and George was grateful. They had time to go slowly. For George to ease into physical intimacy.

He also got in a good laugh when Sporty attacked Levi's feet during yet another "you're not coming yet" tease.

His second orgasm of the day? Epic. Mind blowing. Best moment ever.

They rinsed off separately under lukewarm water, and then spent a lot of time kissing before George realized the time. "We're going to be late for dinner if we don't head back soon," he said.

Levi found his phone and looked at the screen. "You're right. One sec." He swiped a few times, then bit his lower lip in a weird way.

"What's wrong?"

"Nothing wrong, precisely. I forgot to text Wes that

I'd be here to check the cats' food and water. He texted me about twenty minutes ago that he came by, saw the ATV, heard the moaning and left."

George flushed so hotly he thought his face might burst into flames.

"It's okay," Levi continued. "The only person who knows you're up here with me is Reyes, and he doesn't gossip. It's our private business."

"I appreciate you saying that. I'm just…not used to people hearing me doing private things. I can't even masturbate while Orry's home."

One of Levi's eyebrows twitched. "Then I will take you getting off twice with me today as a high compliment. And just to be clear, I do not expect anything else from you just because we had sex today. And expect is the key word. Would I love to do all this again and more? Definitely yes. But no pressure and no expectations."

George melted a bit deeper into his gooey feelings for Levi. "Thank you. I mean, I definitely want to do more, but I appreciate your words more than you know. I spent a good third of my life feeling pressured to be what other people wanted me to be. The very best skater. An Olympic medal winner. Then I spent the last seven years hiding from everyone because I was terrified of other people's expectations. You are a breath of fresh air, Levi Peletier. I am blessed to have met you."

Levi cupped his cheek in a warm palm. "I don't want to control or manipulate you. Not ever. All I want is your friendship. Your companionship. And your honesty. I genuinely like the man you are. Just be you, George Thompson."

"I'll try my best."

"You don't have to try. Just be."

The naked emotions in Levi's eyes prompted George to rise up on his tiptoes and rub their noses together. "I'll be."

"I'll be, too."

They kissed until George's empty stomach growled for food, and while they could have probably eaten at Levi's place, it would look funny to the other guests if they didn't show for the meal. Levi put wet food out for the cats. George also spotted a dry food dispenser situated under the stairs. They both petted and cuddled the cats, especially Ginger, before leaving the tiny house. George enjoyed snuggling against Levi's back on the ATV ride to the ranch, and it was hard to resist his urge to hold Levi's hand during the walk from the barn/garage to the guesthouse.

Dinner was a hearty chicken potpie, and George did his best to get mostly vegetables and less of the crust. Plenty of the other fresh offerings, too. He also allowed himself to indulge in one of Patrice's yeast biscuits, which were soft and buttery and so good. So different from the flaky breakfast biscuits. No one at the table commented on his and Levi's afternoon-long disappearance, likely because they all knew Levi worked at the ghost town. They probably (and rightly) assumed he had special privileges.

After dinner was an evening hike that George kind of wanted to go on but he was exhausted after his long afternoon with Levi. Instead, he settled in the downstairs area with his phone to read. Levi went on the hike, and George was completely unsurprised when Miles and Shawn appeared in the guesthouse. As if summoned. Possibly by a text from Levi. A good guess from the fact that the pair gravitated right over to George's armchair.

"Hey, dude," Shawn said. "How are you enjoying your vacation so far?"

George closed his phone screen. "I've had a lot of fun. The overnight camp was neat, and I really like riding a horse."

"I remember my first camping trip crystal clearly," Miles added. "I was terrified, and these guys kept trying to scare me more with talk of mountain lions, but in the end, I loved the experience. It's one of my and Reyes's favorite things to do now. Camp together."

"I'm starting to see the appeal." He could almost see himself enjoying it with just him and Levi one day. Waking up alone in a tent, surrounded by nature. Maybe in warmer weather, though. "You two don't have anything better to do on a Tuesday night than chill in the guesthouse? Or did Levi ask you to check in on me?"

The pair shared a look that screamed guilty.

"Not check in on," Shawn said. "Just to chill out with. Our guys are up at Mack's place watching a movie."

"And you're not both up there with your guys?"

Miles offered a patient smile. "We both know what it's like to do things outside your comfort zone. And this is not us asking you anything, only offering support. My first visit here, I was a flaming mess because of something a shitty ex had done to me. But there is something about Clean Slate that helped me find a semblance of peace. It let me accept help from my friends and to eventually let my guard down and fall in love with Reyes."

"And finally get said shitty ex tossed in prison," Shawn added.

"I'm glad you found that love, I mean it." George

didn't know much about Miles but the guy seemed like a very genuine soul. Shawn too.

"I lived in my car for two years." Shawn's confession jolted George. "Even while I worked at the ghost town, nobody knew. It wasn't until I let myself be embraced by the generous people here that my life really began to improve. If you ever find yourself in the position to lean on the folks here, and to be part of this family, then do it. It's worth it."

George blinked hard, afraid his stinging eyes would start leaking tears at any moment. "I appreciate the advice. But I'm just here on vacation."

"So was I," Miles replied. "So were Wes and Derrick."

He couldn't deny those truths, and he'd seen firsthand how happy Derrick and Slater were. It was impossible to guess now if George's happiness would be with Levi but he was having a lot of fun exploring the idea. "What are you saying? The horses are matchmakers?"

Miles laughed. "I mean, Tango definitely helped bring me and Reyes together. I adore that horse, but not more than I adore my husband. But if we're bugging you or way off base about something, please let us know. We'll back off."

"You aren't bugging me." George wasn't ready to come out to two guys he barely knew before he told his brother, but he did appreciate how kind and honest Miles and Shawn were being. "I've been...out of the world for a long time. It's nice having friends again."

"You have more than you probably realize. Do you feel up to watching a movie at my cabin? Or would you rather us leave you alone?"

As much as George liked the idea of spending two hours with guys his age, he was exhausted. "I doubt

I'll be awake longer than another hour. Can I get a rain check on the movie?"

"Definitely."

"Please don't be a stranger this week," Shawn said. "Robin and Levi might not be blood related but they are brothers. Levi's been different since he met you. Happier. I hope you've been happier, too."

The pair didn't wait for George to reply; they rose as a unit and left the guesthouse. George stared at some random spot on the wall for a while, turned around by the conversation. By all the things Miles and Shawn hadn't said but had assumed about him and Levi. And it didn't bother him as much as he expected it to, because he was in a safe place. Clean Slate Ranch was safe, just like the place he lived was safe. Maybe the wider world wasn't but he was still experimenting with the wider world. Dipping his toes into it.

One day George would be the man he was always supposed to be. It might take some time but he'd get there. And he'd have friends to help him along the way.

Burt led the evening walk, and he explained that during the summer months they often saw a spectacular sunset. Levi had seen plenty of amazing sunsets in his life, in dozens of different states, but he had to admit Garrett had some of the most beautiful he'd ever seen. Robin had shown Levi his Instagram account and Levi admired the hundreds of sunsets Robin had photographed in tribute to Xander. It had been such a lovely gesture, and Levi had made one of them his phone's background. The sky had been a gorgeous swirl of purples and reds—two of Xander's favorite colors.

He walked a bit away from the other guests, enjoying the crisp night air without making conversation. His thoughts were filled with George and their afternoon together. Sex with George had been different from any of the other sex he'd had in the past, and not because George was a virgin and still figuring himself out. He'd felt genuinely seen and accepted by the younger man in ways he'd never experienced with a partner before. Like he had more to offer than a pretty face and washboard abs. He had come close to something similar with Grant, which was why they'd been together so long before imploding.

Everything about George was special, and Levi wanted to hold on for as long as he could. Do things with George and not just in bed. He wanted to romance him and that wasn't Levi's best event, but he'd try. For all that he'd stopped dreaming of a future with someone by his side, Levi could see flashes of it with George. But saying anything about it this soon in their relationship might scare George off. Be too big for him to handle.

This nebulous future also scared Levi in its own way. He'd bought a house he could take with him because he enjoyed the nomadic lifestyle. Being able to travel whenever he wanted. After living on the road for his entire life, could he actually settle down in one place? Put down real roots? Or would his wandering spirit always tug him elsewhere?

He had no idea, so he'd keep those feelings close for now.

He wanted to talk to Robin about them but it could wait for another day. Once the group circled back to the guesthouse, Levi went upstairs to his room. George was asleep in his bunk, on his left side facing the room. Only a tiny bit disappointed, Levi brushed his teeth and changed into flannel pajama pants—the room was a bit chilly tonight—and a T-shirt. He played a game on his phone until sleepy, and then settled in.

Creaking springs and thrashing woke him at some point, and Levi sat upright. Moonlight showed him George moving around in his bed, and a few soft whimpers made his heart hurt. Levi slipped out of bed and over to George's bunk. "Hey, wake up, you're okay."

George cried out as he came awake, and he blinked dumbly up at Levi for a few seconds. Then he launched himself into Levi's arms, breathing hard, fine tremors racing through his entire body. Levi held him tight, one hand cupped protectively around the back of his neck.

"You're okay, I've got you."

"I fucking hate nightmares," George whispered, his voice a bit raspy. "I didn't mean to wake you."

"Shush, it's fine. It got you out of your nightmare faster." He rubbed gentle circles on George's back. "Do you remember what it was about?"

"Adrian, as usual. He's my bogeyman."

Levi hated that George had nightmares about his former coach, especially knowing the way the man had behaved this past summer. Maybe Adrian's reputation as a coach had been trashed by George quitting, but Adrian had ruined George's life and sense of safety. As much as Levi tried not to hold grudges anymore, he truly wanted to see Adrian punished for still being inside George's head.

George pulled back, blue eyes glistening but also determined. "It was about the night he came to the apartment and hit me. Only Orry was there this time and Adrian started attacking him. I couldn't move to save him. All I could do was scream but I wasn't making any sounds. Just a whimper."

"You're okay now." Levi rubbed their noses together. "Orry's fine."

"He knows where I live."

"Yes, you live in a house full of neighbors who will call the cops if he tries to come inside again. And he'd be a complete idiot to try. He has nothing to gain from seeing you again." Not that obsessive stalkers needed reasons to see their target again and again. Levi had no personal experience with being stalked—Grant had just been a vengeful creep—but he'd heard the stories about Miles's abusive ex last year. Miles being stalked all the way to the ranch and physically attacked.

"I hope you're right." George pressed his forehead into his shoulder. "Thank you. I feel a lot better with you here."

Levi ran his fingers through George's golden hair. "Do you have nightmares a lot?"

"No. Not very often. Usually, it's because something... well, *triggers it* is kind of a loaded way to say it, but yeah. Something happens. Reminds me of the bad stuff."

"Was it that moment you had after our first shower?"

George nodded. "Still not your fault, though. It's all in my head."

"I accept that."

"Hey." He sat up straight. "I know you say you accept it, but do you believe it? Do you believe me when I say it wasn't you or anything you did?"

"Yes." Levi had asked for George's trust; he would offer his in return, no questions. "I believe you. I just hate that you're still hurting over something you can't talk to me about. I hope one day you will."

"Me too." George lightly pressed his lips to Levi's. "Thank you for this. It's nice having someone to wake up to when I'm scared."

"You're more than welcome. You okay to go back to sleep?"

"I think so. Good night, Levi."

"Good night. I hope the bogeyman leaves you alone."

"Me too."

Levi hugged George before leaving his bed and returning to his own. In the dim light, he watched George settle beneath his covers on his back. He watched George for a long time, until sleep finally stole Levi away again.

George woke before the sun had risen, likely because he'd gone to bed early the night before, so he spent time simply staring at Levi, who was asleep facing George. Dark hair a mess, one arm bent awkwardly above his head. So handsome George could barely stand it.

His nightmare flitted back, and he reveled in how wonderful it had felt to be held afterward. To be comforted when he was scared. He didn't have loud nightmares, and they almost never woke Orry. He was glad for that. Orry did so much for him already. And wasn't that partly what this entire trip was about? Getting George into the world and doing things for himself, so Orry didn't have to do it all?

Yes. His brother deserved a real life. George deserved a real life. And by God, they'd get it.

His bladder finally urged George out of bed, and by the time he got out of the shower the sun was rising. Not long after, the rooster call sounded, startling

Levi awake. George was reading on his bunk when that happened, and he couldn't help laughing. "Morning."

"Hey, good morning." Levi rubbed both palms into his eyes. "You know, the rodeo settled on farmland more times than I can remember, but I swear this is the only time I've ever been woken by an actual rooster call."

"I don't think I've ever heard a live rooster call but whatever Patrice uses is effective. How'd you sleep?"

"Mostly like a rock. How was the second half of your sleep?"

George grinned. "It was good. I know I thanked you before but thank you for comforting me."

"It was my pleasure." Levi climbed out of his bed and came over to George's. Leaned down and rubbed their noses together. "I'm glad I was here." Before George could say or do more, Levi straightened and went into the bathroom.

As much as George would have liked a good morning kiss, he loved that Levi was respecting boundaries and not pressing for things. If they kissed today, it would be because George initiated it. And George absolutely planned to initiate kissing. As soon as Levi was washed, dried, and dressed from the bathroom, George initiated a lot of kissing with Levi's back against the wall.

They kissed until George worried about his ability to attend breakfast without tented jeans. "I don't care about my nightmare. Yesterday was amazing. I know we can't sneak off to your house every afternoon but I am definitely up for more physical stuff if we get the chance. Here or after this vacation is over."

"I am very glad to hear you say that."

No good opportunities arose that day. After breakfast, they went on a group trail ride, and after lunch any-one interested in touring the horse rescue down the road was invited along. George definitely wanted to see it. It hurt his heart to see some of the thin, still-wounded horses in their stalls but he also adored watching one of the women in charge demonstrate some of their re-habilitation methods with a horse named Wicket, who would be able to join the Clean Slate Ranch stable soon.

George had never given a lot of thought to horses before now, and he spent a few minutes chatting with the handlers. He could almost see himself doing work like this. Undoing the damage of cruel owners. Giving these beautiful animals a second chance at life.

Kind of how George was finally getting his second chance.

That night he was too nervous about other guests hearing them to do more than kiss Levi for a long time. He went to bed with a woody but it was worth it.

Thursday afternoon, Levi texted ahead to Wes that he'd be at the cabin to feed the cats, and they spent a long time naked in Levi's bed. "Can I touch you?" George asked between luxurious kisses and thrusts of their hips.

"You can touch any part of me you want. Please."

George shifted sideways and studied Levi's erection. For all the porn he'd watched in his lifetime, this was his first experience with another guy's dick. He loved the size and shape of Levi's, and he clasped the root, un-sure but curious. It was somehow both hard and velvety soft. George slowly stroked up and down his length, loving the way Levi's foreskin moved. Levi's breathing deepened, and George understood what sort of power he had right now. He literally held Levi's orgasm in the palm of his hand, and it was an intense thing to realize.

"Tell me what you want," George said, surprising himself with his commanding tone.

Levi moaned. "Whatever you want to give me. Anything, George."

He wanted to make Levi come with his hand, so George did exactly that, twisting his wrist in an unpracticed way. Using his free hand to massage Levi's balls, until Levi came over George's fist and his own stomach. The way Levi gasped for air and his entire body shook was almost too much for George, but he held off on touching himself.

"Wow," Levi said. "Thank you for that gift."

"You are very welcome." Emboldened in a new way—and intensely curious—George did something brand new to him. He leaned down and licked a bit of come off Levi's abs. The salty, slightly bitter taste fascinated him. He tried more, licking Levi clean before concentrating on his own hand.

Levi watched him with wide, lusty eyes. "I love watching your confidence grow. To see you testing boundaries and trying new things."

"It's easier to let go when I know I'm safe." George stretched out next to Levi and rested his head on Levi's shoulder. "You make me feel safe to explore my sexuality. And just be me. No front."

"Do you put up a front for others?"

"Usually. Before this summer, I hardly saw anyone who wasn't Orry, and I was really uncomfortable the first few times we ate downstairs with Derrick, Slater, Dez and Morgan. And when we came for July 4th, I faked it because I could see how much fun Orry was

having when all I wanted to do was go hide in the car."
He traced circles on Levi's pecs. "I don't know why it's
so easy to put my guard down with you."

"I think maybe you do." Levi tilted George's chin
up and kissed him. "But it's new and scary and hard
to admit."

George was smart enough to know what Levi wasn't
saying: George was attracted to Levi and had strong
feelings for the older man. Feelings couched in more
than just being the first person to shine direct—and
positive—attention on him in years. "All of the above,"
George finally said.

"Same here. You also haven't gotten off yet, young
man. Tell me what you want."

George's use of the same words had come across
like a command; Levi's came across more like a rev-
erent question. His courage grew in the face of that
question, and George's cheeks burned when he spoke.
"Use your mouth."

Levi let out that familiar growl an instant before he
began a quest to kiss and lick every part of George's
body. Well, every front part, from his throat to his nipples, and further down to dip into his navel. George
writhed and laughed and enjoyed the exploration, trusting Levi implicitly. They'd connected on a level George
didn't understand and was incapable of unboxing when
his body was soaring with unbridled pleasure and joy.

Levi's chin bumped his erection, and George cried
out from the jolt of stimulation.

Yes, please, soon and thank you.

Warm air blew across his dick a moment before Levi
grasped him in one hand. Levi's steady gaze held his
up the length of George's trembling body. "Thank you

Right Move

for this," Levi said a moment before closing his lips
around the head of George's dick. The intensity of this
brand-new thing short-circuited George's brain a little
bit, and he released a sound part moan and part wail. It
rose from the deepest part of himself that had denied
his feelings for men for so long. Had denied himself
sex of any sort because of his own fears.

He thrashed and made noise and came completely
undone under Levi's mouth and hands and care. He had
no words to warn Levi he was coming before it happened, and Levi sucked him through it, swallowing
every drop like it was the most precious nectar from
the gods. Tiny aftershocks left George a trembling
mess that Levi pulled into his arms. Levi wrapped the
coverlet around their naked bodies and held him while
George came down from the biggest high of his entire life.

"Are you with me?" Levi whispered.

"Think so. Wow. I just...wow." Yeah, no real words
yet.

"I loved doing that for you. You were completely
free for a little while. Perfectly innocent and beautiful."

"You're the only person who's ever made me feel
beautiful. I feel ugly most of the time."

"What?" Levi dropped several kisses on his forehead, cheeks and nose. "You are beautiful all the time,
George. Why do you doubt that?"

"My past." More naked than ever before, George
rolled away from Levi and tried to burrow under the
covers. He felt more than saw Levi sit up as the mattress dipped. Then Ginger was on the bed, her orange
body curling up close to George's head. He nuzzled her

soft fur with his nose, grateful for the comfort from his favorite kitty.

"You don't have to tell me about it," Levi said. "But I'll listen to anything you want to talk about."

"It's not a huge secret if you know where to look online."

"I know, but when I realized who you were, I chose to let you tell me about your past, rather than finding out things from tabloids or gossip rags. I wanted that trust from you."

Hot tears stung George's eyes. "You have that trust, Levi. I just…it's shameful to talk about. And sometimes I don't know why I'm ashamed because none of it was really my fault. It was the fault of all the adults in my life who should have valued my physical and mental health over a fucking gold medal."

"I am so sorry the adults in your life didn't see your value. And I am so sorry they risked your health. What about your brother?"

"It was complicated. Orry and I took different paths when we were kids. I was athletic, while he was musically inclined. When our parents hired Adrian as my coach and he floated Olympic glory in front of them, Orry's passions became less important to them. Our lives became about my training and skating. Orry fell into the background." Old grief bubbled up in George's chest and he sobbed once against Ginger's fur.

Levi carefully turned George until he was burrowed close to Levi's chest, arms tight around each other.

"Adrian was a good technical coach," George continued, finding strength in Levi's embrace. "He was great at turns and jumps and choreography. He knew how to put on a show the judges would love. But emotionally and physically he…was abusive. Praise was few and far between. I was always too slow, too fat, too low on the ice. Couldn't jump high enough. Couldn't spin fast enough. He taught me how to make myself throw up."

A protective sound rumbled through Levi's chest, and his arms cinched tighter around George.

"I was anorexic and bulimic for years, and I was sixteen when it came crashing down. I was supposed to skate at the World Championship, which was my gateway to the Olympics team. But I couldn't do it. I was sick, hungry, stressed out, and terrified of everyone in my life. I locked myself in my hotel room and refused to come out. I remember looking at the glass carafe of the coffee pot and thinking I can break that and make the pain stop."

"Oh, George."

He started shaking, and Levi held him tighter. Never letting go or giving up. "Then I heard Orry's voice. I hadn't seen him in months, because he'd run away from home. I missed my brother so much. He helped me check into the hospital and put my health first. Orry saved my life."

"I'm grateful you had him. So grateful."

"Me too. He survived his own battles and still managed to save me. I owe him so much. He deserves to have a life apart from me. To date and love and live, and I want him to have that. But I'm terrified of letting him go."

"You don't have to let him go for him to have a life." Levi kissed his forehead. "You just…need to take a few steps back. Give him space, not let him go. I cannot begin to imagine what your life has been like, but I do remember how jealous I was when Xander and Robin first got together. I felt like my brother had been stolen away. But he hadn't. He was simply taking a new step. And it scared me because I wasn't taking it too."

George needed to take the focus off himself for a bit. "Have you ever been in love like Xander was?"

"I thought so. But I was wrong." Levi's dark tone intimated he wasn't going into details this afternoon.

"I'm sorry."

"Thank you. And I'm sorry for what your coach put you through. I'm grateful to Orry for helping you, and to you for having the strength to be here today so I could know you."

"Orry's my hero." George raised his upper body and looked down into Levi's shining blue eyes. "But you are someone incredibly important and special to me. You're the only person outside my immediate family that I've ever told about my eating disorder. I still have trouble sometimes, but I'm a work in progress."

"I'm honored you shared your truth with me. One day at a time is often all any of us can do."

"Yeah, it is." George relaxed into Levi's strong embrace, comforted by Levi's candor and acceptance, and the warmth of his arms. Also the weight of whichever cat decided to stretch her body out over his ankles. He was too content to look.

George closed his eyes and soaked in the man holding him, and this little slice of heaven they'd found in a tiny house in the middle of nowhere.

Chapter Sixteen

The following day, Levi did his promised trick riding demonstration for the other guests, and he even got Robin to join him. They didn't do their full show from the ghost town, but the tricks all earned them applause. Little Faith cheered the loudest and when they took their final bows, announced to her dads she wanted to be a trick rider, too.

Rey looked horrified.

George and Shawn followed Levi and Robin into the barn and helped untack the horses. "You guys make it all look easy," George said.

"A lot of years of hard work will make anything look easy," Robin replied. "We're nowhere near as flexible or flashy as in our younger, touring years, but it's still a hell of a lot of fun."

"Agreed." Levi hefted the saddle off Zodiac and carried it into the tack room. He returned with two brushes. "Plus, you have to build trust with the horse you're riding. Not all horses can do what we've trained Zodiac and Apple Jax to do."

"Yup. I tried working with Tude when Mack first floated the idea of the rodeo celebration, but she's too stubborn."

"I think she's just loyal to Mack," Shawn said as he began brushing Apple Jax's flank. "Stubborn people stick together."

Levi chuckled.

"So are you gonna miss the ranch when you go home?" Robin asked George.

"I will." George stroked his own brush along Zodiac's neck, a dreamy smile on his face. "It's gorgeous and peaceful out here. And I feel like I've made a few new friends." He glanced at Shawn, who winked.

Interesting.

"We'll have to find reasons for you to come visit us again," Levi said. "As a friend and not a paying customer."

George quirked an eyebrow at him. "Technically, you're the paying customer."

"Good point."

Once the horses were taken care of and back in their stalls, Robin and Shawn followed them up to the guesthouse for a game of Scrabble. Back in the day, Robin, Levi, Xander and their dad, Doug, would have epic Scrabble battles, all of them super competitive. Levi hadn't played the game since Xander died, and he found comfort in playing again with both Robin and George.

And George's vocabulary skills impressed the crap out of Levi. He won the game with a remarkable 370 points. Their group had plenty of time for a second round before dinner, and Levi just managed to edge George out of the win by using "quixotic."

"I've always wanted a chance to play that word," Levi said.

After dinner, George demanded a rematch, and they played just the two of them, with several of the other guests watching. Levi didn't want to thrash George but he was still a competitive player, and they kept fairly close scores throughout the game as the board filled with tiles. He was confident in his final move—until he saw the way George's eyes lit up. Then he saw his mistake.

Too late. The *N* Levi had put down gave George what he needed to spell "snug" and earn himself a triple word score.

"Nice one," Shawn said. "Why am I sensing more Scrabble tournaments in your future?"

"Because I need to defend my honor," Levi replied. "Right now it's two to one in favor of George."

George's smug grin made Levi's blood warm in a pleasant way. He loved seeing George this confident. He'd blossomed leaps and bounds in the week they'd been on the ranch, and Levi was sad it would all end tomorrow. Well, their vacation would end. This thing they were exploring was only getting started.

And the idea of exploring this thing beyond the magic of the ranch lands scared him on some level. He wanted to be honest with George about his worst mistakes, but he didn't ever want George to look at him with fear or disgust. But if this thing between them was ever going to be more than casual sex, Levi needed to be honest. He told George he'd never lie to him.

"Guess you're out of practice, bro," Robin said as he poked Levi in the ribs. "You used to kick my and Xander's ass without blinking."

"I still kicked *your* ass today."

"George kicked yours worse. Good job, by the way, Master Thompson."

George chuckled. "I haven't played in years. We used

to play with my grandparents before Orry and I moved out. It was fun getting back into it."

"I bet there's an app you can download on your phone," Shawn said. "You can either play the computer or against other people."

"I'll have to look into it. I never thought to do that before now."

Later that evening, Levi waited until they were alone in their room before asking, "Do you think you never thought to play Scrabble again because you missed your grandparents, and it reminds you of them?"

George paused by the big window and gazed out, his body angled slightly away from Levi. "I don't think I did that consciously but it makes sense. This vacation has given me the courage to go out more. To go see them, instead of just talking to them over the phone or a tablet. So playing Scrabble tonight didn't bother me. I had fun." He twisted his head to smile at Levi. "I'm a little sad this is our last night here. It's been the best vacation of my life."

"I'm honored I could give you such a tremendous gift. You are such a special soul, George, and I've loved watching you come alive this week. I'm also sad the vacation is almost over, but I hope we'll continue to see each other when you go home. I know the distance is a bit inconvenient but I..." Levi straightened his spine and took the plunge. "I would like to date you, if that's something you want."

"Really?" George somehow seemed to smile with his entire body. "I've never dated anyone before. I have no idea how."

"Then we'll do what's fun and comfortable for us. Dating doesn't have to be complicated, and with technology it doesn't always have to be in person. As long as we enjoy ourselves and keep getting to know each other."

"And having sex?"

Levi laughed and finally closed the small distance between them. Took George in his arms and inhaled the faintest scents of soap and sweat. "Yes, and having sex. Just like dating, we'll have whatever sex makes us both happy with no expectations."

George's pale cheeks pinked up. "Um, can I ask you something personal?"

"Of course." He had an idea what the question might be but he let George find his own words.

"How do you, uh, prefer to have sex?"

"I like having sex all kinds of ways, depending on my partner at the time. Who they are and what they're comfortable with."

George flashed him an exasperated look. "When you have sex with men, Levi. Do you top or bottom, and what do you expect from me?"

Levi loved this assertive side of George. "I don't expect anything from you except honesty and mutual respect, in and out of bed. And if you're looking for an easy label, then I would consider myself versatile. I like to top and bottom for men. I also love what we do, and I would be perfectly happy if you never wanted to try penetration in either position. I know that penetration is the end goal of most porn, and that you've watched a lot with your job, but it's not the end goal of all relationships. Some couples are perfectly happy never going there."

He ran his fingers through George's hair, enjoying

the way George leaned into his petting. "What are you interested in trying, George?"

"I'm not totally sure." George bit his lower lip in the most adorable way.

"What are things you've fantasized about?"

"Topping." His cheeks flamed brighter but George never looked away. "I'm curious how it feels. But I'm scared because sometimes it looks like bottoming hurts, and I'd never want to hurt another person. Not even by accident."

He kept stroking George's scalp. "The good news is I've had enough anal sex to know how to do it carefully. And if we did do that, you topping me, I would absolutely speak up if something hurt. I've…" Levi struggled to find the right words without lying to George. "I've been hurt a few times in the past, and I never want you to have the same regrets I do."

Anger flared in George's expressive blue eyes. "I'm sorry someone hurt you. Were they punished?"

"Not by the law, but I like to think that karma or the universe has caught up to them." He wanted to tell George more, to share this part of his past, so he led him over to Levi's bunk. They sat, holding hands, George watching him intently. "The same day I found my cats on the side of the road, I took them to a vet in a small town. His name was Dr. Grant Clark, and we flirted a bit. He told me about a campground nearby. I decided to stay close while the kittens were young. Eventually, we started dating and sleeping together. I fell in love with him."

When Levi didn't continue, George quietly asked, "How did Grant hurt you? Did he…attack you?"

"Emotionally, yes." Old hurts flooded back, and Levi

fought to find his center. To get through this conversation without losing his temper in front of George.
"He betrayed my trust. He asked to film us having
sex one night, said he thought it would be super hot
to watch us together later. I thought he was just being
extra kinky, and I trusted him so I said yes. I'm not sure
what changed after that but our relationship began to
go south. He became distant, rude, and he'd pick on me
for my beliefs. My jogging and meditating. I finally had
enough, broke up with him, and hit the road again."

"He didn't like you leaving."

Levi sighed heavily and pressed his shoulder to
George's. "That's putting it mildly. He went the revenge
porn route and posted our sex tape online."

"Fuck." More fury darkened George's expression.
"Shit, I am so sorry."

"I felt extremely betrayed but mostly I was embarrassed for my father and the rodeo, because they were
named in the description. I sent takedown notices but
I couldn't prosecute Grant because I'd agreed to make
the tape. A few months later, I heard from Robin again
for the first time in years, and I knew that leaving had
been the best decision I could have made. Hearing from
my brother, that he was happy and safe, put me back on
my path. And eventually that path led me here."

"I'm glad you're here." George brushed soft lips over
his. "I'm sorry for what you went through."

It wasn't the worst thing Levi had gone through in
his thirty-four years, but that wasn't a story for tonight.
"Thank you. Grant was the first person I truly thought
I'd fallen in love with, but looking back, I think I fell
in love with the idea of him. Being with someone. Having that one great love like Robin and Xander had. Ex-

cept human beings are capable of infinite kinds of love, because now Robin has Shawn, and they are insanely happy together. They give me hope."

"Hope you'll fall in love for real?"

"Yes."

"I've never been in love before."

"I know." *And I don't know if I'm meant to love you but I'm willing to take the chance.* The words couldn't make it past Levi's lips. They were too much for this early moment. "It's scary and exciting, and totally worth it with the right person. I believe that."

"You believing helps me believe it. I know I'm only twenty-three, but I feel so old sometimes, and I want a life. I want Orry to have a life. I want us *both* to have a real life, even if it takes us away from each other for a while."

"The great thing about the time we're living in? Even if you're ten thousand miles from someone you love, you can still see them face-to-face with your phone or tablet. I can tell how much you love your brother, but maybe it's time to put your own happiness first."

George didn't speak, only held his gaze for a long time, before kissing Levi. Levi willingly went to his back, giving George all the control. They kissed for ages with George slotted between his spread legs. George didn't initiate more, though, and Levi didn't press. They kissed until exhausted, and after going through separate bedtime routines, curled up together in Levi's bed. Sharing one space for the first time, with George snuggled up against Levi's back. The big spoon.

Levi fell asleep dreaming of the day George slid home inside his body. He knew to his bones that the experience would be spectacular.

* * *

George experienced the unique sensation of coming awake pressed up close to an adult male body, and he smiled at the back of Levi's head. They were still in the same positions as when they fell asleep, and while George's left arm was a little numb, he was glad. He liked being snuggled up to Levi's broader body. George felt safe and protected in his arms, and he was grateful to hold Levi for a little while. To offer comfort after Levi had shared something personal and painful with him.

George wasn't generally a vengeful person but if he ever stumbled across this Grant Clark character, he was likely to give the asshole a swift kick to the nuts for betraying Levi like that. And while the majority of the subtitle work George did was for name studios, it made him sick to think he could have ever accidentally seen Grant's video.

As comfortable as George was, his bladder gave a kick. Levi grunted in protest when George tugged his arm free, pins and needles already racing through it. Worth it, though. When he returned, Levi was sitting up and smiling at him. "Sleep well?" Levi asked.

"Very well. You?"

"Best sleep in ages."

George slid back into bed and Levi's arms. "That's a high compliment."

"And yet true."

They rested together a while longer, until the sun had risen and the rooster call sounded. Levi went to shower first, because those bathrooms were simply not designed for sharing, and then George took his turn. He left his

things on a towel to dry for packing later—an old habit
he'd started when he was traveling for competitions.

Nope, not thinking about that today. He was going to
enjoy his final couple of hours at the ranch. His phone
had a good-morning text from Orry, which he returned.
Orry had gotten a touch less clingy as the week pro-
gressed, probably because George had begun texting
less frequently. He was safe here and didn't need the
constant reassurances of his brother anymore.

He was safe with Levi for sure, and after having been
around him for the better part of the last two weeks,
going home without him was going to suck. He was attached to Levi and his kitties, and George was thrilled
Levi wanted to date him. A little terrified but mostly
thrilled.

Orry, though, might not be as excited that the first
person George ever chose to date was eleven years older
than him.

At breakfast, Faith was subdued, probably sad that
her vacation was over. But she cheered up when Levi reminded her they had one last trail ride that morning, so
she'd get a chance to say goodbye to the horses. George
was happy to tack and ride Figuro one last time. He and
Levi rode side by side, enjoying the scenery and occasional glimpse of a raccoon or squirrel. Their guide,
Ernie, pointed out a red fox up ahead, but George was
too far down the trail to see it. Damn. He'd loved foxes
ever since his parents showed him Disney's animated
Robin Hood.

His bizarre crush on a cartoon fox at age nine should
have been his first clue he was gay.

It was lunchtime once they were back and the horses

taken care of. George patted Figuro's sleek forehead one more time. "You be good, girl."

She nickered.

Lunch was a smorgasbord of leftovers, since this was the last week open to guests until after the New Year. Patrice encouraged everyone to eat their fill of the cold salads and fresh fruit that wouldn't store as easily as the cold cuts and cheese. Levi and George sat with the Briggs-King family on the porch, despite the chill. George had genuinely enjoyed getting to know them this past week, and he found his courage to ask Mr. Porter to take a picture of their group. Then he got cell numbers from Samuel and Rey and group-texted it to everyone.

"So how was the second honeymoon?" Levi asked once the plates had been collected and returned. They all had about two hours of free time before the buck-board would arrive to take them to their cars.

"I think it was a great success and a lot of fun," Rey replied. "Faith had the time of her life; we got to spend time together as a family with no work to worry about. I call it a huge win."

"Excellent."

Samuel nodded his agreement while smiling fondly at his husband.

Husband. It was too big of a word for George to even consider for himself one day when he'd never even been on a date. Even boyfriend was daunting. He just wanted to be as happy and in love as Samuel and Rey clearly were.

Patrice came around and reminded everyone to have their luggage downstairs by two forty-five so it could be loaded and driven down to the parking lot ahead of

the buckboard. After he'd packed, George gazed around
the room that had been his home this week. It wasn't
very large, and George probably couldn't have handled
sharing with four people, especially if he didn't know
two of them. With him and Levi?

Perfect.

They trotted downstairs and left their suitcases in the
designated spot. George wandered the main yard a bit
by himself to take more pictures, mostly of the bunkhouse and barn. Another of cabin row to give Orry a
better idea of the grounds. George might be leaving
Clean Slate Ranch today but deep down he knew he'd
be back.

Now that he had Levi in his life, George would do
everything he could to keep him.

Levi wasn't sad to climb onto the buckboard for the
return trip, because gods knew he'd probably be back
down this way tomorrow to chill with Robin. He was
more nervous over a question he hadn't managed to ask
George yet, and he wouldn't get another chance until
they were in the privacy of Levi's pickup.

When they reached the parking lot, their luggage was
waiting, the pickup driver idling nearby to watch the
open gate. There was also a taxi waiting for someone.
Faith looked like she wanted to burst into tears once
she climbed off the buckboard. Samuel picked her up
and whispered in her ear while they walked. Levi said
polite goodbyes to the other guests as he grabbed both
his and George's bag. Carrying them both to the pickup
felt right. Faith was settled by the time the Briggs-Kings
luggage was stowed in the taxi's trunk, and they wandered over to say goodbye.

"Despite the long drive to the airport," Rey said, "it's still cheaper than parking a rental for a week."

"Makes sense." Levi squatted and held out his hand to Faith. "It was an honor to meet you, Miss Faith. I hope you get to ride again soon."

"Thank you, Mr. Levi." She shook his hand, then did the same with George. "Are you boyfriends?"

George startled and glanced around, but no one—not even the taxi driver—was paying attention. With a secretive smile, George leaned in and faux whispered, "Not officially but maybe one day."

"Good. I like him. You should like him too and get married like my dads."

"It's a little too soon for getting married, but I do like him. He's a really nice guy. You have a good flight home okay?"

"Okay." She cast a forlorn look at the departing buckboard, barely a shadow on the horizon, and climbed into the taxi.

"It was a pleasure to meet you both and get to know you," Levi said to Samuel and Rey. "You are both very blessed men."

"Considering the rocky start we had, we are extremely blessed to have what we do," Rey said. "If you ever find yourself in or near Harrisburg, give me a call and I'll cook you both dinner."

"He loves to show off his cooking skills," Samuel added.

"It's what I do for a living. I have to be good at it."

They all exchanged handshakes because the meter was running, and then the small family was being driven away. Levi and George were the only guests who hadn't left yet, and the pickup still idled—probably waiting to lock the gate, since they'd be closed to visitors for a few weeks. Levi didn't linger. Once they were in the truck cab, he drove them to the ranch's entrance to Garrett's main road and stopped.

"I want to ask you something," Levi said. "Since it's only three o'clock. I know you probably miss your brother and are eager to see him again, but did you want to spend some time in my home before I drive you back?"

George's bright smile calmed Levi's nerves. "Yes. Please. I'll just text Orry and let him know we're, um, that I want to see Ginger again. Which is totally true."

"Are you going to tell him anything about us being intimate?"

"I will." He sank against the bench seat. "We need to sit down and have a long, serious conversation. Not just me coming out and seeing you, but also him lying to me on Thanksgiving. We definitely need to talk about that."

"How do you think he'll feel about you seeing me?"

"Honestly? I think he'll be upset, and I think he'll blame you because you're older and way more experienced, and it doesn't help that I haven't come out to him yet. I don't think he'll be mad about that but definitely hurt."

"Do you think it will help if I say I have nothing but the best of intentions?"

George snorted. "I don't know, because I *don't* have the best of intentions." He wiggled his eyebrows in a suggestive way that took any possible sting out of the words. "I don't want to go home and go back to being the person I was before, Levi. This week has been too important to me."

"It's been important to me, too. You're the only other person besides Robin who knows what Grant did to me."

"Then, to borrow your words, I thank you for your honesty and your trust."

Levi couldn't resist leaning across the seat to kiss George. "Then let's go say goodbye to the cats."

And that was part of it, but not all of it, once Levi parked his pickup near his home. They spent more time naked in his bed than playing with the cats, and Levi was okay with that. He liked George in his bed and in his life, and he wanted the younger man there as often as humanly possible going forward.

Chapter Seventeen

George was not ready to leave the sanctuary of Garrett, California, but he had another life to return to. As much as he would have liked to chill in Levi's home forever, the real world beckoned him back into its less interesting embrace. After swapping hand jobs—George wasn't quite ready to go down on Levi yet—and playing with the cats, they climbed into Levi's truck for the trip back to San Francisco.

They stopped along the way for a takeout dinner to eat in the cab. George wasn't a huge fan of fast food but the restaurant Levi chose had a grilled chicken sandwich that seemed acceptable, plus a side salad option instead of fries. They entered George's neighborhood a little after eight that night, and George's gut soured the closer Levi got to his place. Their vacation at Clean Slate had been the best kind of dream. The real world wasn't quite as awesome.

Levi found a spot on a side street to park. "Do you want me to walk you to your place?" he asked.

"Okay." They were over a block away from the house, and George wasn't sure about walking around alone, especially after dark. It was a relatively safe neighborhood, but still.

"Excellent."

Levi carried George's bag, and they walked close without touching. Other homes were brightly lit with people moving around inside, testament to all his neighbors living their lives. Cars passed them on the street, carrying other folks to their Saturday evening plans. Or perhaps home from a late dinner in a nice restaurant. So many possibilities for people who didn't hide themselves away from the world.

At the big house's door, George produced his keys. "You don't have to come inside if you aren't ready to, um, I don't know."

"Announce to your neighbors that we're dating?" Levi supplied, smiling. "I'm comfortable with whatever you are. Would you like me to walk you to your door like a proper date would?"

"We weren't on a date."

"Technically, no, dates don't last a full week. But we're also doing our own thing, remember?"

George grinned. "I think I like the idea of our first date being a ranch vacation. It'll be an easy anniversary to remember."

"Then I'd like to walk you to your door."

"Okay." George's belly wobbled with nerves but he slid his key into the lock and turned the knob. He was not surprised to see Derrick, Slater, Dez and Morgan having another Monopoly tournament in the living room, with two mostly empty six-packs and a pizza box nearby. Slater rolled the dice and their quartet looked up to see who was home.

"Hey, you're back," Slater said. "Hi, Levi. What did you think of the ranch, George?"

"It's breathtaking," George replied. "I loved it there, and I am amazed you gave up living there."

Derrick playfully pinched Slater's cheek. "That's because he loves me too much to keep playing with horses."

Slater swatted his hand away. "I lived there for as long as I was meant to, and it was time to move on. Give other people a chance to enjoy its magic. Looks like Levi took good care of you."

Coming from Derrick or Dez, George might have read more into the statement, but Slater was typically a blunt person. "He did. He and Robin even did a trick riding demo for the guests, which was really cool."

"Until Faith announced she wanted to be a trick rider too," Levi added with a chuckle.

"Faith?" Dez asked.

Levi described the family they'd met and befriended, while George kept glancing at his stairs. He'd texted Orry roughly what time he thought he'd be back almost an hour ago and hadn't gotten a response yet, so he had to be working at the bar. "Anyway, I'm going to walk George upstairs. He's had a long week, and I imagine a nice soak in a real tub sounds like heaven right now."

"Amen," Derrick said. "Those showers in the guest-house are utilitarian at best, and not very big. I doubt Morgan would be able to turn around in one."

"Don't say that." Dez reached across the board to punch him in the arm. "I'm still trying to convince Morgan we should make a reservation for next summer. It sounds like fun."

Morgan grunted.

George said goodnight to his friends and led the way upstairs, key at the ready. Other than going downstairs to get the mail, George wasn't used to coming and going with any great frequency. But he was starting to enjoy coming with Levi—in more ways than one. The apartment was expectedly empty and dark. Orry must have been out all day, assuming George would be home before dark, because whenever Orry worked late and George went to bed, he always left the microwave light on so Orry didn't come home to the dark.

At least, he hoped Orry had been out all day and hadn't not left the light on because he was mad at George for some reason.

George hit the light switch by the door, which turned on their floor lamp. Levi put the bag down near the door as George turned to close it, giving them a bit of privacy. He checked his phone but still no reply from Orry. Ninety minutes wasn't the longest he'd ever taken to reply to a text, but George was also used to knowing which job Orry was doing. Saturday night was a good night for driving ride shares or bartending.

"Nothing from your brother?"

George shook his head. "I mean, I'm not super worried or anything. I guess I was hoping he'd be home. I wanted a hug."

"Will a hug from me tide you over?"

"Definitely." George slid easily into Levi's arms now, and he rested his head on Levi's shoulder, nose pressed into his neck.

"I suppose this will have to tide me over for a while too." He ran his fingers through George's hair in the familiar, petting gesture that George was beginning to adore. It made him want to roll over and show his belly like a puppy.

They stayed like that until a key rattled in the doorknob, then broke apart quickly, George's heart suddenly in his throat. Orry didn't seem surprised to see Levi; someone downstairs must have mentioned him still being here. "You must have just got back," he said. "You're still in your coats."

George didn't want to lie and say yeah, they had just gotten back. Levi saved him with, "We got distracted. It was a long week."

"Huh." Orry tossed his own coat over the back of a chair, even though they had hooks by the door, then went to the fridge.

"You don't work tonight?" George asked.

"Bartending gig starts at ten, and I was hoping to eat before then if that's okay."

George took a step back, even though the remarks had been directed toward the refrigerator's interior. It wasn't like Orry to be that snappish with him. Levi briefly squeezed his elbow before letting go. "I'm sorry."

Orry sighed heavily and let the fridge door close. Turned. "No, I'm sorry. It's just been a really long day of ride shares and I've missed you. The apartment has been so empty."

"I missed you too." George opened his arms. "Peace?"

"Of course, dude, we aren't fighting." Orry crossed the distance and hugged him. "I'm glad you're home, and I'm glad you had a good week."

"I had a great week." George squeezed his brother tight, overjoyed to be with him again after almost a full week apart. The longest separation since they were both sixteen. "I took way more pictures than I sent you."

"I bet." Orry pulled back and studied him. "You seem different. More confident."

"I am. I rode a horse and camped overnight, and I made new friends and acquaintances. I was so happy, Or. I felt alive for the first time since... I don't even know. It's been forever."

"I believe you." He shot Levi a suspicious look. "I also need to eat before I got to work again. We'll talk more in the morning, yeah?"

"Of course."

Orry went back to rummaging in the fridge. George took Levi outside to the private landing. "Call me tomorrow when you have a chance to talk to him," Levi whispered. "We'll plan our next date."

"Okay." George brushed his lips over Levi's, wishing he was brave enough to do more. "I'll see you soon. Thank you for everything."

"You're welcome. It was all truly my honor. I'll talk to you soon."

"Count on it." He reluctantly watched Levi descend the steps and disappear from sight. The muffled sounds of Levi saying goodbye to the Monopoly crew drifted up, and then the softer sound of the front door closing. After an entire week close to him, Levi was gone.

George went into the apartment where Orry was eating a sandwich at the small kitchen table while also doing something on his phone. He was tired and the idea of a long, hot bath was appealing, but George plunked his ass down into the chair opposite his brother and asked, "Why did you lie to me on Thanksgiving?"

Orry nearly choked on his food. "What?"

"You told me you had a bartending gig, but the bar you work at was closed that night. I've kept this in for weeks, bro, but I need to know the truth." George couldn't remember the last time he'd been so blunt with his brother, demanding information rather than simply accepting what he was told. And it felt good. Freeing.

Orry put his sandwich down and stared at him for a long time, his identical blue eyes difficult to read for the first time in ages. "I didn't mean to lie. Exactly."

"What does that even mean? Lying is lying." And wasn't he guilty of the same thing by not telling Orry he was gay and now dating Levi? Probably but right now, this was about his brother.

"I know, I just…didn't want to put any kind of pressure on you. About stuff."

"Stuff like what?"

"Dating stuff."

For a split second, George thought Orry knew about him dating Levi. Except that wasn't right. No one knew for sure about their status, which meant… "Are you dating someone?"

"Yes." Orry stared at his lap. "I met her in late October, and a few times when I said I was working I was actually with her. Hanging out. Doing stuff."

For all that George was excited that Orry was dating, he was still confused by the subterfuge. "Why did you think you needed to lie to me about seeing someone? I want you to be happy, and if dating this girl makes you happy then great. I'm all for it."

He looked up. "Really? It's been just you and me for so long. You aren't jealous?"

"No." George didn't have to consider his answer for a moment. "You have taken such good care of me for the last seven years, and I can't possibly be jealous over you finding someone who makes you happy. As long as she makes you happy."

The grin on Orry's face said everything without

words. "Yeah. She's pretty great. Believe it or not, she was a ride share client. We hit it off talking in the car, and she actually told me to call her, so I did."

"What's her name?"

"Zoey. I really like her, George."

"Good." He reached across the small table to squeeze Orry's wrist. "I'm happy for you. Honestly. So, I, uh." His stomach seized up tight. "Hope you can be happy for me, too."

Orry quirked an eyebrow. "Why? Did you meet some hot chick while on vacation?"

"No, I didn't meet a hot chick." Now or never. George steeled his spine and said, "I'm dating Levi. I'm gay."

Orry stared blankly, then pulled his hand away from George's. "You're dating Levi? He's like, a bazillion years older than you."

"Eleven years." And George was a bit turned around by the fact that Orry wasn't reacting more strongly to the whole *I'm gay* announcement.

"Eleven is a lot, dude, especially when you've never dated before. Like, literally never dated anyone."

"Well, who have you dated?"

"I don't know, a few girls casually. Have you ever even had sex?"

George's face went hot all over. "Um."

"Oh fuck, forget I asked." Orry rubbed his palms into his eyes. "I don't need any mental images of my baby brother having sex with anyone of any gender, thank you very much." He put his hands flat to the table and adopted his big-brother stare. "Are you guys being safe?"

"Yes, we're being safe." They hadn't reached a level yet where condoms were essential, but Orry said he didn't need those details, and George left it there. "I really care about Levi. He's kind and considerate, and he has this inner peace that makes me feel comfortable. Safe. I had the best time with him this week, and we agreed to keep seeing each other. I think you'll really like him if you get to know him."

"Okay." Orry frowned. "Twin question. How long have you known you're gay?"

"Known? Maybe a year or two. Suspected? All the way back to skating. Admiring other boys way more than the girls. And not just for their technique. And since we're playing this game, when did you know you're straight?"

His brother laughed. "Fourth grade, when Megan Winkler hit puberty and her boobs got kind of big, and I really wanted to know what they felt like."

"Well, that's vivid."

"Yeah." His mirth faded away beneath another serious frown. "I just need to know you are absolutely okay with everything you've done with Levi. I know the stuff I did when I was sixteen was out of desperation and drug addiction, and I remember how much some stuff hurt. I don't ever want you to be in pain, George."

George stood, moved around the table, and knelt beside Orry's chair. Pulled Orry down to the floor so they were facing each other on an equal level. "I promise you I have never felt pain while I'm with Levi. He is careful. Generous. And yes, he's my first, so maybe it won't last forever with him. But I swear that I am safe with him no matter what. I believe that with my whole heart."

Orry searched his eyes for several long moments before saying, "Okay. I trust you, and I believe you. I do want you to be happy, I swear. I guess I've spent seven years trying to protect you, and I never really thought about what would make you happy *and* safe, rather than just safe."

"Probably because I could never look beyond the boundaries of our apartment. I was terrified of being controlled and manipulated again, and I hid from everyone. But I don't have any of those fears when I'm with Levi. He is…everything I never knew I needed. And I want to be with him for as long as he'll have me. Or for as long as I believe our relationship is healthy for me."

"Good." Orry brought George's right hand up and kissed his knuckles. "That makes me feel better about this whole thing. Not the gay thing, I don't care about that. I just needed to hear you say you want a healthy relationship."

"Because of Adrian?"

"Mostly. You let him in the apartment this past summer."

"I know, and it was a stupid decision. But I promise it won't happen again. He has no more power over me. He's a ghost, part of my past. And if he rings the bell again, I swear I'll call the police."

"Good." Orry hauled him into a hug. "I love you."

"Me too."

"So you went on vacation and snagged yourself a cowboy, huh?"

George laughed as he pulled back, beyond grateful for his twin's easy acceptance of his truth. "I guess you could say that. I think we were both nudging in that direction, but the close proximity kind of forced the issue. In a good way. No bad force."

"Good. So am I allowed to be mad at you for telling Levi you're gay before you told me?"

"Yes."

"Good. I mean, I'm not mad, but I'm glad I have the right to be if I want to."

"You're not?"

"No, dummy. You're my brother and I love you no matter what. I'm glad you're finally starting to get a life. I know how badly Adrian hurt you, and I love knowing that he doesn't have a hold over you anymore. You're living the life you deserve."

George blinked hard as his eyes burned. "We both are, brother. Finally. No more letting the past control us, right?"

"Right. So when do I get to pull the whole 'you hurt my brother and I hurt you' speech on Levi? It's kind of my duty as your twin."

"You only get to do that if I get to pull it on Zoey."

"Never. Got it."

"Exactly. And maybe the four of us can even go out on a double date."

Orry's eyebrows went up, even as his lips twisted into a grin. "Like in a restaurant? You actually want to go out?"

"Eventually. Being at the ranch this past week and around other people in a safe environment…it was something I needed." George was beyond proud of himself for everything he'd accomplished this week. And maybe he'd struggle with anxiety for the rest of his life but he knew deep down he could manage it. It didn't have to control him anymore. He could find new ways to control *it*. "I mean, I'm not ready to go hit up a crowded bar on a Friday night, but a small casual place sounds nice. Maybe even a movie."

"Who are you and where is my actual twin?" But

the excitement in Orry's eyes was everything in that moment. He hauled George into another hug. "I am so fucking proud of you. To be honest, now that I'm seeing Zoey, I've been thinking about a way to bring up you getting out more. Meeting people. I guess you took care of that all by yourself."

"By rescuing a cat."

"And visiting the ghost town. And agreeing to Thanksgiving dinner. You made those choices. You took those steps. You can do anything you set your mind to, you always could. I think you just forgot how for a while."

"A long while." George's stubbornness and drive for success had taken him all the way to the World Championship once. Those traits would also serve to get George out of this apartment and into the real world. Living in it. Not hiding anymore.

And for the first time in a long time, he couldn't wait to see what tomorrow brought.

Chapter Eighteen

Levi didn't sleep well on Saturday night, his body keenly aware of how alone he was. Even though he and George had only shared a bed once, the younger man had still been nearby. A living, breathing presence. Maybe Levi had three cats all over the bed who occasionally purred if he petted them, but it simply wasn't the same.

He finally forced himself to get up, put his running gear on, and head out for his morning exercise. The sun was barely up and he enjoyed watching it paint the sky in brilliant hues of purple, red and orange. Very few clouds yet. Christmas Day was Friday. Would George want to spend part of the holiday together? For sure he always spent it with Orry, but Levi would love to see him for a few hours.

Maybe after he and Robin paid tribute to Xander. They'd already talked about it becoming a yearly tradition, and Levi had agreed without thinking it through. Yes, he'd be here this year, and he was definitely sticking around for another season at the ghost town. But his wanderlust still returned when he thought about Lucky's Rodeo. They were at their winter home in Santa Fe right now. If he hadn't met George, he probably would have hitched up his house and driven out there for a few weeks.

Now he had a reason to stick around the area.

As long as he and George were still together in a year. And seeing as Levi was the guy's first boyfriend... that future was difficult to predict. He could kind of imagine it, though. George had traveled a lot in his youth to various competitions and seen all parts of the country. Then he'd spent the last seven holed up in an apartment with his brother. Maybe he'd want to travel in the tiny home with Levi. See the United States together with the cats.

Maybe.

He usually ran for about half an hour, and despite the cold morning, had a decent sweat by the time he got home. Right into the shower to wash it off and refresh himself, the warm water helping soothe equally warmed-up muscles. Before rehab he hadn't been a runner, preferring the hard work of the rodeo—including swinging bales of hay into a truck—as his exercise. But he'd found a way to center himself when he ran, with peaceful music playing over his ear buds.

Part of him wanted to invite George to run with him, but he remembered the odd look on George's face when they'd first talked about Levi's running habit. Almost spooked. It probably had to do with skating and his bouts with anorexia and bulimia. Bad memories of overexercising, probably. Maybe one day Levi could help him find new, better memories to overshadow the bad ones.

After a bowl of granola for breakfast, he went into the yard and played with the cats for a while. Sporty was stalking something in the grass, and a few minutes later, very proudly trotted over with a struggling field mouse in her mouth. Levi gently extracted the poor thing, then took it into the woods and set it free under a bush where Sporty couldn't get at it again.

She liked to hunt but never killed what she brought him, as if sensing he would disapprove of hunting for sport when she was fed plenty of quality cat food.

He wanted to call George just to hear his voice. They'd spent an entire week together, and it was odd not having him around. But since he didn't want to come across as stalkerish he would wait for George to call him. Robin, predictably, showed up at Levi's house around eleven with an expectant smile.

"How'd the honeymoon go?" he asked.

Levi nearly dropped his mug of tea. "What?"

"The family with the little girl. They were on a second honeymoon or something, right?" Robin winked.

The big jerk had been trying for a spit take and failed, assuming correctly that Levi would think Robin was asking after his and George's vacation together. "Yes, and they told us they had a great time. Even invited us over for dinner if we're ever in their area."

"Us, huh? Are you and George officially a thing?"

"Yes." Levi sat on one end of the narrow sofa, and Robin joined him. "We are officially dating."

"Good for you, dude. I know how gun-shy you were about dating after what Grant did to you." Robin's smiling face when serious. "Did you tell George about that?"

"Last night. We spent some time together here before I drove him home. Talked. Decided we wanted to try long distance. I mean, an hour isn't too bad considering the distance other people have had to overcome, but the Thompsons only have one car, and I get the feeling George doesn't drive much."

"That'll be a lot of driving for you."

"Yeah, but after spending most of my life on the road that doesn't really bother me."

Robin studied his face a beat. "What does bother you then?"

"I'm George's first relationship. I really like him and feel good when I'm around him. He has a genuinely kind soul that's a little bruised, but finally trying to heal. I suppose I'm a little scared I'm…is there an opposite of a rebound relationship?"

"So you're his first and you're worried you're just practice?"

"A little bit. I don't see George doing that consciously or on purpose, but it is a worry. I took a huge chance on trusting Grant so soon in my recovery, and it blew up in my face in a spectacularly painful way."

"I know it did but you have to give yourself permission to take a second chance. I did that with Shawn, and now look at us. About to close on a house in a few weeks."

"True." Levi had fewer years between his heartbreak with Grant than Robin had with losing Xander, but Xander's death had been a much different sort of heartbreak. And Robin had nearly lost his life from the force of his grief. But he was happy now, moving in with his boyfriend, and probably making plans to propose. Xander had resisted marrying Robin for years before Robin wore him down.

Levi had a feeling he wouldn't need to work as hard with Shawn.

Will George want to get married one day?

That was too far into the future to even ponder today. "So did you wander all the way from the ranch just to pick my brain about George?"

"Nah, Shawn and I were invited to lunch at Mack's place. I figured I'd pester you while Shawn visits with Wes and Miles."

"No Reyes? The ranch is closed to guests so he doesn't have that excuse."

"I'm sure Reyes will be there to pester Mack. You should come up with me."

Levi shook his head. "No thanks, I wasn't directly invited and don't like to crash other people's gatherings."

Robin whipped out his phone and started texting. Sure enough, about a minute later, Levi's phone pinged. A texted invite from Mack for Levi to join them for lunch. "You are such a dork."

"A dork who looks out for my brother. Seriously, though, I do hope things work out with George. He's a great guy, and you two always look happy when you're together."

"Unlike whenever you're with Shawn and you always look constipated?"

Robin growled softly. "Those are fightin' words, Peletier." He lunged, and Levi found himself wrestling with his best friend on the house's small living room floor. They tickled and pinched like kids having a brawl, neither of them really trying to win, and the entire production made Levi hoot with laughter.

"Okay, uncle," Levi said. "I was joking. You two are adorable together."

"That's better." Robin stood, then offered Levi his hand for a boost up. "Friends?"

"Nope, you attacked me. We won't be friends again for exactly five minutes."

"Now who's the dork?"

"Still you. I'm defending my pride here."

Baby came in through the cat door, probably to see what all the fuss was about, and Robin scooped her up. "Your daddy is being silly, little girl."

"Yes, well, you technically started it." Levi reached over to scratch under Baby's chin. "Why am I friends with such a silly man?"

"You keep me around for my charming good looks."

"You wish." A head bumped Levi's ankle and he bent to get Ginger, careful of her injured leg. She instantly began purring. "Hey, princess. Are you jealous?" That got him an adorable chin nuzzle. Then she squirmed until Levi put her down.

She went up the stairs and stood at the top, and she began to yowl. As if sensing someone else wasn't there who was supposed to be.

Cats know, and she misses George.

"He'll be back again soon, girl," Levi said.

"Come on, it's getting close to lunchtime." Robin kissed Baby's head and put her down. "When are you talking to George today?"

Levi led the way out of the house. "This afternoon probably. George wanted to talk to his brother about us and a few other things, and I said he could take his time and call when he was ready."

"He's coming out?"

"That's the plan." He didn't know Orry well, and hopefully, the conversation went in George's favor. He imagined Orry would fully support his twin, but just in case things went badly, Levi would be there for George no matter what.

* * *

Lunch was fun, as was every meal Levi shared at the Garrett-Bentley cabin. Good food, good friendship, and always amusing stories from Wes about his acting adventures, or from Reyes about that week's guests. No one asked him directly if he and George were dating, but he did get curious looks from Wes and Miles when Reyes talked about the adorable Briggs-King family and their daughter.

Levi would answer if they asked but he wasn't much on freely sharing certain personal details of his life. He hadn't even told his own father what Grant had done to him, only that they'd broken up. Dad would love George, and he'd be thrilled Levi was dating again.

"What kind of cookies are you guys baking this afternoon?" Miles asked Shawn.

"We're doing double-chocolate crinkle cookies," Shawn replied. Last Christmas, as a way to perk Shawn up when he was missing his late mother, Robin had asked Shawn to teach him how to bake. They ended up doing Nine Days of Cookies, one new cookie each day leading up to Christmas, and they left them in the guesthouse kitchen for all the hands to share. They'd decided to make it a tradition.

"Oooh, yum," Wes said. "Chocolate cookies. I'm definitely popping down to steal a few."

"Feel free, they're for the entire Clean Slate family. Including you, Levi."

Levi smiled. It warmed him to be considered part of this big, eclectic family. "I appreciate it, thank you. I missed them all last year but I promise to try some this week. I've had your food and know they'll be excellent. Hopefully, you've taught Robin a few things."

Robin mimicked throwing something at his head from the other side of the long table. One of Levi's favorite things about the cabin was the long, wooden dining table that stood in front of a huge picture window, giving them all a perfect view of the outdoors. The beauty of the land was on full display and always helped Levi feel a little bit freer.

Far away from that hospital room before rehab.

Around one thirty, Levi's phone rang with George's assigned ringtone and he grinned. Excused himself from the table, Robin smirking at him the entire time, and went outside to the front porch. He was warm inside despite the chilly air, and he happily answered the call. "Levi Peletier's answering service. How may I direct your call?"

The joke was worth it for the joyful laughter from George. "Cute. Hi."

"Hey, yourself. How are you?"

"Great, actually." He still sounded perfectly upbeat, and that gave Levi hope for a positive conversation with Orry. "I would have called you sooner but I wanted to get caught up on some work, and then Orry and I went out for lunch."

"I'm glad you got some work—" *Wait.* "You went out for lunch? As in a restaurant?"

"Sort of. We did pickup from a local place and then ate in the car in the parking lot."

"How was that?"

"A little nerve-wracking. I can't remember the last time I walked into a restaurant, even for the five minutes it took to grab our order. But I was around a lot of strangers, both inside and in the parking lot, and I think

I was okay. It helped that I was with Orry. He keeps me grounded. Kind of like you do."

Levi could easily picture his shy smile and leaned against the porch railing. "Good for you. So can I assume your conversation with Orry went well?"

"Super well. Honestly, he was more annoyed that you're eleven years older than me than he was about me coming out. That surprised me a little but also not really. He's protective, and you have so much more life experience."

Of that, Levi was keenly aware, and he worried what George would think of him when he found out how much experience Levi had. "What about Orry's Thanksgiving lie?"

"He's dating a girl named Zoey, and he was afraid to tell me because he didn't want to pressure me to get out of the apartment and try to find a life of my own. I was able to do that all by myself, and he was proud of me. I even suggested the four of us go out on a double date sometime."

Levi smiled across the yard, beyond proud of George and everything he'd accomplished this week. "I'd like that. I want to get to know Orry better, and I'm sure you'll enjoy meeting the woman who caught his eye."

"Yeah. Orry deserves someone special. He's been my rock, but I want him to have a life almost more than I want one myself. Orry went through bad stuff of his own, and I want him to be happy."

"I remember you mentioning that about Orry. And I love that you want your brother to be happy, but it's okay to focus on your own happiness first. Take the slow steps you need to proceed comfortably. If you push yourself too hard, too fast, you could backslide and undo all your progress."

"More advice from rehab?"

George's voice was light and curious, which kept Levi from taking any offense. "Yes. I fell very, very hard at one point in my life, George. You let fear send you into hiding, but I let grief send me into a very different place. I'd like to tell you about it one day."

"I can tell from your voice how painful it was, and I appreciate your honesty and trust. When you're ready to tell me, I'll listen. I care about you, Levi."

"I care about you, too. And I am thrilled that your conversation with Orry went well, and that he's accepting you. All parts of you."

George chuckled. "Well, I think he's still a tiny bit hesitant about me dating you, but it's all about the age difference and experience difference. But I assured him you aren't taking advantage of me. I have been completely consenting in everything we've done together. And I hope we can do more soon."

"Yeah? Like what?"

If someone could blush over the phone, Levi was pretty sure George had mastered it. "You know. Other stuff. In bed."

"Hmm. Next time we're alone together, you'll have to elaborate. And we'll talk about next steps."

"Cool, okay." George sounded relieved, as if he thought Levi wanted to talk about hyperprivate stuff over the phone. Levi had never been a fan of phone sex or anything similar, especially not these last few years.

"Since I have you on the phone," Levi hedged, "Christmas is Friday, and I know you probably always spend the day with Orry, but I was wondering if you wanted to see me for a little while? Mack and Wes have a new tradition of hosting dinner on Christmas Day, because Reyes and Miles go camping on Christmas Eve, and I didn't know if you'd want to come." Okay, he'd kind of rambled that but Levi was a little nervous about this. And considering the dangerous trick riding he did, it took a lot to make him genuinely nervous.

George was quiet a moment. "You don't have family you need to be with on Christmas Day?"

"I'll be here with Robin, and I consider a lot of these guys here to be family now. My blood family is wintering with the rodeo in Santa Fe. I won't see them but I'll definitely talk to my dad. I'm assuming you don't speak with your parents anymore?"

"No. Just our grandparents. I think I'd like to go visit them on Christmas morning. It's been ages since I've seen them in person." Levi could almost picture George standing straighter. "Yes, I'd like to have Christmas Day dinner with you. Orry usually works part of the day, anyway, so maybe now he'll spend it with his girlfriend."

"And you'll spend it with your boyfriend."

George made a noise of delight that wasn't quite laughter. "God, a few weeks ago I never thought I'd hear or say those words. Or do anything for Christmas except sit around in the apartment with a frozen turkey dinner."

Levi wanted to reach through his phone and hug George. "I'm beyond thrilled to offer you new experiences, this week and beyond. You give me more than you realize, George. Part of me died when Xander died, and I lost a part of myself for a while after. Then Grant happened, and I wasn't sure how I'd trust again. But you make it easy to trust you, and that has nothing to do with how sheltered you've been these last few years. It's all about you and your great big heart."

"I'd kiss you for that if we were in the same room."

"And I would absolutely let you. I adore your kisses, George. Never doubt that you're desirable simply for being the man you are." *Especially if this delicate thing between us doesn't last.*

But Levi didn't want to think like that this soon into their developing relationship. Maybe a few weeks into the future but not now. Not yet.

"What are you up to today?" George asked. "Playing with the cats?"

Levi chuckled. "I did for a bit this morning. Then Robin came by and kidnapped me to lunch at Mack's house."

"Shit, did my call interrupt your lunch? I'm sorry, I didn't mean to."

"It's okay. We were done eating and just talking around the table with drinks. You didn't interrupt anything, and I was happy to hear from you, I promise. I worried about you speakin' to Orry, and I can tell now I was wrong to worry. You and he have a very special bond."

"If I can get personal for a second, did Xander know you were bisexual?"

Levi considered the question briefly. "I don't remember us ever talkin' about it explicitly. He was very much openly gay since our early teens, but I was less open about the people I chose to be with. I just let the person speak to me. But I also never really dated anyone that seriously. With our traveling lifestyle, it was impossible to establish a real relationship with anyone who wasn't part of the company, which is why Robin and Xander worked so well and for a long time."

"Thank you for answering my question."

"Of course. There are certain parts of my past I'm not ready to talk about but my time with Lucky's isn't one of them. I loved that life." *And sometimes I miss that life, but I also enjoy having roots for a change.*

"I can hear that in your voice," George said. "How much you loved the rodeo. I can't imagine how much it hurt to lose your brother and then leave that life. And to have it happen on Christmas. What a horrible day to lose your brother."

Old grief squeezed Levi's heart, and his mind flashed to the expression of utter devastation on Robin's face as he held a limp Xander in his arms. "It was an accident, and it made the holidays hard for a while. But it was better last year because I was here with Robin, and Robin finally spoke to Dad again. They'd been at odds since Xander died, and I think the reconciliation helped all three of us heal more. No, I'm positive it did."

"I'm glad." George cleared his throat hard. "Well, I won't keep you any longer from your friends. I'm sure we'll talk again before then, but what time Christmas Day? And, um, I did get my license but I haven't driven on my own in ages."

"I don't mind picking you up. I'll double-check the exact time of dinner and text you. And if you want to spend the night, that's okay, too." It was a bold comment for Levi but he didn't regret it. Two hours of driving to bring his boyfriend to Christmas dinner was no hardship but he truly hoped George would want to spend more time with him and the cats.

"I'll, um. Let you know?"

The way he phrased it as a question was intensely adorable. "Of course, and no pressure at all. It's just an idea, if you're game. And even if all we do is share my bed, that's fine. I want everything between us to always be consensual."

George made a soft noise. "Because of how Grant betrayed you?"

"That's part of it." *And I am not going into the rest of it today.* "But I've always been a fan of enthusiastic consent. Only what you agree to. Heck, I'll sleep on the couch if you want to stay over and sleep in the bed, just so we have more time to spend together."

"That's actually kind of romantic. You sleeping on the couch. I liked how we slept the last night at the ranch, all close together. But I, uh, like I said I'll let you know what I want."

Levi fought back a tiny nugget of disappointment. "Of course. No pressure ever. This is our relationship, and we'll go at the pace that's right for us."

"I didn't say that because I'm scared of spending the night with you, Levi. We spent six nights together in a small room, and I always felt safe. But that was also in a house full of other people. You live in a clearing with no one else in sight."

"I hear you and understand." He didn't completely but this was George's truth, and he'd listen and absorb. "I promise you're safe alone with me but I do hear you."

"I know you do. Even though we aren't talking in person, I can see the reassurances in your eyes. I'm excited to see you on Christmas Day."

Levi fought a tiny nugget of disappointment that they wouldn't see each other again until the end of the week but that was part of dating someone long distance. And even if they didn't see each other in person, they may still "see" each other with their phone apps during the week. He hoped so. He missed George's smile and wide blue eyes.

"I'm excited, too," Levi said. "And call or text me anytime. I don't have any big plans leading up to Christmas Day other than tasting Shawn's cookies."

George laughed. "Why does that sound like a euphemism?"

"It's literal." He explained the cookie tradition.

"That's really cool. A fun way to spend the holidays with your partner. Just like Miles and Reyes going camping. Did Lucky's have any kind of traditions?"

"A few. On Christmas, we did up a big dinner for everyone who was wintering with us. Some people had other family to get to, but a lot of folks are like the ranch hands here. This is their home and their found family."

"I'm glad places like that exist to take in strays like you and Slater. He opened up a bit about his past to me and Orry, and I don't know what you know so that's all I'll say. But Clean Slate was a soft spot for him to land until he met Derrick and learned to craft."

"I don't know either man at all, but I'm glad they found each other. Everyone who wants one deserves someone special."

George let out a long, low breath. "Yeah. Anyway, I won't keep you from your friends any longer. I've got work to get back to. Getting ahead means more time off leading up to Christmas and beyond."

"Enjoy your porn."

He laughed. "Talk to you later."

"Bye." Levi reluctantly put his phone in his back pocket, a bit adrift after hearing George's voice again.

But they'd be together again on Christmas, and that was a gift. "Thank you for putting George in my life," he said to the bright winter sky. "Just when I needed him."

He went back inside to join the others, excited for what the rest of the week would bring.

Chapter Nineteen

George was freaking out a little bit on the ride to meet up with Levi, which was kind of ridiculous for two reasons.

One, he'd just had a fantastic Christmas morning with Orry and their grandparents. George had hugged them for the first time in years. They'd shared small presents, talked about all kinds of things, and Orry even showed off photos of Zoey. George kept Levi under wraps for now, unsure how his grandparents would feel about him being gay. That was a reveal for another time, not their first holiday as a quartet in years.

Two, Orry was driving him to the same rest stop for an afternoon dinner with near-strangers without the buffer of his twin. But he'd have Levi there, and that was everything. Still. Strange freak-out happening, and he did his best to hide it from Orry. He didn't want Orry to change his mind about having dinner with Zoey's family out of guilt over George's anxiety. He could do this.

I need to do this.

A few days ago, George had done some online research, and he'd found a worksheet of coping skills for anxiety. The progressive muscle relaxation was a favorite but it would have been a bit too obvious with Orry right there. Challenging his thoughts and fears seemed to be working, as his stress levels went down a fraction.

"You still feel okay about this?" Orry asked as they neared the truck stop. "Staying over?"

"Yes." His voice wobbled a bit. Mentally, he was great with this but something else—emotional, maybe?—was nervous. He'd napped with Levi in his bed but never slept over with a guy somewhere this remote. He believed Levi with his whole heart about respecting what George would and wouldn't want. No, this nervousness was rooted in his past with Adrian and the way he'd disrespected George's boundaries.

"And I'm looking forward to spending time with Levi's friends," he continued. "Really spending time, not standing off to the side like at Thanksgiving. I've been to the cabin, so it's not a completely strange place, and I saw a lot of the other guests at the ranch last week. I promise, if I start to get overwhelmed, I will call you."

But I don't think I will because Levi will be with me.

In only a few weeks, Levi had become his dearest friend, other than Orry. They'd texted frequently during the week, spoken on the phone every day, and even Skyped a few times. They talked about important things, goofy things, and everything in between. Levi loved telling him stories about Lucky's, and he spun vivid pictures of the men, women, and horses he'd worked with. So many good memories of his entire life, up until Xander died.

George told him a few humorous stories about awkward moments in scenes he'd captioned. He was limited on those, though, because many of the studios had him sign a confidentiality form, especially for scenes that hadn't released from the company yet. It wasn't always easy figuring out how to describe the way some people grunted or groaned.

Orry pulled into the parking lot and found Levi's truck already waiting close to where they'd swapped the first time. "Thanks again for agreeing to meet halfway," George said as he leaned between the two front seats to grab a gym bag he'd borrowed from Orry.

I need to buy one of my own for future overnights.

The thought made him smile.

"No problem," Orry replied. "Zoey's family's house is on my way back, anyway. It's fine. Have fun, I mean it. Merry Christmas, bro."

George hugged Orry, then climbed out. Levi impressed the hell out of him by having gotten out of his cab, walked to the passenger side door, and he was waiting with the door open. So gentlemanly and adorable that George had to greet him with a kiss. "Hi."

"Hi back." Levi's bright smile settled a bit more of George's strange freak-out. "Take your bag?"

"Okay." He handed it over and climbed into the truck. Levi shut his door.

Instead of putting his light bag in the truck bed, Levi carried it to his side and put it on the seat between them. Thank God. George would have spent the whole drive wondering if it would fly out the back on the interstate— especially since it had Levi's present in it. Orry drove away first, and after a quick look around, Levi leaned over and planted a long, sensual hello kiss on George. The kind that might have led to more if they'd been somewhere with privacy.

"I've missed doing that," Levi said after they pulled apart.

"Me too. Missed you. Merry Christmas." They'd spoken earlier that morning after Levi's run, but George needed to say it in person.

"Merry Christmas, George."

They shared another quick kiss. George waited until they were on the interstate before asking, "How did your tribute go this afternoon?" He'd been so moved when Levi told him that he and Robin had stood in the corral at the exact time of Xander's death and remembered him. Shared stories. Last year, it had been the moment Robin reconnected with his former father-in-law, who still considered Robin his son.

"It was lovely. We talked about Xander again. Then Dad called and we all spoke together on speaker. Remembered him as a family."

"Cool. I'm glad you had that."

"Thank you." They were on a smooth stretch of highway so Levi reached over and held George's hand. "How was your visit with your grandparents?"

"All four of us cried." George chuckled, unashamed of himself or his emotions. "It was beyond amazing to see them again. To hug them. Even Orry cried a little. We brought them a miniature Christmas tree, and we sang a few carols. Orry told them about Zoey." He bit his lip, uncertain how Levi would react to this. "I didn't tell them about you or that I'm gay. I was scared they'd react badly and I didn't want to ruin our first visit in three years."

Levi squeezed his hand and tossed him a warm smile. "I'm not upset or offended. This is your family, and you need to do this at your pace. Rebuild your relationship with them. Let them get to know you better. If they took you and Orry in for years, they must love you very much. Believe in that love, all right?"

"I'll try. Thank you."

"Of course."

He loved Levi's positive attitude about life the most, and George basked in it for the rest of the trip to Garrett. The road to the ranch and ghost town were becoming familiar to him now. The beauty of the land soaked into his bones, and that deep-down anxiety calmed a little bit more.

Other vehicles were already parked in front of the cabin when they arrived for the three o'clock dinner, maybe ten minutes early. Less time for George to have to make small talk before the meal began. George's hands twitched with nerves as he climbed out of the truck, but he steeled himself with a few deep, calming breaths. Four-second inhale, four-second hold, six-second exhale. Repeat. He knew these people. And he had Levi as a touchstone.

I can do this. I want to do this for me, for Orry, and for Levi. Come on, Thompson. Focus. You know what you're doing, so do it.

The last three lines were a familiar pep talk from his competition days, words he told himself over and over as he warmed up and waited for his turn. Words he'd come up with himself, not words given to him by Adrian. Adrian's pep talks often went along the lines of "Don't let me down, kid."

No. No Adrian thoughts on Christmas Day.

Levi didn't have to knock. Robin opened the door wearing a bright smile and a Santa hat. He also had more similar things in his hands. "No admittance without a Santa hat, elf hat, or reindeer antlers," he said. "Wes's orders and it's his house."

George started laughing at the hilarious absurdity

of it and asked for the antlers. Levi plopped an elf hat on his head, and it definitely didn't look as good as his cowboy hat. Robin let them inside and, sure enough, everyone had something on their head. George recognized a lot of the guests, but a few were only vaguely familiar from Thanksgiving and he couldn't remember their names. Two very unexpected faces approached, and maybe he shouldn't have been surprised, but George warmly greeted Derrick and Slater.

And of course they'd be here, since Derrick was Wes's brother-in-law, and the rest of the family was lingering near the kitchen. Neither man made a big deal out of George showing up with Levi beyond an obvious wink from Derrick. George would get questions from his neighbors this weekend, for sure.

Wes, on the other hand, had no such tact. As soon as he realized George was there—and not with Slater and Derrick—he bounced over with a smear of flour on one cheek and asked, "Oh my God, are you two dating? How cute are you both?"

"Down boy," Derrick said. "Forgive my brother-in-law his rudeness but he's got a never-ending romantic streak, and he's constantly trying to couple people up."

"Hey, I totally called Miles and Reyes before they happened."

A little overwhelmed by the attention, George blurted out, "Yes, Levi and I are dating. Okay?"

Wes squealed. "I knew it! Congrats, honey, Levi is a keeper. This one." He poked Derrick in the chest. "Meh."

Derrick tried to pinch him and Wes darted back to the kitchen. George glanced at Levi, whose gentle smile told him he'd done and said the right thing. Revealing their relationship at George's pace. George stuck close to Levi during the big sit-down meal, more intimate than the huge shindig of Thanksgiving. Shawn sat on George's other side and the familiar face helped keep him relaxed as he ate the amazing food. He usually chose small portions of the healthiest, least fatty foods, but it was Christmas and George was here. Happy.

He took a scoop of macaroni and cheese for the first time in years, as well as a thick, buttery biscuit. Delicious.

Conversations happened mostly around him, and George replied to the occasional question thrown his way. Mostly, he concentrated on eating and observing the other faces at the table. And trying to remember all their names. He recognized everyone from the ranch or ghost town, as well as Wes's parents, Wes's sister and her husband, and their adorable little girl. But there were too many, and he was out of practice.

Thankfully, no one seemed to hold it against him or ask direct questions about his relationship with Levi. He allowed himself to enjoy these moments with a family created by blood and friendship and marriage. Nothing in his life had ever been as boisterous or genuine, and he ached to be part of this. A true part of it.

He caught Slater watching him a few times from the far end of the table, a knowing half smile on his face. Slater had resisted being folded into the Clean Slate family for a long time, preferring to remain at arm's length until he'd realized how many people cared about him.

George half smiled back at his neighbor.

Various desserts accompanied the meal but George was full of food and curious about a different sort of dessert. A private one with Levi. He refused offers of different cakes and pies. When Levi cast him a curious look, George held his gaze and tried to put his thoughts into his eyes.

This isn't about food. This is about privacy. Please.

Levi's expression shifted into understanding, and he also passed on dessert. It was rude to leave right away, though, so they sat through several minutes of the others eating, George's pulse racing with anticipation.

"I hate to be the early party pooper," Levi said, "but George and I need to be heading out. Wes and Mrs. Bentley, the meal was amazing. Thank you for your hard work."

Thankfully, no one questioned why they had to leave, whether because George needed to get back to the city, or for other personal reasons. George shook a few hands, and accepted hugs from both Shawn and Robin on his way to the door. He'd genuinely enjoyed the meal and the companionship, and he adored Levi for getting them out of there before he could possibly become overwhelmed.

"You did great," Levi said on the walk to the truck. "You were ready to leave, right? I didn't read you wrong."

"I was ready." George grabbed Levi's arm by the fender of the truck to stop him. Met his gaze. "I wasn't overwhelmed by the company, not exactly. They're all lovely people. More like ready to spend some time alone. It's been a while."

Levi's expression went predatory for a flash before settling into a sexy smirk. "Alone, huh? Just you, me and my three cats?"

"Exactly. All five of us in your bed?"

"That might be a little crowded."

George's belly flipped with want. "Then we'll kick the cats out and barricade the cat door."

Levi quirked an eyebrow. "It actually has a lock for when we're traveling. The last thing I need is for one of them to try and get out when I hit a red light."

"Good thinking." As much as George wanted to lean in and do something sexy, he was very aware of their open surroundings. And that anyone could be watching them from a window or the front door, and anything beyond quick kisses were still private for him. For now. "Can we go?"

"Definitely."

Even though it was a one-minute drive up to Levi's place, it seemed to take forever. Probably because George was eager to spend time with his boyfriend. His first-ever boyfriend, who was kind, patient, spiritual, and who seemed to always want to see the best in people. So different from George, who was skeptical of everyone at first meeting. It's why he'd shied away from all his neighbors until the night Slater and Derrick came to his rescue.

The simple fact that they'd cared enough to check on a stranger had told him a lot about their character. And it had helped him build trust with them.

The strong trust he had with Levi stemmed from the fact that the man had allowed a near-stranger to care for his beloved cat for a week, without knowing more than surface facts about him. If George hadn't taken a walk that day, he wouldn't be here now. Socializing with new friends.

Happy.

Levi carried his bag into the familiar little house,

and they both left their shoes by the front door. It didn't take long for the cats to swarm inside. George bent to lift Ginger into his arms and she head-bumped his chin, already purring up a storm. "Did you miss me, sweetheart?"

"We both did," Levi said. "Do you want your bag in the loft or bathroom?"

"Down here for now, actually. I have something for you." His cheeks heated, and he tried to hide his face in Ginger's fur.

"Oh? I have something for you, too. Your present."

"Yeah?" George had hoped for a gift but hadn't expected one. "Can I be super-duper cheesy and say being with you today is already a great present?"

Levi carded his fingers through George's hair in a tender, affectionate gesture. "I feel the same way." He put the gym bag on the sofa and approached the bookshelf stairs. A paper Christmas tree was taped to it and a rectangular, wrapped box leaned against the shelf beneath it. It jangled a bit when Levi picked it up.

They were doing this now. Stomach tightening, George retrieved his own gift from his bag and dug out a small, square box he'd wrapped in the candy cane paper Orry had left over from last year. They sat close together on the sofa. It wasn't the same as waking up together on Christmas morning, but George couldn't complain. Or think too far ahead about doing that next year.

"I wanted to do—" they both said in stereo. Levi laughed and deferred to George. "I wanted to do something meaningful," George continued and handed over the small box. "Merry Christmas."

Levi put George's gift aside and accepted the box. He examined it slowly, as if trying to solve the puzzle of what was inside, instead of simply tearing into it and finding out. "Thank you for this gift, George."

"You haven't even seen it yet."

"Doesn't matter. It will have a great deal of meaning, because you mean a great deal to me." With an adorable bite to his lower lip, Levi carefully unwrapped the paper and put it on the sofa, showing off a white jewelry-style box. The sides weren't taped so he pulled the lid off. George held his breath as Levi folded a piece of red tissue paper to the side.

Levi's breath caught, his blue eyes widening in wonder. "Oh wow." He lifted a metal keychain from the tissue and held it up.

"I found an artist online who does commissions. I was the last person she could fit in before Christmas, and I really hope you like it."

"It's amazing." Levi looked as if he wanted to cry. "Oh, George, thank you."

George let out a relieved breath. He'd sent pictures of all three of Levi's cats to an artist who specialized in metal jewelry engraving, and she had cut each cat's face out of the same piece of metal in a circle, kind of like a wreath. Then she had lightly painted each cat to the correct colors. "You're welcome. You can actually use it if you want, because she has a guarantee on the work, instead of just keeping it around as a trinket. Unless, uh, you don't want to run around with three cats on your keys."

Levi answered that question by dragging him into a long, possessive kiss that seemed to say thank you and many other things at once. "I'll definitely use it. I want to show it off. This is a lovely gift, thank you so much. Gosh, it makes my gift seem kind of ordinary."

"Nah. To paraphrase your own words, it's special because it's from you. Now gimme."

"You're adorable." Levi handed him the bigger, somewhat noisy box.

George resisted the urge to shake it and simply unwrapped it. His breath caught. It was a Scrabble Onyx Limited Edition board game. The box itself was jet-black with white lettering and it just looked expensive. "Holy shit. Wow."

"Is it okay?"

"Are you kidding? It's amazing. I've never seen this version in stores."

"It came out ages ago. I went looking online for fun, interesting Scrabble boards, so I didn't have to settle for the basic big-box-store sets, and I really liked the look of this one."

"I think it's beautiful." George laughed and kissed Levi's cheek. "Now I can keep beating your ass at Scrabble."

"You wish."

"I don't wish, I know." He put the game aside and snuggled in closer for a proper hug. Levi held him close, and George tucked his head under his chin, loving the feel of the man beside him. He'd loved everything about today, and he hoped they kept enjoying themselves right upstairs.

Sporty jumped onto the couch and began to battle the wrapping paper, paws lashing out, teeth gnashing like an animal possessed. She fought it right into George's lap, where her claws pierced through his jeans. George's yelp was high pitched enough that it startled a hissing Sporty to the floor.

Levi chuckled. "That's what you get for clawing him, girl."

Sporty gave him a betrayed look before flouncing out the cat door.

"You never lack for entertainment with them around, do you?" George asked.

"Never. You should see the epic fights they get into when they're stuck inside the home during traveling time."

You should see was a turn of phrase that everyone used when they thought a person should witness an event, so George tried not to read too much into the comment. Into the idea of traveling in this tiny house with Levi and the cats. The idea intrigued him. Seeing the country like he had when he was younger. But this thing between them was still too new to dream that far ahead. "I can't imagine how crazy it gets," George said.

"Crap, I'm being rude. Are you thirsty?"

He surprised himself by blurting out, "Not for a drink."

Levi quirked an eyebrow, his eyes flittering briefly down to George's lips. "Thirsty for something else?"

"Yes." George had watched what probably amounted to a full year's worth of porn, and he'd heard every possible way of someone asking for what he wanted. But for some reason, words failed him. He felt like a foolish kid, which only made his face flame.

"Hey." Levi squeezed his wrist. "How about we go upstairs and relax on the bed? We can just chill, kiss, whatever, until you're sure it's what you want."

He wanted to say, "I am sure," but what came out instead was, "Okay." Maybe initiating it would be easier than asking for it. He did want it but…ugh, why did sex have to be so complicated? "Let's go upstairs."

Levi led the way, and George eagerly followed, taking a moment to ogle Levi's ass during the ascent. He had a perfect ass that bunched and swayed beneath tight denim, and not for the first time, George wondered what it would feel like to be inside Levi. To experience that unique pleasure with someone he truly cared about and trusted.

The familiar, low-ceiling loft quickly filled with all three cats, and George couldn't help laughing at the way the three furballs started wrestling all over the mattress. "Am I going to have to lock you three out?" Levi asked as he shooed them away. They didn't go farther than the top of the stairs, as if unsure of what was happening.

"Your cats are voyeurs."

"They're clingy." He pulled his cell out of his pocket. "It's getting late and too chilly to lock them out, especially if I get distracted and forget to unlock the cat door later."

George shrugged as he stretched out on the bed. "I don't mind. I love Ginger, and the trio keeps things interesting."

Levi's eyebrows twitched. "They really do. May I join you down there?"

"You better." He rolled to his right side as Levi slid on the bed facing him. Each of them had a different pillow, and it felt like too far away. But also just right for now. Levi inched closer, and George did the same, hoping Levi made the first move. Except Levi seemed content to wait for George's signals. Giving George all the power when he was used to having none.

"I've never had a Christmas like this," George whispered.

Levi brushed a knuckle down George's cheek. "Like what, sweetheart?"

Sweetheart.

"Full of joy and love. Between this morning with Orry and our grandparents, and then dinner at the cabin. Being here with you." George didn't want to delve too deeply into the past, but... "Growing up, Christmas was stiff. We had a tree. Stockings. One present each because, as our parents said, they were spending so much money between my skating and Orry's musical interests. There was just no real joy. Not like today."

"I'm glad I could help give you a portion of today's joy. This is the best Christmas I've had in a long time, too. For different reasons, but the emotions are similar, I think." Levi's eyes went soft lidded. "You were very unexpected, George."

"You were too. Very unexpected, but in the best way." George rested a hand on Levi's shoulder, enjoying the warm contact. "I wanted to get a life so badly but had no idea how to go about it. How to tell my brother who I really am. How to even attempt to take what I want."

Desire burned in Levi's eyes. "What do you want?"

"You." George waited for embarrassment over his bluntness that never came, so he grabbed on to his confidence with both hands. "I want you, Levi."

"I'm all yours."

George lunged, rolling Levi to his back and covering the bigger man with his slimmer body. Knees on either side of Levi's hips, he rubbed their groins together as he came in for a long, exploratory kiss. Deeper than their first kisses and far more meaningful now. Tonight was about more than spending a holiday together. It was a new step toward something bigger between them.

Levi ground up into him, hands loose on George's hips, giving George all the control. It endeared the older man to him even more and gave George the confidence to be aggressive. To lick and stroke into Levi's mouth, plundering and seeking, their erections riding each other through two layers of denim. He kissed his way around Levi's neck, tasting hot skin and the slight tang of sweat, and he wanted more. More skin to taste, more of Levi's body to admire and enjoy.

Curbing his natural instinct to ask, George instead demanded, "Clothes off. Under the covers."

Levi released a gentle, growly sound that sent wiggles of arousal through George's belly. He rolled off Levi and tugged at his own belt. The mattress bounced as they both got naked as quickly as possible without bumping their heads on the low roof of the loft. Levi pulled back the covers and, after they both climbed into the middle, tugged just the top sheet up around their waists. George didn't know how the home's heat system worked but it was warm up there.

And it was about to get warmer.

They both lay on their sides, heads propped up on one hand, facing each other. Levi's eyes gleamed, and he seemed to vibrate with the need to act first, but restrained himself. Waited for George to move. George studied the tan swaths of Levi's bare chest. The work-hardened muscles of his abs and arms, and the smattering of dark hair on his chest. He never stopped marveling at how beautiful Levi was, and that he'd chosen someone as plain as George.

With a single finger, George traced a line from the

base of Levi's throat, slowly down between his pecs to his navel. He swirled into that navel, and Levi huffed, not quite laughing. Down farther into the thin happy trail that led to his destination. He ran his finger up the length of Levi's dick and paused to rub around the slit. Levi inhaled sharply, hips jerking once, silently asking for more.

"Whatever you want, sweetheart," Levi whispered.

"I want to try sucking you." The bold words popped out but George didn't blush. He meant them. He really wanted to share this with Levi. To know what it felt like. What Levi tasted like.

Levi licked his lips. "Are you sure?"

"Positive."

"Then yes, please." He rolled to his back, then scooted a bit higher up the bed so he was half reclining against the two pillows, his legs spread lewdly. Showing off his hard, red dick. George knelt between his legs and reached out, but Levi caught his wrist. "I don't have anything but I do have condoms if you want to use one."

"I believe you and no, I want to taste you. Have for a while but I've been too nervous to try."

Levi pulled him up for a soft kiss. "It's not something you have to master or even enjoy. If you don't like it, you can stop, okay? I don't want you to feel pressured to finish something you've started. Consent can be revoked at any time during sex."

"I know." George kissed him again. "But thank you for saying it. You are…amazing."

"You're pretty amazing yourself."

Inspired by his position, George took his time kissing and licking his way down Levi's torso. Tasting his way across smooth, sun-kissed skin. Loving the way

Levi's belly quivered with want. It stoked George's own arousal, and part of him wanted to quit the foreplay and get to the main event, but he was enjoying himself too much. Enjoying having complete control for a little while. A different kind of control than hiding in his apartment and avoiding people.

Control over his happiness.

Levi's cock bumped his chin, and George smiled. Then he dipped his tongue into Levi's navel just to hear him chuckle and feel his abs ripple. He was doing this for Levi as much as himself, giving Levi pleasure, and George loved it. He reveled in it in a way he hadn't since his first first-place skate in a national competition. But this wasn't about impressing his parents, his coach or the judges.

This was all for him and Levi.

George sat back on his ankles and wrapped his hand around Levi's shaft, stroking lightly while he watched Levi's face. Levi held his gaze, lips parted, panting lightly. Aroused and anticipating. It fueled George's desire to make Levi soar—even if he wasn't very good at it at first.

He continued stroking him as he leaned forward and inhaled the spicy scent of Levi. His mouth watered, desperate to put that scent on his tongue and experience this new thing. A small pearl of fluid appeared in the slit, and George couldn't help himself. He licked it, and a burst of salt hit his tongue. Levi gasped.

Oh yes, I like this.

George made a soft, almost desperate sound he didn't recognize from himself before taking the head of Levi's cock into his mouth. Soft, sharp, and exactly right. He used a bit of his day job knowledge and rubbed his tongue against the underside of Levi's glans, against that sensitive bundle of nerves, and that earned him a long moan from Levi. Fingers brushed through his hair but didn't stay. Didn't direct or force. He worked the glans until Levi lost a bit of his previously perfect control and thrust up into George's mouth.

Not too far, though, and George stilled him by wrapping his hand around the base of his dick and holding firm. He took a bit more of Levi's length, loving this new exploration, as the heady taste of his boyfriend filled his senses, leaving him a bit lightheaded from the experience. He went down as far as he could before his gag reflex said no more, then pulled back to suck on the glans again, because Levi really seemed to like that. Levi's upper body thrashed, and his hands clenched at the bottom sheet. So much control that George's heart swelled with even more affection for the man.

Using his hand as a gauge, George worked steadily up and down Levi's shaft, wetting the skin, enjoying the way his tongue glided over heat and steel.

"So good, sweetheart," Levi panted. "So fucking good."

The fact that George had managed to get Levi to swear again spurred George on even more. Fueled by every gasp and cry he earned from Levi, he used his free hand to massage Levi's sac until his balls were high and tight.

"Gonna come soon," Levi said. "You don't have to—ah!"

Oh yes, he did. George used both hands and tongue to work Levi harder, faster, doing his best to bring his boyfriend to a messy, spit-soaked orgasm. Levi cried out and thrust up, into George's sure grip, and George did his best to swallow the salty, slightly bitter load.

To lick and suck and drag every single second of pleasure out of Levi, whose body trembled from his release.

He didn't want to stop, but Levi let out a soft protesting noise, and George released his softening cock from his mouth. Sat back and marveled at what he'd done. Sparkling eyes stared at him down the length of Levi's body, his face red and expression almost dazed. George licked his lips, unsure how he looked or if he'd been as good as—

Levi lunged, knocking George over on his back, mouth covering George's in the most intense, claiming kiss of his life. Levi's tongue licked into his mouth as if trying to get his own come back, and George surrendered. The pressure of Levi's thigh on his groin became too much, and George moaned as he came, coating their bellies and smoothing the way even more. Levi didn't relent for a long time, but the kisses gradually slowed. Became calmer, more sensual and less frantic. When Levi finally released his mouth, George's lips felt swollen and he didn't care.

"Thank you," Levi panted. "That was the best sex of my life, I mean it, George."

Levi had never lied to him, so George took the compliment. "I loved everything about it. It's easy with you, Levi. And we are definitely doing this again."

"Oh yes, we are." He nuzzled his nose against George's. "It's still early. Do you want to rinse off, make hot chocolate and watch a cheesy Christmas movie?"

"Absolutely."

They did exactly that, and George couldn't remember a better, more relaxing—and satiating—Christmas Day ever.

Chapter Twenty

Levi couldn't remember a better, more relaxing Christmas in his entire adult life. First waking up to find Robin had left him a gift under his paper tree—new running trainers—and then a long run in the crisp winter air. A hearty breakfast with his friends in the guesthouse, eventually followed by an amazing conversation with Robin and Dad to honor Xander. His trip out to get George. Dinner at Mack's.

The incredible sex he'd shared with George later. George had seemed like a completely different person that night, full of confidence and taking control. Telling Levi what he wanted. Giving Levi so much pleasure he'd lost his mind a little bit. Even such a simple thing as watching *It's A Wonderful Life*—because George had never seen it—while drinking cocoa had been everything Levi never knew he needed.

And he wanted to protect it.

He watched George sleep, his face faintly lit by moonlight that filtered through the loft's various small windows. George looked peaceful, almost like an angel with his shaggy blond hair and strikingly fair skin. They'd gone to bed in their boxers, and Levi marveled at the amount of trust he'd earned with George in only five weeks. He was nothing like the shy, panicked boy he'd first met on Thanksgiving.

George was alive and thriving, and while he recognized that George had done the bulk of the work, Levi loved knowing he'd helped George on his journey. But would their journeys always travel the same path? He hadn't told George yet, because Levi still wasn't sure what he thought about it, and he needed to sit on it for a while. There was no hurry for a decision anyway.

After he, Robin and Dad had conference called as a trio, Dad had asked to speak to Levi privately. Robin had headed back to his cabin, leaving Levi alone in the corral. Levi had perched on the set of steps the horsemen used for shorter riders or greenhorns who couldn't mount on their own.

"What's up, Dad?" Levi asked. "Everything okay at home?"

"Nothin's wrong, son, but I've come to a decision that I think you deserve to hear first." Dad's voice was clear, no hint of worry or stress. "It's about Lucky's."

His heart began thumping against his ribs. "Is the rodeo in trouble? Can I help?"

"No, we're not in trouble. Far from it. Potter's already working on a full spring schedule, and we've got all our regular summer spots lined up. The business is solid, don't worry about that."

"Then what kind of decision?"

"It's a promise I made to your mother before she passed."

Levi closed his eyes and pinched the bridge of his nose. Mom had passed away from ovarian cancer when he was seventeen, and it had been a hard time for their family. He still missed her and hoped she would be proud of the man he'd become. When the land was quiet around him, he liked to think it whispered that she was.

"She always supported the rodeo and you boys being part of it," Dad continued, "but we did have arguments about it. When she first got sick, I promised her and God that I'd retire early enough that she and I could travel, just the two of us. See the places around the world we never got to see, because I was always too busy with the rodeo."

"And then she died."

Dad cleared his throat hard. "Yeah. But the last time she was awake, I told her I'd keep my promise. I told her I would retire when I turned sixty and see the places we talked about."

"You're retiring?" He turned sixty next September. Levi was glad to be sitting because his head spun a bit with shock. He never thought his dad would retire, not even after he dislocated his shoulder two years ago. "But what about Lucky's? You're the heart of the rodeo."

"I want Lucky's to go on, and Willard has offered to buy me out on more than one occasion. Take over when I'm ready to retire."

Levi nodded even though Dad couldn't see him. Willard was one of the most senior guys in the rodeo, and he'd been with them since Levi was a child. "I think he's a good choice. And you could use the money to travel."

"Yup, I could. But I also invested your mom's life insurance as a future retirement plan, knowing I couldn't go on with Lucky's forever, so I'm covered. It's not about the money, it's about family. My father started it, and I'd hate to be the last Peletier to own it. Willard taking over and eventually buying me out is my second choice." Levi saw the request sailing toward him before Dad lobbed it his way. "I want you to take over running it when I retire, Levi. It was always supposed to be your legacy."

A reflexive "I don't want it" died before it passed his lips. Levi had walked away from Lucky's after Xander died, allowing his grief to carry him far away from his family and into a long year of terrible decisions. Even after he got sober, Levi had never entertained the idea of going back to Lucky's—at least, not seriously. His wanderlust still existed, and the idea of traveling again...of performing in front of audiences of thousands...

"I have a job here that I love, Dad," Levi said. "I can't just leave before the season is over. I can't do that to Robin and Mack."

"It wouldn't happen the day of my birthday, son." Dad's tone had changed into something almost hopeful. "I'd stay with Lucky's until the end of our season, too. This will be my farewell tour, one last visit to places I've been traveling to my entire life. Saying goodbye."

Levi blinked several times, affected by the new grief in his father's voice as he spoke about another hard goodbye. Dad had already lost his own parents, his wife, and one son. Now he was losing his rodeo—if he sold out to Willard. If Levi took over, it would stay in the family longer.

He couldn't bring himself to break his dad's heart by saying no to taking over Lucky's, but he also couldn't commit to it. Not without a lot of meditating, soul searching...and more time with George. What would happen to his relationship with George if Levi ended up traveling ten months out of the year?

"Are you sure this is what you want to do, Dad?"

"It is. If my accident didn't tell me I should step

back, then my promise to your mother has convinced me. Besides, you're safe and happy and dating again, and Robin is safe and happy and in love. I can leave the country knowing my boys are well."

I will not cry. I will not cry.

"You know how much I love you, even when we were estranged," Levi said, voice too rough for his liking. "And you know how much I treasure my time at Lucky's. I am honored that you want me to run it but I can't give you an answer today."

"I understand, and I did not expect a yes or no today. You've got plenty of time, months, to decide what you want to do. I also haven't decided if I want to sell out to Willard or not, he's just the best second choice to run it."

If he didn't know Dad as well as he did, Levi might think his father was trying to manipulate him into saying yes. Saying no meant Dad potentially selling Lucky's to someone else, and there went Levi's inheritance. But money wasn't the most important thing to Levi. It never had been and never would be. If Dad walked away from Lucky's without another Peletier in charge, it was because he simply wanted a clean break from his old life.

Levi couldn't bear giving him a disingenuous "Let Willard run it for a few years and then I'll decide" kind of answer. It jerked everyone around, especially if Willard was prepared to buy Dad out now. As much as Levi wanted to travel again, he wasn't sure if running the rodeo was how he wanted to do it. But Dad had said he had a few months to decide.

"I'm definitely going to need time," Levi said. "There's just so much to consider."

"I know there is. And I don't want to steal you away

from the life you have if it's what makes you happiest, and I mean that. All I've ever wanted is for my boys to be happy."

"We are." Happy and—at least for Levi—now a little bit confused.

"Good. Well, I won't keep you much longer. I'm sure you've got your man to get back to soon."

They'd chatted briefly for a while longer, and then they had said their goodbyes. Levi had wandered the corral for a while, before he found himself heading toward one of the walking trails. But even out in the beautiful lands of Clean Slate Ranch, he hadn't been able to collect his swirling thoughts. He'd pushed the conversation with Dad aside and tried to enjoy the rest of his day.

A day that culminated with George asleep in his bed, a half smile on his face, eyes twitching as he dreamed about something that seemed pleasant. Levi was slowly, but surely, falling in love with George Thompson, but what did that mean for Levi's future? For the future of Lucky's? No, he couldn't give Lucky's more weight in his decision than his relationship with George, no matter how new and delicate it still was. Lucky's was his past; his future was still yet to be written.

"I want you in my future," he whispered to George. "I hope you want me in yours."

George snuffled once, then settled.

Content with his boyfriend by his side for now, Levi relaxed against his own pillow and tried to fall asleep.

Levi spent all the next morning lounging in bed with George—minus a quick break to eat an instant oatmeal breakfast for fuel—occasionally having sex, but mostly existing. Watching videos on Levi's tablet. Talking. Existing. They reluctantly left their bubble to clean up and dress, so they could drive down to the ranch for lunch at the guesthouse with their friends. George practically glowed with confidence, and it made Levi's heart swell.

He hated driving George back to the truck stop, but he'd agreed to meet Orry there at two. "I feel like a kid being swapped by two divorced parents," George joked.

"I'd drive you the entire way if I had to," Levi replied. "You're worth it."

That got him a smitten smile that Levi didn't allow himself to read too far into. They kissed for a while as they waited in their usual side of the parking lot, until a familiar car pulled in on the passenger side. Orry sprang from the car to give George a big hug, as if the pair had been separated for weeks instead of twenty-four hours. George leaned into the cab to grab his gym bag, blew Levi a kiss, and then followed his brother to their car.

Levi sent a quick text: Best Christmas ever. Talk to you soon, sweetheart.

George's reply came before Orry had completely left the lot: Same. Can't wait for next time.

With a goofy grin on his face, Levi texted Robin to ask if he was able to go riding in forty-five minutes. About ten minutes into his drive, Robin texted back an affirmative, and Levi returned to the ranch. Since it was the off-season, he parked near the guesthouse and headed for the barn, where Robin was already tacking his favorite horse Apple Jax.

"Hey, man," Robin said. "Wasn't sure if you wanted to ride Zodiac or another horse."

"Has she been exercised yet today?" Levi replied as he strode into the corral.

"Yeah, I saw Scott with her earlier."

"I'm not picky, so any of the mares who haven't been out yet."

"Cool. Finish these straps for me."

Levi completed saddling up Apple Jax for Robin while he went into the barn. Robin returned a few minutes later with Figuro, the horse George had ridden last week during their vacation. They tacked her together with few words spoken, both of them able to do this task in their sleep. Robin cast him a few curious looks, aware Levi needed to talk to him, but he didn't ask.

Yet.

Robin waited until they were about a hundred yards down one of the employee paths before he said, "Okay, what's up? Everything okay with George?"

"Everything is perfect with George. We had an amazing Christmas together. Zero regrets, and I think we're even stronger than ever. I hated dropping him off today and can't wait to see him again."

"So, not George. You and me aren't fighting. Do you have any other friends you could be having issues with?"

Levi snorted. "I'm not having issues, exactly. Yesterday, when I talked to Dad he told me something that I'm having trouble with, and he didn't swear me to secrecy. I need to talk it out with you, brother."

"Now I'm intrigued." Robin slowed Apple Jax so they were riding side by side along the trail. He tossed Levi a curious look. "Hit me."

"Dad's retiring at the end of the season."

Robin's entire body jerked with shock. "He's what? Why?"

"A promise he made to Mom before she died." His chest squeezed with old grief. "They were supposed to spend their retirement traveling the world. Now he plans on traveling alone in her honor."

"But…what about Lucky's?"

"That's the thing." He reined Figuro to a stop and it took Robin a few steps to pull Apple Jax back. "He asked me to take over the rodeo when he retires."

Robin's lips parted, his eyes going comically wide for an instant. "I mean… I knew he always intended for you and Xander to take over Lucky's one day, but this soon? What did you say?"

"I told him I couldn't make a decision, and I can't. I walked away from Lucky's for a reason, just like you did. I never intended to go back. I love working at Bentley, and I love being here. I've got George. But sometimes…"

Robin backed Apple Jax up until they were next to each other, his expression intense. "Sometimes what?"

"Sometimes I miss traveling." A bit of weight left Levi's chest with the admission. "Sometimes I miss the road. To be honest, if I hadn't met George, I probably would have driven down to Santa Fe during this break to see Dad. I don't know if I'm the kind of guy who will ever have permanent roots, like you and Shawn are gonna have with your house. It's why I hitch mine to the back of my truck."

"So you're considering it?"

"I don't know. I'm not dismissin' it outright. Dad said he's considering selling to Willard, but that's his number two choice."

Robin scowled. "Sounds like emotional—"

"Please don't say emotional blackmail, because you know that isn't Dad. He was laying out his options, and selling is an option. He'll be done and can move on, do something new with his life. He's happy knowing you and I are safe and enjoying our lives, he really is. I didn't get any sense of pressure from him to take over. I hate the idea of someone else who isn't a Peletier running the rodeo, but... I don't know if I can do it. Or if I even want to."

His best friend and brother studied him for a long time. "But you also aren't sure if you don't want to."

"Pretty much." Levi let out a long, slow breath that did nothing to focus him. "A part of me wants to say yes, to go back to that life. But the rest of me chafes at the idea of going back to such a stressful lifestyle. Always on the move, always trying to make the next gig. Praying for good weather and a good crowd so we can break even."

"Sounds like the part that chafes isn't stronger than the part that wants to say yes."

"I wish it was." And Levi meant it. He wanted to settle down and have roots, but what if that wasn't him? Or his future? Maybe his future was traveling across the country. But what about George? This was why he needed to talk to his brother. "I honestly don't know what I want."

"Have you talked to George about this?"

"No. Dad just brought it up yesterday, and this thing I have with George is still so fresh. I don't want to pressure him, and Dad said I have a few months to decide. I wanted to talk to you, because you're the most likely to get it."

Robin quirked an eyebrow. "George might surprise you."

"Maybe, but he's still young and figuring himself out."

"You know, if Shawn found out I was withholding

something this big because I didn't think he was mature enough to handle it, he'd probably deck me."

The mental image of the much slimmer Shawn decking Robin made Levi snort. "I don't think George is immature. Far from it. It's just…" Levi struggled to find the words to describe his feelings. "I don't want him to make a decision based on what he thinks *I* might want."

"Do you trust George to know his own mind?"

"Of course."

"Then talk to him about this. I had a similar problem last year with Shawn. When I flew out to New Mexico to drive back with Lucky's for opening day? I made the decision and travel plans before I told Shawn about it, and he had real, genuine fear that I was going to decide I wanted to go back to the rodeo. It didn't exactly drive a wedge between us, but we did have a few tense days where he thought I was leaving him."

"But you weren't and you didn't."

"I know that, and he knows that now." Robin reached out to rub Apple Jax's neck. "Sometimes fear is not rational, especially when it comes to relationships. If you can't say no straight out to Dad, then you need to talk to George about it."

"I will. Soon. I want us to get through the rest of the holidays first. And maybe see how things go once I'm back to work full time. Neither of us has ever done a long-distance relationship, and when Bentley opens again, I'll be a lot busier than I've been since I met George."

"Yeah, you will. And even busier if you go on tour with Lucky's."

"Unlikely."

"But not impossible?"

Levi shrugged, annoyed at himself for being unable to turn Dad down flat. He loved the life he had right now; he also loved the life he used to live with the rodeo. And he couldn't make himself turn Dad down flat, once and done. He hadn't been this turned around and confused since before rehab.

"I want to sit with this for a while," Levi finally said. "Just allow the information to exist in my head and do its own thing. One of the things I learned about myself in therapy is that I can't force a decision. Reacting impulsively is why I left Lucky's and ended up in jail, Robin."

"Shit, man, I'm not trying to push you. Just…be thoughtful."

"That's what I'm trying to do. I'll talk to George about it when it feels right. Now is just too soon for us and for how new and fragile everything is."

"You're right, and I have one more question, and then I promise I'll drop it."

"Ask."

"How will George react when he finds out you got the rodeo offer on Christmas, but he doesn't hear about it until weeks after the fact?"

Levi tilted his face to the sky. "I don't know, brother. I truly do not know."

George spent the week between Christmas and New Year's in a state of immeasurable joy. He worked on his caption assignments during the day as usual, but his lunch breaks were often spent video chatting with Levi while they both ate their meals. Sometimes Levi ate outside, but mostly indoors, as Garrett was apparently experiencing a cold snap. Even the cats were spending more time in the tiny house than usual, and it was fun watching Sporty try to snag bits of Levi's lunch.

Twice, Levi drove into the city and they shared dinner together. Both times they got takeout, found a spot near a public park, and ate in the bed of the truck. The picnics were chilly but also a lot of fun, even if he still battled the occasional panic attack. George could be out in the world without being too close to crowds of people like they would in a restaurant.

Like he would on New Year's Eve.

He and Orry had agreed on a double date that night. A locally owned restaurant Orry delivered for was doing a ticket-only buffet dinner that began at nine o'clock, and he'd scored cheap tickets for the four of them. Orry had promised George that it was a maximum of a hundred people, and the restaurant was spacious enough that they wouldn't be jammed in like so many New Year's crowds seemed to be. George was nervous as hell about the dinner but also excited to both meet Zoey and hang with his brother in a real social situation. And to show off his boyfriend a little.

Levi drove into the city on New Year's Eve and arrived at the apartment at seven so they could hang out for a while. Someone, probably Dez, had decorated the downstairs living room with festive white and gold decor, and they chilled down there with Derrick and Slater, who were heading for Derrick's brother's house in a little while for a small family celebration.

Around eight, Orry showed up with his girlfriend and George finally got to meet Zoey. She was taller than Orry, with a lean frame, short purple hair, and heavy makeup that dared you to criticize anything about her. George liked her immediately. They hung out and chatted until it was time for their two groups to split for their evening destinations.

Orry drove, since their shared car could hold four people, and George didn't mind sitting in the back with Levi. He held Levi's hand, happy to have his boyfriend nearby while his insides bounced all over the place. Levi watched him the entire way with an adoring smile that made George feel so seen he almost couldn't stand it. As they neared the venue, George closed his eyes and did a few rounds of deep breathing.

The restaurant had valet parking, which was kind of cool, and Zoey checked her coat just inside the building. George practically adhered himself to Levi's side once they entered the throng but there was enough room that it wasn't oppressive or claustrophobic. They all got drinks, and when the buffet opened at ten, George treated himself to samples of things he'd never tried before: mini spinach quiche, fried mushrooms, sausage and squash skewers, and so many other things.

All the food was amazing, and George genuinely liked Zoey. She told an abundance of stories of her earlier life as a waitress in a restaurant similar to this one, and George almost couldn't believe how horribly people could act. And how rude they could be to waitstaff for simply doing their jobs.

At eleven, the food began to clear, music came up, and folks started dancing in the open space. While they weren't the only same-sex couple in the restaurant, George was still nervous to go out there with Levi. They stayed at their table even after Orry and Zoey went out to dance.

"I'm proud of you," Levi said to him. "Just for being here but you also seem extremely calm."

"I'm a little jumpy inside," George admitted. "But it helps having you and Orry both nearby. A month ago, I never imagined I'd be in a place with this many people, but I am. And I think I'm doing okay."

"Good. Being sociable really does suit you, George. You're practically glowing right now."

"I used to love being the center of attention. Once upon a time, I was a kid who knew how to ice skate really well, and people watched me. They applauded me. They threw flowers at me." His smile dimmed. "But then it stopped being fun. And I hated people staring at me. Glaring at me. Mocking me for quitting. And I disappeared." George took Levi's hand and squeezed. "You helped me find myself again. I'll always battle with my anxiety but I don't have to let it control my life."

"It has been my genuine pleasure and honor to know and help you. You get to begin a brand-new year soon. Fresh start, clean slate. The new George Thompson." He held up his glass of sparkling water. "To you."

George grinned, joy bubbling up inside him like the fizzing liquid in his champagne flute. "To me, and to us."

They tapped their rims together and drank. Sat side by side and watched others dance. At five minutes to midnight, they joined Orry and Zoey on the dance floor with their drinks. A television screen mounted for the occasion broadcasted the ball drop in Times Square. With more joy in his heart than George ever expected to feel, he counted down the last ten seconds with the crowd, his arm tight around Levi's waist.

He counted down the end of his old self, his old secluded life, and he rang in the New Year with hope for every day yet to come. That he would continue to grow, to embrace his new life, and to be the very best person he could for his family, his boyfriend, and for the new friends he was making both in the city and at Clean Slate Ranch.

To my future. Please, let it be a great one.

Chapter Twenty-One

George expected to spend the night at home with Levi, but Levi surprised the hell out of him by willingly driving them both all the way to Garrett and the privacy of his tiny house. They slept in, both too tired to do more than collapse with all three kitties somewhere close by, and it was the best night of George's life.

The best next day, too. They spent New Year's Day doing a whole lot of nothing other than snacking and sex. Leading up to the new year, George had given serious thought to taking the next step into anal sex, but he couldn't see them taking that step yet. Maybe one day in the future but not now. He loved the sex they had, and Levi seemed perfectly content with it, too. They were creating their own relationship, their own rules. They didn't have to measure what they did or did not do against other couples.

An orgasm was an orgasm, and George adored everyone single one he shared with Levi.

The next week passed in a similar way to the previous one with two big changes. First, Shawn and Robin closed on their house, and George enjoyed a celebratory teleconference call with the pair plus Levi to toast the good news. George even got a phone tour of the house, which needed a lot of TLC but was charming and just the right size for the couple. The second change, which George kept to himself for now, was a cold call to Arthur Garrett's horse rescue inquiring about employment.

George still thought about the rescue and the horses they brought in for rehabilitation. Some of those beautiful animals ended up at the ranch. Others were sold to vetted owners. Some retired at the rescue for the rest of their natural days, and George was interested in the process. While they didn't have any current openings for someone like him (with no actual experience with horses or rehab), it was tangible proof to George that he was open to a new career. To doing something bigger than closed-captions for porn. Maybe even moving closer to Levi.

With the ghost town due to reopen in roughly two more weeks, Levi's spare time was dwindling. George decided to take a bit of extra time off—and by time off, he crammed in as much work as he could into three whole days so he could take three more off—and spend a few days with Levi. That turned into spending time with Shawn and Robin, and helping them do some work around their new house.

The house was midcentury, one story with two bedrooms and one and a half bathrooms. Their patch of land was small, but the backyard showed remnants of what might have once been a vegetable garden and could be replanted if the pair got ambitious. The floor plan was a little boxy, compared to how open George's apartment was, but Shawn and Robin also didn't have the budget for a huge renovation to open it up. For now, the pair said, this house would work for them.

George loved getting his hands dirty. The biggest job

was renovating the kitchen, which had come without working appliances and with outdated cabinets that refused to be cleaned to matter what they threw at them. Their quartet spent a fun morning demolishing the kitchen and hauling the debris to the dump in the back of Levi's truck. After a long day of hard work, George slept like a rock next to Levi and the cats.

The next day, they yanked up a ton of old carpet to reveal gorgeous hardwood floors that needed some sanding and refinishing. Shawn was beside himself with joy over the discovery. "I will never understand why people covered gorgeous wood floors with carpet," he said during their lunch break that day. "Wood floors are so much easier to sweep, especially if we get a pet."

"A pet?" Levi parroted.

"We've discussed options but made no decisions," Robin replied. "As much as we'd both like a dog, neither of us is keen on keeping the poor thing kenneled for eight or more hours a day while we're at work."

"Cats are great and very independent."

"And they tear up furniture."

"Not if you train them not to. My girls are very well behaved."

"We're still discussing it," Shawn said. "And we're nowhere close to a place where we can get a pet. The house still needs lots of work and we haven't even moved in completely yet."

"Did Judson give you guys any kind of deadline on leaving the cabin?" George asked.

"No, because he's that amazing, but Robin and I agreed we want to be moved in here by mid-February. That way, if Judson needs to hire any new horsemen before the summer season gets into full swing, he'll have the space. He's been more than generous letting us live there for as long as we have, considering neither of us technically works for the ranch. We work for Mack."

"The good news is," Robin added, "neither of us has a lot of stuff to move over from the cabin. Once we've got the floors and kitchen situated, all we need to do is buy furniture. I mean, I'd carve it all from wood if I could but a couch is a lot more complicated than a chess set."

George startled. "You play chess?"

"Not me, but Shawn is really good. He even taught Slater's old roommate Hugo how to play."

"My grandfather taught me to play," Shawn said after he ate a handful of kettle-cooked chips. "We'd play late into the night and snack the whole time. It's a game I enjoy, and I like spreading that joy to other people. Do you play, George?"

"I don't but I'm willing to learn," George replied. The more he hung out with the other couple, the more he admired the strength of their relationship. "I remember watching the film *Searching for Bobby Fischer* when I was a kid and being fascinated by the game. But my parents wouldn't let me try it because my focus needed to be on skating the whole time. No distractions."

"You mentioned skating once before. Is that what you used to do?"

George popped a chip into his mouth to give himself a moment to collect his thoughts. He wasn't ashamed of his past anymore, or of the impulsive decision he'd made to quit. And he didn't want to keep hiding from his new friends. "Yes. I was a figure skater, and I could have possibly made it on to the Olympic team, but I chose another path." *A path that wouldn't kill me.*

"Wow, that's impressive. I'm about as athletic as a worn sneaker."

"You do pretty damned good on a horse," Robin said. "You got yourself up in the saddle on your first try, unlike a lot of other people I know. I remember the week that Wes and his crew were here for a vacation-slash-bridal shower. Talk about a bunch of greenhorns who either needed a boost or the steps."

"George did pretty darn good his first time mountin' a horse," Levi added. "You and Figuro made a fine matched set."

"I do love riding," George replied. "Horses are amazing animals." He nearly brought up his interest in a possible career change but he didn't want to get too serious on such a fun-filled day. They had a lot of work left to do once lunch was over, and he hadn't told anyone—not even Orry—that he was interested in the horse rescue.

"They are that. You can look a good horse in the eyes and see they've got an old soul." Levi held his gaze a beat. "Kind of like with some people."

George grinned.

By the end of the day, all the old carpet was gone, most of the staples were removed, and there was only a bit of crusty glue left to be sanded off before the floors could be restained and varnished. George was exhausted in the very best way, and he fell asleep on the tiny home's couch while attempting to watch a movie with Levi. Levi woke him, and they stumbled upstairs to bed with the cats.

The next morning, they made love in a familiar, tender way. George adored how they had sex. It was exactly what he wanted: unhurried, passionate, and perfectly right for them. Occasionally, he worried that his disinterest in anal sex would wear on Levi, make him resent their relationship, but Levi never pushed. Never pressured George into anything he wasn't comfortable with, and that was something he was only used to from Orry. The lack of pressure. Everyone else in George's life had always pushed him. Pushed him to skate better, faster. To lose weight and be slimmer. To be the best.

All Levi ever asked George to be was himself.

The last day George was in town, their quartet mostly worked on the floors. The kitchen cabinets were due to arrive tomorrow, and they'd hired professional installers to do the work. "Absolutely worth the money to do it right," Robin said. "Shawn deserves the best kitchen we can afford."

"Any kitchen is fine," Shawn replied, his cheeks red. "But this new one is infinitely better than what used to be here. And don't they say that kitchens sell houses? So if we decide to move in the future, we'll have a great selling point."

"You just bought the house and you're thinking about moving?" George asked.

"No, not anytime soon. But we both know that the future is malleable, and we probably won't work at the ghost town forever. I could get a kitchen job offer, Robin could get some other sort of offer. This is our home for now, though, and we're going to take life one day at a time."

"Best way to take it," Levi said. "One day at a time. One issue at a time." He caught and held George's gaze. "One promise at a time."

George smiled.

Being driven back to the apartment—home no longer felt like the right word without Levi there—sucked but it was a necessary evil. Since Orry was working until eleven, they spent some quality time in George's bedroom before Levi had to leave. He'd enjoyed the last few days helping Shawn and Robin fix up their house, and he hoped to spend a few days next week if possible. But George needed to work, and the ghost town opened for the new season a week from tomorrow, which meant Levi, Shawn and Robin would all be busy preparing.

He worried a bit about Levi going back to work full time after getting used to him being available at the drop of a hat. That was part of being in an adult relationship, though. Managing their schedules with their personal time.

Part of being an adult was also facing his past and, that night, alone in his room, George searched for a video of his last big skate. The footage wasn't the best, and his stomach ached as he pressed play. Then the music filled his room the same way it had once filled his soul and his muscles, and it eased that ache. He recalled the joy of gliding across the ice. Of performing perfect jump combinations to thunderous applause. Of spinning so fast on one skate he thought he'd fly away into the heavens.

And he smiled. Truly, genuinely smiled. He'd been talented. He'd had potential. But skating hadn't been his future. Maybe one day he'd have the courage to find a rink and put on skates again. To remember what he'd loved for so many years—until he lost that love.

Not yet, but at least now he could look at his past self and see beyond the shame. See the joy he'd once possessed for the sport. Maybe he could even teach Levi to ice skate the way Levi had taught him to ride a horse.

I think I'd like that.

Orry impressed the hell out of him by taking off all his varied jobs for opening day of the ghost town. He, George and Zoey drove out to Garrett for the event. Even though Robin and Levi did trick riding demos every day, they had a more elaborate demonstration planned for opening day, and George was pleasantly surprised when Levi led their trio into the town before the official opening time of ten o'clock.

At the corral where Levi and Robin performed, Levi introduced George to Doug Peletier. His father. Doug had flown out to support his sons, just like he'd been there last year, and George was absolutely floored by the kindness of the older man.

"Never thought I'd see the day Levi settled down with someone worthy of him," Doug said as he shook George's hand. "I never heard him talk about that Grant fellow the way he talks about you, George. You must be a special person."

George's face blazed. "Levi is amazing, sir. He's talented and kind and I'm honored to be in his life. He gives me so much."

"Don't sir me, son. Doug is fine." Something in his tender expression suggested that maybe one day, George would have the honor of calling him Dad.

His heart turned over in a weird way at that thought. George hadn't spoken to his own father in years. Not on holidays or birthdays. And as much as part of him missed his biological parents, George was content with the separation. It was healthier for all of them. George wasn't going to reach out to people who'd always treated him like a prize instead of a son. He had more pride than that. And a hell of a lot more self-worth.

They hung around the corral until the first demo at

eleven, and George was elated when Slater and Derrick joined their group. Levi and Robin were amazing, performing all kinds of roping and riding tricks, a few of which required volunteers from the audience for simple tasks. As much as George wanted to volunteer and interact with his boyfriend, he'd long ago lost the desire for others to stare at him. The show received loud applause, and George hung around long enough to give Levi a kiss.

Afterward, Orry and Zoey wanted to wander the ghost town, and George ended up with Doug. They walked up and down Main Street, visiting the shops and tables of locals who were selling their arts and crafts, similar to the big July 4th celebration. The weather was sunny and crisp, and George basked in the joy of parental pride, even if the pride wasn't directed at him. Doug told him new stories of the rodeo and George soaked in every single word.

They had lunch at the saloon, and Shawn served them personally so he could chat with Doug for a few minutes. George didn't know Shawn's entire backstory, but he soaked in the very father-son dynamic between the pair, their connection through their shared love of Robin. So much love existed between the people who worked at both Bentley and Clean Slate, and George had somehow found himself caught up in it. All because he'd stupidly allowed Adrian into the apartment.

While that encounter had been terrifying, it had set George on the path he now walked, and he couldn't imagine being anywhere else. Or with anyone except Levi.

George cheered his boyfriend on during the second big demonstration, which was similar to the first, but just different enough that he didn't get bored. After the applause died down, Levi came over and planted a long kiss on George that left his face hot and his libido up. Levi was practically glowing and George soaked in his positive energy.

"You did an amazing job, son," Doug said. "I think you're even better than you were last year."

"I've had a lot more practice since then," Levi replied with a bark of laughter. "Muscle memory woke up a lot this past year. Plus, Zodiac has been a dream to train and work with. You've gotta trust your animal and have them trust you for this stuff to work."

"True words, my boy. You'd be an asset to the rodeo, but I also see the passion you have for the work you do here."

Levi's eyebrows furrowed briefly, and George wasn't sure why. Doug had simply paid him a compliment about his performance today. It wasn't as if Doug was trying to lure Levi back to Lucky's.

Was he?

Nah, that was George being paranoid. He couldn't spend time thinking of ways in which his relationship would fall apart. He had to do exactly what Shawn and Levi had both said: take it one day at a time. One promise at a time. And right now, the biggest promise he'd made was to take care with Levi's heart. George wasn't sure if he was in love with Levi or not, but he had incredibly strong feelings. Strong enough that losing the man would hurt. Immensely. But he didn't want to think about that possibility on such a gorgeous, fun-filled day.

As much as George wanted to spend the night with Levi, it didn't work out logistically. Levi had to work tomorrow, and Doug was only in town until Monday.

George couldn't be selfish and deny Levi time with his father, so he went home with Orry and Zoey. He genuinely liked Zoey, who was positive, funny, and made Orry laugh. A lot. Orry deserved to laugh as much as he could, after working his ass off these last couple of years.

For the next few weeks, George figured out a driving schedule with Orry and Levi that allowed George to stay over during the ghost town's "weekend." They were closed on Tuesday and Wednesday, giving all the staff got proper time off, and it not only gave George time with Levi, but it allowed them to continue helping Shawn and Robin renovate their house. Once the kitchen was complete, they moved on to the hardwood floors in the rest of the house, sanding and staining, and George enjoyed the labor. And the company. Miles occasionally joined them for a few hours too, since his own husband was busy running the ranch on those days off. George had never felt so accepted by a group of people in his life.

Never truly felt like part of a family who loved him for who he was, not for his potential.

Levi came into the city for Valentine's Day, despite working a long day at Bentley. They shared a late dinner at a nice restaurant—George was a touch nervous about it but no one stared or cared who he was or used to be—followed by a lot of time in George's bedroom. Touching and moving and sucking and simply making each other feel good. Afterward, they lay together under the covers, tangled into one person with George's head tucked under Levi's chin.

"Does it bother you that I don't want to try anal sex?" George asked before he could censor himself.

"No." Levi didn't hesitate for a second. "We have sex the way that makes sense to us and that feels right. Sex isn't one size fits all, George. There's no have to, there's only what we want and desire." He slid a hand down to gently squeeze George's hip, prompting George to prop up on one elbow and look his boyfriend in the eyes. "I desire you, George Thompson. Your mind, your spirit, your courage, and yeah, your sexy body. I love what we do together." His blue eyes glimmered in a brand-new way a moment before Levi said, "I love you."

George's heart trilled with joy and adoration, and he kissed Levi breathless before saying, "I love you, too. I've never been in love before but this feels right. I love you, Levi."

"Yeah?" Levi rolled George to his back and kissed him for a long time, until their cocks both took notice of the friction. They came close together, rutting through their releases, creating something unique to them. A relationship defined by their own terms.

And George would fight any battle necessary to protect it.

Chapter Twenty-Two

For as much as George missed Levi's physical presence—and kind of envied Orry's frequent interactions with Zoey—they were making a long-distance relationship work for them. Frequent Skype dates, texting and phone calls throughout the week helped ease the ache he felt from Levi's absence. They communicated constantly and George had reworked his own schedule so his personal weekend off was now identical to Levi's.

Win-win.

Shawn and Robin's house was also shaping up in the best way, and the pair was hoping to have a housewarming party soon. Scheduling was the issue, because most of the planned guests either worked at Bentley or Clean Slate, and the days/nights off didn't exactly mesh. Maybe multiple parties to accommodate schedules? Whatever, it wasn't George's problem to fix. All he needed to worry about was getting from Garrett to San Francisco and back again, based on who could drive him where.

Not for the first time, George considered looking for a really cheap car. He wanted to stop relying on rides from other people. Orry always had dibs on their car, because of his various jobs and his need to be mobile.

And George hated how many miles he was constantly asking Levi to drive for him, whether halfway or all the way to the city. One day, a deep-down part of him wanted to call Garrett home.

He wanted Levi to be home.

The second week in March, George and Shawn were painting the bathroom while their guys worked outside in the yard, pulling weeds and preparing what Shawn hoped to be a nice little vegetable garden. They'd randomly paired off that way, and George enjoyed Shawn's friendship. He was about two years older and had a familiar wariness of the world at large, while embracing the people closest to him that George sympathized with a lot. Shawn had chosen a pale yellow paint for the home's full bathroom, and George liked how it complimented the shower curtain and rugs Shawn had already picked out.

Will I ever have a house like this with Levi? Or will he always want to live on top of wheels?

They needed to have that conversation sometime in the near future. George adored the tiny home, but its placement was temporary. It might always be temporary.

"I think it looks pretty damned good," Shawn said once their task was done. They both stood back and admired the walls. "It's bright and airy."

"I love it." George put his roller in the pan and wiped his hands on a rag. "It makes the room seem bigger than it is."

"Yeah."

"I can't imagine how stressful it is to pick so many things at once. Kitchen cabinets, paint colors for a bunch of rooms, furniture and curtains."

"It's definitely a chore but worth it." Shawn wandered out into the kitchen and grabbed a canned soda from the fridge. "Thirsty?"

"Sure, thank you." He accepted a cola and popped the tab. Took a long drink to both wet his whistle and get the smell of paint out of his nostrils.

"I guess the bonus of a tiny house is there isn't a whole lot to worry about changing in terms of colors or décor. It's all kind of set in stone." Shawn peered out the kitchen window to the backyard where Robin and Levi were wrestling in the grass instead of working on the garden. "God, they're like a pair of kids sometimes. I can't imagine Robin trick riding with anyone else up at Bentley."

"Well, Levi's not going anywhere, so you don't really have to imagine it."

An odd kind of relief came over Shawn. "Levi told you he's turning his dad down?"

George blinked, confused by the question. "Turning his dad down for what?"

"Taking over running Lucky's Rodeo when Doug retires at the end of this season." Shawn's eyes popped wide. "Fuck, Levi didn't tell you about this?"

As confused and unsure as he was, George didn't want Shawn to think he'd said or done anything wrong, so he obfuscated. "Yeah, sorry, it slipped my mind. He didn't say anything, um, specifically about his decision. I meant right now. We aren't going anywhere."

That seemed to placate Shawn for now, and George tried not to dwell on it. But it stuck in the back of his mind like a sliver of wood beneath his skin—irritating and present. Doug was retiring and apparently wanted Levi to take over running Lucky's when he did. When had Doug said this? Why hadn't Levi mentioned it yet? And what did that mean for their future as a couple?

George had no idea and that terrified him.

Levi couldn't put his finger on when things between himself and George changed. George was slower to respond to his texts. He didn't answer Levi's calls as frequently as Levi was used to. And the third week in March, George begged off their usual "weekend" together, citing a heavy workload. If everything else had been normal, Levi might not have worried about that. They couldn't spend every bit of time off with each other; they needed to have life and work balance.

But this wasn't their established normal, and Levi spent a lot of time either running the various trails, or playing with his cats and worrying he'd done something wrong. Upon reflection, he couldn't think of a thing he could have said or done. Maybe George was having a minor personal crisis, and Levi hoped he trusted Levi enough to come to him. To talk about it and try to find a solution.

They saw each other the following week for their "weekend" and George was upbeat but also...not? Levi couldn't put his finger on it because he wasn't used to this side of George. The hard to read side who said all the right things but whose eyes were distant. Uncertain. Had George changed his mind about being with Levi but he didn't know how to say it? Levi didn't want to believe that, and when he tried to bring it up with George, George insisted he was fine. They were fine.

Levi didn't agree they were fine but they also weren't fighting, so what was this distance?

During that Friday's routine demo at Bentley, Levi

nearly fell off Zodiac during a standing run—a trick he could do in his freaking sleep—and once they finished, Robin dragged him away from the corral. "What is wrong with you, pal? You're distracted, and it's going to get you hurt."

"I'm not sure." Levi shrugged out of Robin's hold and took a few steps away, closer to the tree line. "I get the sense that something is off with George but when I try to ask him about it, he says everything is fine. But I don't think everything is fine."

Robin crossed his arms. "What do you think could be wrong?"

"I don't know. Orry and Zoey are doing great, so it's not about them. George and I see each other as much as we can. I honestly don't know how to make him talk to me, and I won't see him in person again until Tuesday."

"Do you think?" Robin shifted his weight, face pinched. "Do you think he found out about you being arrested? Or the attack?"

Levi's gut rolled, and he pushed against those painful memories. "Maybe. It isn't something I've talked to him about yet, and I need to. I also don't see George pulling away if he found out about those things. That doesn't feel like him. This is something else."

"I didn't figure on you two having issues talking to each other."

"I didn't think so either until recently. When I see him Tuesday we'll go somewhere and talk about this. I ignored the weird vibes I got from Grant and we both know how that turned out."

"George is nothing like Grant, though. George sees you. He's with you for who you are and not just for your ass."

"That's for sure."

Robin tilted his head to the side. "Wait, you guys don't fuck?"

"No, and I'm perfectly fine with it, considering my history." Levi ran a hand through his hair. "Maybe that's it. Maybe George thinks I'll get bored with us not having intercourse and leave him, so he's keeping his distance? Ugh."

"Talk to him on Tuesday, brother. Tell him everything. Let him absorb it and understand your perspective in the most informed way possible."

"I will." Tuesday felt like weeks away but at least he'd have work to keep him distracted for the next few days. George was the most important person in his life, and Levi would fight to keep him in it.

The weekend, naturally, slithered along like a drunk turtle, with phone calls and texts to George that left Levi both hopeful and uneasy. He spent a lot of his free time meditating, trying to clear his mind of worry and stay positive. Monday evening, after they returned the horses to the Clean Slate barn, Robin invited Levi over for a late dinner at the house. They were officially moved in and slowly decorating.

With Shawn still closing down the saloon, Levi drove Robin to the house in his pickup, and they ended up making rice bowls out of the various remnants of take-out and other dishes littering the fridge. "We need to go shopping soon and stock up," Robin said of their bare pantry. "We've just been so busy with the house, there's never time to really cook."

"You don't have to explain to me." Levi sipped at his cola. "You and Shawn have had a busy few months getting settled in. Give yourself time to nest."

"Believe me, we're nesting. Neither one of us has ever really had our own space like this. Shawn went from living with his grandparents to renting a room from a cousin to living in his car. I went from sharing an RV with three other people to rooming with Ernie at the ranch." He looked around their sparkling new kitchen with gentle affection Levi kind of envied. "This is our space. Our home."

"I'm happy for you, Robin, I meant it. You both deserve this."

"You deserve it too, man. And I expect George does, too." He quirked an eyebrow. "Unless you decide to go on the road with Lucky's."

"I haven't made any decisions about that."

"What does George think?"

Levi's heart skipped a beat. "He doesn't know."

"He doesn't? But…"

"But what?"

Robin fiddled with his fork. "Something Shawn said a few weeks ago. He was talking to George and brought up Lucky's, assuming you'd told George about the offer, and he said George reacted oddly. Surprised, but then he brushed it off like he knew exactly what Shawn was talking about."

"What? Why didn't you bring this up sooner?"

"I guess I assumed you actually tell your boyfriend about important shit, dude. Are you saying George has no idea Dad offered you Lucky's?"

"Well, he obviously knows now." Levi dropped his forehead into his hand and sighed. "That explains it all, I think. George's odd distance these last few weeks. Fuck." He leapt up from the table so fast he nearly toppled his chair over. "I have to go."

"Where?"

"Into the city to talk to George. It can't wait until tomorrow. It's waited long enough."

"Well, drive safely and get there in one piece, okay?"

"I will." He passed Shawn coming inside the house just as he was barreling out and tossed him a quick, "Hi, bye," as he hightailed it to his truck, desperate to talk to his boyfriend.

George mostly deconstructed the grilled chicken sandwich Orry had brought him for dinner, too stressed and upset to eat. Orry had a rare evening off, and he wolfed down his own sandwich and fries, while also texting. Probably with Zoey. The pair was in each other's back pockets whenever possible, and their joy only made George more and more jealous.

Jealous and stupid, because George was the idiot who wouldn't simply talk to Levi about his fears. That he knew about Levi taking over Lucky's next year, and he was terrified of being dumped. But George had never been in this sort of position before, and he loathed confrontation. He didn't know how to tell Levi what he knew or to demand answers and clarification. His anxiety monster insisted he was going to lose the best thing in his life soon, and he didn't want to face that.

So he moped when he was alone and tried to shine when he was with Levi, and the whole thing had left his stomach a mess this weekend. He'd downed antacids several times today, and the few bites of his sandwich he'd managed were not sitting well. Thankfully, Orry was distracted enough by his phone that he didn't notice.

It also hurt a little that he didn't notice. Orry had always been attuned to George's bad moods. But George also wasn't the sole focus on Orry's life anymore. George had to learn to share his big brother's attention.

Still hurt.

Orry left the table first, phone in hand, and went to his room. George scraped the rest of his sandwich into the trash, the simple sight of it making him queasy. He was ahead on his current assignments in preparation for Levi picking him up in the morning for their weekend, so he spread out on his side on the futon and watched TV. Whatever was on, mindlessly flipping channels during commercial breaks, unable to settle on one particular thing. Work was even proving a challenge some days. His mind wandered during scenes and he'd miss the dialogue—such as it was, sometimes—and have to go back.

He'd started dozing during a rerun of *Everybody Loves Raymond* when the doorbell buzzed. They almost never had visitors, and George trudged to the call box. Fully expecting it to be Zoey, he hit the button to unlock the front door and trudged back to the futon. But Orry didn't emerge from his room. George's gut cramped. Had he made a mistake not asking who it was? What if he'd just let Adrian into the building again?

He jumped when someone knocked, his heart pounding hard. George inched closer to the door. "Who is it?"

"It's Levi," was the unexpected, muffled response.

"Levi." George turned the deadbolt, opened the door, and gaped at the unexpected sight of Levi on his landing. "You're here." And way early.

"I need to talk to you about something important, and it couldn't wait."

His insides shriveled up. This was the moment Levi confessed about taking over Lucky's and leaving him.

He took a step back, allowing Levi to come inside. Orry popped his head out of his room and said, "Hey, dude, I thought we were meeting up tomorrow morning."

"Change of plans," Levi said. "I really need some privacy to talk to George."

"No sweat. I'll chill downstairs in the living room." Orry flashed George a curious look on his way out of the apartment. George had no idea what his own face looked like. Probably a combination of glum and terrified.

"I know what you're going to say." George moved to put the futon between them, needing the physical barrier and unsure exactly why. His hands started shaking. "You're going away with Lucky's next year, aren't you?"

Levi took a single step closer, hands loose by his sides, his expression determined. "I have not made that decision, George. It was wrong of me to keep this from you for as long as I have, and I own that mistake. I accept and acknowledge your hurt, and I am so sorry for causing it. My father did offer me the chance to take over running the rodeo next season after he retires, but I did not give him an answer."

"Why not?"

"Because of us. Because when Dad offered, we were still feeling each other out. Still becoming an us that made sense."

Annoyance crept up to overcome some of George's fear. "How long ago did he offer?"

"Christmas Day."

"That was almost three fucking months ago!" He hadn't meant to yell, but what the actual fuck? Three months of sitting on this secret?

"I know, and I am so sorry. And I'm even sorrier you found this out from Shawn and not me. The only person

I told was Robin, and he obviously let something slip, and that's not an excuse. I didn't turn my dad down flat on his offer, so I should have told you about it sooner. Especially after I said I love you. I owed you that truth and I know I broke your trust by not sharing it."

George wanted to rage at his boyfriend for keeping something this important from him but he didn't have the energy to do it. All he had was anger and defeat, and defeat was winning. "You didn't tell Doug no because you're considering it."

"It's my family's legacy. I loved my time with Lucky's. I love being on the road, on the move. But I also love you, and I love living in Garrett. I suppose I foolishly hoped all those loves could come together somehow. I didn't want to disappoint my dad or disappoint you."

The conflict in his heart played out all over Levi's face, and it dimmed some of George's anger. Not all but some. He circled the futon and sat on one end. Levi sat on the other, a long distance between them. "I think I understand why you didn't say anything in December," George said. "We were still feeling things out, falling in love. But these last few weeks, Levi? I didn't expect you to keep a secret this big from me. Stuff about your past, sure, those things are private, but something that affects both of our futures?"

"You're right."

"I know." George picked at seam of his jeans. "But I'm also wrong. When Shawn first let it slip, I should have said something to you about it, instead of letting it fester. You always say people shouldn't keep things bottled up and I did that. Just like I let Orry get away with the Thanksgiving lie for weeks before I confronted him. I don't like confrontation. It always ends badly."

"It didn't end badly with Orry."

"True. I guess I keep comparing everything to my last encounter with Adrian."

"That was a traumatic moment for you. Him attacking you." Levi scooted a few inches closer. "But I need you to know and believe me when I say I will never be physically, verbally, or emotionally violent with you, George. Not for any reason. I've survived too much violence to ever want to hurt another human soul."

George's chest ached for the new misery in Levi's blue eyes. A flash and gone but it had been there, and he wanted to know more. "What sort of violence?"

Levi inhaled deeply, then let the breath out slowly. "After Xander died and I quit the rodeo, I went on what I can only describe as a year-long bender. I drank heavily and for a long time. Did some drugs but alcohol was easier to find. Spent all my savings. Ended up living in my car for a while, too angry and proud to call my dad for help. When my car got impounded for unpaid tickets, I started tricking out for a place to sleep. Prostituting for alcohol money."

Shock jolted through George's core at that confession. Levi didn't look ashamed of his actions, though, more resigned to the fact that they'd happened. George also didn't know what to say so he stayed silent. Grateful to Levi for sharing these painful truths.

"It all ended when I woke up in the ER, bloody and brutalized, and I had a perforated bowel injury that they treated endoscopically, so they kept me in hospital for a few days. After I detoxed, I called Dad and he came. I went straight into rehab, and I have been sober ever since. I turned my whole life around and I stopped being angry at the world over Xander's accidental death. I didn't even blame Robin anymore for goading Xander into getting up on a horse for the first time. I couldn't hate and blame and be able to move forward."

"I'm so sorry you went through that." George raged and ached for the pain Levi must have gone through after his attack. "Did they ever catch the people who hurt you?"

"No. But I like to think that karma has or will soon catch up with each of them. I don't have room in my heart to hate them anymore. Only to hope that they'll change or face the consequences."

"Then you're a better person than me. I can't imagine ever forgiving my abuser."

"Adrian?"

"Yes." His stomach twisted up tight. "Not only for berating me into an eating disorder but sometimes he'd lose his temper and shove me. He'd…grope me during practice. Obvious gropes, not accidents."

Fury blazed in Levi's eyes. "Did you tell anyone?"

"I told everyone who would listen after I quit skating, which I think is a huge part of why Adrian hates me so much. That last night I couldn't bear the idea of working with him anymore if I won. Or the possible illness or violence if I lost, and I fell apart. Had a massive panic attack. My accusations of both the groping and the anorexia ruined his reputation as a coach. I obviously couldn't prove anything but it was enough. No one would hire him."

"You did the right thing." Levi moved to the center of the futon. "You are a strong, strong man, George. Never doubt that. You have been battling your anxiety for so many years, and I am in awe of your strength."

"Thank you. It's a never-ending battle, but thank you." George rested his hand on Levi's thigh, needing the physical contact while his mind sorted through all this new information. "Since we're bleeding our souls all over the place tonight, I have a confession to make."

Levi covered George's hand with his own. "Okay."

"I called up Arthur Garrett's horse rescue to inquire about working there. Working with horses. In Garrett."

"You did?"

"Yes, and I'm honestly not sure why I did it. I mean, I love the ranch and being around those horses, and I love the work they do. Saving those beautiful animals and giving them a better life. They don't have any job openings right now, and I don't have any experience other than some YouTube videos I've been watching, but I also don't want to close-caption porn forever. I mean, sure, it's something I can do anywhere as long as I have Wi-Fi, but I also want to be part of something bigger."

"Yeah?"

"Yes." George closed the rest of the distance between them and pressed his shoulder to Levi's. "I'm still upset with you for not telling me about the Lucky's offer sooner, but I understand why you didn't. And thank you for telling me what happened to you."

"We both shared our truths tonight. Thank you for trusting me with yours, too."

"You're welcome." They shared a single, tender kiss. "I guess you still don't know what you want to do about Lucky's, huh?"

"I really don't. Like I said, I love livin' on Garrett land. I love workin' at the ghost town with Robin, seeing my brother every day. But the rodeo life is in my blood, and I hate the idea of Dad selling it off to some-

one else. I also hate the idea of being on the road for
months at a time and not seeing you. Not holding you.
Kissing you. Makin' love to you."

"Then let's keep talking about it. Not necessarily tonight but going forward. I don't want you to ever resent
me for the choice you make about it."

"I don't think I could ever resent you, and I adore
how supportive you're being when you have every right
to still be pissed."

"There's no point in staying mad. You weren't being
deliberately cruel. That's not who you are. We talked.
Maybe a little late, but we did talk. Honestly talked. And
I think we're in a really good place to move forward.
To create a life unique to us as a committed couple."

"So do I." Levi leaned in and nuzzled his nose
against George's. "Forgive me for keeping my secret?"

"As long as you forgive me for already knowing it."

They sealed that with a long, tender kiss George
didn't want to break. But he also didn't want to end up
humping his boyfriend on the futon when Orry could
come back at any moment. George sent Orry a text that
the coast was clear, then dragged Levi into his bedroom
for a proper make-out session. They moved together
in bed in a familiar way, worshiping each other's body
with hands and mouths and tongues.

Creating something wholly unique to them and their
relationship. No one else's. Perhaps they'd both stumbled a bit along the way, but George fell asleep that
night positive they'd finally made all the right moves.
They were on a united path toward a future that would
make them both happy.

And George had never been more joyful in his life
than with Levi by his side.

Epilogue

Nine Months Later

Levi brought two mugs of steaming hot cocoa to the sofa where George sat, Ginger already curled up on his lap. George's laptop rested on a small C-shaped table he'd bought for ease of use in the tiny home's limited workspace, and their scheduled Zoom call was still waiting on one person.

George accepted the mug and kissed his cheek.

Shawn and Robin were already on the call, both dressed adorably in elf hats and ugly Christmas sweaters. In another window, Orry and Zoey were relaxing on the apartment's futon, casually teasing Shawn and Robin about their chosen attire. Levi had missed commemorating the anniversary of Xander's death with Robin in person, but he also understood it was time for them both to move on. They'd always love Xander in their hearts and that was good enough.

Now it was time to look to the future.

"Doug's late," Shawn said. "Did he get the right link?"

"Yeah, he's probably just having issues figuring it out," Robin joked. "He'll be on in a few, I'm sure."

Levi snuggled up close to George and wasn't surprised when Baby planted herself on his lap. Sporty was somewhere, probably outside enjoying the New Mexico sunshine. They'd joined the rest of Lucky's Rodeo at their winter spot in Santa Fe last week, after driving the house and contents to their new location. The cats were still getting used to the unfamiliar terrain and tended to stick close.

Finally, Dad jumped into the call and they were complete. He was reclining on a bed with some sort of tapestry on the wall behind him. "Greetings from Venice," Dad said with cheer in his tone and eyes. "Never thought I'd live to spend Christmas Day in Italy but this is what your mother wanted, Levi. To follow her heritage home."

"Is Italy as beautiful as the pictures I've seen?" George asked.

"Even more beautiful than words can describe, son. It's worth the trip if you find yourself able to come."

"Maybe next winter. We've got a busy season coming up."

They truly did. With Levi now in charge of Lucky's Rodeo, he was actively working with both Potter and Willard to build next year's travel schedule. Levi wanted to do more small shows, more local venues, interspersed with the bigger, more prestigious state fairs and events. To boost smaller economies with their attraction, and they could definitely afford it. And everyone who'd worked with Levi in the past was happy to have him back.

Some folks were a bit standoffish with George, but George was also shy around the staff as a whole. He was working on it, shoring up his courage and battling his social anxiety. He loved working with the horses, though, and Levi had never been prouder of his boyfriend. Proud for taking a chance on a mobile life that took him thousands of miles away from his brother. From the quiet, contained life he was used to. For facing his anxiety monster head-on and trying something brand new.

George still did closed-caption work and he'd go part-time once the rodeo season began next year so he could help with the horses. Levi had sat downstairs in the living room with Slater and Derrick for close to an hour while George said goodbye to Orry in their apartment last week. It had been hard, but worth it for the way George glowed. He was happy, thriving, and living his life, and Levi was blessed to know and love him.

"So what's better in Italy, Dad?" Robin asked. "The pizza or the pasta?"

"Pasta, hands down," Dad replied. "It's an art form over here. Doesn't matter what the sauce is, the pasta is exceptional. I've never seen so many different shapes."

"I am completely jealous," George said. "Our Christmas dinner is takeout turkey and stuffing from a local place that we ordered ahead from."

"Hey, it's the perfect meal for two," Levi retorted. "Besides, my oven only fits so much food at once. You could have a homemade turkey or sides but not both."

"Fortunately, we don't have to cook," Shawn said. "We're due at Wes and Mack's place in about three hours for dinner. Just like last year."

"Yeah." It was hard to believe that a little over a year ago, Levi and George had begun their flirtation, and that they'd nurtured it for so long. Talking and asking and checking in when they sensed a problem. They'd had a lot of long conversations about Levi taking over Lucky's and, in the end, George had agreed to travel with him. To keep their family together all year long, instead of Levi going off alone with the cats.

Levi had done a lot of running, meditating and soul searching before he told Dad he'd run Lucky's. And he didn't regret his decision for a single moment. Not when he saw how happy his whole family was.

Twelve sixteen rolled around and the call went silent for about a full minute. "Five years since we lost you, Xander," Dad said. "We'll never stop loving you but I think we can all feel you smiling down on us from wherever you are. You and your momma. Keep loving each other until we see you again."

Levi pictured his brother's smiling face and sent positive energy into the world on his and his mom's behalf. *Wherever both you are, I hope you're at peace.*

"How do you think training is going?" Dad asked Robin.

Robin groaned. "Can I report back in a few more weeks?"

Once Levi announced he was leaving the ghost town for Lucky's, Robin had put out an ad for a new trick riding partner. He'd gotten a reply from a young man named Sam, who had a lot of promise but still needed a ton of training to truly develop his skills. Levi had hated leaving Robin and Mack in the lurch like that but they had over a month before Bentley re-opened for the season.

"You know exactly what I'll do if Mack asks," Levi said. "Bring the entire show to Bentley for opening day."

"I know you will but Mack trusts me to keep our

demos running, and I'm gonna do it." Robin tilted his chin up. "Sam's good, he's just got to work on his balance a little bit more. We'll be fine."

"I'd call that Peletier stubbornness," Dad said, "but you aren't blood."

"Hey, some things are acquired traits. I've known you nutcases for thirteen years now. Some things stick."

Dad burst out laughing. "Yeah, I guess they do. George, how are you liking Santa Fe?"

"I can't complain," George replied. "The weather is great. The company is even better. The only thing I'm really missing is a hug from my brother."

"Yeah, well, you'll get a huge one next time I see you," Orry said. "It's been a long time since we've been apart on Christmas but that's part of growing up, right? Moving on and trying new things."

"It is. Orry, you are the best brother I ever could have wanted. Thank you for protecting me when I couldn't protect myself. You've done so much for me, and all I want is for you to be happy."

"I am happy, bro. More than I can say."

"Good. Did you see Grandpa and Gramma today?" George and Levi had both visited them before leaving the city, and they'd been delighted to meet Levi. And to hear about George's new adventure in life. The charming elderly pair had wished them both all the best.

"This morning, yes, Zoey and I visited. They're good. They miss you, but they're excited about your new job with the rodeo. Getting out of the city and state. Doing something new."

"I love what I'm doing." George pressed his shoulder into Levi's. "Some days I surprise even myself."

Some days he still surprised the crap out of Levi.

George had taken an interest in the physical work involved in the rodeo. With his young age and physical flexibility, George could learn to participate in the rodeo shows, and they were slowly easing him into a few of the tricks. He would likely not perform this coming season but maybe the next. With a little more training, practice and time.

Lucky's Rodeo was Levi's to shape and form, and he absolutely wanted his partner's input. For them to create a show worthy of Dad's legacy and be as inclusive as possible going forward. An attraction that would make every past and future Peletier who worked for it proud.

"So did you get anything fun in your stocking this year?" Robin asked, seeming to direct the question to Levi.

Levi chuckled, not about to tell him about the spectacular blow job he'd gotten from George under their tiny Christmas tree. "Nothing but coal. Apparently, I was a bad boy this year and Santa didn't approve."

"Yeah, right."

"There actually was one gift Levi hasn't gotten yet," George said, a funny hitch in his voice. "I wanted to give it to him with our family around to see."

Curious, Levi angled to face George more fully. George put his left hand in his pocket but didn't bring out anything yet. Whatever the gift was, it was small.

"This is going to stay PG rated, right?" Levi asked.

"Yes, it is," George replied. He clasped Levi's hand with his free one and squeezed. "The first time we met up at the ghost town, I knew there was something special about you, Levi, but I had no idea exactly how special you were. That you'd be my mythical knight in shining armor, saving me from my isolated life high up in a tower that I couldn't escape from alone. You give me so many things I never knew I needed and other things I never thought I deserved. You give me peace and joy and courage. And we're about to start a brand-new life together. Before we do, I wanted to…well…" George pulled his left hand from his pocket and held it out. On his palm were two gold bands. "I want to put a ring on it."

Levi's lips parted, stunned by the gesture and that George had been the one to do it first. To take another huge leap forward into his new life.

"Holy shit," Orry squeaked. "Did you just propose?"

"Not yet," George replied, his clear blue eyes never leaving Levi's. "Marry me, Levi?"

"Yes." Levi closed his free hand around the rings and held tight, his eyes burning with joyful tears. "Of course I'll marry you."

The call erupted with cheers and shouts, and Levi ignored it all in favor of kissing George. A long, promising kiss that only ended long enough for them to each put a ring on the other, and then they were back in each other's arms. The laptop eventually went silent as everyone else dropped out, because Levi couldn't stop kissing his fiancé.

Until Sporty crash landed on his lap, claws up, and he broke free with a yelp. Her job done, Sporty jumped onto the back of the couch and settled by George's head. "You sure you're ready for this?" Levi asked. "Three step-cats is a lot of work."

George stroked Baby, who'd resettled on the cushion beside him. "They're worth it. You're worth it. Some days my life still doesn't feel real. I think I'll wake up in my old bed, alone with no one but my brother to defend me. Never satisfied with how my body looked. A year ago, I never would have, in my wildest fantasies, thought I'd be here. In another state, far from Orry, newly engaged, happy with who I am, and so in love my heart wants to burst."

"I never expected to be here, either. You helped me open up and trust again, and I will always treasure that. As I'll treasure you for the rest of our lives, George Thompson."

"I'll treasure you, too, Levi Peletier."

They sealed those perfect words with another long, sensual kiss that eventually led them upstairs to the bedroom. As they moved together with all the time in the world to reach climax and no rush to get there, Levi sent silent thanks after thanks to the universe for leading him here, to this exact moment. To George.

To a future he couldn't wait to see and experience with his husband by his side.

* * * * *

Reviews are an invaluable tool when it comes to spreading the word about great reads.
Please consider leaving an honest review for this, or any of Carina Press's other titles that you've read, on your favorite retailer or review site.

For more information about A.M. Arthur's books, please visit her website here:
https://amarthur.blogspot.com/
Or like her on Facebook:
https://www.facebook.com/A.M.Arthur.M.A/

Acknowledgments

Huge thanks, as always, to my amazing editor Alissa. We've been on quite the journey these last few years, and I am forever grateful for your guidance and friendship. To the Clean Slate Ranch fans who have followed me along on this crazy journey, thank you guys too. This found family means the world to me, as does your loyalty and support. If only CSR was a real place, I'd take you all on vacation. —A.M.

About the Author

A.M. Arthur was born and raised in the same kind of small town that she likes to write about, a stone's throw from both beach resorts and generational farmland. She's been creating stories in her head since she was a child and scribbling them down nearly as long, in a losing battle to make the fictional voices stop. She credits an early fascination with male friendships (bromance hadn't been coined yet back then) with her later discovery of and subsequent love affair with m/m romance stories. A.M. Arthur's work is available from Carina Press, SMP Swerve, and Briggs-King Books.

When not exorcising the voices in her head, she toils away in a retail job that tests her patience and gives her lots of story fodder. She can also be found in her kitchen, pretending she's an amateur chef and trying to not poison herself or others with her cuisine experiments.

Contact her at am_arthur@yahoo.com with your cooking tips (or book comments). For updates, info and the occasional freebie, sign up for her free newsletter: https://vr2.verticalresponse.com/s/signupformynewsletter16492674416904

A series of failed relationships with women has left Detective Nathan Wolf still single at thirty-four— because he's too scared to admit to his longtime crush on his best friend James.

Read on for an excerpt of Getting It Right, *the next installment in the Restoration series by A.M. Arthur.*

Chapter One

Never said I'd let you fuck me...Get off...Let go!

Ezra's words chased themselves around James Taggert's mind as he stalked down the sidewalk, away from Pot O Gold, desperate to stuff his hands into his too-tight jeans pockets to keep them from trembling. Never in his life had he acted like such a selfish asshole and allowed a situation to get that out of control. He stopped a few blocks from the bar he'd abandoned and leaned against the cool bricks of a closed Mexican grocery store. He needed to apologize to Ezra, but he was too embarrassed and too drunk to make it as genuine as Ezra deserved.

His phone was at his ear, the other end buzzing.

"Jay?" Nathan Wolf's voice was a balm to his frazzled nerves. "What's wrong? It's after midnight."

"Price is getting out."

"Shit, when did you find out? Where are you?"

Having a best friend who knew all of his sordid backstory made times like this so much easier. "This afternoon. I'm outside the Pot. I'm fucked-up, Nate, and I did something. Something bad."

"Stay put. I can be there in under ten."

The phone call ended, but the calm of talking to

Nathan was taking some of the edge off his panic. He tapped a cigarette out of the crumpled pack in his back pocket. Thumbed the lighter. He took a long drag, letting the smoke fill his lungs to choking before releasing it hard through his nose. The stinging helped sober him up a bit more. He stared at the smoldering end of one of his worst habits.

I really need to quit. Again.

He'd quit five times in the past ten years, but kicking a habit he'd picked up at fourteen was hard. And not even a serious consideration when the cigarette in his hand was the only thing keeping him from pacing like a lunatic while he waited for Nathan. He shouldn't have come out tonight at all, not after the news he'd gotten, but what else was he supposed to do when he found out Stephen Price had made parole? Sit home and stew until the anger made him crazy? He'd dressed up, splashed on his best cologne and come down to his favorite watering hole for peach mojitos and cock. Irish pub by day and popular gay bar by night, Pot O Gold was his preferred destination for both.

He had walked in, ordered his first drink from Riley, one of his favorite bartenders, and then perused the pickings. A lot of familiar faces. A lot of guys he'd already fucked. He didn't have a rule about fucking someone only once, but too many repeat performances and some guys got a little clingy. He wanted sex, not a relationship.

Ezra Kelley had caught his attention immediately. He'd seen Ezra around the Pot on and off for the past year or so, sometimes alone and sometimes with other people. Bar chatter said Ezra was a good fuck. James had taken in the tall, lean body, the spiky blond hair and silver stud in his eyebrow. Even the purple sleeve-less top that matched the strange purple contact lenses had turned him on. Perhaps because Ezra was the exact physical opposite of what James really wanted and could never have.

He had claimed Ezra quickly. Dancing with him, drinks in hands, practically fucking with their clothes on. James downed more mojitos than he usually allowed himself, because the rum brought numbness. Numb-ness from the pain of today's news, the pain of old loss and the violence churning inside him, aimed directly at Stephen Fucking Price and everything he'd taken from James's family.

Alcohol, adrenaline and Ezra's wood had made James temporarily lose his mind. They'd walked into the bathroom stall together. That had definitely been mutual. And Ezra hadn't minded that blow job one bit until James had put Ezra against the wall and pulled the guy's pants down to fuck him. He'd been too damned drunk to see the surprise in Ezra's eyes, or hear the real fear in his voice. And then James had been an asshole, trying to argue with him about what they were going to do. Accidentally scaring Ezra into barfing up all of his night's drinks.

And like a fucking coward, James had fled. Fled down the sidewalk to this spot to wallow in his shame and try to keep the acid in his stomach from erupting.

He dragged on the cigarette, watching the tip flare orange. The whole world still listed a bit to one side. He'd moved all of his morning appointments to the af-ternoon, clearing his schedule until noon, but drink-ing himself into a hangover on a weekday was idiotic.

Then again, how often did he find out that the bas-

tard who molested his sister when she was thirteen was
being paroled? None of his psychology textbooks had
given him an answer for how to react to that kind of
news, so he'd done exactly what he always advised his
patients not to do—mask the pain. His mask of choice
was alcohol and sex.

Except he'd overdone it on the alcohol, and he'd hurt
Ezra in the process.

I am a douche bag.

He smoked his way through two more cigarettes before Nathan's beat-up Ram pickup pulled alongside
the curb. For a city cop, he was still adorably country.
Nathan leaned across the console to shove open the
passenger side door, and James gratefully slid inside.
The simple, familiar presence of Nathan nearby made
James's nerves unfurl a little bit more. Nathan was the
one thing in James's life that had always made sense.
Had always been easy.

Weariness settled into his bones, turning his drunken
daze into extreme fatigue. He wanted to pass out and
soon.

Nathan shoved a bottle of water at him, then eased
the truck back into the street. He cracked both of the
front windows, probably because James reeked of
smoke. Nathan had never been shy about telling him
how gross his habit was. Nathan was also smart enough
not to engage in conversation until they were shuffling
up the short sidewalk to Nathan's half of a two-story
duplex. Nathan slung an arm around James's waist, and
the heat of the other man's body so close felt amazing.
Real. Not like the fake closeness of dancing with strangers in a crowded bar.

He finally got a good look at his friend as Nathan crossed the narrow living room to the kitchen in the rear. Flannel pajama pants and a spring coat. James had woken him up.

Yeah, I'm a douche bag.

"You hungry?" Nathan shouted from the kitchen.

"No." In the familiar, somewhat cluttered warmth of Nathan's home, he had a safe place to wallow in the shame still burning in his gut.

Nathan's place was the definition of a straight bachelor's pad—which worked since Nathan was a straight bachelor. Dark leather furniture right out of a magazine's page, decorated exactly the same because he couldn't be bothered. A monster, sixty-inch flat screen mounted on the wall over an entertainment console boasted two gaming systems, alongside a Blu-ray player and hundreds of movies. Only a handful of photos hung on the wall, mostly of his rather large extended family that lived in southern Delaware.

James paused to stare at a familiar photo of himself with Nathan, taken right after Nathan had graduated from the police academy. They were both grinning, arms slung around each other's shoulder. Nathan so handsome in his uniform, James in a gray suit that hadn't been stylish in a decade. Because that's how long it had been. Nathan had made detective last year, so he didn't wear his uniform anymore. James sort of missed it.

Nathan came back into the living room sans coat, a white wifebeater showing off his muscled arms and flat stomach. He was one-eighth Nanticoke Indian on his mother's side, which gave his skin a lovely golden hue. His short hair was shiny black, and was always soft on the rare occasion James had a reason to touch it. His dark brown eyes often seemed to be smiling at him, even when things were serious, like right now.

He was carrying a bamboo tray loaded down with two shot glasses, a bottle of Kentucky bourbon and a bag of barbecue potato chips. He settled the tray on his magazine-covered coffee table, then poured them each a shot.

James sank onto the couch next to Nathan and accepted the glass. After a silent toast, he threw it back. The harsh, smoky liquid burned its way into his stomach.

Nathan refilled both glasses. "Does your mom know?"

"She's the one who told me." Grace had been sobbing when he answered his cell, and it took more than five minutes for him to understand what she'd been babbling. *The bastard is getting out.* The statement had punched him in the balls and tipped his world upside down.

"How is she?"

"Took it like a champ."

"Liar."

James downed the second shot, thankful for the burn. "She was a mess. I stopped by to bring her dinner, because she doesn't feed herself when she gets depressed. She wouldn't get out of bed. She still fucking blames herself for what happened to Laurie, and it's been almost twenty years."

"And you don't?" Nathan shot him a pointed look before knocking back his second drink. He poured them both a third.

"I was her big brother." James picked up the shot glass, mesmerized by the amber liquid. His mind was soft again, a gentle fuzziness very different from earlier. The fuzz wrapped around him like silk, coddling him, relaxing his tongue because this was Nathan, and Nathan was safe.

Nathan is everything. "I didn't protect Laurie."

"Yes, Jay, you did. You stopped Stephen that day. You stopped it from happening again."

His eyes burned. "Shouldn't have happened in the first place. Fucking piece of shit." Third shot down the hatch. A fourth sounded nice, but his hands were shaking and he'd already fucked up once tonight because he'd drunk too much.

Nathan pried the shot glass out of his hand, then angled his body toward him and put a warm hand on his knee. "The only person to blame for what Price did to your sister is Price. He pretended to love your mother. He pretended to be a friend to you and Laurie. He violated your trust because he's a sick fucking pervert who deserves to rot for touching her."

"I wish I'd killed him."

"Don't say that."

"I could have. A quarter-inch to the left, and I'd have killed him. The doctor said so." James flinched away from the memories bombarding his liquor-pickled brain. Coming home from tenth grade early because it was a half day. Stephen's car in the driveway when he should be at work. Laurie had stayed home with a sick stomach, so he went to check on her right away, only to find Stephen in her room. In her bed. On top of her.

A harsh noise tore from his throat, leaving it raw. His eyes stung, and he blinked against furious tears. "After I left Mom's place, I headed home and got dressed up for the Pot. I wanted to dance and to get laid, and I thought if I could channel my emotions into that, then it wouldn't hurt so much." He sounded hoarse, as if he'd gargled sand.

"What happened at the Pot?"

"I targeted my guy, danced and drank way more than I should have." *Shouldn't have been drinking at all.* "I practically dragged him into a bathroom stall." *Douche bag.* "Sucked him off. After, I wanted to fuck."

James's throat hurt as though the words themselves were laced with razor wire. "I shoved him against the wall. He started protesting, and I was too drunk to really hear him at first. Then he freaked and said *no* and I finally heard him. I stopped, but fucking Christ, Nate."

The hand on his knee squeezed. "You stopped."

He never had to explain things to Nathan because Nathan always *got it*. And he never got weird when James talked about sex or other non-straight-guy things, because that was Nathan. "What if I hadn't? I was so close to doing it. So fucking out of my mind I almost—"

"You. Stopped. You didn't do anything irreversible. You definitely owe him one major apology, but you didn't have sex with him against his will."

Nathan's hand flew from his knee to his cheek. "You did not become Price tonight, you hear me? You're still you, Jay. You're you."

James shuddered. Arms wrapped around him, pulling him forward, and James went. He pressed his forehead against the hard line of Nathan's collarbone and wept. Harsh, angry sobs that shook his entire body. Nathan held him together, hands rubbing his back, touching his hair, whispering comforting words that made no actual sense. James clung to his best friend, needing the comfort. Needing the familiar body and heat and scent of Irish Spring soap.

"I've got you," Nathan whispered.

"Please." James didn't know what he was asking for. The bourbon was making his brain soft, his actions slow. Instincts were taking over, urging him to find the comfort he'd sought out earlier. The logical side of his mushy brain was trying to argue that this was Nathan.

His very straight best friend Nathan, whose hand pressed against the back of James's neck. A thumb stroked firm circles against the skin, over the bumps of his spine. Tense muscles relaxed, allowing blood to flow more freely, and a flash of arousal warmed his gut.

Something prickled up James's spine, and he gasped. He'd been attracted to Nathan for years, ever since their junior year in college when they'd played Truth or Dare at a party, and Nathan had been dared to kiss James for a full minute.

The dare had been a joke perpetrated by Nathan's then-girlfriend Paula, who'd insisted it would be hot seeing her boyfriend kissing his gay best friend. She'd then whispered something into Nathan's ear which, he'd told James later, had been a promise of oral sex later that night. Maybe the whole thing had been about getting laid for Nathan, but the kiss had meant so much more to James. He'd wanted Nathan badly afterward, so naturally he'd gone out and fucked the first willing guy he could find. He'd still gone home with the taste of Nathan's lips lingering in his mouth.

Nathan's other hand drifted from his back to his waist, then up again, as if it wasn't certain where to linger. James straightened enough to see Nathan's face. To see the concern and confusion in his coffee-colored eyes. Nathan licked his lips, probably without meaning to, and James's pulse raced.

This isn't real. He'll do anything for you, because you'll do anything for him, so don't take advantage, you giant douche.

He told his conscience to take a flying fuck, and he did the exact wrong thing. He pressed his lips lightly against Nathan's and stopped. Waited. Instead of pulling away, Nathan held steady, just like he had in college. Except no one had dared him this time, and they were alone. Nothing to prove to anyone.

Adrenaline and arousal zinged through James, wrapped up in the fog of alcohol, demanding he take this further. Turn it into a real kiss before his chance was gone.

Just one real kiss.

James closed his eyes and slanted his head for a better angle. Nathan moved, warm lips whispering against his. Reacting to the most natural act on earth. James parted his lips and gently flicked his tongue against Nathan's mouth. He caught the faint flavor of bourbon and chips, and something behind that. Something all Nathan. His gut tightened with want. He clutched the back of Nathan's thin shirt, part of him wishing they were naked in a bed somewhere so he could taste every inch of Nathan. Lick him until he was moaning with desire. Swallow his cock down. Suck him. Make him come so hard he'd never want another lover.

Nathan gasped into his mouth as if he'd heard all of James's plans. He clutched James's hip, then let go, uncertain. James fumbled for Nathan's hand and gave it a firm squeeze before putting it back on his hip, liking it there. James slid his right hand down over soft flannel to grab Nathan's ass. Nathan groaned and jerked, his free hand threading into James's hair—to pull him off or keep him there, it didn't matter, because Nathan tasted so good and James didn't want it to end.

Except Nathan ripped away from him, his cheeks flushed and his lips wet. He pressed a palm to James's chest.

"You're drunk, Jay," Nathan said. "You're drunk and you're hurting, and this isn't what you want."

"I don't?" He was pretty sure he did, but only if Nathan wanted it, too, and he didn't look like he did anymore.

"No, you don't. You can't."

"But you feel so good, Nate. Taste good, too, and not just like bourbon."

Nathan lifted a hand toward his face, and James leaned into the touch that never came because Nathan dropped his hand. "I think you need to go to bed and sleep this off."

"Bed sounds good." He reached for Nathan again, all spaghetti arms and determination, and he got a solid face-plant on the sofa. Being horizontal started shutting down some of his higher brain function, because he suddenly couldn't quite recall why he was on the couch and not in a bed.

"Roll over."

"Woof."

"Jesus, you're wasted."

"I know you are, but what am I?"

"For fuck's sake."

Arms rolled James onto his back. He reached for the shape looming over him, only to get the corner of a blanket in his mouth. Flat on his back felt nice. Swimmy. Everything all swirly and floaty.

"Nothing happened with us tonight, Jay," Nathan said. "It was all a really nice dream."

James tried to protest, but the light went off and Nathan was gone. He was alone again, on the one night when he didn't want to sleep alone.

Moonlight glinted off the bottle of amber liquid left behind on the coffee table. His sister's cries filled the too-quiet room.

Just one more shot...

Don't miss Getting It Right *by A.M. Arthur,*
available wherever books are sold.
www.CarinaPress.com

Also Available from A.M. Arthur
Unearthing Cole, *a Discovering Me novella*
He only came back to get her ashes; he never thought he'd find a reason to stay.

Cole Alston swore he'd never return to his childhood home in rural North Carolina—until he inherits his mother's hoarded property. He hopes to sell everything and use the money to start over in Canada, far away from his abusive ex-boyfriend. It's a daunting task, and Cole has no idea where to start.

Luckily for him, the local antique store owner, Jeremy Collins, offers his services in sorting and selling the hoard in exchange for a fee. Their chemistry soon turns their professional relationship into a personal one, but Cole must overcome his past and his anxiety before he can accept a new man in his life.

Or the possibility of a happy future.